Reviews for
The Triempery Revelations

"Two elements elevate this work above standard fare. First, it's a character study at its heart, driven by the growth and evolving relationships of complex people, vibrant and varied, without any reduced to stereotypes of good or bad. Second, the mysteries of the Rill and the Wall are compelling and drive readers to explore this world more deeply. Stephens serves up a terrific first entry to a fascinating new series."
—*Booklist*

"An incredible introduction to a new fantasy series... layered, flawed characters within a fascinating world with a rich history and intriguing magic system that you can't wait to learn more about."
—*Smyco*

"*The Kheld King* takes all the elements that made *Sordaneon* great and expands them. A character-driven story with high stakes, with politics as the main focus of this fantasy."
—*Jamreads*

"If *Dune*, *Lord of the Rings* and *Game of Thrones* all got together and made a book baby, it would be rather like *Sordaneon*, which is to say that it's brilliantly done. ... It was easy to sink into the world along with Dorilian and the others. I'm absolutely in awe of how many layers Stephens brought to the strange world of the Rill and all those fighting for power."
—*Rebecca Crunden*

BIBLIOGRAPHY

The Triempery Revelations

Sordaneon

The Kheld King

The Second Stone

The God Spear

The Walled City
(forthcoming)

Moon Blood and Salt Flowers

THE
GOD
SPEAR

THE TRIEMPERY REVELATIONS
- BOOK -
IV

L. L. STEPHENS

Copyright Information
THE GOD SPEAR
Published by

FOREST PATH BOOKS

Forest Path Books publications may be purchased for educational, business, or sales/promotional use. For information, please address the publishers at:
info@forestpathbooks.com
or
Forest Path Books, LLC
P. O. Box 847, Stanwood, WA 98292 USA

Stay informed on our releases and news!
Join the reading group/newsletter at:
https://forestpathbooks.com/into-the-forest

Front cover art © 2024 by Larry Rostant *https://rostant.com*
Map of Amallar © 2024 Thomas Rey *https://www.artstation.com/thomrey*
PR Compass Rose font © Peter Rempel (licensed for use)
Cover and interior design by Mahli *https://bookdesignbymahli.com*
Cover content is for illustrative purposes only, and any person depicted on the cover is a model.

Library of Congress Control Number: 2022923555
ISBNs:
978-1-951293-78-9 (hardcover)
978-1-951293-77-2 (trade paper)
978-1-951293-76-5 (e-book)

Map of Amallar

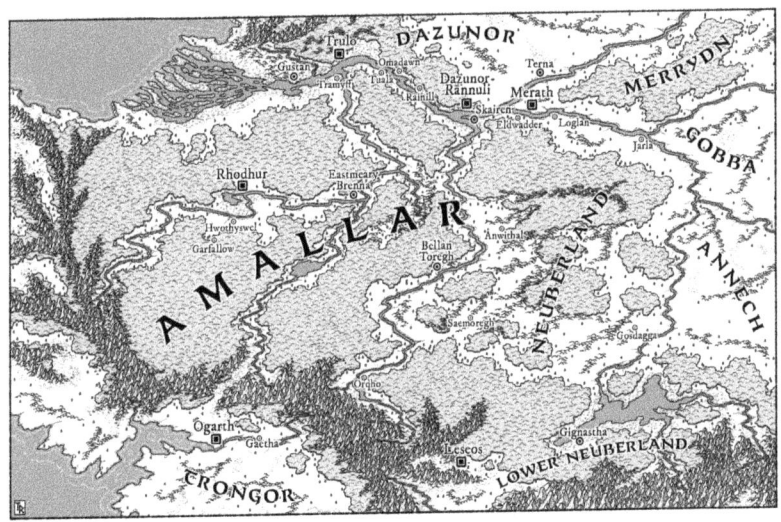

For my mother, Betty Capelle—who never quite understood my drive to write these books, but who ended up in them anyway.

THE
GOD
SPEAR

Amallar is a wild land, a tangle of trees into which no
light—even that of knowledge—can penetrate. It will be
no loss for the King to give it to the Khelds, who are little
better than beasts. They follow a god called Lud, whom
they believe led them through a door of stone into this
land. For that reason, they claimed our land god-given to
be theirs.

RAMMELON OF AVERRN,
LETTER TO HIS COUSIN THE BAS OF NALAPAR

("I thought there'd be an actual road," Hans said. The line
drawn on the maps he'd looked at in Sordan and Trongor
had hinted at something better than this sorry excuse for a
highway. "No wonder Amallar has trouble building trade with its
neighbors."

Herberth's answering chuckle earned a scowl from Arne.
Herberth ignored the warning and proceeded to elaborate. "King
Stefan ordered a better road to be built in the early years of his reign,
but Stefan withdrew the funds later to pay for his wars. It didn't
help that his trade minister in those later years was incompetent
and never resumed the work. From what I hear, the only finished
parts of the road lie east of the country."

Clearly no one had finished the part of the road leading to
Trongor. From maps and talks with geography tutors, Hans knew
that Amallar's claim to a seacoast consisted of sheer cliffs topped
either by more mountains, or by vast bogs with not one serviceable
harbor. He got the sinking feeling that he had exchanged a
frustrating situation for an impossible one. He hadn't expected
Amallar to be *this* isolated and backward. Sordan, for all its

uncertainties and treacherous politics, had infrastructure. Sordan not only built armies with which to defend itself, it built roads to move them.

Only now did it occur to Hans why Marenthro had sent him to Sordan. It had not been just to enlist Dorilian or learn more about the Rill. Marenthro wanted Hans to gain the backing of a powerful *state*: a leader, nation, and people capable of mounting a successful war. So far, Amallar didn't look like it had much to offer in the powerful-state department.

At least Amallar didn't feel dangerous. The Trongor Pass had dumped Hans and his party into a vast, hilly country thick with ravines and mist-shrouded forests. There might be people and villages to be found among the folds and hollows of those grandmotherly skirts, but the comforts of civilization would be few. Even the trade road to Trongor, important enough to have a name, was barely more than a track.

The few encounters with fellow travelers along the road had been with the occasional small trader or people, generally women, intent on reaching the next town to treat the sick. As for hospitality—the most pressing inconvenience was that the handful of inns along the road were inadequate establishments wholly incapable of sleeping or feeding the number of men Hans and Herberth had with them. Save for Herbeth and his captain Farrl, both of whom Hans insisted be housed under a roof each night, the Trongorians ended up camping nearby. At least, as Hans had predicted, the people they met along the road were more curious than suspicious and never seriously challenged his progress.

A brisk, chill wind had kicked up overnight, reminding Hans and his party that they were in the northlands now. The farther north they rode, the more the trees wore autumn colors, so that the hills looked to be afire. They made good progress along the dry track and stopped at midday to water and rest their horses.

"You'd think someone would wonder who the hell we might be or what we might be up to," Arne commented, noting the lack of scrutiny as they prepared to move on. His riding skills had improved and he easily swung atop his sturdy horse.

Hans patted the shoulder of his own dapple-gray mount and checked the girth strap one more time.

"We're being watched," Farrl assured the party. "Essera's kings have long ordered Kheld rangers to not interfere with mercantile or diplomatic missions." He gestured to the banners that proclaimed them so. "They act only if they suspect trouble. Consider too that it was not so long ago this land was protected by powerful interests. Highborn promises on the one hand and Essera's might on the other are effective deterrents."

"Seems to me, both of that lot are dead and gone," Arne countered. "Guess it's a good thing Trongor doesn't have a craving for land over the mountains."

"Our folk prefer the sea and the riches mining brings. We are interested in your country and people only for what trade we might share." Herberth lifted his hat to wipe at his brow. "Can you tell me how far we are from Rhodhur?"

"Day or so." Arne scratched at his head as he considered. "We should reach the Rhodhur Road tomorrow once we get to Uggwil's Pitchfork today. The road branches there. One road will head up Rhodhur way, one will cross the Brennan to the Toregh Trail, and the other will run over to Eastmeary." Just speaking the name made him brighten. "That's where I grew up. Eastmeary Brenna. Good land, all farms and towns." He slapped a hand to his forehead. "Damn it all, but I should've thought of this before! We don't have to stick to this road or wait to get to the Fork to turn north. We're going northeast now. All we have to do is set out cross-country from here, point ourselves north, and intercept the Rhodhur Road about halfway. We could cut a day off our time, easy."

Herberth eyed the surrounding hills. "The forest is thick. We could get lost in it."

"Nah," said Arne, "I have cousins in these parts. Had an uncle too, near Uggwil. My brothers and me visited every year until a bear got him. Point being I got a map in my head. The hills are taller not far from here, and I know *those* hills with their insides out and backwards. I can find Rhodhur blindfolded."

"I sure hope so," Hans said. "I don't remember it being quite this tucked away." He was willing to count on Arne as a guide. None of the Trongorians had deep knowledge of Amallar whereas Arne, at least, was a native.

"And I'm for staying on the Trongor Road," Herberth insisted. "We know where *it* goes, and there are certain to be inns along the way, as there have been thus far." He generously did not question the quality of that housing.

Arne refused to be swayed. "We'll make Rhodhur by tomorrow night if we get a good start today. You can't do better for inns than Rhodhur's and you can't do better for food. We should travel fast while we can. This time of year the weather can change like a mad goat's temper and when it does it'll rain like the heavens come falling in, or I'm not a Kheld!"

Herberth turned to his captain. "Farrl?"

"I think it safe to cut overland, sir. At this point any course that takes us north will bring us to the Rhodhur Road."

Herberth then nodded his assent and returned to join his men. Hans mounted his horse and gave Arne a weary, hopeful smile.

"I'm not making trouble," Arne said in his defense. "This is better. It's a shortcut. There's a trail and all. You'll see."

"There should be a road."

"There should be a lot of things, if people did a better job of getting them done."

They set out riding north into forested hills that seemed never-ending. The sun nudged just above the trees as they began to ride downhill into bottomlands, where a river tributary rushed swift and cold. One of Farrl's men, riding ahead, returned to say he had spotted people on horseback on the other side of the narrow valley between the hills.

Herberth turned to Arne. "Should we be worried?"

"Nah. We're too far from the road to start running into ruffians."

"What if they followed us and are now circling to cut us off?" Herberth's words prompted the Trongorian rangers to exchange glances and nods. "Is there any way to turn back and go around?"

"We'd lose a day or more," said Arne, looking put out. "Aside from the bridge at Eastmeary Brenna, the only place to cross is at the Frendel Fords."

"Perhaps you should have thought of that when you proposed this adventure," Herberth snapped.

Arne's ears burned bright red. "Look, I might have groused a lot, but we never seriously thought we'd ride all this way without nobody seeing us. It might be someone who's followed us, and it might be someone who don't even know we're here. Lots of folk use the Fords."

"I have no wish to be set upon by bandits."

"And I tell you bandits wouldn't want to be set upon by *us*!

Whatever that lot is, they're not Staubaun robber lords." Arne looked affronted by the thought. "There aren't enough rich travelers in these parts to make a business of robbing folk. It's young hooligans, mostly, and nothing your swords here wouldn't set to running."

"I say we go ahead," Hans decided. "He's right about us being well armed." He suspected forty veteran Trongorian soldiers could hold their own against even Staubaun robber lords. Meanwhile, standing here was getting them nowhere. Hans had adjusted his own sword and tested his grip. Even though he, like Arne, had never used a blade in actual combat, it wouldn't hurt to look menacing.

They set out again, more cautiously than before. The rangers riding in front and behind the party, respecting the possibility of ambush, rode with their weapons ready at their sides. Herberth, at least, was mollified. In weather dry and cool enough to not overtax the horses, they covered ground quickly. By afternoon they rounded a bend and were thankful to see the trail broaden to become a path. As they began to wend downhill, they glimpsed the glittering trace of a river.

"That's the Frendel," said Arne.

The Frendel didn't seem mighty, but Hans remembered from childhood that it was barely navigable. Rhodhur itself was not a river port. The Fords were located below the town. So were the gentler, useful parts of the Frendel. What they saw below them was wild, untamed, a young torrent of water imprisoned by a narrow valley. It presented churning stretches of whitewater only a fool would attempt to cross.

Herberth frowned. "After three days of rain, I hope your fords are passable."

"They ought to be," said Arne. "But we should aim to cross today before it rains again. Those clouds are awful dark." They had only to look to the north and west to see the threat. "We'll be glad once we're over. There'll be proper inns. The road on the other side is well traveled."

The path down the hill was steep and followed a deep ravine thick with oak, maple, and wild apple trees. A fast stream flowed along the boulder-strewn bottom and the tree-crowned hill loomed above. Hans wanted to get through it and out into the open again.

They had just emerged from trees into an open patch dense with young pines and low, fruiting scrub when a spray of dirt and stone erupted on the trail ahead of them. A second shower, this time of splintered rock, shattered from the stony hillside close above their heads. The party rapidly dismounted and sought shelter—along with their horses—among a stand of mixed beech and sturdy maples just off the path.

"Madrock's Hells!" Arne swore. "They've got us pinned and proper all right!" Below them, precariously near, was the stream. Above, the path was wide open to attack with only two outlets, both narrow and easily bottled.

"Maybe if I get up and talk to them..." Hans moved to push to his feet. The attack had been sudden but not entirely unexpected. Their attackers had merely bided their time, knowing there was no way out of the ravine but to go forward or back, and able to control both from the surrounding bluffs. They'd even made a point of sorts by not killing anyone with their first barrage.

But Arne held on to Hans and did not let him rise. "No," he said. "This is my job, remember. If they ain't friendly, it's better me getting a rock to my head than you."

Arne stood up and stepped out onto the path again, where he took off his hat and waved it. When no one took a shot at him from the surrounding bluffs, he hollered in his native tongue, "What the hell, you damn cowards! Haven't you ever seen a Kheld before?"

Hans broke out laughing. It was perfect.

A voice from the bluffs hailed across the stream. "You're the first damn Kheld I ever saw come out of Trongor at the head of their folk! If you're an honest Son of Alm, give me a name!"

Arne flashed Hans a huge grin. Brigands would not have trailed them all the way from Trongor, nor would they have bothered to ask for a name. He threw out his chest and shouted back at the cliff. "My name is Arne! Arne Thegn Anseldson! I was captured in Neuberland, but now I'm back!"

"Like hell!"

"The Mother's Truth! My mother is Wyneghan Thegn Aelfricsda of Prydoahn, and I have seven brothers and five sisters"—with pure defiance Arne thrust his hand over his head, finger pointing to the sky—"and I can name them all!"

A long silence answered him. Hans wondered if whoever listened was waiting for Arne to continue. Then there came a different sort of shout. "Go on up the trail until you come out near the first ford. We'll deal with you there. And don't try to turn back. We'll damn kill any who do!"

One by one, with Hans going first only because no one was near enough to hold him back, the rest of the company emerged with their mounts out of hiding and rejoined Arne on the path.

Only Herberth, however, openly grumbled about the reception. "Your countrymen extend a harsh welcome," he snorted to Arne.

"Yeah, well, they got good reason." Arne followed Hans's lead in remounting his horse. "We have to give them a chance to look us over, to make sure for themselves that we mean no harm."

As the day slipped toward its end, it dissolved into fine drizzle. The swirling water of the river ahead of them took on a heavy, leaden cast as they left the stream behind and the sodden trail broadened into a lowland clearing.

"They aren't here yet," Herberth observed as they reined to a halt within paces of the water. Here the Frendel was wide and appeared to be shallow, lined by rushes and river grass, with an area of silt and gravel that marked the Ford. The open flat was unmarred by either foot or hoof.

Hans shifted in the saddle and searched sharply up and down the line of the river, attending every thicket and patch of weeds, every stand of sapling elder. Khelds owned these woods; he'd seen for himself as a child how they walked and lived and breathed the ways of their forest. They would stand among the oaks and one might think the trees had eyes as blue as the jays that chattered in the branches. Even the woodland sounds might be no more than Khelds signaling each other from hill to hill. As Hans heard a clacking birdcall break across the clearing, he looked to Arne, whose gaze met his with the shared knowledge that they were, indeed, being watched. All around them, hidden by the thickets and shadows of the wood, men of Amallar waited, bows drawn and slings ready, watching to see if the strangers would prove to be bad guests or welcome friends.

A short time later, a dozen or so men emerged from the woods around the clearing. They were Khelds, with skin browned by lives spent out of doors, dark haired and dark-bearded beneath their hoods and various head coverings. A few had pushed back those hood to reveal eyes of every shade of blue.

One of the men, unusually big and burly for a Kheld, ordered Hans's party to dismount and step away from their horses. As he and his companions obeyed, Hans noted with some surprise that they were not deprived of their weapons.

Another man emerged from the shadow of a thicket beside the river—compact, hooded, and cloaked. When he spoke, they recognized him as the man who had shouted at them from the bluffs. "Which of you claims to be Arne, son of Wyneghan?"

Arne stepped out from among his companions. "I'm Arne," he boasted with just the right hint of Kheld bravado. "And I'll rattle off a whole list of kin if you need me to."

The observer held his silence only for a moment, then he threw back his hood. His resemblance to Arne was so marked that one could have passed for the other but for the smattering of freckles on the newcomer's nose.

"Brec!" Arne burst out at once in recognition, his face wiped clean of all but joy. "It's my own brother!"

"Thought I recognized your voice, Arne," Brec said. "But I never hoped to see you again, and not in all the world with men of Trongor!"

They embraced many times, Arne jumping around with a quick energy only puppies and excited Khelds were known to possess. Brec's wide smile perked up his round face when he turned at last to the others. He faced Hans in good-natured perplexity.

"You look familiar, and I suspect I should know you—but I don't."

"You probably saw or knew my brother." Hans returned the smile. "I'm your cousin Hans, Handurin from Gustan. I visited Rhodhur a few times as a boy."

Brec's blue eyes grew rounder. "Hans Erwanson? *Stefan's* brother?"

"That's me," Hans acknowledged, not sure if he should grin or frown. "Stefan's brother."

Wonder transfigured Brec's pleasant exuberance in a way Hans already disliked. "Do you even know what that means these days?"

"More than you do, Brec Anseldson."

"But we heard you were a prisoner in Sordan!"

"Not anymore."

The other Khelds all crowded near, wide-eyed with welcome and awe. No one questioned whether he was in fact Prince Handurin. *Do I look that much like Stefan?* Hans wondered. Endelarin had implied he did not. More likely it was Arne's presence that gave his claim added weight.

Brec clapped Arne soundly across the back as if determined to show he had not forgotten him, though his gaze lingered on Hans. "Madrock's Hells! We'll have a ringing party in the old Hall tonight in your honor. The both of you! I'll bet there's a story in how that happened. In one day we not only get back Stefan's brother, but *my* own brother too! All hells, Arne, we thought you dead in Neuberland—they let some prisoners go last summer, but you weren't one of them. And of course Mother cried for days, and the girls too, all of them! All that damn sobbing... that's why I couldn't take your word back on the path there—to have some total stranger try to pass himself off as my dead brother! But what a tale! You turn up to be not dead at all."

Herberth ventured an aside to Hans as Brec chattered. "My Khelda is not good enough for this. Is this young man some sort of brother to your friend?" Even though he had whispered discreetly, that the Trongorian had spoken in Stauba brought instant, reflexively hostile, attention.

"Better introduce these Staubaun speakers to us." Brec frowned as his fellow Khelds pressed nearer, their grips on their weapons visibly tightened. "That tongue ain't something we like to hear inside our borders—or out of them. Where'd you pick these men up, anyway?"

"This man," Hans placed a hand on Herberth's beefy shoulder, "is Herberth Estol Tammett, Elector of Trongor. He made Arne and me welcome when we came to his country, and now he has given us an escort to Rhodhur."

Brec and the other Khelds peered at Herberth in slack-jawed wonder. "Heard they had an Elector but never seen the like. Don't think Stefan ever took any of our folk their way."

Herberth replied in rough Khelda. "No. King Stefan and I met only twice, both times in Permephedon."

Wide-eyed, Brec nodded in the direction of the other travelers. "And them? Allies?"

Hans nodded. "If we're lucky. I would like to make Herberth and his men welcome in Amallar. It's the hope of all who ride with me that we reach Rhodhur, or some other place with food and shelter before nightfall."

"Well, that we can do!" Brec turned at once to his Kheld companions, all of whom had relaxed and were now grinning. "This sounds good enough for me. Let's get them to Rhodhur before the moon rises and they get a night chill in their bones. And the river isn't so high yet that we can't have you there for late supper," he added to Hans and Arne.

Once they were mounted and had forded the Frendel, Brec and his men led them surely to the road. Riding swiftly, they passed farms and villages along the road. Dusk and rain had begun to settle heavily over the hills by the time they entered Rhodhur. The rutted, muddy streets were lined by jumbles of wood and stone buildings. Ahead of them loomed the town's Great Hall, the heart of Khelddom itself. Through gray veils of rain, the rustic building's hundreds of golden windows beckoned, suggesting warm beds and downy pillows and hot breads fresh from the oven, as well as the friendly company of people exchanging laughter within its walls.

Though Hans had returned to his birth World months ago, only now did he see a place that looked like home. While the sight of Rhodhur Hall didn't inspire the same sense of grandeur and storied glory as did Staubaun seats, or present the enduring stony strength of Ogarth's Old Fort, it did impress visitors with its sheer size and fortitude. Wood and stone raised formidable stories and framed its many windows. Rooflines sharp against heavy winter snow challenged the sky. The main building was solid and reassuring while the Hall's courtyards led to enough outbuildings to rival that of a Sordaneon palace.

The hills and approaches were steep and easily defended. No foreign troops had ever occupied Rhodhur, though it was also true that none had ever tried. Brec had sent a messenger ahead, so they found the timber gate that usually barred the deep stone portal open to admit them.

Hans remembered the flagstone courtyard and watched with a grin as Arne celebrated their arrival by riding once around on his horse. Though the courtyard opened before them in a dim circle of hazy lantern light and the Hall's covered entry was murky with shadow, lighted windows peered out from rugged walls and beneath ornamental cornices. Elaborately carved wooden beams supported the eaves of four stories of overhanging roofs. Everything was exactly as Hans remembered, complete with that Kheld love of ostentation which they so steadfastly denied. Rhodhur and Gustan, not Sordan or any other Staubaun place, had seemed in his childhood the height of magnificence. To his delight, he found that he could still think so.

They dismounted and handed the reins to one of Farrl's men, who then rode off with several of Brec's men and the remaining rangers toward the rear of the Hall and the stables.

"Remember?" asked Arne.

"Yes." Hans was grateful to be off his horse and standing stiffly on ground again. "This place hasn't changed at all. It's every bit as big as I remember it."

"Let's go tell folk you're here!" Brec tried to run off, but Hans managed to grab hold of his sleeve.

"No," he said. "Don't tell anyone yet. I want to speak to Robdan Aelfricson first."

"Uncle *Rob*?" Brec's lively voice dropped in disbelief.

"Come on, Hans," urged Arne, "you can talk to him later. I mean, he might not even be here. He's probably off to the Archhalia or somewhere."

Brec shook his head. "Just got back from High Council a week ago, or else he never got there. Strange goings-on in the north, word has it. I don't know what you want to see him for. He won't do you much good." He frowned at Hans, ignoring Herberth and Farrl, who had stayed with them. "Times have changed, cousin Hans. You should pay your courtesy visit to Nalf Rhys—he's head of the Thegnkeld these days. Stefan counted on him and so can you. Don't know where you got the idea that Robdan's somebody. He's just filling in until we find someone better."

Hans fought a sigh. He was bone-tired and not in a hurry to meet anyone Stefan had counted on. "I think I've learned to recognize a somebody when I see one. And I don't believe in nobodies."

Brec looked at him with fresh, if bewildered, respect—as though genuinely surprised to hear him voice an opinion. "Okay, Hans Thegn," he said, with more deference than any of them had yet heard in his voice. "If that's what you want."

Glancing at Herberth and then at Arne, neither of whom had anything to add, Hans nodded. "That's what I want," he said. "There'll be time for me to meet others later. But I want to talk to Robdan now."

"All right, then. But you might not have long. My lads are already spreading the news." Brec led them along a puddle-strewn path to the back of the Hall, where rainwater cascaded from overflowing gutters. At path's end he showed them a side door into a narrow alcove, from which ascended a closed and somewhat musty stairway. The stair was little used, and Hans didn't remember it. At the top of the stair an oil lamp hung from iron chains, casting sullen shadows along a hallway lined with closed doors of rough-hewn timber.

Brec stopped in front of a door bearing brass clan-marks and rapped twice on the heavy wood planks. "You can go on in," he told them. "Old Rob don't hear the knocks but half the time anyway. He always has his nose stuck in a book and his ears wrapped around the pages."

2

Immediately following his transformation, within weeks of
inhabiting the Rill corpus and thereby creating the Entity,
Derlon resumed communication with his brothers and
sons. He appeared to them at Permephedon and Sordan
and together they decided on where to raise the next
mounts. Derlon himself chose the mount at Heb to be
raised first of all because the fen dwellers had treated him
well during his travels.

DEBEN III SORDANEON, *LIFE OF DERLON*

"Where is Dorilian?"

Of all the questions afire in Nammuor's mind, that one burned hottest. Far hotter, for certain, than the temper of the angry crowd that ringed the Rillhome. Cacophonous chants hurled against the residence, penetrating its formidable walls and giving Nammuor yet another reason to dislike Dazunor-Rannuli. The main reason for his dislike glowed with smug, intolerable light on the other side of the palace's glass windows.

Subdued and silent, the Rill hunkered atop Dazunor-Rannuli's Mount like the abandoned toy of a changeable god. Nammuor had journeyed to the Rillhome from the Emrysen Palace, a more pleasant destination. Though the distance between the two palaces was not great, he had kept his presence in the city concealed by allowing himself to be cocooned inside the rough jolting of a common carriage. That means of passage, bypassing the Lago and the Lower Canal, had been uncomfortable, but necessary because proximity to the Rillhome—and its Entity—made wearing the Diadem pure torture.

At a nearby table, Essera's Prince Regent, Erenor Tholeros,

poured a stream of ruby wine into a goblet of flame-gilded crystal. Rill glow cast highlights and shadows upon his sharp, noble-born features. "Last word I had of the Hierarch, he was in Sordan, sitting pretty with an imprisoned prince."

"He could have used the Rill before it entered this problematic state—left his City and entered yours—right under everyone's noses."

"For what purpose?" Erenor scoffed. "To invade us? Look around you. Do you see any sign of him here? Or in Permephedon? The World knows Dorilian's every move. He never travels but with an army to protect him. Put your mind at rest; the man's so paranoid he never leaves his island."

Nammuor scowled. Although likely true, the assumption felt dangerous.

Separated from the Rill Entity by glass and stone, Nammuor narrowed his gaze, then trained his Diadem's razor-edged perceptions upon the crown of inert structures—and encountered a wall of power. Blue-white. Violent. Veils of torment blocked any further incursion. *Back! Back!* The necessity of retreat stung even as doing so bolstered his hunger to someday prevail. Without exception, his attempts to fully *inhabit* the Diadem—to use it, to have the device's arcane energies amplify his mortal brain and body—ended in this way, in pain. When pitted against an Entity, unfortunately, his failures were even more ignominious, but at least they were invisible. Though every space within Nammuor's skull screamed in protest and red agony flooded his vision, he stood without flinching. He had chosen wisely to stay at *this* end of the palace. Any nearer to the Rill and the pain would have been intolerable. Closing his eyes, he turned his head and stepped away from the window.

"Yon Entity is *not* dead," Nammuor said. Obtaining that verdict for himself had been the sole reason for his having traveled to this bloated, miserable seat of power.

"It might as well be." Erenor drew another deep drink from the goblet before he threw the vessel against a tapestry-embellished wall. The goblet survived the tapestry, but not the floor; it shattered into shards of glass and gold. "Look at it! The thrice-cursed Rill might as well be stone. Even its glow is less! Nights here have become dangerous. There's more crime on the streets, more collisions between gonds on the canals. And don't get me started on the warehouses." A feral growl entered Erenor's voice as he shot Nammuor a glare. "Winter is on the doorstep and Dazunor-Rannuli's damn food supply is either running out or rotting in storage!"

Complaints and more complaints. Erenor dwelled on nothing else. Food. Violence. The sheer *inconvenience*. Was Nammuor the only person in Essera able to comprehend what was really taking place?

"Your city's stockyards overflow with meat on the hoof. And what grain your overfed population can't ship out by Rill, they can now eat. They can gorge upon the contents of a nation's worth of warehouses and eat up all the profits they can no longer make. Your people won't starve; they'll all be fat before solstice."

"They're rioting! Listen to them! They want my blood!"

The howling of voices outside the walls had picked up volume. Nammuor grimaced. "They're even more simple-minded than you are. They actually think you can do something if they scare you enough. They may even be wondering what idiocy you did to bring this down upon them."

Nammuor noticed that Erenor looked uncomfortable at that precisely worded remark. There was something there, a telltale shift of gaze, a lift of the chin and squaring of the shoulders. Defiance and fear. Fear of what? Discovery? Or reprisal?

What did you do?

The last genuine news Nammuor—or anyone—had heard out of Sordan was that Prince Handurin had been placed under arrest and imprisoned in Sordan's Citadel. Had Erenor done something to spark that action? Something threatening enough to have spooked Dorilian into taking *this* drastic step with the Rill?

Of one thing Nammuor was certain—in doing so Dorilian had tipped his hand and shown a card that, perhaps, he had not wanted to reveal.

Nammuor clenched his teeth and bit down hard as newer, sharper pain shot through his forehead. He could not stay here much longer. As a former Sordaneon palace, the Rillhome—constructed to bathe the godborn in the energy of their nearby Entity—was almost as unbearable as its namesake. Impatiently, he rubbed at the three jewels set into an elaborate device that curled behind his ear. It wasn't mere jewelry. He had seen and heard enough and now wanted nothing more than to escape this hellhole.

He addressed Erenor again. "So you know nothing—and will

know nothing, because nobody will. Nobody *can*. Not with the Rill in *that* state." Nammuor walked away from the window and its view. Coram Barzanes, who had traveled with them from the Emrysen Palace, waited beside the door with two red-robed mages of Nammuor's ever-present entourage. One of Erenor's lackeys, a lord named Kondros Bragord, also stood at hand. Coram had already gathered Nammuor's cloak of heavy velvets and furs and held it at the ready.

"Henceforth we will communicate by array," Nammuor continued. "We still have that. Sordan doesn't have one, of course." Famously, that device had been destroyed by loyal Sordaneon forces during Labran's ill-fated rebellion; Mormantalorus had also destroyed its array. "The nearest array to Sordan is in Askorras. What a pity." A new thought crossed his mind and he frowned. "Don't you think it odd that *Permephedon* doesn't have an array?"

Erenor shrugged. "It never needed one. It had the Rill. Even better, it has the wizard Marenthro. He talks to Entities."

Nammuor gestured to the window. "Even now?"

"According to the Epoptes. Exactly what I told you when you arrived. I'd just gotten the messages myself by courier. Marenthro talked with it, and he claimed that he wouldn't—or couldn't—restore the Rill to service."

"This time."

"Yes. *This* time. The Epoptes are flummoxed. Those stranded in the north no longer possess any means to communicate or reason with the Entity or each other. The Rill has a long history of *not* doing anything unexpected. It has always been compliant to resolving our needs. Dorilian, on the other hand..."

Nammuor let the rest of that sentence fall as intended. Yes. Dorilian. Back to where he had started.

Dazunor-Rannuli could starve for all Nammuor cared. All of Essera could starve. Now that the Rill was unresponsive, Nammuor needed to find some other way to feed and supply *his* troops. He would instruct General Zel to begin seizing Esseran harvests and storehouses. Let Erenor complain about that.

He signaled to Coram, who spread open the great cloak of crimson velvet and black fur so that it might settle over Nammuor's shoulders.

Before fastening his cloak clasp, Nammuor looked over at Erenor's pinched, nervous face. "A pity you wasted your spy in the

Serat. Did you really think getting your prince thrown into a cell would make him less of a threat to you?"

For once, Erenor simply pressed his lips and exercised prudence by not rising to the bait.

Nammuor finished with the clasp. "Placing any informant into the Serat is almost impossible, far less one with the level of access we need—but I will attempt to get a transmitting crystal to Sordan and into position. I might even share news with you, especially if you can provide information on Sordan's troop movements. Dorilian could well seek to invade Essera, you know. The Wall still stands and as a Highborn Prince he might have an eye to that Entity's gifts. As for the other," with a crisp motion, Nammuor pointed to the window through which the Rill shone with eerie stillness, "you are far from safe. Eventually he is going to want to use *that*."

He strode toward the arched exit, only to see the argentstone door fly open. The captain of Erenor's Regent's Guard stood in the doorframe, his broad body filling that space.

"You cannot leave, my liege. Nor you, Nuarch. Rioters have seized the bridge to the Lago Rim Road. They will soon overrun the palace esplanade."

Erenor confronted the captain. "There's no way out?"

"We can still cross the Grace Bridge to the Mount. And you could leave by water. You need do neither. The Rillhome is secure and well defended. I have sent to the Emrysen garrison for reinforcements."

Coram came to Nammuor's side. "I can leave with you, Master."

As Nammuor's representative, Coram was to have stayed in Dazunor-Rannuli. For him to flee now would be wasteful. Doubly so. Translocation crystals such as Coram wore were difficult and costly to produce; Nammuor did not have a limitless supply. Neither was now the time to leave Dazunor-Rannuli and its Entity unwatched.

Though he wanted nothing more than to depart, it would be imprudent to leave Coram and Essera's still-useful puppet of a Regent in danger.

"No." To the captain, Nammuor said, "Take me to a place from which I can see the problem for myself."

With every step delivering cuts of pain behind his eyes, Nammuor followed along vaulted corridors of green marble veined with silver, through arches of onyx and gates of jade. Sordaneon wealth still filled these halls. Stefan's pillaging had barely begun the process of dismantling it. What irritated Nammuor most was hearing Erenor and Bragord's urgent whispers to each other as they scurried in his wake. Their impotence… rankled. He wondered how much longer he could tolerate their limitations.

Nammuor strode out upon the stone balcony that overlooked the imposing land entrance to the Rillhome. From there he gazed upon a wide court flanked by manicured lawns that rolled from the gated palace entry to a picturesque canal. Across that canal the stately Sanctuary of the Sisters of Mercy raised azure cupolas above serene bluestone walls. A bridge joined the paved road of the Sisters of Mercy to the mall leading to the Rillhome, and also to the Lago Rim road that, lined by palatial residences, ringed Dazunor-Rannuli's lake and the Malyrdeon Illystri palace like a jeweled necklace.

Irate citizens had crossed the bridge to besiege the Rillhome. Nammuor looked upon those thousands as they thrust high their torches and flimsy weapons, voices raised to howl their grievances. They had been told the Prince Regent was in the palace and they wanted him to answer for the state of the Rill. To give them answers.

Nammuor overheard the slavish Bragord mutter to Erenor.

"At least we can be heartened, sir, knowing the Sordaneons are good at building fortresses."

Yes. Even fools could be right on occasion. Sordaneons were builders. Architects. *Creators.* But more dangerously, they were not yet extinct.

"We'll leave by boat," Erenor decided. "Unless the rabble have launched watercraft and made that impossible."

"No need," Nammuor said. If Erenor could not control this wretched city's population, Nammuor would do it for him. *These* people too were creating—aimlessly, without intelligence, pathetic imitations of their god. They were creating disorder. Inciting complications and outcomes and unpredictability. The Diadem clamored to instill order, to sweep clean the chaos.

Nammuor stretched out his hands.

He could not remove these flesh things of Leur from existence— even the crystals of Highborn blood in his Diadem did not enable him to do that—but he could alter them, slay them, reduce them to their raw materials. Fry them. Freeze them. Open the ground to swallow their numbers. He could… exhaust himself by doing these things. Drain his body of resources and his Diadem of precious power it might not restore for weeks, perhaps months.

If Dorilian was making moves, Nammuor needed to be more prudent.

Using the bridge as a terminal point, he pulled free energy from the surrounding air and earth. Simple magic. The Highborn could do it and by using his device, so could Nammuor. The chants from the crowd below stilled as the troublemakers noticed him on the balcony and that he was generating a giant orb of swirling blue. A few of the wiser among them screamed. Some people began to run... toward the bridge. Nammuor released the gathered power.

In a thick bolt, crackling light leaped toward the bridge and the singular void Nammuor had created. Tendrils spilled over into the crowd, outracing the scurrying fools, passing through their mostly liquid bodies and causing scores to fall, screaming, many sliced into halves or with gaping holes where their torsos had been. Where the bolt found the bridge, the stone arch shattered, laced by blue violence. Stones dropped with loud splashes into the canal to crackle and hiss beneath the cries of the dying.

Dropping his arms to his sides, Nammuor staggered and propped his palms onto the stone balustrade. White heat behind his facial bones and skull screaming from the Diadem's incursion, he kept his eyes open to see what he had wrought. Survivors desperate to escape jumped into the canal. Others fled toward the scant protection of a small woodland at the Rillhome island's western edge. Those who had not survived, and those who would not, littered the grounds.

He had done enough. No one would attack this palace again, not tonight. All he wanted now was to leave this glowing, sickly place and return to Aral.

"What have you done?" Erenor came to stand just behind him. "How are my soldiers supposed to cross? How am I supposed to get home?"

"I don't care. Walk on the bodies of the dead. Swim." Nammuor touched the gems of his translocation device. Before his eyes Erenor and the destroyed bridge faded from view, to be replaced by the ocean outside the windows of his Aral work chamber. His ears were filled by the cries of gulls. But most welcome of all was that he no longer felt the Rill's oppressive presence.

3

One might argue that Khelds are a provincial culture:
insular, focused on internal struggles and ambitions, hostile
to outside influences. Yet Triemperal merchants would do
well to consider that Khelds are well-famed for their
hospitality, their ready laughter, their lively minds and
music—and also for the unsurpassed generosity of their
tables. No one sets a better table, nor prepares food more
deliciously, than a Kheldish innkeeper.

MARC FREDERICK STAUBERG-RANDOLPH,
OPINION REPORT TO THE MERCANTILE QUORUM

Hans lifted the latch and slowly entered. Herberth and Farrl,
and lastly Arne, filed in after him. Though the corridor was
murky, the room was bright. His first impression was of a
cozy, cluttered hole inhabited by a not-so-orderly packrat. The room
was taken over by books. Those overran the shelf-lined walls and
were stacked in every available corner. But a fine fire spread its warm
light from a stone hearth, and oil lamps cast a softer glow.

Robdan rose from his desk in a far corner of the room, a pen
clutched in one hand. A short, spare man on the older side of middle
years, with curling hair thinning at the top, a pale face worn into
grooves of worry, and inquisitive eyes of clear, bright Kheld blue,
Robdan watched, stock-still, as the four men entered.

"Arne-lad, sister's-son, is it really you?" Putting his pen aside,
Robdan stepped from behind the desk and extended his arms in
greeting. When Arne came into his embrace, he clasped him warmly.
"Wyneghan cried for weeks until she learned you were safe."

Arne's jaw dropped. "She learned? How? I never got to write
nothing even after I learned how."

"Neither of us did," said Hans, noting Robdan's lack of surprise. A possible answer nudged into place and he said to Arne, "Word got out to my mother, though."

Wide-eyed, Arne snorted. "That woman we met with, the Kheld man's wife!"

"That could well be," said Robdan. "Wyneghan claims to have heard it from a woman's tongue, even before I had official word." He chuckled at their bemusement. "Sordan is not exactly the back hills of the world. News does get out of there." He turned to Hans. "You don't know how welcome you are here, Hans-lad. Your coming is an answer to our prayers." To Herberth he said, "Welcome, Elector. We are honored by your visit."

Herberth returned the greeting and introduced Farrl, whom Robdan also welcomed.

"So you *knew* we were coming?" Hans could not believe it. Certainly Brec and the others had not feigned surprise. He looked at Herberth, who shrugged his ignorance of the whole affair.

"Not the Elector. He's quite unexpected." With a sheepish smile, Robdan pointed to the faded chairs. "Please be seated, all of you. The fact of this is that a few months ago—quite apart from Wyneghan's news—I had contact with someone who, in exchange for certain… cooperations, on my part, let me know that you—and Arne here—would not be held prisoner in Sordan indefinitely. That you were going to be let go."

Hans, who alone remained standing, continued to stare at him, completely at a loss. "Dorilian?"

"I think so." Robdan's expression apologized for not being surer. "By way of intermediary, you understand. Amallar has no official relationship with Sordan, of course, but there've always been informal exchanges. What I was asked to do was to buy time for him, to keep the clans from doing anything rash when it was heard that you were being kept prisoner in Sordan. The hardest part was that I couldn't tell anyone what I knew—and especially not Wyneghan!"

Dorilian had tied as neat a knot as Hans had ever seen—the unbelievable bravura of the man to have secretly directed events in Amallar! If the Khelds ever found out, they would be livid… and Robdan even more under fire than he already was. It occurred to Hans that Robdan just might be as naive and misguided as Arne and Brec seemed to think.

"Uncle," he said, using the Kheld word for any older male blood relative with whom one was familiar. "I don't know what kind of game Dorilian is playing or what he planned to do. Arne and I escaped from Sordan—he didn't let us go."

"He didn't?"

"No."

Robdan's expression fell and he looked away. "Is he as treacherous, then, as everyone believes?"

"And you don't?" Arne challenged, wide-eyed.

"No. I never have." Robdan spoke with thoughtful consideration. "He has always been rather... predictable where Amallar is concerned. On his own terms, he's more to be trusted than any of Essera's shifty lords."

"Well I don't know anyone who thinks that," Arne persisted.

"And I know many. In one way or another I've been on the fringe of Esseran politics for most of my adult life, much of it in the Archhalia. I watch, I read, and I learn. Sordan's Hierarch is brutally honest about what he thinks. He never comes to the table pretending, as many Esseran lords do, that he has Amallar's best interests at heart. I may not always like the answers I get from Dorilian Sordaneon, but I can count on those answers to mean what they say."

Herberth agreed. "The Sordaneon eagle has yet to pretend to be a dove, that I know. Your own men trust the Hierarch's word in the field."

Arne grimaced. "That's because there's a code about such things, the King's own."

"And at the moment no king to enforce it," Herberth pointed out.

With a shake of his head, Robdan gave Hans a weak smile. "See? You've only just come home and already there is argument."

"Nothing I haven't heard before."

"And more of it to come, I'm afraid. By now surely word has spread that you are here. That sort of news travels quickly where every wall fronts on some neighbor's ear. My little apartment is fortunate in its privacy." Robdan took a seat upon the raised stone hearth and rubbed his hands before the fire. They were scholar's hands, unhardened and stained by ink. "By keeping my people from doing anything rash, I haven't gathered much favor. The clan chiefs think me a coward. A few accuse me of being in Staubaun back pockets. To everyone else I'm just an old fool too immersed in fanciful politics to see reality. But I do see it. I see it clearly. People easily forget that reality is a giant beast and that those who stare it in the face may become so frightened of its teeth that they never see the claws—and it is the claws that strike soonest. Therefore, I like to look for claws." Robdan indulged his notion with a self-deprecating laugh.

Hans sat on the hearth facing him. "Uncle, I don't know if Dorilian Sordaneon will prove to be the blackest betrayer that ever lived, but I doubt it. And the men in his pocket, he scorns for being small enough to fit in it. He never even tried to put you there. And I think I know why—there's no man in the world who owns a pocket big enough to hold an honest man. And that's what I need, Uncle. I need honest men. Honest *people*. I don't need to be told what Stefan would have done; I need to find out what Stefan *should* have done. And I don't need to be told what to do; I want to gain the wisdom to help me figure out what needs doing. Once I have that, I can steer my own path."

Watching relief break into Robdan's kindly gaze, Hans knew that he had opened the right door, said the right things. That he had taken the right advice. Dorilian had been on the mark about one thing, at least: Robdan was a man whose guidance could be trusted. Unfortunately, Hans needed more than guidance.

"I want an alliance with Sordan, Uncle."

Though Arne loudly groaned and Herberth bowed his neck at hearing Hans state aloud what he had already said to Trongor's governors, Hans kept his focus on Robdan. What Hans saw in Robdan's expression was pure, unconcealed hope.

"Did I hear you correctly? You *want* an alliance?"

Hans watched the shifting patterns of firelight on Robdan's face—and those of the others. "I don't want to tear the Triempery further apart. I want to put it back together."

"Oh, lad, do you think you can?" Though the others in the room leaned forward, listening intently, it seemed only the two of them sat before that low fire in the heart of Amallar.

Hans spread his hands. "I have to try. I *want* to try. And this is where I must start. Here in Amallar. I've been trying to sort things out and... well, there's an old saying I know about getting one's own house in order."

Robdan gave a nod and a tilt of his head that said he was interested in hearing more. "Did you accomplish anything in Sordan? Toward that end?"

Hans looked at Robdan sharply. He had yet to meet another Kheld capable of asking that question, simple as it was.

"I think that Dorilian and I are capable of talking to each other without dragging up the past. We got most of that out of the way in Sordan, and I would call that an accomplishment of sorts. I may have made a mistake in leaving him on bad terms—but I don't regret it. I'll just have to deal with those consequences. I think that if I can go to him, having proven that Amallar will listen to me, maybe even follow me, he will regard seriously any proposal I make. He's ultimately political. He wants peace with Amallar, and he wants it badly. We may be able to reach an understanding."

"But that talk of you being a prisoner in Sordan—were you?"

It was time for Hans, too, to be honest. "I don't know. It didn't always feel that way, though at the end it did. But people have told me that Dorilian might do one thing and mean another. I can sometimes judge his intentions, but not always—he's too complex for me to fully unravel."

"Yes. Many say the same," Robdan admitted. "Indeed, the entire Archhalia."

Hans smiled at his uncle, finding him an unlikely politician. And very possibly an effective one.

Robdan returned the smile, though his was wry, and sad. "There have been only a handful of Archhalia meetings since Stefan was murdered and I took office as representative for my people—and the Hierarch attended only *one* of those meetings. Tensions were very high. He arrived late and left... abruptly. Though I was there to witness that session, I regret to say the Hierarch and I have never actually met in person." Robdan's blue gaze steadfastly acknowledged Hans's surprise. "The Archhalia is a public bed, but no one wants to sleep with me. In the Archhalia, every word, every gesture, every moment of every glance is measured and assigned significance. And not just by Staubauns. Were I to initiate a conversation with Sordan's Hierarch, even if I *could*, and the Stefanites here in Amallar got wind of it, they would see me stripped of my post—and that would do no good to anyone." He gave Hans an apologetic look. "I have far more hope that you can get something done. A dialogue is the only foundation for lasting peace between Sordan and Amallar. Yet it is the one thing we've never had."

But Hans had picked up on another term Robdan had used. "Stefanites?" he asked, though the name suggested the answer. "Has some sort of cult or something grown around my brother's reign?"

"Not a cult, no. But followers. Stefan had a great many supporters among our people, you see, and when he died... let's just say they didn't stop supporting him, even though at the end he didn't value their loyalty to the degree they thought he should. It was largely to oppose the power of the Stefanites—especially the ones he had raised to lordships—that the Staubaun lords of Essera resisted Stefan's reforms. And afterward... well, his friends died with him, may they rest in peace, because the turmoil goes on without them. His followers who remain will look to you now to fulfill their aspirations."

"And what might those be?"

"Lands. Titles. Influence. And a few will also want Dorilian Sordaneon's head on a pike."

Hans battled a twist of nausea when he saw that Robdan was not joking. Across the room, Herberth and Farrl looked disgusted but not surprised. Even Arne did not look disturbed by the suggestion, though he, more than any of them, should have known better. "Well, they can forget about that one." Hans was surprised by the sheer power of his own reaction. He had heard Staubauns speak as violently, and with more immediate threat, against his own life.

The threat fed images still bright in his mind. A sword cleaving fingers. Dorilian reaching for Marc Frederick across a chasm, begging him to take his hand. Hans caught himself, astonished where his mind had wandered. The connection then had been so intensely *personal*....

That explained it, of course. Drawing back, he noticed that his hands were icy cold even though they rested upon stones warmed by a fire. It took an effort to pull his thoughts away.

"What is it?"

He felt Robdan's hand on his shoulder and shrugged it off, though there was nothing in it but a steady, utterly human warmth.

"I don't know. I can't explain it." There was something almost hypnotic about the dancing gases of the fire, the conversion of common things—of wood and air—into heat and light. Into magic. Hans shook his head. "I just know something's waiting for me in Essera. Something beautiful and terrible and powerful. Marenthro didn't tell me what I would find because I wasn't ready to understand.

I still don't, but I know it's there; I can feel it. And I'm not sure how he fits, but Dorilian is part of what I'm here to do."

Robdan stared at him, seemingly at a loss, but with intense interest. Nearby, Herberth and Arne were looking at Hans quizzically, straining to hear. He must have been talking to himself, almost whispering. He met Robdan's gaze. "Marenthro knew what would happen when Dorilian and I came together—he knew it would be strong. It's part of why he sent me away, he and my mother. They wanted me far away for a while, not just from dreams or Nammuor, but Dorilian too, maybe because we might become enemies the way he and Stefan did. But now Nammuor is stronger, or our enemies have gotten to be too many. Something. So Marenthro decided to throw me into the fire—with Dorilian, together. I'm here to forge something, Uncle."

"Forge what?"

"I haven't figured that out yet. An alliance, to start, against the people who want to kill *me*." Hans stood and stretched. His body felt both taut and supple again, as if the fire had seeped into his muscles. "I'm going to send a messenger to Sordan tomorrow. With any luck, Dorilian will send an emissary right away and we can get a head start on this thing."

"But that will take weeks, even just to open a dialogue." Robdan appeared worried. From the chairs nearby, Arne and Herberth still heeded the conversation. Farrl maintained watch at the door. "Time already is growing short. The situation in Essera has been worsening for months. And Sordan is very far away. To go there and back again—"

"It should only take a week to get to Sordan. Maybe Herberth would do it—" Hans glanced at the Elector, who nodded. A faded but beautifully drawn map hung mounted above the mantelpiece and Hans gestured to it. "You could even go with him, Uncle. You could ride to Dazunor-Rannuli—that's the closest Rill city, right? —and then go by Rill."

Rising from the hearth, Robdan ran a hand through his graying hair. "Even if I could do that—if they would *let* me…. You haven't heard, have you?" He looked at Hans, then at the others. "The news only reached Rhodhur two days ago, though there were rumors before that. The Rill has stopped running."

Herberth swore something dread and foul. The others gasped. Robdan might as well have said that the Dazun had ceased to flow.

"When?" Hans asked.

"A little over two weeks ago. It happened while the Epoptes were convening at Permephedon. Naturally everyone is saying that Dorilian did it."

"He could have." It so completely fit. Hans realized he should have guessed it. Dorilian wasn't a man to just sit still and do nothing.

"I did hear, by way of a message from Trulo, that the Rill still runs at Randpory Crossing." Robdan volunteered what he clearly hoped was helpful information.

"He just cut off Essera—and Neuberland." Hans looked at the map again.

Herberth snorted. "He kept Sordan's share intact."

"And yours." Robdan pointed out Trongor's proximity to Randpory Crossing. From his seat, Herberth merely raised both eyebrows and sank his chin into his hand.

Hans, too, juggled thoughts that refused to stand still. His situation had just gotten either better or worse. His first thought, and fear, was that Dorilian had stopped the Rill in some sort of retaliatory strike at him. How better to stir up Essera than to cut its Rill out from under them—and then cast the blame on someone at whom they could lash back? But another, far more tantalizing possibility suggested itself. He remembered Dorilian in a rage at the Epoptean leader, Quirin, and threatening to shut down the flow of supplies into enemy hands. And not just supplies....

Information. Dorilian had made sure Essera would not know what was happening.

My escape, Hans realized. He licked dry lips. Stopping the Rill was the first strike in their war. But were he and Dorilian allies... or enemies?

"Looks like you're in rather a hole." Herberth glumly eyeballed Hans from across the room. "Your murdering regent on one side and him on the other, and Nammuor looking to jump in." Hans could almost read Herberth's mind—that Trongor was in the damned hole with him.

"Nammuor should take a good look before he leaps," said Hans. "The hole may be a hell of a lot deeper than he thinks." *It may reach all the way to Sordan.*

A knock on the door interrupted them. After heaving a sigh, Robdan went to answer it. He had opened the door but the tiniest of cracks when it flew open, several men thrusting Robdan aside so they could barge past him into the room. Involuntarily, Hans's hand flew to the hilt of his sword. Herberth and Arne jumped to their feet at the sudden intrusion, Farrl placing his body—and sword—between the room's occupants and the newcomers.

A stocky man, his full brown beard streaked with strands of gray, planted himself before them with eager brusqueness. "Hans Erwanson?" The man turned his small, narrowed eyes on Farrl and gauged the Trongorian's steel. "Tell this man to put his weapon down. I'm Nalf Rhys Thegn, Thegnard of this land, and you're in my house. Under my protection! No harm will come to any man here."

Hans shoved his half-drawn sword back down into the scabbard and gestured that Farrl and Herberth should do the same. If ever Hans hoped to win over the Khelds, or earn the support of Trongor as an ally, he needed to act like a leader. A prince.

"Nalf Rhys Thegn," he acknowledged. He assigned that name as one he must remember. "I don't appreciate when people force their way into my company."

It was, he thought, the sort of thing Dorilian might say—and he liked the way it fit.

Nalf angled back, head up, heavy eyebrows lowering across his rough face as he stopped to take another look. *It worked*, thought Hans, only a little surprised. He had borrowed from a master, after all.

"Hans Thegn." Nalf reworded his greeting to the politest form. "We didn't realize that you would find our welcome too abrupt."

"Actually, I think Robdan found it so."

Nalf's glance at Robdan displayed neither annoyance nor concern. "And I think he expected it. Hans Thegn can't return to the land his brother ruled first and best and not be welcomed for it! We're here, all of us, and we're ready to stand beside you where you stand, or march at your side against all manner of those who would oppose you in your destiny!"

"My friends and I have just traveled all the way from Trongor, Thegnard." Hans granted the title, if only to demonstrate that he knew it. "What we are is *tired*. We only just arrived."

Nalf laughed and strode forward to throw an arm across Hans's shoulder. "And you need a place to stay, lad! That's why you'll room with me, in my best quarters."

Robdan looked affronted. "I think Prince Handurin should have his own quarters. And the Lord Elector of Trongor should be quartered with his men. There are apartments enough in this jumble of an inn."

Nalf's smile didn't quite mask his impatience. "Those rooms will be filled by morning, what with the harvest and the hunt and folk hearing that their prince has returned! He needs to stay with those who can do him the most good."

"Isn't that for him to decide?"

"Once he knows the facts."

"I know one fact," Hans interrupted the exchange. Beneath the thin facade of this argument, he sensed issues far more heated. He could guess the nature of those problems which moved men like Nalf Rhys and Robdan Aelfricson to oppose each other. *Stefan*, he thought. *Stefan's memory divides them like a wall divides a house.* He moved to lighten the atmosphere surrounding his return to Amallar. "The fact is that neither I nor my guests can eat arguments. And the thing I remember best about Khelds is that it isn't good manners to let guests go hungry."

"You remember well." The expression in Nalf's blue-gray eyes was shrewd and left no doubt he sensed the redirection. "There's a feast being set in the Hall even as we speak. When Brec told us that you'd come and young Arne here was with you"—he acknowledged the presence of his other countryman— "we thought to give you a welcome to fit the occasion. We'll have ale pots all around tonight! Come," he said, "meet your people. They've waited long enough for you to put in an appearance."

Nalf led them down a series of narrow hallways built with little respect for aesthetics but with great regard for space. They came out at last onto a balcony overlooking the Great Hall, the main gathering place of all Khelddom and as noisy and crowded a room as could be found in the Triempery and perhaps the known world.

From one end of the room to the other, great iron wheels hung from beams each hewn from a mighty oak and darkened with age and smoke, and those wheels carried dozens of burning oil lamps to cast a somewhat dingy golden glow over the scene below. Tall walls built of rough-hewn granite were grandly covered with wool tapestries woven by many generations of Kheld artisans. The tapestries depicted the everyday lives of their people in colors as vibrant as those that met Kheld eyes when they stepped into a brilliant autumn day. On each facing wall, three yawning fireplaces roared with heat. Stone mantels joined into a single ledge the length of the room and bearing the mounted drinking horns of ancestors. Trophies gathered from battle covered the walls. And milling about the tables and chairs below feasted more Khelds than all but a few Staubauns had ever seen in one place.

With Robdan on one side and Nalf Rhys on the other, Hans stepped out onto the landing and into a din of loud ringing voices and clattering plates. Then, all of a sudden, a great cheer arose. Hans looked down upon a vast roomful of people, men and women, elders and children who had obviously gathered just for this, all lifting their arms to greet him. The intensity of their feeling burned so fiercely and so brightly that all he wanted at that moment was to find some cool dark corner in which to soothe the lie of not being who they wanted to see. Nalf Rhys's hand clamped upon Hans's arm like an iron fetter.

Nalf spoke and the crowd hailed him loudly. Hans barely heard what Nalf said to the crowd, only that they responded with wild joy. *There are so many of them!* Numbed, Hans let Nalf and his lieutenants lead him down the wide stair into the main Hall. An entire room full of Khelds surged forward, hundreds of hands reached out to touch him, to determine that he was real. It was too much, too many. The sheer pressure of so many wants and needs brought home to him the enormity of the task ahead. In their hopeful gazes he glimpsed another man. Saw him in the lift of their heads, the swagger in their walks, and the defiant way they raised their tankards high.

For the remainder of that night, though his name rang from the rafters, Hans did not hear it. Though Nalf never strayed from his side, not once did Hans hear his name upon the Thegnard's lips.

The only name he heard was *Stefan*.

4

When the world turns around, friends vanish, and enemies appear.

STEFAN STAUBERG-RANDOLPH, LETTER TO GOFF HORVADSON

"The situation is... delicate."

Emyli perused the furniture around her and wished she had met Sinon Kouranos in a room with more projectiles. This side chamber was small and sparse, purposed for the keeping of secrets. It lacked even an inkwell or any other means of making notes. "I can't believe this. You're telling me Dorilian Sordaneon doesn't know where my son is?"

"As I explained..."

Hans had escaped. Or sought to escape. Emyli had listened to the Sordani ambassador's explanation and wasn't sure she believed either the part where Hans had somehow engineered a flight from Sordan or the part where Sinon had outlined Dorilian's "deception" about the disappearance. Nearly always, princes who disappeared while in the custody of powerful rulers turned up dead, if they turned up at all. Just because Sinon had explained the story soon to be passed around on every tongue—that Hans remained a prisoner—did not remove the chance it could be false.

"If that man has thrown my son into a cell and thinks he can let him rot—"

"Of course not. Please hear me out."

"Is that why the Rill has stopped? Is that part of *this*?"

Emyli had only to look out the window to see the Rill's shocking transformation, silent and dimmed, utterly unmoving. Day in and day out, all of Permephedon stared helplessly at the frozen god. Emyli had listened for days—far too many days now—to every manner of panic and speculation. She had wondered if Hans might be tied to it somehow, but her demand for Sinon to come to her residence in the High Citadel and provide an explanation had met only with delays and postponements. The privacy of this hidden room, accessed from two equally secretive chambers established in ages past by two branches of now-sundered Highborn kindreds, today served them both well.

Now at last she might get answers.

"I want to speak with Dorilian," she said. "Surely you have some means, surely *he* does."

"None."

Emyli looked at Sinon sharply, sensing more to the answer than that Dorilian Sordaneon would not capitulate to her demand.

"My Hierarch cannot travel by Rill, not currently. Neither can he use it to communicate. As things now stand, *no one* can... travel or communicate. Surely you comprehend this already."

"I just thought... I hoped maybe you would know more or have some way. I cannot believe even Dorilian would be this reckless. There will be war over this."

Sinon slowly spread his hands. "If there is, you can be sure he has taken it into account."

Of course. War... might even be the point of it all. That Dorilian might someday be capable of commanding the Rill had worried all of Essera since the day of his birth. That he would do so now meant... something. But what? Marc Frederick had warned Emyli that Dorilian would tear down expectations—only to erect new ones.

"He's hamstringing us, all of us. Enemies and friends." Emyli's mind raced as previous understandings acquired complex and chilling dimensions. "He's created a darkness the better to move in the shadows—and us *with* him."

"Which instructs us to consider the reason." Sinon steepled his fingers before his nose while his dark eyes met Emyli's across them. "Consider too the significance of his having sent a message to you— one I received in advance to deliver to you."

"I doubt I'm the only person who will hear he has imprisoned my son."

"Ah, but you may be the only person, besides myself, to have heard—from him—that your son *escaped*."

Yes, there was that. The possibility of Sinon's news being true multiplied severalfold.

"And what is he telling me with these words or his deed? Does he want me to sit on his revelation? Do nothing so that events unfold as he sees fit? For months I allowed speculation that Hans might possibly be his prisoner," Emyli reminded Sinon, "and yes, I used that speculation to advance my son's cause! But Dorilian used it too. I let him play his humiliating game. But this—"

"May all be to your son's advantage and protection. We have no way of knowing more, not as things stand. Not *now*. Your Royal Highness, my Hierarch's message tells me he is not playing games with your son's life. But he *is* plucking the strings of what people believe of him."

Enemy. Vengeful. Manipulator. Oh yes, Dorilian was that. Always that. Dorilian had lived his whole life surrounded by deceit, murder, and lies—and he was expert at employing all three.

Marenthro, where are you? Now, when Emyli needed him, Marenthro was nowhere to be found. After letting her know he had brought Hans back to this World, after an embrace and a promise of trust, Marenthro had disappeared. *In their hands.* Those were his very words. *We have done all we can... what happens now is in their hands.*

Theirs, not his. Not hers. But surely, neither had Emyli done everything she might do.

She must be true and pure of purpose. Herself. Essera's Princess and mother of an endangered son.

Whatever she did—or did not do—she must not alert those enemies who watched her. Whether Hans was indeed Dorilian's prisoner, or in danger from him, or was in fact loose in the World and making his own way, there were monsters afoot in Essera— monsters Emyli must convince not to act. About that Sinon was very right. Hans was safer if his regent, the Seven Houses, and Nammuor all believed that Dorilian had locked Hans away, never again to let him see the light of day.

As soon as possible, Emyli must correspond with Asphalladra. Gather more information. Passing messages between them would be challenging now that the Rill was silent and there were no more Highborn Princes in Essera through whom to avail secret message cylinders. But it could be done. There were riders. Ships. Birds. Arrays in Merath and Askorras.

As for Dorilian… Emyli was not about to let that man reign upon his throne in mighty Sordan like some master of puppets. If Sinon could not, or would not, tell her his Hierarch's grand design, Emyli would find someone who would. Tiflan, perhaps. She refused to believe that Dorilian had merely retreated into self-protective paranoia.

"There is another matter, Your Royal Highness."

"Something to do with my son?"

She watched as Sinon fought a smile. "No, at least not directly. My Hierarch, in advance of this development, has secretly transferred significant assets into your name and moved them to Permephedon." He extended a large message cylinder. "The documents within indicate which vaults and give you ownership of the deposited assets. They formerly belonged to your father and have gained value over the years. You will find titles to those original properties, minus the Songbird Palace, and to additional properties, several ships, and a great deal of gold and other commodities."

"And Dorilian is giving these back? To me?" Emyli's heart ached. Stefan had needed this fortune. Had fought during his entire reign to have these assets restored to him.

"He is returning them. He has vacated the trust. You are Marc Frederick's heir."

"What about my sons? My father adopted them. *Stefan* was Marc Frederick's Heir! And Dorilian withheld this money out of spite. He did it so he could enjoy watching Stefan suffer. I don't want it!"

Sinon sighed and ducked his head, then lifted his gaze to hers. "But don't you think Handurin might?"

Lips parted, Emyli let the rest of her retort die between her teeth. Her personal fortune was substantial and sufficient to maintain her, yes, but only that. She could not pay to mount a war. Soldiers. Horses. Weapons and wagons. Too many things. War had drained Stefan's accounts, leaving nothing to his Heir. Only Essera itself still had a treasury, and Erenor would make certain that Hans had no access to it. Hans would need this money. She could use it to help him.

"You will, of course, let your Hierarch know I received these assets."

"As soon as it is possible, yes."

"I hope you understand my lack of gratitude. I have just learned my son is missing—and you can no longer communicate with your Hierarch. There's nothing you or I can do at this moment."

"The day will come, may it be soon, when that will change. I hope you believe that, if you need anything, I will do whatever I can to assist you."

"My poor son." Emyli believed Sinon and trusted him well enough to share her greatest worry. "I pray every day that Hans finds help along the way. My father was given time to learn this World. He had a Wall Lord to teach him and he had people who wanted him to be King. After he defeated Labran Sordaneon and kept Sordan in Essera's orbit, they all wanted him—the Malyrdeon Princes, the Seven Houses, and Amallar too. Even Stefan had the Khelds, at least, and friends and family still in Essera.

"But my poor Hans. Who does he have? Only me? I have not seen him in nine years. This World barely knows him—and he barely knows it. He has no one."

5

Great civilizations are not destroyed by great enemies.
They are nibbled to death by tiny things. By disease or fear
or lies.

EPIRADES, *HISTORY OF THE MALYRDEONS*

I t was afternoon when Dorilian reached the Frendel lowlands. For
the first time in a week, he followed a fresh and direct trail. Small
things scampered through wet leaves that flecked untidy
meadows with gold. He dismounted atop a low ridge and studied the
silver thread of the river below. As his horse cropped at nearby tufts
of grass, Dorilian searched the flats along the river for signs of the
party he followed.

He was much farther north than he had ever planned to go. But
his perverse temper, whether it would prove to be his salvation or
his undoing, had prodded him to catch up with Handurin before he
reached Rhodhur. Unfortunately, the Trongorian party had made
good speed, traveling light and long, and now they were almost to
their destination. It now appeared clear that Dorilian would not
intercept them.

Whatever else would come of it, he did not look forward to having
to deal with Handurin among Khelds. It was little better than not
being able to deal with him at all. There would be need for secrecy
and more secrecy. Good as Dorilian was at it, he knew no secret long
stayed that way. *Damn Handurin for having left Sordan too soon. We
could have settled this whole thing among civilized people!*

Nor did Dorilian feel safe among Khelds. He had not brought
with him such things of power as would protect—but also identify—

him. Only the Rill Stone, carried concealed within a less conspicuous piece of gear. Without access to enhancers, he must depend on his wits and the discretion of others, in addition to his innate ability to emotionally influence situations around him. And looming over all of this, he was hampered by Erydon Malyrdeon's ancient Promise to the Khelds: that in Amallar they would not be attacked or harmed by any Highborn land or person.

That Dorilian had been able to penetrate this far into Amallar at all was revealing. Erydon's Promise remained in force, powerfully so. He discerned its weight within the Mind; the Promise resided in his mind also, so that every time he so much as saw a Kheld along the road, his awareness sharpened to an edge keener than any knife pressed unerringly to his nerves. Much as Dorilian wondered what might happen if he attacked one of the barbarians, he was in no hurry to test the prohibition. He knew not what might follow. All the more reason to find Handurin quickly, conclude their business, and leave this Leur-forsaken land.

Leaden clouds darkened the hills by the time Dorilian had rested his horse and remounted. After making his way downhill, he skirted the flats nearer the stream and kept to the woodlands for cover. Crags looked down on him like angry sentinels, lowering and gray with mist. He found the trail heading toward the river, a narrow track leading downhill. He had almost reached the river when he pulled up on the reins. Two Kheld riders—as shaggy as the small, sturdy horses they rode—emerged on the trail ahead of him.

Dorilian focused on their faces. The men exchanged fox-sly glances and hard-lipped snickers, neither the restrained caution of men intent on their own business nor the determined stance of men employed in the honest stopping of strangers. It was easy to guess what they thought of him: a lone traveler, obviously not a Kheld, probably a stranger to these hills. Easy prey. Dorilian relaxed his hands on the reins and pondered his course. He had never been beset by robbers before. Prior to these last two weeks, he had always traveled with scores of armed guards. A novel situation, and one for which he had no precedent.

If he could not attack them, intimidation might work. He carried a discouragingly serious array of weapons and rode the better horse.

The men approached with their clubs crudely concealed. Just as he placed his hand on his sword hilt to dissuade them, Dorilian detected movement on the hillside above. Other riders moved along the bluff. An ambush, then. The oafs had not looked that cunning. Dorilian quickly reconsidered his plan. Breaking between the two approaching riders so he might continue on the road would only lead to his being caught between the two groups and the towering bluff.

The would-be robbers, accustomed to easy prey, did not yet suspect that their intended victim had no intention of submitting. The Khelds had almost reached him when, with a hoarse yell calculated to startle, Dorilian spurred his larger, stronger beast off the trail.

Though it didn't look like much, the dun gelding had been chosen for utility. Tiflan had made certain Dorilian would have a mount that could outrun his enemies or jump common obstacles with ease. The first two attackers barely had time to gape as horse and rider charged past them, off the road and downhill toward the flats along the river.

The other riders, coming down from the bluffs, emerged onto the flats in pursuit.

Storm clouds loomed, one of those fast storms off the Northsea that drenched Amallar with the wealth of rain that Trongor's arid hills never saw. It came upon Dorilian quickly, fat drops pelting his face and clothing. He could only wish Handurin was having to ward off as many nuisances.

Patches of native grasses and extravagant wildflowers flashed past as he guided his mount past stands of scrubby ash and hardapple trees. Sodden ground, puckered by past floods, threw up the tangled remains of trees now rotted like wrecks of grounded ships.

Dorilian cut along the tree break, heading upstream, back toward the woods and possible concealment. He had left behind the first two men who had accosted him, but had not lost his secondary pursuers. Nor did these Khelds ride like opportunists. They were organized and determined.

He gave his mount its head in the flats. Three men on dark horses pursued him. The rest of the Khelds, reading Dorilian's intent, rode along the base of the hill, racing as furiously as he. Soon he saw the reason. Ahead, the floodplain ended, the hill looming as a wall of green as the river curved toward it. They would engage him there.

Damn! He reined in, turned his mount quickly. Though the gelding bucked and jumped in protest, Dorilian kept his seat. He heard his pursuers shout their alarm at his sudden maneuver. Left with no other course, he charged back at the Khelds immediately pursuing him. The men challenged with their spears, but he spurred his horse around them, gaining the flood plain again before seeing several Kheld horsemen break from the trees, riding toward him. He had no choice now but to make for the river.

To the accompaniment of whistles and hoots, Dorilian headed into the twisted maze of tree trunks and roots, his fleet mount's advantages negated by the terrain as he headed for the river. The three Khelds were again on his heels.

He pressed flat against his mount's neck as the Kheld riders charged again, their horses spurred to full gallop, their spears extended. One spear he dodged as the Khelds gave a shout that he could liken only to a sporting cheer. Again and again, the riders cut him off as he was forced to change direction until, seizing an opening when one rider swung too wide, he broke through and the dun horse leaped forward, sprinting for the water. Ahead loomed a tree trunk, a mass of wood and branches and roots. Too late to turn, the dun horse jumped. Dorilian clung to its neck as the horse pitched forward, front legs giving way as they plunged badly into the hollow on the other side.

A blinding red haze of sheer agony exploded up his left leg and into his brain as he fell sideways into a tangle of soft earth and twisted roots, landing in a sprawling heap beneath the oncoming Kheld horses. Dorilian had a vision of flying hoofs and dirt clods erupting over his head as one of the horses leaped over him, landing with a splash in the muddy marsh grasses beyond. The other Kheld, too, managed to turn aside his horse, leaving Dorilian thankful to not be trampled. That rider returned first, dismounting to approach. The dun gelding screamed and thrashed upon the ground, blood frothing its mouth, its front legs broken. The Kheld called to his fellow, who tossed him a club. With a swift, clean swing, the man brought it down behind the dun's ears, crushing its skull. The horse collapsed and was still.

Grinding his teeth against the pain, Dorilian struggled to a sitting position, the best he could manage. He doubted he could run. Simply to stand might be asking much. He gazed up at his captors, stocky, bearded, blue-eyed men who stared at him with harsh, yet equally intense, curiosity. *Go ahead, look.* He granted them that much due for having run him down.

The good news was, he had hurt none of them. Erydon's thrice-cursed Promise was intact.

When the Khelds did not appear ready to kill him, Dorilian

unbuckled the sturdy Trongorian sword still strapped across his back and with his fingers gripped around the sheathed blade, he offered it to them. It was precisely the sort of gesture that Khelds with their intense love of statements liked to see, and the first horseman nodded with grim respect as he took the weapon. The other man cut loose the saddlebags and spare weapons from the fallen horse and tossed them to one of the other riders. Another galloped away, no doubt to tell the others what had happened. Then both horsemen assisted Dorilian to his feet and lent support as he limped back to where the rest of the Khelds waited at the edge of the flood plain.

Once or twice one of his captors leaned a shaggy face near and attempted a simple question in Khelda. Falling into the hands of barbarians was humiliating enough, but Dorilian would be damned before he made any effort to speak. He needed them only to help him walk. The marshy ground gave way to firmer turf and he stumbled, barely able to stay upright, through clawing, thorny grasses. When they reached the half circle of mounted men, his two captors gave him a shove and forced him to his knees before the others.

Concealing a wince at the sharp tearing in his injured knee as it hit hard ground, Dorilian swallowed the indignity along with the pain. He, who had never in his life knelt to any man not more than he was, was on his knees before louts who would never know the difference. Partly to conceal his distaste, partly to control the pain, he kept his eyes and mind focused on the ground. *A Trongorian*, he reminded himself, committing to that misdirection. *A soldier, a courier, a minor lord—what would it mean to one of those?*

He must be careful. What they saw or heard, they would interpret onto him.

Leather creaked as one of the Khelds dismounted, boots crushing wet stone and soggy twigs underfoot. When those boots emerged into his field of vision, Dorilian was fairly certain that this time he merited the attention of the leader. Even through his forced preoccupation, he sensed the other impatiently waiting. The boots took one step closer. Abruptly, cold steel pressed under Dorilian's jaw. A dagger forced his head back and his gaze up to meet that of a young woman.

She raised her eyebrows above dark-lashed eyes of startling deep sky-blue. Her lips parted slightly with surprise, openly curious.

"Who might you be?" Confidence framed the question, spoken in crisp Trongorian Esta. She must have recognized the trappings of Dorilian's horse or gone through his bags. Though the question was neither polite nor patient, he could no longer pretend not to understand. He was disposed not to answer—until the young woman pressed harder with the dagger at his throat. The blade bit skin. "A name?"

"Thron Estol Bevvan." Dorilian was glad for the way she'd framed the question.

She did not withdraw her weapon. "What are you doing in Amallar?"

Having satisfied his momentary curiosity, Dorilian averted his eyes again and refused to answer. In addition to being uncouth, the woman's tone was undeserving of cooperation.

She released a snarl of frustration but apparently realized her dagger would not answer this question for her and withdrew it. He had given a name, and it matched that on the papers in the saddlebags taken from his horse.

He heard the quiet caress of leather on metal as the young woman returned the dagger to its sheath. "Search him."

His captors tightened their grip and a third man, who'd been standing beside the woman, stepped forward. Reduced to staring in helpless outrage, Dorilian forced himself to remain motionless. The man rummaged through each outer garment, finding and prying into every pocket before feeling down Dorilian's breeches. Had the man gone any further, actually touched him flesh to flesh, Dorilian would have thrust him aside with no more thought to danger than a dying man has of gasping for air. But the search was mercifully brief, more so because it brought forth results: a finely stitched leather envelope thick with papers, a compass, an engraved medallion, and a flask of golden liquid. The compass was examined and quickly set aside. A closer look at the medallion disclosed it to be a token of the Electorate of Trongor, an item one in the Elector's service might conceivably carry. The packet of papers interested the Kheld leader more. There were two messages within and she examined each quickly, using her body to shield them from the rain, scrutinizing colored wax closures imprinted with official seals of state.

One of the seals was that of Trongor—the other, Sordan's.

She froze. Her mouth pulled into a frown of disapproval and undisguised loathing. She was educated, then, for a Kheld, to be able to recognize the state seal of a nation with which her people had no official traffic. *Careful*, Dorilian told himself. But the young woman had caught some nuance of his expression.

"Do you think all women simple... or just ours?" she asked archly. Her fingers tapped the slender documents. "The map in your bags is marked out for Rhodhur. Who there dares to receive a message from Sordan?"

At hearing her speak the hated name, the other Khelds stiffened and their glances, cautious before, turned hostile. Not a question Dorilian cared to answer. But neither was silence an altogether successful strategy. He wanted to be escorted to Rhodhur, not taken off to the woods to be executed as a spy. The time had come to shift tactics.

When the Kheld leader took the Sordani letter in hand and moved a finger under the fold to break the seal, he rewarded her by breaking his silence.

"Those are official documents and not meant for you."

"How can you be sure? You don't know who I am."

"I know who you are *not*."

Dorilian watched the way the young woman's lips parted with a retort that cool sense prevented. She widened the fold, though her gaze stayed locked on his. "Which is more than I know about you. If you won't tell me who this message is for, then the message itself will do it. I read Stauba and Esta."

"Your languages will do you no good." It gave him great pleasure to inform her why. "The document has been encoded."

That answer earned a far from friendly smile. "I suppose *you* could read it?"

"If I would choose to do so."

Which he wouldn't.

Her gaze narrowed. "All right, then." After tucking the documents into her jacket, out of the rain, she held up Dorilian's flask of ambrosia restorative. "Tell me what this is."

"Disgusting. Go ahead. Taste it."

A horse galloped up to the Kheld party. "Thegna Aubrey!" the flustered rider shouted as he pulled to a halt before them. "Thegna Aubrey! Tidings from the Fords!" He barely seemed to be able to control his horse, which pranced from side to side before the group. "Brec at the Fords sent me to tell you—those intruders we saw, just about the same time you started chasing this one? Kin of yours!"

The young woman looked up at the rider, her rain-bright face wiped clean of pique and suddenly pretty, with laughter in her eyes. "I thought you said they were Trongorians!"

"Turns out some were, some weren't. They came up Trongor way. But you'll never guess who was with them."

"Probably not," Aubrey replied with a hint of impatience. "Why don't you just tell me?"

Dorilian did not bother to show interest. He knew what the man would say: that they had found Handurin and that Kheld of his, that they were thrilled with the prince's return, that Handurin would be at Rhodhur within the hour if he was not there already.

The rider did not disappoint. Finally managing to calm his nervous horse he puffed up his chest. "All right. But it's worth waiting for. It was Arne Anseldson, for one, Brec's kilth that was lost in Neuberland. And Hans Erwanson—that's right! King Stefan's brother, the very one!"

But the Khelds around him merely exchanged glances. At last the woman, Aubrey, spoke. "That's impossible, Rudell Cohnachson. Hans Stauberg-Randolph is prisoner in Sordan. Under arrest. That news was the talk of every trader on the Slowpike."

"He must've escaped! Or maybe they let him go. I don't know about that. But he came here, and he'll be at Rhodhur now any minute. Thegna Aubrey," the man said solemnly, "I wouldn't tell it wrong to you, with you being a faetha and holder and all."

"I'm not saying you're lying, Rudell. I'm saying maybe *he* is. He may not be the prince at all and we're buying it." She crossed her arms and turned her face aside as a gust of wind brushed slashes of dark hair down from under her hood and across her cheek.

Her men, however, looked as though they wanted to believe it, and they stared at the messenger hopefully. But poor Rudell was at a loss to verify anything, having heard it secondhand himself.

"I heard him mention the prince." Dorilian spoke up in Esta, drawing startled glances from Aubrey and a few of the men. "I was following Handurin and his party."

"Aren't you informative all of a sudden!" Her hand dropped to her dagger as though she were contemplating using it. "Would you mind telling us what you were following them for?"

"To deliver a message."

"Stones! We're back to that again!" She sorted through the papers in her hand and walked over to where Rudell sat astride his horse. "His papers say he's Trongorian." The papers crackled in the wind as she waved them. The sound mimicked that of the wildly skittering leaves stirred by the coming storm.

Rudell nodded as though that made sense. "I cannot read, Thegna Aubrey, so it won't do no good to show me these. But one of the fellows with Hans and Arne was Herberth of Trongor—yes, himself that heads their lot—and there were other Trongorians with them, a fair number of 'em. And it doesn't look like your man is Staubaun."

"No, it doesn't," Aubrey agreed. She refolded the papers and tucked them into her jacket alongside the envelopes. "I thought for sure he was until I saw his eyes."

"'Sides," Rudell said, smiling. "I never saw one that would dare set foot this far into Amallar. As soon find a Kheld in Sordan, I say."

"You say Prince Handurin is at Rhodhur?" Aubrey tucked her hair back under her hood as the rain pelted down upon them with greater force. When Rudell nodded, she turned to the man who had searched Dorilian. "Wodd, fetch five horses and gear enough for the ride. Rudell can ride with us to rejoin his band. We're taking this man to Rhodhur. Tonight. He has some explaining to do, and he's shown us that he won't do it here."

Wodd hesitated, pointing heavenward as thunder rumbled overhead. "Lud's own Hell, Aubrey! The weather—"

"What of it?" Aubrey looked up at the roiling sky, her profile neatly etched against the rain-heavy clouds. "We've ridden through worse."

"May be, but it'll be nasty. And this fellow is in no shape for hard riding. Look at him!"

"He's in shape enough to talk when it suits him. He'll ride." She spared not a glance to determine her prisoner's condition. "I didn't journey all the way from Saemoregh just to chase down and spend the night standing guard over some tagalong while half the Thegnkeld whoops it up about Hans Erwanson in the Great Hall. I, too, intend to be at Rhodhur when and if anything is to be decided!"

As Aubrey returned her attention to Dorilian, it was impossible for him not to pick up on the resonance of her thoughts. She did little or nothing to dampen them. Impatience, suspicion, and a subliminal prickling of doubt.

While Wodd prepared the horses and gear for the long ride to Rhodhur, two other men helped Dorilian hobble over to a nearby hunters' lean-to, a bare shelter he had not seen from the clearing. A latticework of boughs, some still thick with the previous year's leaves, shielded them from an increasingly persistent rain. It was a narrow, dank space, and in view of his aptitude for escape, Aubrey stayed with him. Having no other option, Dorilian sat upon the rush matting of the floor and leaned against the hard tree bole at his back. He could do little else. It took his full concentration to block the throbbing pain of his knee and the bones broken in his leg and ankle. His Highborn ligaments and tendons would knit in the next several hours and be sound before another night fell. His scratches and scrapes would heal quickly also and even the deepest gouges would be nearly gone by morning. It would be another day at least before his bones fully mended. Fortunately, only the smaller leg bone was broken and it was well supported by his boot; the ankle bone was but a crack. All he really needed was rest.

He wanted only two things from this young woman: to get him to Rhodhur and to be left alone. But when Aubrey closed the flap of the lean-to, it became wearyingly apparent that she wanted to engage in conversation.

She knelt on the matting and emptied the contents of a crude ceramic pot into an even cruder bowl of hollow and discolored wood, which she offered to him.

Dorilian looked upon a thin bean gruel endowed with occasional trespasses of meat, the rank smell of which he found offensive. Hunger battled distaste. He had not eaten since morning. Distaste won out. "No."

"You're not hungry?"

"Not hungry enough to eat that."

"It's your stomach." Aubrey set the bowl aside. She had pushed back her hood to reveal thick dark hair knotted at the right shoulder where a large, ornate brooch held her cloak in place. "We won't be here long."

"Good."

"Are you always this charming?" Her vexed gaze swept across his face and evoked a frown of concern. "At the very least I can take care of some of those cuts."

"No!" It was bad enough he must endure this Kheld wench's questions and her vile food. He was not about to let her touch him as well.

At first taken aback, Aubrey set her jaw. She reached her hand under his chin and wrenched his head to the side so she could look at his cuts in somewhat better light.

"You want those to fester?" she snapped. "I really don't care, you know, but I'm a healer and the Mother has charged me to tend the wounds of fools. Some woman might find you appealing one day if I can get these to heal well. Let me look at your hands."

In the end, Dorilian permitted Aubrey's ministrations because it seemed likely he would get no peace otherwise. He didn't fight when she bathed his facial cuts with what clean water was to be had. Her touch wasn't as bad as he had feared it would be and he barely flinched beneath it. She stroked the deeper cuts clean of blood and dirt with cat's tongue expertise before smearing them with a pungent, stinging salve. She would no doubt take credit when the cuts healed quickly. Aubrey then took hold of his wrists and did the same for his hands. When she finished her attention to his torn fingers and gashed palms, her inquisitive gaze fixed on his with shrewd speculation.

"What kind of life do Trongorians lead these days? These aren't the hands of a soldier."

"I never claimed to be one. It so happens my duties keep me very much occupied with administrative work."

"In what capacity? You don't look like a clerk, either."

Silence seemed the best answer to that question. Aubrey cocked her head and fixed him with another frown. "You're very poor company, Thron Estol Bevvan."

"When I am treated as a guest, I shall respond as one."

"Guests don't run away from their hosts. Let's see that leg."

"That's not necessary. It is quite sound."

Aubrey would no more be dissuaded from that task than the others. Her hands worked calmly and efficiently, pushing up the fabric of Dorilian's trouser leg, firmly kneading torn muscles and bruised, healing flesh. But as her hands pressed through his boot leather into the ankle, she hesitated. When Aubrey pressed again to confirm her findings, he stiffened his abused muscles against further prying.

"The leg will have to wait." She sounded reluctant. "The knee and ankle are swollen and a bone might be broken, but it doesn't feel to be displaced and the boot's an adequate splint for now." From outside the shelter came the sounds of horses being led up to the lean-to and the clatter of armed men and riding gear.

Aubrey turned to heed the arrival of Wodd and two other riders. Their heavy outer garments glistened with rain. Wodd glanced from Aubrey to Dorilian.

"This means we've given up on riding to Garfallow, I suppose."

"What's happening at Rhodhur is more important. Cewitha can

ride with the lads to Garfallow in the morning. She can claim the loom and deliver the coin. They can take it straight back to Amundhal or rejoin us at Rhodhur."

With a crisp nod, Wodd went to make that arrangement. Dorilian watched Aubrey quickly pack together her own gear, thrusting his papers and other confiscated belongings into a leather satchel she carried strapped beneath her heavy cloak. Though rustic, her woolen garments were of good weave and belted with expertly worked leather. The gilded brooch that clasped her cloak hinted of prosperity. So did her education. Aubrey spoke three languages—that Dorilian knew of—and might, for a Kheld, be well born.

Well born and of mixed blood. For all their deeply held hatreds, Neuberland's Khelds were more likely to have mixed with Staubauns than their brethren born in Amallar. Dorilian had noted from the first that Aubrey, though not tall by Staubaun measures, was taller than all but one of her men. Her hair was dark, her eyes blue, but her oval face and narrower nose gave evidence of Staubaun blood. So did the subtle amber undertones in her hair. It was not unheard of for pretty Kheld women to capture the interest of Staubaun men, only to have the offspring farmed out again among their Kheld kin. That would explain her lack of refinement.

"Come on, man." One of the Khelds reached to help him to his feet. But when the man moved to bind his hands, Dorilian forestalled him.

"That won't be necessary." Only twice in his life had he been bound, and he refused to allow it now. "I will not attempt to escape."

Aubrey assessed him in the half light. "You tried to escape us before. Why should we trust you now?"

"You have my word. It has always served to bind me—and more surely, I might add, than those things could."

"Your word is worth so much?" She didn't sound like she believed him. "We shall see. Leave him be, Molloc, but if he makes a move, aim for blood."

Dorilian stumbled worse than before when they led him out, his injuries exploding into sharp new pain with every step. But his hands were free, and by using his uninjured leg he was able to mount the Kheld horse on his own. Aubrey emerged from the lean-to under a layer of rain gear. Lashing the saddle bags she carried to the back of her horse, she mounted with a light energy that defied the storm.

"One of my men will ride forward. I will guard you myself."

"Is that an honor? Or a precaution?"

"Call it what you like." Aubrey took the reins to Dorilian's horse into her gloved hand. "Have you ever been to Rhodhur?"

"No."

"It's not an easy ride, even in good weather. The hills are steep and the road rough, and the Fords may be dangerous in this storm. Because the way will be difficult, I'm going to give you the reins. But I won't be far behind you, and—" She held up a glint of curved metal. Dorilian recognized the sleek horror of a *skifr*. He had last seen one in Sordan, covered with Palimia's blood. "If you try to escape, Thron, I'll skewer you."

He met Aubrey's gaze with new appreciation. "I believe you would."

Aubrey studied him through the rain-wet lashes of her narrowed lids, her irises gleaming blue fire in a flash of distant lightning. Her lips curved into a light smile of distrust and something else, more womanly and less reassuring. "Don't test me, Thron. These are dangerous times, and Amallar is a dangerous place to be—but not as dangerous as Neuberland. I have a feeling about you that just won't sleep—and if I catch the scent of what it is, I just might skewer you anyway."

6

Marc Frederick did not command Kheld loyalty as a
matter of birth. For the first thirty years of his life, neither
Khelds nor Staubauns were aware he existed.

ROBDAN AELFRICSON, *THE STAUBERG-RANDOLPH SUCCESSION*

Hans knocked and, a few moments later, the chamber door
creaked open. Seeing Robdan's face appear in that opening
was relief: it meant Hans had knocked on the right door and
not that of one of Nalf's cronies. Robdan looked surprised to see him
but gestured he should enter.

"Come in, come in. What a pleasant surprise! You're up early. I
don't usually get morning callers." Combing his fingers through
disheveled hair, Robdan ushered Hans into his cluttered front room.
The gloom of a dreary dawn barely drove off the shadows.

"Nalf Rhys is still sleeping it off."

"The ale didn't get to your head, then, given you found your way
back to my place."

"It's funny, but once I've been anywhere, I almost always know
how to get back."

That wasn't strictly true anymore, given Hans didn't know how
to get back to the Qullasuyu or any other part of the First Creation
world he had left behind—but he had just proven he could navigate
Rhodhur Hall. He sank down onto an upholstered chair and watched
Robdan pick up one of the implements next to the hearth. The
morning was damp and cold. Any heat coaxed from the remains of
last night's fire would be welcome.

"I've reached a decision," Hans announced. "A big one. I have
to do something about getting my own room."

Robdan sighed and prodded the coals. "Yes, I think you should."

"I would've done it last night but there was too much confusion. Nalf Rhys made it impossible for me to refuse him. And there were so many people." Hans felt again some of the acute discomfort he'd experienced when Nalf, taking advantage of the chaos and Hans's inexperience, had maneuvered him into spending the night in the Thegnard's quarters. They were impressive as Kheld accommodations went and Nalf had boasted that Hans would have his own bedchamber. "Last night, after we retired from the Great Hall, I really thought I was going to get some sleep. That's all I wanted, one night's sleep in a real bed. But Nalf called in half the Frendeli Cruihcil to begin laying plans for my coronation. I'm not sure because I fell asleep on them, but I think they appointed themselves to positions in my court, or my staff, or whatever."

"Nalf is very ambitious. Stefan allowed him a great deal of authority in that last year, though only in Amallar. I sometimes think—" Robdan cut short what he was saying and put the poker aside.

"Think what?" Hans asked.

Robdan shook his head. "No matter. I was about to be unkind." He padded over to a wardrobe and rummaged within for clothes suitable for the day. Even on short acquaintance, Hans already knew what Robdan would wear. Probably something dark, probably brown, and comfortably well worn, but it would be clean and in good repair. Last night Hans had overheard someone snicker that Robdan aspired to invisibility. He'd also overheard that Robdan was the best customer of the Hall's washwomen.

"Did you sleep well?" Robdan had dug out a brown overtunic to go with his faded trousers.

"No." Hans rubbed his eyes. "Just snatches here and there. When I awoke, I couldn't wait to get out of that bed, out of that room. I believe Nalf Rhys watched me as I slept."

"You might as well get used to it. You're going to be watched in everything you do." Robdan knotted a belt of woven leather strips about his middle and then, because that feature was hardly his best, he bloused the tunic above it. "But we can get you a room of your own. Privacy is available, even in this Hall, if one knows where to look for it. I'll ask Gerd, our innkeeper, what he can do. We've been friends for many years and he will probably tie himself in knots to accommodate you. In fact, now would be a fine time to seek him out.

His breakfasts are famous!" Robdan was clearly eager to move on to more pleasant pastimes.

Hans grinned. "Would you believe I'm starved? I thought I'd never be hungry again after stuffing myself so shamelessly last night."

"You but prove your heritage, lad. There are few things in this world that a proper Kheld would not just as soon accompany with a good meal. I've been told it's because we have little bodies but big hearts."

Hans was familiar with the saying, meant to imply that the taller and leaner Staubauns had big bodies and little hearts. Not entirely untrue, taken altogether. "A little early for breakfast, isn't it?"

"It's never too early for breakfast. You're up, I'm up, and there are herdsfolk and smiths who rise before the sun does. We'll not be alone at the table." Before they stepped out into the dark hallway, Hans following, Robdan covered the grate and lit a taper. "Of course, considering how much drink went down last night, I suspect most of this Hall will sleep until the cows come in."

With Robdan leading the way, Hans traveled the empty, narrow halls. Predawn draped the slumbering Hall with a muffled, gray-edged silence. Unlike most places of government and decision, people actually lived in Rhodhur Hall. Most of those residents were men. Women generally found housing in the Barrowwood, the Thegn Motherhome, more to their liking. Men who had no family with whom they might board often found it easier to take a room at the Hall than seek out one in town. Though they varied in age and occupation, the Hall's inhabitants were generally law-abiding; many were seasonal residents or travelers passing through.

Robdan knew where to find Herberth's room, which the Elector shared with Farrl. As expected, the Trongorians were awake and eager to leave their small quarters.

When they reached the cavernous dining hall, Hans spied Arne already seated at a table with two stalwart young Khelds and his brother Brec. The latter was still suffering from last night's celebration and had braced his head in his hands. A few more men gathered at tables nearer the kitchen, but they were well into their meals, leaving the innkeeper free to join the newcomers.

Gerd Vesl Ralfson was the most robust of cooks and innkeepers, a rotund, indefatigable man with curly dark hair thinning on the top. According to Robdan, Gerd rose before dawn every morning to set his porridges, stews, and griddles to warming. This day was clearly no exception. The man all but popped to his feet when he saw Hans and Robdan coming down the stairs into his domain.

"Good morning, Hans Thegn!" he announced. "And Rob! Did you sleep well with all that commotion last night? What would you have for breakfast? Anything you want, anything at all. Sorry I don't remember the names of your friends. There's so much happening around here lately and so many new people that I simply can't keep track."

"Herberth, Lord Elector of Trongor, and Farrl, Captain of the Elector's guard." Hans named the Trongorians, who had gotten short shrift of the introductions the night before. Nalf had clearly stolen the show for his own purposes. After exchanging pleasantries, Farrl said he must see to how his men had spent the night and left. Hans slid onto the bench beside Arne, with Herberth seated to his left and Robdan across the table. "Do you have any eggs for us?" Hans asked. Just yesterday, his companions had voiced missing that delicacy.

"If I don't have eggs, I'll lay them myself!" The innkeeper hastened off to the kitchen.

Robdan pulled at his loose tunic and glanced around the nearly empty hall. "Am I wrong, or is there a draft this morning? A chilly draft?"

"Just not enough people here to heat it up, Uncle," Brec said morosely.

"Where is everybody?" Herberth scanned the cavernous emptiness that last night had seemed to be a bottomless well of Khelds.

"Sleeping it off," Brec replied.

"As you should be, I think."

Brec shrugged. "Wish I could. Mother knows my head could use that mercy. But I've men at the Fords to get back to." He turned a bleary eye on Hans. "If you came that way, no telling what's coming on your heels. Doesn't hold together that you could get out of Sordan like that and they wouldn't send something after you."

Hans had decided last night it was best to speak carefully. "There's a lot going on that folk here in the kelds don't know about." He used the word that loosely meant a community of their people. "The world outside has gotten complicated. Sordan has other problems, and bigger ones than Stefan's little brother come home."

"I sure as Madrock's Hells hope so!" one of the other Khelds snorted.

"I suspect the Rill is *your* bigger problem," was Herberth's contribution. Since hearing that news the night before, Herberth had been tense and unhappy. That Trongor needed Sordan—and the Rill—was something Hans would soon need to address. If only he knew how. "Essera will not be so welcoming now that the Rill is stopped. Sordan's message is clear: You are on your own."

"That ain't such a bad place to be," said Arne. He punctuated that statement by biting into a hunk of jam-slathered bread.

"Did you say the Rill's been stopped?" asked Brec. Hans could only surmise that out in the wild on patrols, Brec had not yet heard that bit of news. Few in Amallar paid attention to Rill talk.

"Cold north of the Randpory," Arne told him.

"You don't say," marveled Brec. His two men sitting with him at the table also looked amazed. "Thought that was a lot of talk, that the Sordan folk could do such. Never thought nothing could stop it. I knew a fellow once that got in the path of one, at Bellan Toregh where it flies. Top of the tor, among the cold trees. Climbed up there drunk when he should've known better, used rope and arrow and then hung down and tried to hitch a ride. Only it doesn't work that way, goes too fast. You can hardly see the damn thing coming 'til it's on you. So there he was hanging and something seemed to throw him in the air, like, and just tore him to blood and pulp, not even enough left to interest a crow." He shook his head. "That's when I thought to myself there ain't no way to stop one of those things. It just bounces back and forth, and it'll go on forever, 'cause there ain't no way to stop something you can't even see."

"Never did us no good, anyways." Another of the Khelds plunked his mug down on the table.

"It could," said Hans. Heads turned to stare at him and he knew that he had been right all along. The Rill. Essera's golden goose. The silver jewel of Sordan's crown. The Triempery's beating heart, Dorilian had called it. What if Amallar could be brought into that shining circle?

"At Bellan Toregh," Hans explained. "Think about it—the Rill already runs there." The faces watching him showed only disbelief, but Hans turned the idea over, and then over again, wondering if he could get them to embrace his vision. "Bellan Toregh was a Rill port once. It's a node. I saw it on a map in Sordan, a map of everywhere the Rill used to run. But Amallar was so sparsely inhabited for so long that there was no need for it, no reason to awaken a node for the Rill to stop here."

"And it won't never stop here, neither." Clearly, Arne's wider knowledge of the world hadn't improved his opinion of the Rill. "Us being backward weren't the only reason. Even the Staubauns say it can't run nowhere 'cept the way it does. There's no one can wake it up and no changing it. Besides," he reasoned, "it's all stopped now, so what's the use?"

"Maybe I can get it unstopped."

Fortunately, Hans didn't have to say more. Gerd chose that moment to bustle in with a tray piled high with covered plates and steaming mugs. Dishes clinked and utensils clattered as Gerd and two helpers set plates upon the table. Fried golden eggs smiled sunnily upon beds of toasted biscuits, golden fried shredded potatoes nestled beneath slabs of cured, spiced pork side. Pots of potent honey-laced grog bumped up against crocks of cider and deep cups of branroot, a thick dark drink made from the ground tubers of a plant that grew in these hills. Baskets of apples and late peaches sat within reach of every hand. Gerd had outdone himself even by Kheld standards, which were generous. All thoughts not having to do with food, even dreams of the Rill, slunk under the table, embarrassed by any pretensions of importance.

Rain splashed against high windows, distorting the scant sunlight. Following the Kheld custom of not allowing conflict or controversy of any sort to disrupt a meal, Hans and his companions spoke quietly together. Enemies had been known to meet across a dinner table, exchange pleasant conversation, and then kill each other in the street after. They barely attended the sounds of horses being ridden into the stone-paved courtyard. Only Brec, whose appetite lagged behind the others, looked up from his plate when the main doors opened and a rain-drenched party stepped into the Hall and onto the landing. When Brec jumped to his feet and dashed toward the newcomers, Hans lifted his head to watch.

"Hey, Aubrey!"

At Brec's greeting the other diners looked up, some surprised, others curious.

One of the new arrivals turned at the sound of the name and pulled back a sodden hood to reveal a young Kheld woman with disordered strands of loosely knotted wet hair trailing across her travel-worn features. Arne turned to Robdan with a questioning gape.

"Probably business of some kind or other. She's forever improving her holding," Robdan told him.

"Last I saw her," Arne said, "she was a skinny brat in braids!"

Aubrey spoke animatedly with young Brec as they approached the table, her two men coming behind. A third man, head bowed and hooded, apparently a prisoner, bent over and leaned upon the two men as he limped between them.

"Hans Thegn Erwanson—or should I say Stauberg-Randolph?" Aubrey greeted when Brec pointed him out to her.

"The first, I think. Here, anyway." Hans smiled up at her, but he was more than a little curious. "Aubrey...?" he prompted, unsure of her relationship to him and following Kheld custom to first establish if there were kin bonds to honor.

"Aubrey Thegn Amundda. If you ask Robdan, he will admit me cousin to his kilth, and so also to yours."

When looked upon to confirm this, Robdan nodded, his broad smile welcoming. Aubrey smiled back before she resumed attention to Hans. "I would ask pardon, Hans Thegn, for disturbing your meal, but the matter is important, and it seems to me only your attention will solve it. Yesterday my men and I ran into Brec south of the Fords. He was going after your party and wanted me to intercept a second man who appeared to be following you."

Hans turned on Brec. "You could have told me!"

Brec shrugged. "About what? Could've been just about anything, this time of year. We've had reports of ruffians about, too, stealing travelers' purses. Figured we'd know soon enough with Aubrey taking care of it. And it was too soon to wonder where she'd got to. With that storm hitting and all, I thought she'd wait it out 'til morning anyway."

"I would have, except for these." Aubrey reached inside her bulky rain gear and drew forth a dark envelope and a bundle of papers, which she placed on the table. "The top paper says he's Trongorian. There's also a letter attached to a bunch of mining reports."

From beside Hans, Herberth stared closely at the prisoner.

"He ran away from us at the Fords and, except for the name, has refused to grant us any two words resembling a straight answer. And one of the documents in the envelope is marked with Sordani seals."

"Hells! Let me see that." Brec reached for the papers.

"Wait," said Hans. The sealed documents looked official. He turned to his right. "Elector?"

His rank acknowledged, Herberth picked up the papers and began to leaf through them. He frowned over the identification and handed it to Hans, along with a heavy mining report and two sealed documents. Though wrapped in an envelope of treated leather for protection, the fine ivory parchment was damp and stained by handling—still, there was no mistaking that silver eagle stamped into the emerald-green wax seal upon the fold. The symbol glowed. *Sordan.* Hans cradled the letter in his hands. It was plainly an official correspondence, and he didn't doubt for a moment whose hand had sent it.

Dorilian anticipated me, or his spies found me. It must have reached Ogarth after I left. He looked at the messenger who had followed him into Amallar to deliver it. The man had been forced to kneel on the wooden floor, where water from his soaked clothing was rapidly forming a puddle about his knees. It was difficult to tell much about him. Hans glanced away, only to feel Herberth's fingers dig into his knee under the table, demanding that he take another, closer, look.

Hans's indecision alerted Aubrey who, puzzled, attended the captive herself. She shook her head. Her men, in their excitement at meeting the Stauberg-Randolph prince, had neglected to remove the prisoner's hood.

"You can show him," she admonished her men before she yanked back the concealing leather.

Hans swallowed hard. Beside him, Arne's mouth dropped open and he might have said something had Robdan not leaned forward to ask for butter and gained Arne's attention that way. Hans caught a brief glimpse of Robdan's pale face and mouthed warning to say nothing.

Dorilian? Not even rough clothing and rain-darkened hair, or a face marred by already fading cuts and bruises, could mask the contemptuous recognition in those silver eyes. They locked onto Hans's with an entirely unsubtle appreciation of his dilemma. *Both* their dilemmas. But surely Aubrey and her men didn't know who Dorilian was, or they would have announced it to the world. Hans tried to think clearly—but could not think at all.

One slip and these people will tear him to pieces!

7

Stefan will not listen to reason. He points to the Wall and
how it survived the deaths of its Highborn kindred, so he
says the Rill will survive the deaths of the Sordaneons. His
desire to remove Dorilian I at least understand. They've
torn at each other's throats for years. But why kill the boy
too? Stefan's fear of the Highborn is such that he wishes to
murder even babes in the womb.

CULLEN BRODHESON, LETTER TO HIS WIFE ASPHALLADRA

Impossible.

Hans tried to force his mind to accept what he was seeing. A
man. One man on his knees being stood over by armed guards
while Hans enjoyed breakfast at a table in Rhodhur Hall in the
company of boisterous Khelds. This man didn't fit with any of it.

That Dorilian Sordaneon could even *be* in Amallar shattered
possibility. Dorilian famously had not left his fortified island for several
years. He was *always* heavily guarded. Always richly dressed. Always
clean. It was inconceivable that he should show up—alone and filthy—
in Amallar, a country he vehemently hated and that hated him in turn.

Most impossible of all was seeing Dorilian on his knees. To anyone.

Aubrey might have yanked back her prisoner's hood in irritation,
not triumph, but that was all the evidence Hans needed. It really
was Dorilian on the hardwood planks, glaring at him to say or do
something. Preferably something that wouldn't put an end to his life.

I won him over, Hans realized. *I succeeded after all.* Going to
Sordan had *not* been a waste of time.

But what the hell do I do now?

"Release him." Hans thought he did a passable job of keeping the
tightness in his throat out of his voice. "This man is known to me."

With renewed interest, he glanced again at the Trongorian papers in his hands and noted the name written there. Thron Estol Bevvan. Such a fragile thing, a change of name. An interesting choice, though. Thron meant "eagle" in Ardaenan, a tongue commonly spoken only south of the Telarkans. Bevvan was probably derived from the Esta word, *bevar*, for "commander."

The men who'd brought in Dorilian, at least, appeared ready to accept their wet, disheveled charge as Trongorian. And if Arne kept his mouth shut, probably other Khelds would as well. They'd have no reason to think otherwise. Dorilian certainly *looked* rough.

With a warning look at Arne, whose dumbfounded stare promised to do whatever Hans wanted, Hans handed the papers to Herberth. For what were probably the same reasons as Hans, Herberth too was tense-jawed, saying nothing. The Khelds around the table showed more interest in some of the papers than in the man who had brought them. For now, Hans had no real choice but to let the situation play out.

Something indecipherable warmed in Aubrey's eyes and she gestured to her men to release the prisoner. Her former captive shot her an icy glare that would have made a Sordani Haliast shrivel on the spot. Hans almost did. It was obvious Dorilian felt he had been subjected to less than suitable treatment. How unsuitable, Hans wished he could know, but Aubrey Thegn Amundda had received a look that in Sordan would have seen Legon disjoint her pretty neck. Undismayed, Aubrey helped Dorilian to his feet and assisted him as he limped to the table. When Dorilian took a seat beside kindly Robdan, who had scooted over, Robdan poured himself a second crock of cider and immediately took a deep gulp.

What happened to make him limp like that? Hans indulged one horrible thought after another. *If they mistreated him, trying to get him to talk...*

"Well, Thron." Hans used the Esta dialect of Trongor to promote the masquerade. "You look like somebody has given you a hard time."

"I would gladly claim so, except that every bit of this is my own fault."

Hans blinked. Dorilian had replied in faultless, high clan, and perfectly inflected Khelda. Few outsiders ever mastered the language with that degree of fluency; Hans wasn't even sure he had. Aubrey shot Dorilian an annoyed stare and Arne openly gaped, no doubt recalling all his and Hans's secret talks and snide asides during their time in Sordan.

"What happened to your leg?" Robdan's unfeigned concern did a better job of keeping things mundane.

"Nothing serious. It will heal, given proper rest. Do you think I may be permitted to eat before I collapse?" Dorilian was utterly sincere—and unused to asking. One look at his glassy eyes and the paleness of exhaustion beneath a layer of mud moved soft-hearted Gerd to trot off for plates of hash and a pot of Rhodhur's strongest branroot. Aubrey, who had taken a seat alongside Dorilian on the bench, shoved a basket of biscuits in front of him.

"As I told you before, he ran away from us above the Fords," she explained. "He rode his horse off the road on one of the hill slopes, then tried to outrace my men on the flood plain below Hwothyswel. He's one hell of a rider. Wodd, my second, said Thron's horse stumbled and broke its legs among some roots when just a stone's throw from the Frendel, and that's what nearly got him killed. Swears that your friend would have taken to the water if he hadn't been hurt."

"I can also swim." Dorilian's tone told every man at the table the statement was meant especially for her.

"I'm glad you caught him." Mostly Hans was just glad he wouldn't have to explain to the world how Sordan's Hierarch had broken his neck.

"So am I. This man needs to be watched." The way Aubrey's smile turned over when she looked at Dorilian bore all the warning marks of danger.

Dorilian wasn't paying attention; he was eating like a man half-starved. Hans knew the feeling, but more than that, he felt his own hunger gnawing at his vitals, demanding to be fed. The reason hit him upside the head. He was seated with a projective empath... they *all* were. Projected hunger had just moved Hans's hand to break open a biscuit, slather both halves with wild berry jam and eat it without thought. Across the table, Dorilian poured honey onto an already sweet roll and ate that. A few of the Khelds were doing the same. If Hans didn't put a stop to it they would eat the Hall down.

"Herberth?" Hans addressed the Trongorian Elector. He also glanced up at Farrl, who had just rejoined them. "Don't you think we should get him... this man, your man, to bed? He can take his breakfast with him. I mean, he must be exhausted."

"He certainly looks it." Herberth picked up on the offered opening.

"We'll take him up to my room and tend to him there." He and Farrl excused themselves from the other men at the table and immediately went to lend Dorilian any help he might need in getting to his feet.

They had no trouble convincing Dorilian to leave the table, and with it a Hall rapidly filling with curious Khelds, although it required the assistance of both men for him to make the stairs. Robdan, after watching their painfully slow progress, sighed. "He isn't going anywhere for a while, is he?"

"No, probably not." A flash of orange caught Hans's eye. Nalf Rhys was coming down the stairs, accompanied by several followers. They stopped at the landing to let Herberth and his charge pass. Nalf stopped again at the bottom of the stairs to glance back over his shoulder before proceeding to where Hans and the others still shared the morning meal.

Gods, thought Hans, *if Nalf Rhys ever met him, he isn't likely to have forgotten it.*

The Thegnard offered polite good mornings before filling the place Herberth had vacated.

"More Trongorians?" He gestured at the stairs before he helped himself to a plate of ladled eggs and potato dumplings. A kitchen lad hurried in with clean dishes and mugs of fresh grog, which he passed around to Nalf Rhys and his group.

"A courier," said Robdan, neatly bridging the gap. He passed Nalf Rhys a pot of jam.

"I caught him following Hans." Aubrey smiled at Nalf when he raised his head from his meal to look at her. "Hello, Uncle."

To Hans's surprise, Nalf Rhys threw back his head and roared with laughter. "Damn, girl, you turn up at odd times. Past summer's solstice night and now a thunderstorm!" His gaze narrowed as he studied Aubrey, all the while working on his meal. "What brings you to Rhodhur at this time of year?"

"A new loom. I bought a mechanized one for my weavers from a man in Garfallow. But mostly I'm here because of what I learned on the Slowpike. The Rill stopped."

"No news. Heard tell of it days ago from ears near the Toregh. Nothing going on at Leseos or the High Hole. But good news to your lot, eh? Now your cruihcil can worry on closer things."

"Not good news. Arms shipped by way of Leseos supplied *us* too."

"So now you find some way else."

Hans had a good idea what they were talking about. Leseos, a domain in the Telarkan mountains, possessed a Rill port and was the primary depot for men and supplies deployed by Essera in the Neuberland wars. So, this Aubrey was from Neuberland. And she had contact with the local government there. That probably meant she held clan status in her own right.

"Maybe, maybe not." Aubrey deferred to her kinsman's satisfaction. "Still, it's not the worst thing in the world, not for us, though it defies explanation. The Rill doesn't just stop—and when it does, so does everything else. Leseos was in a panic from what I heard, which is reason enough for me to believe it was unexpected. But," she added with a frown, "someone, somewhere, knew ahead. More supplies and men have poured into Leseos in the last two months than we first guessed. That's why I was headed there, to look into what was going on—though I turned when I heard the Rill had stopped."

"And who do you think did it? Sordan?"

"Who else?" Everything about Aubrey smoldered with resentment. Watching, Hans was arrested by the clear color in her cheeks, the way anger brought her looks into sharp focus.

Nalf Rhys didn't miss the admiring glance. "Aubrey Amundda, my brother's daughter from Saemoregh," he said proudly. "She holds fine land with good herds and industry. She'd be married by now, could the Neuberland Cruihcil provide a man who could keep her sitting at a hearth."

Aubrey laughed and, like a cat who knows the security of her seat, smiled smugly over her cup of grog.

"I'd still like to know what's in that Sordan letter," Brec interjected in a voice meant to be heard around the table. He peered across at Hans. "You ain't opened it."

"It's for Herberth. It was brought by his man." Hans was happy he could pass along that source of contention. His hand fled to the letters where they rested, still within their leather envelope, on the table.

"Wouldn't hurt to look at them, now would it?" chided Nalf Rhys. As their gazes locked at close range, he too placed his hand on the parcel.

"Oh don't, please," said Robdan. "The letter is clearly for the Elector and he is our guest. It would be a diplomatic insult, as well as one of hospitality, if we violate another domain's official correspondence."

"And that might be," Nalf Rhys agreed wholeheartedly though

his eyes narrowed. "I don't doubt for a moment it would be frowned upon by Trongor. But in case you haven't noticed, all our arses are sitting here in Amallar. And you know what that means? It means if there are Sordanish letters here, it's for me to decide who gets them." He slid the letters out from under Hans's hand.

"Don't do it, Nalf Thegn!" Hans surprised them by raising his voice. His tone drew stares from other parts of the Hall. "We can't afford to offend friends!"

Nalf disregarded him and worked his thick finger under the emerald green Sordaneon seal, breaking the silver eagle. A spark of white light burst at his finger. Though startled, Nalf paused but for a moment before he pried loose the parchment fold. Inside he found a single sheet of pure white vellum with not a mark upon it. "What joke is this? It's blank!" He threw the paper down in disgust. "A fine piece of nothing!"

Hans stared. He saw writing on the page, faint but clearly visible.

Aubrey laughed, drawing a glare from her scowling uncle. "Thron said it was encrypted. But he said nothing about being unable to see it."

"Who is Thron?" Nalf's temper little improved to know that someone had known of this farce ahead of him.

"The courier that Aubrey caught," said Brec. "The one that limped upstairs."

"It must be some sort of special ink," Hans interceded. He retrieved the paper, which he folded without looking at it. For his own part, he was glad that "Thron" had gone upstairs and couldn't be called upon to explain the document. Perhaps by the time anyone sought him out, Herberth would have set matters right. Hans slid the paper back into its envelope. "I'm sure the Sordaneons have devised ways to ensure the privacy of their correspondence."

Nalf stiffened but did not answer. His transgression had not just embarrassed him, but it also put Hans in a better light for having observed proprieties.

Hans was relieved to see Herberth descend the stairs. When he came to the table, the Elector took a seat on the bench opposite and gave the group a taciturn nod. "Washed, fed, and fast asleep," Herberth said to those who cared enough to listen. "Looks like we're stuck with him."

"Our gain," said Hans. "I'm sure we can make use of another of your officers." To get off that subject, which had all but set Arne to openly snorting, Hans took up the letters and handed them to the Elector. "I believe these are yours. The curiosity at this table is killing some people by slow turns."

"Truly?" Herberth spoke with a forced coolness that hinted somewhat at his aggravation. First the Hierarch, and now the unwelcome scrutiny of a hall full of nosy Khelds. He turned over the letter and noticed the broken seal. His broad face colored red as he scanned the men at the table. "This document has been violated!"

"It is my business," Nalf Rhys growled with quiet warning, "to know what passes in these lands and under this roof. That letter grossly violates our goodwill."

Stiff-lipped, Herberth held up the second letter, the one bearing his own Trongorian seal. "Then I submit that this one does *not*." He worked his finger under the seal, cracking it, and withdrew the document within. All could see that this paper, at least, bore obvious traces of ink. By the slight smile that barely lifted one corner of Herberth's mouth, Hans knew the man was examining another perfect forgery, one worthy of admiration and study. Hans never doubted for a moment that the paper would be pronounced as genuine. When he glanced up at last, Herberth did just that. "'Tis from the Vice-Elector, written in Ogarth after I left there. I have been approached by His Thrice Royal Grace, the Hierarch of Sordan, to convey *this* message to Prince Handurin." With exaggerated duty, even pleasure, he extended the second letter to Hans.

The parchment envelope felt newly heavy and hot. All eyes at the table watched his hand as he took it. For the second time that morning, the vital paper within was brought forth into the dim light of the Hall, but this time it was Hans who unfolded that smooth, white sheet.

"Use this." Herberth lifted a chain from around his neck and brought it over his head, holding it out to Hans. The oddly shaped object dangling from it glinted like a lump of dull lead in the pale morning light. "It is a codestone. A man in my position sometimes has need of one."

The chain passed, lightweight but strong, into Hans's hand. He saw at once that it had been crafted more for security than decoration. The codestone itself was a lumpish chunky trapezoid with one flat surface.

"Ugly, isn't it?" granted Herberth. "But pass it over the page and then decide its worth."

Unfolding the paper, Hans moved to do as directed, then stopped. He had not yet touched the stone to the paper, but he saw the words on it clearly: a pale yellowish-blue ink, but readable.

"Go ahead," said Herberth. "You have to touch the stone to the document."

A quick glance at the Elector's face, and at other faces around the table, showed that they still thought the paper blank. To satisfy those who watched him, Hans lightly set the stone to the smooth surface of the paper, covering the first words of the letter, and moved it across the page. Where the codestone had passed, black markings appeared, exactly mimicking the writing that flowed there, filing across the page as he proceeded. By the time he had finished passing the stone over the page, the letter had revealed itself in its entirety.

"Only a codestone can reveal it." Herberth looped the chain back over his head after Hans passed it back to him.

"Where can I get one of those things?" Brec was clearly entranced by the magic he had just seen performed before his very eyes.

"Yes," said Aubrey. "Where?"

Hans wondered if Aubrey recalled papers captured in Neuberland, as blank as this one, that she and others had been forced to dismiss as dummies or decoys.

"Such stones are not bestowed outside of need," Herberth explained. "They must be obtained from Highborn hands—and those, as you must also know, are now very few. This one is an accessory of my office."

The Khelds crowded close. Nalf Rhys leaned over Hans's shoulder as he read.

"Madrock's Hells!" Nalf Rhys burst out in renewed rage. "It's not in Sordanish! It's not even in Stauba!"

"That's right, it's not." Hans realized now why Dorilian had made him study the dead language of Aryata. It had been for more than allowing him to read a few musty, incredibly ancient texts. The Highborn wrote their correspondence in the language their ancestor Amynas had spoken.

"What does it say?" Arne wanted to know. He'd determined by now that Hans, at least, could read it.

"He wants to talk." Hans condensed the substance of the letter considerably. "He proposes meeting at Leseos." Arne scowled, but Herberth looked astounded. There was little doubting the reason for his surprise, now that Dorilian himself had turned up at

Rhodhur. But Hans knew this piece of paper for what it was: an official document, not a secret missive. An opening, an offer, and—in its own way—a gift.

"He must think we're uncommon idiots to believe we'd take him up on that." Nalf Rhys rapped his mug on the table, calling for more grog amid a chorus of agreement.

"Well, I must be an idiot then," said Hans. How long had Dorilian been laying the groundwork for an opening such as this? Neither could Hans ignore that he must begin laying some groundwork of his own. "And if Leseos is unsuitable, some other place can be found. Amallar will never be secure if we can't find a way to move past our troubles with Sordan." Only when he'd said it did he realize that he might have plunged too soon into forbidden waters. Vast disapproval stabbed at him from every gaze and frown.

"We're securer for having no dealings with that monster at all!" This time Nalf Rhys slammed his mug on the table, startling the boy who had come to refill it. "We are powerful and numerous. Sordan fears us? Well, let them fear, I say. We have a place in Essera, a high place! And all the Highborn Princes, Sordaneon or whatever, cannot deny it to us. Nor to you, if you have the balls to stand and take back what's yours! Stefan never bent his neck to Sordan, though his enemy shot him with sorcery and burned him with lies." He reached over and ripped the letter out of Hans's hands. "Like this, words on blank paper! Sorcery! Sorcery! It's demon's blood that runs in those veins!"

While Hans watched, stunned, Nalf Rhys tore the letter into pieces. Tatters fluttered to the floor and table like the scattered feathers of a slaughtered bird. All around the Hall people stared and exclaimed their disbelief that Nalf would bring a conflict into the open at a meal at which he presided.

Hans forced himself to remain calm. Control was by far the more potent response. "If you destroy every proposal that crosses your table," he said, "it's small wonder that Amallar receives so few. Do you even know how you are regarded beyond your own borders? Do you care? Khelds are looked upon with contempt. And why? Because of things like what happened just now! Every word you said smacks of childishness and ignorance." Hans caught a glimpse, barely in the corner of his vision, of Aubrey watching him intently.

"Childishness! Ignorance!" The color in Nalf's face rose higher, making the whites of his eyes stand out even more angry and pale.

"Aren't they the same thing?" Hans responded. "Talk of demons and sorcery will make you a laughingstock among people who know what these things really are." He drew the Permephedeon *deiknya* from the pouch he wore on a cord around his neck. He turned to Robdan. "Give me your hand." When Robdan did so, Hans placed the *deiknya* into the older man's lined palm. "Go ahead, take it." Hans withdrew his fingers and the colors of the medallion faded. "Pass it around. You won't damage it, and it can't hurt you."

Hand to wondering hand, the *deiknya* passed around the table, touching a dozen persons that reached out to hold it, the colors bleeding away until the unknown substrate took on a grayish, metallic cast. Then Hans took it back into his own hand and held it in his palm in clear view. The colors flooded back, warm and vibrant and rich, its mysterious markings renewed.

"Marenthro gave this to me," he told the amazed listeners. "It serves to identify me among people who have knowledge of such things. It bought Arne and me our passage to Sordan and once we were there it was recognized as proof of my claim. Sorcery, some might call it, but it's not. I have an idea of how it works, though I don't have the knowledge or skill to make such a thing." He tucked the *deiknya* back into its hidden safe niche next to his skin, aware of the wonder in their eyes and their deep pride that he, their Hans Thegn, was versed in the ways of Highborn lands.

"Pretty magic," said Nalf Rhys. His temper had settled, though the way he smiled through gritted teeth continued to shout opposition. "It so happens Marenthro Dru'vida is a great sorcerer, gifted in arts no others understand. I've seen him make dead men and every drop of blood they'd spilled disappear! Bespeak the damn Wall! Saw and heard with my own ears! But Sordan is another beast, and by that document you threaten to perjure yourself before your brother's memory. Would you treat with those who destroyed him, by whatever the means they did it?"

"No," said Hans. "And I haven't."

"Dorilian Sordaneon—"

"Didn't kill Stefan. Or my grandfather. I won't deny that Dorilian and Stefan were enemies"—Hans said it before anyone could interrupt him—"for all the world knows that they were. *I* know that they were. But it's far too simple to lay blame on the man left standing, just because he wasn't the one who fell. Marenthro doesn't, or he would never have sent me to Sordan."

"Marenthro sent you?" Brec looked amazed. "Arne here said

something like that, but I didn't quite take it. Permephedon's
wizard... are you telling us you saw him yourself, and he talked to
you?"

Hans nodded and leaned forward to explain. "Marenthro came
to me in... the place where I was. He told me it was time for me to
return, here, to my World and my people—and I don't think he
meant Khelds only. He said that Essera was too dangerous, that I
had too many enemies there. If I went to Essera I'd end up dead.
And he said if I went to Amallar without having allies, I might never
get any. Then he told me to go to Sordan because that was where I
would find what I needed."

"And did you? Find whatever that was?" Doubt furrowed
Aubrey's brow.

"Yes. I think I did." Hans thought of Sordan's gleaming crown
of towers and the Rill—and Dorilian, about whom Hans had many
questions and one irrefutable proof: Dorilian had followed him *here*.

"I'll tell you what that wizard did! He sent you into the pit to
show you the ways of your enemy and the shape of the demon breed
that dwell there," Nalf Rhys maintained. "You were made captive,
mistreated, imprisoned—such is the path of heroes. Alm himself
trod such a path. Straight into the jaws of the Great Beast of
Madrock's Hells he strode! If to go to Sordan was what you needed,
it was but to show you the power of the creature you must oppose.
Stefan knew. He knew the true face of the enemy. Dorilian
Sordaneon is not human, he said."

Hans felt his heart empty as a chill crept through his veins. He
himself had heard Stefan say those words. But if that was what
people thought.... "That's absurd. Dorilian's human. He's a man
just as we are. I spoke with him, ate with him—for months I lived
in his house. I even fought him once and drew his blood. Ask Arne
his opinion if you doubt mine."

All eyes turned on Arne, who looked uncomfortable. Reluctantly,
because he hated to admit it, Arne nodded. "Well, I weren't around
him that much, not like Hans here, but to me he looked human
enough and mostly acted like it. Talked funny, though, like a gods-
damned lord."

"All them Staubauns do," Brec concurred with the only thing he
could.

Another man spoke up. "But he has six fingers, folk say, like
demon kin."

Gerd, who had stayed nearby, snorted. "That's not what I heard. I heard that on one hand he has only three."

Arne shook his head. "Naw. He has five, same as us. On both hands too. Hans counted 'em to be sure."

"And why is that?" Nalf was not backing down. "It's because the abominations appear howsoever they wish to appear! What looks like a man and talks like a man may still not be one. The Highborn may appear like men, but they're monsters: their flesh is fashioned by dark arts, their eyes shine in the dark, their skin's cold to the touch—you but saw what he wanted you to see. They're demon seed, and they practice the ways of the damned!"

Hans tapped the *deiknya* where it lay against his breastbone. "You thought this was magic? Or that letter?" He shook his head. "They're toys, Nalf Thegn. Trinkets. Sordan is full of them. So is Permephedon. They're remnants of another age, when such things were common to all men. The Rill was a way all people traveled then; it went to every city—every nation. It may even have gone to other worlds. So much was destroyed that the remnants now seem magical. But power then was many times the power now, and there are things of power in the World today that make your talk of demons real."

"What things?" Nalf's eyebrows lifted.

"Crystals. Devices. Weapons. Things not all in the hands of Permephedon or Sordan—or of men who will use them wisely."

"I've heard talk lately of a blood-crowned sorcerer in Essera." All eyes again turned to Gerd, who folded his arms, unsmiling. "I hear a lot."

"That's the one," Hans concurred.

Nalf Rhys scowled. "Nammuor the Mormantaloran has extended the arm of peace to Amallar. Says he has no quarrel with us, though I would see him and his ships out of Stauberg and Aral. That throne is yours, not his—or Erenor's."

"Then help me fight him. Help me fight them both," said Hans.

"We'll help you fight Sordan," said Nalf Rhys. "We'll help you fight the enemies of Amallar. We'll have your back when it comes to the Regent Erenor. But I won't go with attacking those who've not attacked *us*! You've come back with crazy ideas, and I'll not listen to you over a good man's meal. Stefan sought this Nammuor's alliance, sought it and got it—and the Sordaneon killed him for that."

Herberth snorted at this interpretation. Khelds throughout the room, however, nodded and grunted at what to them made sense.

"An alliance? People said it in Sordan, but I didn't think… Is it true? Stefan sought Nammuor out *first?*" Hans stared at Robdan and hoped for him to deny it.

"I'm afraid so, yes." Robdan looked as apologetic as if he'd made the alliance himself.

Hans closed his eyes, overcome by the enormity of his brother's mistake. He could not reconcile the horror of Stefan's death, or his memory of Nammuor and his mages wielding sorcery and ruin, with the image of Stefan extending the hand of alliance to the man who would murder him.

"I'm afraid so!" Nalf Rhys's voice took on a mocking tone. "Was there ever a man more filled with fear than you? You were afraid of everything that might've meant Stefan's success. No wonder he never listened to your advice!"

"Then, tell me, why did he not succeed more?" Robdan did not need to raise his voice in the silence that surrounded them. "Which was more flawed—my advice or his judgment? What I advised Stefan to forgo, he went ahead and did. What I begged him to do, he would have no part of, favoring other counsel. I tried to warn him about this Mormantaloran. I, and many others, including Marenthro Dru'vida."

"And did you warn him about Dorilian Sordaneon, growing rich and mighty in the south? No, you had your mouth full of other worries. 'Make peace,' you said. 'Before it's too late,' you said. Damn lot of nonsense, and Stefan would've been a damn fool to listen to it. The Sordaneon's got nothing to offer that he wouldn't as soon stick in our backs. And I'll tell you something else—and Hans Thegn here, too, long as his ears are open — what Stefan did, he did as King. He was *King!* And he got things done for us that no one else ever did."

"Did he? Then why have we so little to show for it?" Robdan sat with jaw tight and chin lifted. "No man of the Khelds now holds position in Essera, where in Marc Frederick's reign we held dozens of offices, minor though most were. Once there were Kheld merchants in Stauberg and through the whole of Tahlwent, and Kheld craftsmen too—but now no Kheld lives nor goes to either domain, nor are we welcomed as peers in Merath or Dazunor-Rannuli. And Hans is right when he says we're held in contempt. Contempt!" Robdan's gentle face looked pained. "Not even hatred, which at least in its way is a form of respect. If we are feared, it's because we're looked upon as looters and plunderers. And as murderers too. The men who beheaded the Dannutheon Princes walk among us to this day. Yes! Is it any wonder we are seen as barbarians unfit to live side by side with civilized folk?" Barely concealing a glance at Herberth, Robdan said, "Sometimes I don't wonder that they think it."

"How dare you!" Nalf Rhys half rose from his seat.

"He dares because he's telling the truth!" Hans ground the words to a sharp edge without even trying, stopping even Nalf Rhys in midsyllable. "Yes, Stefan tried. He tried hard to rule well and he made some good choices. But he also put many Khelds into offices and titles which those men didn't understand and could not manage—as high magistrates, as tax collectors. He gave great estates to many men who didn't know how to handle their responsibilities, men who wasted so much wealth and wielded their new power so bluntly that people thought Stefan was doing it on purpose. From what I can tell, all he left Khelds with was a bad name!"

"But you're his brother!" someone reminded him.

"That's right," Hans said. "Stefan was my brother. I loved him, but I don't love everything he did. His legacy is something to which I am bound by name and blood. Until now it hasn't done me one bit of good. And somehow I don't think it's going to."

The hundreds of Khelds in the Hall, as many women now as men, stared at Hans, stunned and wary, not knowing what to think. Many viewed him with suspicion. But in some of their eyes Hans saw signs of their inclination to respect a man who showed a mind of his own. Above all else, Khelds took pride in a reputation for stubbornness and independence, even flaunting it at times. He had not hurt his standing by speaking his own point of view. Better yet would be if he threw a few punches in defense of that view. No doubt he would have to before he was through. But for now, Hans had stated his piece, and only those early risers who had come down to the main Hall or wandered in from the street had heard him.

Nalf Rhys cupped his thick hands around the hot curve of his refilled grog cup and blew upon the thick steam that rose to his lips. His pale blue gaze stabbed at Hans across the rim of the massive vessel, showing anger carefully held in check. That much of a truce yet ruled the table. "You've only just arrived, keldan. Sit back in the warmth of your kilth and forget these small disagreements. Your time will come. And when it does, you will know for certain which path to take."

8

Political ideals are not a belief of the Mind, but of Men.
What we believe, the Mind upholds. It does not create
beliefs to impose upon us.

ZAMENES, *On the Nature of Gods and Men*

Hans sought out Dorilian as soon as he was able. He waited until after the Hall had emptied before making his way to the room where Herberth and his captain stayed. Farrl guarded the door but, after speaking with Herberth, went downstairs with his Elector to eat. Arne waited outside the room to make sure Hans's meeting with Dorilian would not be disturbed or overheard.

"I can't believe he's trusting us. Trusting *me*. After we ran away." Hans paused at the door. "I mean, this is crazy. I think people here would kill him if they knew."

"Probably," Arne admitted.

"I could hold him hostage, I guess. It would serve him right."

"Why don't you? He could use a taste of his own hard ways, if you ask me. He's put you in a proper spot."

"I wonder if he understands the spot *he's* in. Where I come from, men in his position just don't do things like this!"

Herberth had left Dorilian asleep in the room earlier, but when Hans entered Dorilian was awake, dressed in a simple tunic, seated in a chair before the window and wrapping his injured knee. A basin of mostly melted ice and some rags left over from chilling his swollen joint littered the floor. He glanced up only briefly when Hans walked through the door.

"I was wondering when you would come by."

"And I'd like to know what the hell you're doing here."

Dorilian continued to attend to his wrapping. "Speak Stauba, will you? I have had my fill of speaking Khelda today. I came after you. It was you, after all, who left Sordan."

"I'm not going back."

This time Dorilian shot him an icy glare. "I'm not inviting you back. The only reason you were my guest at all was because Marenthro tossed you into my lap with no more than a 'Here you go, blowhard, let's see what you can do with this rare mess.' Well, now it is your turn to worry about whether your Kheld friends will dash not only my skull but your hopes along with it. It serves you right for not having the sense to stay where your prospects were good. Coming to this backwater of the World is not my idea of a healthy change in climate—but you and I have unfinished business."

"You've got a great sense of timing, you know."

"The timing was all yours, Handurin." Dorilian knotted the end of the binding, securing it, and sank back in the chair to face him. "I planned to catch up with you at Ogarth, but you left before I could get there. You left Sordan mere days before I would have set you free. You upset some very elaborate planning, young man."

Hans pulled over another chair and placed it behind Dorilian's, away from the windows. It was the best they could do for privacy. The noise of daily comings and goings—added to the fact that this was a guest wing with low occupancy during the day—made eavesdropping unlikely. "All right, what were you planning?" He spoke quietly when Dorilian had turned to face him. "You didn't see fit to let me in on it. You kept me in the dark, cut off, isolated. You *used* me."

"I used you well, if for nothing more than to set up your own departure. You would never have made it into Amallar and the bosom of your Kheldish friends had that planning not been in force, the results already in motion. Street talk and rumors are meant for the ears of those who strain to hear them. Real plans are held in secret. And it was *my* plan to have Essera and Nammuor—and yes, these Khelds who talk so boastfully it is a wonder they heed any rumor at all—believe that you were my prisoner. Believe that you were being held, without hope of freedom, in Sordan, under my thumb. Only then would Nammuor move slowly, confident that you would not move at all. All was devised toward that end, to have them think that Sordan was where you were." Dorilian turned on

Hans, his mouth firming into a frown of deepening displeasure, his gaze cut from cold, clear glass. "At least in Essera they still think as much. Trongor knows better since you made your entrance there so brazenly. And your Khelds, of course, know that you are here. But Essera, I dare to hope, can be held silent yet for another week. It could have been more but for your foolhardy haste to be gone."

"If that was your plan, why didn't you let me know? Did you trust me so little that it became safer in your eyes to blind me along with the world to what you were doing?" Hans clenched his fists, almost thankful for the pain of his nails as they dug into the thick skin of his palms. How long had he waited, certain that something, maybe even something like this, was going on? "I held on for weeks waiting for you to give me the chance to do something, be something more than just another prop in one of your convoluted plays, until at last I was convinced that *I* was the game, that you were playing with *me*. The night I found poison in my drink, the night I *drank* it—" Hans inhaled sharply and looked out the window to where sunlight was struggling to break through the clouds. Memory of that night wrenched at his bowels, twisting. He noticed that Dorilian looked disturbed—but not surprised. "You knew?"

"The next morning. We found blood-tinged vomit in a bowl and still some poison in the cup. Legon traced it to one of the kitchen staff." Dorilian frowned, then added, "The woman left in haste, but I'm certain Legon will apprehend her and learn who was behind the deed."

Hans believed it. He stared at his fists. "After that, Arne and I had to leave. I was too afraid even to ask for help; I didn't know who to trust. I thought the next person who came in the room might try to finish the job. Once I'd stared death in the face, nothing, not even Marenthro, could have persuaded me to stay. I thought of telling you—I almost did—but I couldn't be sure, and part of me didn't want to know."

"Know what?" For the first time Hans could remember, Dorilian sounded defeated, and weary of it. "Whether it was my hand that tried to poison you?"

"That was part of it. I couldn't bear to think that you would, but I couldn't afford to believe blindly that I would be safe any longer in your keeping. More than anything, I was afraid that you would clamp down the guard, force me to stay—and there were too many rumors, maybe, too many lies and too many hard words. I didn't

know what to believe anymore. I—I didn't know who to trust."
Hans looked up, asking for understanding. "My every instinct told
me to leave, that someone there wanted to kill me."

Dorilian nodded. In his silence and long stare, Hans sensed that
the Hierarch believed him, that he weighed more than Hans's
words. "Now you see how we must live. Are you still certain you
want to be a prince?" Shaking his head, he looked away. "Someone
underestimated what it would take to kill you. I would not have
made that mistake. I did not poison you, Handurin, nor did I order
it or know of the deed. I came after you as much to tell you that as
anything else."

"I believe you." Seeing this man before him, hearing his words,
Hans couldn't do otherwise. *He's been accused too often... of too many
misdeeds, by too many people....*

Dorilian bent his neck and absently began to knead the aching
muscles below his knee.

"Does it hurt?" Hans dared hope the injury was minor.

"Not much. The ice helped."

"We could get a faetha to look at it."

"No, it will heal. It's better already; the ankle likewise. By
tomorrow I will be much improved." The scratches that had marred
Dorilian's face that morning had vanished, as if they had never been
there.

"Improved enough to leave?"

Dorilian's smile displayed a rare appreciation. "Are you anxious
to be rid of me?"

"Yes!" Hans couldn't say it emphatically enough. "I keep
thinking that any moment now someone is going remember having
seen you somewhere before."

"The chance I take. And if by that chance someone should
stumble onto me, I would suggest you move quickly to place me in
chains"—Dorilian pinned him with words as sharp as any
sword—"as I did you in Sordan."

"There were no chains in Sordan."

"A polite difference. People thought there were. I suspect Khelds
require more blatant proofs." Dorilian pushed himself out of the
chair and onto his feet.

Hans rose, ready to help, but Dorilian motioned him back.
Apparently, being treated as an invalid annoyed him more than the
injury itself. But he looked uncomfortable, and Hans thought it

wouldn't hurt to distract him. "That correspondence you sent, the invisible one—"

"Special ink." Dorilian grunted as he put weight on his leg.

"What I don't understand is how I was able to see lettering on the paper when no one else could." Hans saw Dorilian glance at him and knew that he was not mistaken. "I did see writing, before Herberth's codestone revealed it to the others."

Dorilian nodded. "Yes. The ink is visible only to the intended reader."

"How does it do that? Is it magic?"

"No. Have Marenthro explain it to you sometime."

Hans hesitated, wondering how to bring up the other matter on his mind. "Speaking of blatant proofs." He stayed at hand as Dorilian tested a few more steps. "You were rather blatant yourself, shutting down the Rill while the Epoptes were convening at Permephedon."

To Hans's surprise, because he had expected Dorilian to be pleased with himself, the Hierarch frowned. When he spoke, it was as if he spoke from somewhere else—not from a sparsely furnished room in Amallar, but as he had spoken on the terrace in Sordan, looking out upon a City built for gods. "Yes, I was blatant. As blatant as any man who ever freed a bone of his own body from the very jaws of the dog that gnaws it. And I blatantly enjoyed doing it. For too long, the Epoptes have treated the Rill like a sublime beast of burden—and the Seven Houses treat it like their private whore." Angling toward the wall, Dorilian hopped over, the better to lean upon it. "Men hold nothing sacred forever. You know what the Cibulitan Initiates say, don't you? That the Rill, even Sordan, even we ourselves, are only Permephedon dreaming. But all men twist the ramblings of mystics to their design."

"There are some Mentans who say the same thing, that the world is but a dream of the gods."

"Or that gods are but the dreams of men." Dorilian straightened, coming back to himself. "The gods are benign. The Aryati vanquished them long ago and the stars swallowed their memory. We create our own gods now. But the Epoptes forgot a cardinal rule of godhood: that those who create a god are thereafter obliged to serve it, or the god ceases to be. Derlon Sordaneon gave immortal life to an Entity, but it was the Epoptes who created the god. Over time complacency corrupted them—complacency and the greed of common men, and they forgot that their god was ever other than they conceived it. They began serving themselves and other men, not the god. They forgot one other thing as well: Derlon may be a god, but he is Sordaneon still, and I stand to inherit the Entity."

"Which allows you to use it for your own ends?"

"Do you wish to discuss the interpretations?"

A subject best avoided for now. It was late afternoon, so would probably take all night, and Dorilian was too touchy not to take offense.

Hans frowned at him. "What I really want to do is keep you safe. I've heard enough already to know it's dangerous for you to be here."

"And where not dangerous, tell me? As I recall, upon our first meeting there was an attempt on my life, and that was in the heart of Sordan, on the very eve of First Day, the Coming, when my person should be held inviolate. My murder would serve any number of ends. I count my enemies to be more numerous by far than my friends. Seen through such a lens, I am safer in Amallar where none know me."

"But for how long? How long can you keep up this charade?"

"Among Khelds? Perhaps indefinitely."

Hans watched as Dorilian put weight on the leg, then attempted to walk a few steps. The leg obviously still bothered him, but Hans could see that he was indeed much improved over that morning.

"I would even go so far," Dorilian gave Hans a wolfish grin, "as to say that they would have a hard time believing *you* if you told them the truth."

Hans sank against the wall beam at his back and shook his head, exasperated, because if anything, Dorilian had a point. The truth was too far-fetched. "Look," he said, "your secret is safe so far because no one who knows about you is going to say anything. But what if you run into someone who does know you, from, say, an Archhalia meeting? Or that year you were in Gustan? And don't try to tell me it can't happen. You speak the language like a native! Obviously, you've met a few Khelds in your day."

"Two or three. However, these past several years, none could have seen me except in Sordan. I did not travel to Essera, not even to Permephedon, while Stefan was King. Since then, I have been to Essera once—and that was the Archhalia meeting that voted on your return. From that meeting, only Robdan would know me on sight. Whatever Khelds saw me before then, when I went to school at Permephedon, or when I was at Gustan, or confronted Stefan—all of those men are dead."

"How do you know that?"

"I know who they were. I knew their names, the titles he gave them, their kin. And I know that they are dead. Erenor cleared his path to power ruthlessly. Stefan's friends did not long survive him."

"Asphalladra. Her husband Cullen—"

"I knew Cullen from Gustan. Her too. He broke his leg playing *pelekys*. I was bored, so during his recuperation, he taught me Khelda and I taught him better Stauba and how to play a game called courses. He was intelligent and loyal, and Stefan rewarded him with titles and lands, including two of my palaces. Erenor killed Cullen first of all." Dorilian moved to the corner of the bed he'd apparently slept on, where he sat down and began putting on a fresh shirt and trousers. "I didn't come here to mingle with barbarians. I will stay out of their way as much as is possible in this rabbit warren they call home. Who built this place, anyway? It lacks cohesion."

"Oh, I don't know." Hans looked in admiration at the room's carved walls and different-sized windows. "I think Rhodhur has a certain rustic charm."

"You would." From the edge of the bed, Dorilian glanced up at him. "Listen, Handurin, I will not stay here any longer than I must. I don't like my being here any more than you do. There is danger, though not the kind you fear. If Nammuor should find me here undefended, I'm lost in more ways than you can imagine. He still thinks I am in Sordan if my plans have gone right. But there is much to be done and very little time left to do it. I have proposed talks, for all that I'm convinced your Khelds will not accept them. They are not my concern. I cannot bind them, nor will I try. That is for you to do. All I want is for Amallar to stay out of any conflict in Essera. And in return, I will acknowledge you as rightful ruler of that land, including the Stauberg Principalities and the Royal North. That is no small matter. Stefan never had that from me. Such a declaration would assure your ascension in the event of victory."

"So you will graciously allow me to be the king the Khelds want so badly, and in return they have only to accept the presence of yourself and your armies in Essera? That's not going to happen. Lip service is cheap. No one is going to believe it. What if following the victory, you choose to turn against me and Amallar? Who's to say that Essera and its Staubaun lords would not fall in behind you? Am I to take such a chance?"

"Play the game as you see fit. Here I sit. Slay me now and save yourself the trouble later. I am a dead man already if you cannot be trusted. We are on the board together, you and I. As the pieces now stand, I cannot move until you do."

"Wrong," said Hans. "I can't move until you move."

"How is that?"

"Later. You and I are going to turn that board of ours upside down, and then there'll be plenty of room to move. But discretion is the better part of policy until we get you settled. My main concern right now is what to do with you. Do you want to bunk here with Herberth, or may I make a suggestion?"

"Suggest as you will. The innkeeper inquired as to my accommodation earlier and informed me that there are no rooms to spare, else I would have procured one for myself." Dorilian rose again to finish dressing.

Watching, Hans saw little to remind him of the man he had known in Sordan. That ruler and Highborn Prince, so resplendent in the bejeweled silks of royalty, had been replaced by a man equally as striking, but differently so, as he donned garments of homespun wool. To Hans's eyes, Dorilian Sordaneon had become an intriguing, far less constrained, stranger. And one to be handled very carefully.

"You could stay with Robdan." Hans didn't want to rush the idea. Dorilian's first reaction would almost certainly be to reject the proposal, simply on the basis that Robdan was a Kheld. However inconvenient the sleeping arrangements might be, however crowded, Herberth, as Elector of Trongor, was an ally of long standing and by far more acceptable a roommate for Sordan's Highborn ruler. "Please, hear me out," Hans said when Dorilian hesitated on the verge of apparent refusal. "Robdan has an extra bedchamber in his apartment. And he said you're welcome to use it."

"Considering the general crowdedness of this place, I appreciate his generosity." Dorilian stopped short of accepting the offer, though Hans could see he was considering it. The lure of separate sleeping quarters obviously tempted him.

"We may need to use Robdan's apartment anyway," Hans told him. "It's one of the few private places to be had in this Hall. I can justify being with Robdan, if only to say I have to look at his maps or his books, not to mention that we're kin—but how am I going to explain that I need to spend a lot of time with you? A Trongorian not even remotely involved in policymaking?"

"And my being his guest will eliminate the need to seek me out.

I understand that. But why would a man of Robdan's rank take in a Trongorian of no discernible position?"

"Because the Trongorian is injured, maybe?" A clatter of cart wheels rolling across the stones through the gate drifted up to the window from outside. "Because his apartment is on the second floor and Herberth's is on the fourth? I don't care how fast you heal, that leg could easily bother you for weeks if you play it up. And it hurts enough for now that I think you should do it."

"Is Robdan so commonly charitable that his fellow Khelds will believe this?"

"Believe me, he is."

"Then it might be well if, on that pretense, I accept his offer."

"Good. Robdan will be pleased, I think."

But the real pleasure was Hans's, at laying the foundation of his own plan. Dorilian might have met a few Khelds, even studied their language and ways, but that was a far cry from really knowing them. If Dorilian knew Khelds better as a people, he might even make a friend or two. At the very least he might be more receptive when Hans proposed to open the Rill to Amallar. Hans didn't want to appear too eager, though. Dorilian was too sensitive an observer not to notice, and would play along with subtle manipulations, if only to see the directions they took.

"It's going to take time anyway." Hans watched as Dorilian gathered his belongings. "A few days to get the feel of this place, a few days to fit in. I only got here yesterday myself. But I think the Kheld leadership is fragmented—not badly, not that an outsider would easily see, but the cracks are there. A man named Nalf Rhys is Thegnard—that is, their leader—and he dominates the Witan. This morning he made it very clear that he opposes negotiations with Sordan. Unless I can get the upper hand on him, we won't get anywhere."

"Then take the leadership upon yourself. That shouldn't be so difficult, given your relationships."

"You'd think so. I guess it's true in a way because Stefan is all they want to talk about." Hans took the saddlebags Dorilian handed to him and slung them over his shoulder as they prepared to leave for Robdan's quarters. "What I need to decide is how to go about this. Do I want to start splitting off factions or have a try at binding them together? Nammuor is splitting off factions already—and if I try to do the same, the whole thing could shatter. The last thing we need is a clan war." The last few days had taught Hans that he still had a lot to learn about Amallar and how Khelds fit into the whole Essera-Triempery puzzle. "One more thing, before we go," he said. "Try, if you can, to steer clear of Aubrey Amundda. From what I saw, she isn't entirely satisfied with your story. And while it could just be a bad case of feminine intuition, if she's as smart as I think she is, you could be in deep trouble."

Dorilian looked away. "Are Kheld women, then, more excellent at subtlety, at soft, hidden traps and the insensible lure, than have been other women through the ages? Staubaun women, when one gets to know their ways, are far more vicious than the beasts we kill to robe them. Don't lecture me on a woman's ways." Hans thought that perhaps Dorilian was referring to his own marriage, nearly erased from people's memories, which Endelarin had hinted to have been disastrous. "I'm well armed against women's attentions. And I was not reared in the Esseran habit."

Hans knew the practice to which Dorilian alluded, wherein Staubaun lords in Essera, but also in Neuberland, trafficked in Kheld women for purposes of pleasure. Many of these women were never seen again; the lucky ones were simply discarded. The idea that Dorilian might have engaged in such behavior had never crossed Hans's mind. Thinking that he might have offended, he sought to apologize. "I didn't mean to imply—"

"The matter is not a new one. I would, however, warn you similarly."

"About Aubrey?"

"About women. Your Khelds will not seek to get an heir from me because they do not know who I am. But you are another matter. I expect they will move quickly on it."

"I'll remember, if it comes to that." Hans felt somewhat embarrassed by the nature of the advice. But as he looked at Dorilian, he knew. *It happened to you, didn't it? Is that what your marriage was?*

As if to answer that thought, Dorilian said, "It will come to that, Handurin. It always comes to that. I was conceived in cold-blooded propagation of a dynasty, after all. So was Levyathan." He turned away. "And so were you."

9

The Khelds are skilled at midwifery and believe children conceived by a union freely entered are gifts bestowed by their Goddess. Children belong to the clan of their mother, with women of high status being much sought as wives. If a man wishes a child from a woman of a status higher than his own, he must gift the woman's kin with cattle, swine, or other substantial property. In this way clans increase their wealth.

ELDHAN MALYRDEON, LETTER TO KING ERYDON

Aubrey walked into Nalf Rhys's room to find him staring out a window at fields awash with the last warm glow of sunset. Standing beside her uncle, she watched workers trudge home past lengthening shadows, leaving behind their livelihoods until morning. Far below, in the pens of the village, cattle lowed as herd boys and girls brought them in from the meadows. Maybe Nalf also felt the world growing smaller as day drew to a close. He scratched his head and rubbed his fingers through his beard before he turned to speak.

"Might be a good thing after all that Hans Erwanson turned down my hospitality," he grumbled. "Damn boy moved into quarters of his own—but at least that means the rest of us are free to have meetings without him."

The rest of us. Aubrey knew what that meant: Stefanite members of the Frendeli Cruihcil, and Old Mother Ewlys, who sat near the hearth all the while measuring the gathered men with bird-bright eyes. It had become clear enough at breakfast that Stefan's successor was going to require a harder hand and a lot more rope than any of them had first hoped. Although Aubrey had just ridden in from

Neuberland and had not rested the night before, she'd decided to accept Nalf's request—odd though it was. Her uncle had never sought her out before for this sort of council. Choosing a chair beside Mother Ewlys, Aubrey openly watched Nalf pace the carpeted floor, waiting for him to enlighten her.

For all that Nalf was her closest kin, he and Aubrey had never become close. For one thing, Nalf had not approved of Aubrey's mother. His brother Amund's choice of a wife had been a half-Staubaun young woman whose high clan mother had given her no father name. Neither had she been born under the Hill as Nalf and Amund had been. Partly to escape his wife's dubious origins, Amund had sought Neuberland and the far settlements where things such as parentage mattered less. Aubrey had met Nalf only a few times all told. After her parents's deaths Nalf had arranged to get her into the school at Aurdollen—and when Aubrey was fifteen Nalf had sought to marry her off to Stefan Stauberg-Randolph. The events of that day still formed an uncomfortable barrier between Aubrey and her uncle.

The way Nalf looked at her now caused Aubrey to think he might be about to try something like that again.

"Rannuf." Nalf turned to his chief man, a short thin former warrior with a limp and a patchy beard. "Mulled cider, if you will, and dash it with brandy." When Rannuf had left, quietly closing the door to the Thegnard's private sitting room behind him, Nalf renewed his attention to his niece. "Aubrey," he began pleasantly, though she could tell his mood hadn't yet recovered from the morning. "Tell me, lass, what do you think of our young Hans Thegn?"

Aubrey settled deeper between the arms of her upholstered chair. She already sensed what ground Nalf intended to plow. "What is there to think? I first met him this morning."

"Come on, woman, stick your neck out. Give us an opinion. I know you've got a journey bag full of 'em. You certainly had plenty to say at breakfast."

"Fine. I'm not all that sure whether the prince is the answer to our prayers—or Sordan's. I didn't like all of what I heard this morning, but he holds strong views and he may find support."

Cadal Andweson, one of Nalf's fellow Thegn chieftains, raised a different concern. "Are you sure he's the real Hans Erwanson? Maybe Sordan, or someone in Essera, has sent us an impostor."

Nalf Rhys walked across the room and rifled through a few pages of a book on his worktable. He returned with a square of paper the size of a child's palm, which he handed to Cadal. "See that? The Princess Emyli gave that to Robdan at the last Archhalia session. Tale is, Marenthro Dru'vida brought it from the netherworld."

When the paper came around to Aubrey, she touched its glossy finish and stared in wonder at a perfect likeness of the young man they had all met that morning downstairs. The image had even captured his self-conscious smile and the exact color of his hair and skin. She passed it to Mother Ewlys, seated beside her. The Old Mothers held sway over Amallar in ways that made men like Nalf and his cronies uneasy. Mostly because they feared to offend the women, he had invited one of them also.

"Damn fancy magic, that thing." Nalf Rhys took back the image from a clearly contemplative Ewlys. "Emyli told Robdan that boy's her son and that he'd be coming back soon. I may not think much of Robdan, but he wouldn't lie about it."

"No," concurred Aubrey. "He wouldn't. And that medallion Hans Thegn showed, that he said Marenthro gave him? That's no phony, either. Only folk of importance own them. I've seen such before, in Leseos. Staubauns consider them truer than birthmarks. What's more, Hans says this one was given him by the hand of the Dru'vida himself. What reason would Permephedon's wizard have to send an impostor?"

Nalf Rhys snorted. "I won't even guess about that. The thing is, I knew Stefan. I knew the look of him. If this Hans isn't his brother, then I'm a blind man—same shape of the eyebrows, same smile. That damn gold in his hair, though, I don't know where he got that from. Not only that, but he used to spend winters here as a boy, and last night half the Hall was saying they remembered him. That's not even the best proof of it. Arne Anseldson got picked up by him in the southlands somewhere, and he's sworn right and left to whoever would listen that this Hans is Stefan's real live brother, that he was almost killed for it in Sordan. Hell, the boy's been nobbing with the likes of Trongor and Ardaen—not to mention that bastard Dorilian in Sordan, who I'm damn surprised didn't kill him. If he isn't Hans Stauberg-Randolph, he sure as all hells is trouble."

"So even the Sordaneon believes he is Emyli's son." Mother Ewlys clearly knew a corroboration when she saw one. "What are we going to do about this?"

Nalf Rhys returned the paper to his book before seeking his big chair in front of the fire. "What the hells *can* we do? He's got the damn Esseran kingship in his hands. What I or anyone else wants can't change that fact a spit one way or the other. Nor the fact that he's Stefan's brother. People will follow him blind for that alone. And it's plain as day he's got plans he wants to do in Amallar. Thing is, how far do we let him go?"

There was a brief creak as the door opened. Aubrey looked over to see Rannuf return with a tray bearing bright ceramic drinking bowls filled with spirits. The warm curve of the bowl as Aubrey took it into her hand caused her to smile. One of the best things about colder weather was that it occasioned so many pleasant ways to find warmth.

Like this one. Cider and *charen* — chider, some called it — was considered a woman's drink and a great favorite served daily at the Barrowhome. Most men would rather quaff ale. But it appeared Mother Ewlys approved Nalf's choice, as there was pleasure in the way the old woman handled her cup. Seeing Aubrey's nod of approval, Nalf cleared his throat and proceeded to make his point.

"Hans Thegn started this morning already, making noises about a deal with Sordan. I can't see it, and I don't think the Witan would allow it, but there's no knowing what kind of trouble he can cause with that sort of talk. Sordan blab and Staubaun blather! He's talking alliances that we'll have no part in. We can't let him get out of hand, not if we want a say later. We can't have a king with more Staubaun ties than Kheld ones—but I'd sure as hells hate to throw him away. Look at him now. Stefan's only brother and he's got Sordan written all over him. It's a hell of a thing!"

"Throw him *away*?" Aubrey set her drink on the raised stone hearth beside her chair. What were these men thinking? She looked at Rannuf, whose plain, guarded face revealed nothing, and Mother Ewlys, who showed no hint of what her thoughts might be. Aubrey returned a scathing glance to her watchful uncle. "You can't throw Hans away. Throw him away and you throw away the only Kheld claim to the throne for the next thousand years!"

"You think I don't know that?" Nalf Rhys groused. "Of course I know that! *He* knows that! And if we don't make him one of us, there are others out there looking to snap him up 'cause they damn well know it too! That's why we need to come up with a damn hard plan to tie him down—to get him over to our side and keep him here."

Retrieving her chider from the hearth, Aubrey traced the cup's gilded lip with a deliberate finger. "You still haven't told me why I'm here for this conversation." Though she knew already where things were headed, she could make her own points on the way. "The Neuberland settlements can't make alliances with anyone. We're a country without a government or representatives."

"Neuberland, hells. This has to do with bigger things than Neuberland. This is a Kheld matter, and that includes us all. You, her"—Nalf waved his hand to include Ewlys— "all of us! What we've got on our hands is a man who's hardly old enough to be one, a man we hardly know, and that means playing him day by day as he goes." He scowled and picked up the heavy, brass-tipped Thegnard's staff he carried at all formal occasions and used that to rap out his plan upon the table, punctuating each point with a solid crack. "When Hans Thegn goes north, he goes north to be King. That's what we've all wanted for longer than any of us can remember. Not a Staubaun King, a Kheld one! King of mighty Essera. That's what we got with Stefan and that's what we lost. Well, I for one want it back. This Hans has support, noble support—Robdan told us that—and if we can put him in front of us, he'll open Essera for us. Open it! We'll have a part like before. We'll have a say! And if it's true Essera isn't what it was, well, it's still worth the having. But we won't have it 'til we have him."

"*Have* him?" Aubrey snorted. "What if we do have him? What then? We can't leash and muzzle him and expect him to perform tricks."

"Who wants tricks? You can get a Staubaun to do tricks. Show a gold-hair some coin and they do tricks aplenty. And don't you worry about how we get Hans Thegn to do right by his Kheld kin." Nalf combed at his beard. "I'm not talking about that. He'll find Stefan's legacy here a hand more than he bargained for. He'll do just fine, or he'll find himself marching into Essera without an army at his back." As Nalf squinted across the firelight with a long, lingering appraisal, he met and held Aubrey's gaze. "But say all things come together and we get him up and on his throne. What happens then? What if he becomes King and takes a Staubaun woman to wife?"

"What makes you think he would?"

"I'm not Thegnard for being the kind of man who'd think he *wouldn't*! Hell, think of the alliances he'll need to make. And those he's got he'll want to strengthen. Essera's high lords are probably planning it already, damn the bastards, and most likely he got away from Sordan in the nick of time too. Those Staubauns would marry off their daughters to curly-cocked goats if it'd secure a domain, much less an empire. Not a few of them tried to get their claws into

Stefan, throwing their blonde girls his way, but he was smart enough to marry our Nilla. Too bad the babes...."

Aubrey read the look that crossed Nalf's face. As did most Khelds, Nalf thought the deaths of Stefan and his heirs the work of Sordan. Or maybe the Staubaun barons of Essera. She remembered Nilla Lowenda as gentle and kind, easily flattered and easily led. Silly Nilly, Aubrey had called her as a girl, though they'd been friends. Sadly, Aubrey had never seen Nilla again after she became Stefan's queen and went to Essera—Stefan, not Nilla, had seen to that. All Kheld folk had hoped for a child from the match, an heir to the throne they held so precariously through Stefan. But the first child, a boy, had miscarried because of poison, and the second child, a daughter, had died before her first year. The final blow had been the terrible end to which Nilla, along with her husband and unborn son, had come.

Aubrey's friend Lark Rappeleye had forewarned Nilla's fate because of the way the union had been created. But no one, it seemed, had taken the proper lesson from it.

Poor Silly Nilly. Aubrey couldn't help but feel a chill. Perhaps Ewlys felt it too, the lingering shade of the Mother's Inconsolation. That would explain why Ewlys's gray head bowed over her gnarled, tense hands as she cradled her cup of chider. *Lark spoke true when she said Nilla didn't choose her own man. She didn't follow the Mother but let men choose for her and became a brood mare to their hopes of dynasty. She was as helpless as a doe. All she ever wanted was to have children at her knees. And men in their plots and their greed didn't even let her have that.*

Nalf Rhys coughed to gain Aubrey's attention again, then fixed her with a piercing, probing glance. "I think you know what we want from you."

"I want you to tell me, just to be sure."

For a moment Nalf said nothing, then he leaned forward, putting aside his half-empty bowl. "What if I say I want you to find out what Hans Thegn's about?"

Aubrey refused to flinch from his gaze. "Why me?"

A deep bull roar of a laugh escaped Nalf's bearded throat. "Why the hell? Because I think you can do it, that's why! Look at her, she's a gods-damned beauty—isn't she, Rannuf?" His appraisal was accompanied by a calculating smile that chilled Aubrey's blood, making her only too aware that her woman's shape and looks were being subjected to scrutiny—by Nalf and the three other men in the room. Only Ewlys, at Aubrey's side, radiated coiled offense. "Those eyes, that hair, the pretty color of her mouth. One thing for Staubaun blood, it breeds good-looking women."

Aubrey glared. "Look, Nalf—"

"Beast!" Ewlys interjected. "This woman's gifts are not yours to use, neither as weapon nor profit!" She assailed Nalf with a snarl and a swat of her bony hand. "Her body and talents are hers alone! Such is the Mother's Law. Have you learned nothing from your failures?"

"A world more than you! Mother of Us All!" Nalf lifted his burly arms to the heavens, even though the Mother's domain was earth. "Is it a crime to ask a woman to use her damned gifts? You ask us men to use ours often enough. 'Dearie, fetch that loom from the rafters.'" Nalf spoke in a high voice. "'Dearie, plow that field.'"

"Neither of those purposes is to circumvent the Mother's Law!"

"Oh? Well, last I heard, the Mother tells women to seek out men for the purpose of hopping under the covers with them."

Ewlys looked upon Nalf as she might a child. "For themselves and Her blessing. For pleasure and the furtherance of life. For joy and love of the World She has gifted unto us all. Not to further the designs of men to shape matters to their own purposes. Such paths lead to the creation of wicked things as bring only destruction and ruin."

Cadal hunched and grumbled. "We have wicked things anyway, fuck all Her rules."

Ewlys hissed disapproval.

Nalf gestured, signaling Cadal to cease. He drew a deep breath before turning his full attention on Aubrey. "Don't you ever look in the mirror like a normal wench? Well, next time open your eyes and look good! It's to your advantage this time. Men look at women— with all the Mother's blessing," he said pointedly and with a hard glance to Ewlys, "and Hans Thegn will look at you. I saw the way he looked at you this morning."

Aubrey waved him off. "Lud's Stones! Who wouldn't have stared? I looked like something the floods turned up."

"Don't give me that bosh. He's a man, ain't he? He's young, but the younger the man, the hotter the sap—and the more it addles the brain. Once you have him seeking you out, maybe find out what he's planning to do." Nalf pushed to his feet and stalked to Aubrey's side. He looked older, thicker, now that the sun had set and only firelight illuminated the room. "We need to shine a light inside his head."

Ewlys was having none of it. An old woman and tiny, but still sapling straight, she rose to face the half circle of men. "It goes against the Mother's Law for a woman to mislead a man, to taint his choice—and hers."

"Damn it. I'm not asking that. Just to find out if he's a proper Kheld. Get a feel for what he's after and what plans he has for getting it done. Where's the harm in that? Hans Thegn has plans or he wouldn't have Trongor's Elector with him."

Aubrey frowned at the observation. She wasn't sure what to make of Hans's Trongorian company, but she'd been thinking about it. There was trade in that direction, though not enough of it, and Stefan, though he had pursued ties with lands south of the Telarkans, had been wary. Khelds had long harbored a suspicion that Trongor paid more than lip service to Sordan. Like most merchant states, Trongor depended heavily on commerce from Sordan's Rill ports and allies. Yet that country had more than once provided Stefan with ships when Sordan had harassed Essera's vessels on the high seas. And Trongor had run blockades when Dorilian placed an embargo on Esseran trade in his domains' seaports. Though Trongor's neutrality was not of a flavor Khelds found to their liking, neither did they regard Herberth or his people as unfriendly.

Which was why this morning's letters were both innocent and troubling.

"Hans could have gone into Essera on a Trongorian ship." Aubrey explored the basis of her still-diffuse grasp of things. "Hans could have gone to Essera but instead he came here. That tells me he knows he needs us."

"And Sordan too?" The chieftain asking the question led a keld from towns just west of Eastmeary Brenna. He knew as much about Sordan as any of them, which was to say very little.

Nalf huffed into his chair and plunked his staff on the table. "I believe him about what he says, that Marenthro Dru'vida sent him there. Had a little talk with Arne Anseldson last night. Got himself captured by Staubauns last fall around some town down by Gignastha and ended up by a long story at some foul port on the river road to Sordan, where Hans Thegn saw he was a fellow Kheld and bought him off. Hans even then was dead set on going to Sordan. Arne said he tried to talk him out of it, but Hans's story at the time was that Marenthro had told him there was something to find there. So he had that tale about the wizard sending him to Sordan long before he got here." Nalf scowled and ran his fingers through his beard. Aubrey could see that very little about any of what Nalf was telling them sat well with him, except the part where Hans had bought young Arne's freedom.

"So we're within a wizard's plan." Cadal surveyed the others unhappily. "If so, even Hans Thegn may not know what path has been laid for him."

"The Mother's Path perhaps." Ewlys tugged her orange woolen cloak over her shoulders, a concession to old bones, and included them all in her sharp blue gaze before taking her seat again. "People are too often intent on paths of their own to see Her designs."

"Could be, could be," Nalf acknowledged.

"I don't believe this is only the Dru'vida's work," was Aubrey's opinion. "Hans is making his own decisions."

"But from what basis, eh, girl?" Nalf pounced on that key point. "Arne also said that Dorilian Sordaneon himself saved their lives once he knew who they were. Taught 'em to use a sword too. Now if that doesn't suggest that Sordaneon devil has some use for Hans Thegn, I don't know what does."

"They say they escaped." Aubrey heard her own edge of doubt in that answer. That same doubt showed in Cadal's heavy-lidded eyes and in the guarded looks of the other men. Only Ewlys looked unconcerned.

Nalf admitted suspicion. "So they say. So they may well *believe*. And who the hells would even know if it's true or not, but that demon in his City of Lies?" He attempted to drink from his cup again but was too distraught and put it aside on the mantel. Instead, he fingered the knob of the knife at his belt. "It doesn't stand to reason that Dorilian Sordaneon let him go."

"And even less that he could escape," Cadal insisted. "Our spies tell us the island is a fortress, so mighty it challenges Permephedon. Every approach is heavily guarded, and the Hierarch's walls, too tall to scale, are seamless, not made of mortal stone."

"Except that the Rill stopped," Aubrey said. As she had hoped, conversation fell short and every gaze turned to her.

Nalf scowled. "What's that mean, 'except that the Rill stopped'?"

It fell on her to explain it to them. "I don't know. I haven't figured that out yet. But Hans Thegn leaves Sordan—and the Rill stops. It could have been to prevent him from using it." Aubrey met their questioning gazes with an arch of her eyebrow. "Or it could be a diversion."

"Diversion?" Nalf obviously weighed every word. "To hinder his escape?"

"Or to keep people from knowing that he had. Don't expect me or any of us to read the Sordaneon's mind."

Nalf nodded at that. None of them would ever be that subtle, that soaked in treachery and its ways. "But he sent that letter after, didn't he? Pony-quick with his spies and always has been. What we need to know, and know soon, is whether we're watching a puppet at work—or if we're watching a prince." He singled out Aubrey again. "There are ways to bind young Hans to us. He's already bound by blood, and damn if I don't think he's bound by his heart as well. He wants us to have our place, even if he has his own ideas about that. But wanting is not enough. It's only good if he can become king in Essera and there's no Sordanish plot to snatch it from him. If he dies, we have nothing."

"And we don't have much more than that since Stefan died," said Rannuf.

In their gazes, Aubrey felt their male suspicion of the power women wielded, of what a woman might yet take from them. A Staubaun woman, breeding Staubaun heirs. It was just like men to think prevention would also come in the form of a woman. The presumption infuriated her, though for different reasons than inflamed Ewlys. Those who sought to secure the future through a man's seed would seek also to secure the woman who bore its fruit. Before Marc Frederick had put the taste of power on their tongues, Khelds had regarded children as the Mother's Gift, new lives entering the world in the spirit of the union that had created them, products of no design but Hers. What could any product of such plotting as this be but soulless? Aubrey clamped down on her distaste before Nalf and his cronies could see it. She knew better than to try to argue for the Mother before men such as these, who did not realize the extent to which they had adopted Staubaun patriarchy—and priorities.

"I will seek to find out what Hans is thinking." Only agreement would appease them, and this one was easy. "I'm as interested as you in knowing his plans—particularly on how he plans to deal with Neuberland. But I won't insinuate myself into his life. I will present myself to no man falsely."

"And what falsehood in it? You're a Kheld, damn it! The Staubauns killed your father in Neuberland. Dishonored your mother and killed her too. A woman with blood to answer for won't turn to froth once she's got a man in her or a crown on her head." Nalf looked Aubrey cold in the eye. "And haven't you always wanted it? A little of what the Staubauns have? Just to throw back at them? Power's better than spit, girl, a damn sight better."

"Nilla didn't think so."

Aubrey saw Ewlys's jaw tense and understood. The Old Mothers had failed Nilla that day too.

Nalf Rhys glared at both women. "Nilla was a sweet girl and I'll hear no sass about our choice of her. She was our queen! She couldn't see the wickedness in men and she died at the hands of that wickedness." To Aubrey he said, "It's a gentle fault that you certainly lack. But that's why you'll outlast her."

No, Aubrey wasn't like Nilla. In so many ways, she was not like Nilla at all. Nilla had only wanted a gentle Kheld husband who would build her a house but men like the ones in this room had thrown her into a pit of wolves. And for what? So that some of them could be given estates and raised to titles? Was that what Nalf saw in Aubrey?

"I told you what I'm willing to do, and I'll do it," she snapped. "But I don't believe Hans Thegn is half the idiot you seem to think he is. If he wants to marry a lord's daughter, he'll marry a lord's daughter and there won't be a lot any of us can do to stop him. For all we know, his mother the Princess Emyli has already arranged a noble marriage to some Esseran house that will solidify his support there. All I can do is put myself in his path. Now excuse me, Uncle, *bancutha*." She bowed her head when using the old word of respect for men familiar to her but not of her kilth. "I really didn't get much sleep this morning."

Standing, Aubrey lent her hand to Ewlys. The Old Mother accepted Aubrey's help and they left the room together, wool skirts sweeping about their ankles.

No sooner had they closed the main chamber door behind them than Ewlys turned to Aubrey and sighed. "It has begun."

10

It is not true that Khelds have no knowledge of the lands
beyond their borders. Every traveler to their land is eagerly
waylaid and questioned as to what he has heard or knows.
Towns open their gates and inns are meeting places for
talk; the common people welcome traders to their houses,
not only to purchase wares but to hear news of other
places. From such bits and pieces, Khelds form opinions
about every important subject.

MERGAN STAUBAUN PAZOR, REPORT TO KING ESTEVAN II

The next day dawned full of the promise of fair weather. Hans
woke eager to explore his surroundings, but the only sound
that greeted his rising was Arne's quiet snores from a cot
across the room. By whatever means Gerd had procured the room,
it was a large one and Hans appreciated having a good friend nearby.
He donned his clothes in silence and left Arne behind. Dorilian, he
was sure, would have risen with the first rays of the sun, and Robdan
had offered the night before to take them both on a morning tour of
Rhodhur and its surrounding villages.

They left on horseback before the sun cleared the trees. Dorilian
rode one of the Trongorian horses, a handsome bay roan to replace
the one he'd lost, and Farrl—who said he wished to learn more of the
lay of the land—rode with them. A back trail led from the more
populous valley and into the hills. After a time, they emerged from the
trees on a rise overlooking a large, open pond. A flock of ducks
paddled on the surface, joining a gaggle of black-headed geese and a
family of what looked like muskrats gathered among a stand of reeds.
The water looked like gray glass in the bottom of a bowl, the land
surrounding it rich with grasses, bright patches of heather, and late

blooming asters. Past the smooth expanse, the Hall rose as a collection of brown planes and angles, partly obscured by outbuildings and trees.

Dorilian, who until then had said little, abruptly swung down from his horse. He kicked at the ground, then stood on the ridge at that point where it began to slope toward the water, appraising the shoreline.

"Is something wrong?" asked Hans.

"No." With a wince, favoring his injured leg, Dorilian stooped and, using the knife from his belt, scraped a hole in the earth, sifting the loam between his fingers, then looked again around the boundaries of the lake, scanning for something. A bit stiffly, he rose to his feet. He turned to Robdan. "Do you know the source of this water, Master Aelfricson?"

Robdan looked perplexed, though he had lived within sight of this pond most of his life. "We call it Duckbutt Pond. Its water comes from a stream out of the taller hills to the west."

Dorilian looked past his companions' shoulders at the autumn-tinted hills. "Does the stream reach this edge, and then run downward into the bowl? Or has it cut a course?"

"It's a ground stream only," Robdan replied. "There's rock all around, not that far down. That's why no trees grow near. There is a fan of falls where the stream comes in. If you look closely, you can see. Over there." They looked to where Robdan pointed, to a place where water tumbled in the sun.

"I thought as much."

"How's that?" Hans saw nothing out of the ordinary here.

"See how very round it is."

Hans thought it a good time to trot out his Mentan education. "Glacial action will do that. Or perhaps this is an old volcanic crater."

"The geology speaks differently. This region was not formed by geothermal activity. And the valleys in this area exhibit a distinctly nonglacial formation. In fact, the valleys are what give the answer away. The one I rode through the other day had very little natural rock. However, I did see a great deal of what miners call *skellai*, or cinder. See those hills?" Dorilian gestured at the surrounding elevations. "Those are the remains of a pre-Exile city."

"That explains much," said Farrl. "It must have been a great one in its day for us to have ridden through so much of it."

Hans blinked. He had never suspected. He looked more closely, seeking some telltale patterns of streets or buildings, but all he saw were low hills clothed in ranks of trees. If Dorilian was correct, such patterns, if they existed, might be discerned from the air, but from ground level they were invisible.

"Pre-Exile?" Hans drew on what little he knew. "You mean Aryati?"

"No. I should guess that this one predated the Aryati."

"It was here before the sorcerer lords?" Robdan looked amazed.

"Devastation erased some cities from the face of the World. Others it merely broke and leveled. Such cities may still exist in degraded form."

Farrl had his own opinion to offer and said to Robdan, "Not only Aryati cities underwent ore flows. Your folk might find some good metal here."

Dorilian lost interest in the hills and turned his attention back to the pond. "This pond, however, may be the remains of an Aryati construction. I have seen for myself such great bowls in Sansordan and Teremar, standing on the edges of grassland or dune, holding the sky in vast stone cups. As a boy, I thought maybe the ancients had used them to catch water, but I was later taught that they were ears, the ears of the Aryati, listening to the stars. But the Aryati died and their ears went deaf, and the stars for all we know went out. Devastation reduced the city that once stood here to rubble, and Time made it possible for water to flow into your bowl—and out an overflow at some other point. Your basin, Master Robdan, is in the process of filling in, first with water, then with silt, and now with soil and growth. But then, it makes a very pretty pond, does it not?"

"We... like to think so." Robdan looked askance at the gleaming surface of Duckbutt Pond, then at the hills, as if he were imagining ghostly cities underneath.

But Hans found himself studying Dorilian anew. *Is he ever satisfied with just the surface of a thing?* More and more Hans suspected that Dorilian lived in a world of layers, wherein he saw not just the surface but the linearity of time through its fabric, underlying structures and socially constructed projections. Here in Amallar, among people for whom conclusions were generally drawn from less informed observations, Hans felt a special kinship with a man who could say he stood upon the lip of a dish once used to listen to the stars.

And why shouldn't he know that? He's related to the Wall Lords. He lives in a city that puts anything the Dominion had to shame. And the Rill is something even beyond that.

But Hans didn't know what the Rill might be. About the Rill and the Wall, Hans still knew next to nothing. He didn't even know what Dorilian had done with the Rill, or if it could be undone. *I didn't ask the right questions.* Hans felt a sinking deep in his chest as Dorilian remounted his horse. *I didn't ask if he could start it up again.*

The north gate loomed less grim, and the grass had lost its frost by the time they drew again near to Rhodhur Hall. The rear yards bustled with activity, ringing with the clang of farriers' hammers, clattering with farmers' carts and the shrill voices of women calling for laundering. Dorilian excused himself as soon as they entered the yard and headed with Farrl to the opposite side to stable his horse with those of the Trongorians. Hans and Robdan were left to face a growing crowd of Khelds attracted by their late arrival. Never again would Hans enter Rhodhur unnoticed or unannounced. From now on his mornings would be spent engaging in vague discussions of the weather or prospects for a good harvest with people he hardly knew.

The crowd took several minutes to thin, people drifting away to pursue work that would not wait, before Hans and Robdan could finally lead their horses to the stable. A light voice hailed across the yard as they approached.

"Robdan! Hans Thegn!"

They turned to see Aubrey, her legs straining against the faded fabric of a long skirt, a loose jacket flapping carelessly as she crossed the stable compound. "I was hoping I would find you."

"Our misfortune," Robdan lamented quietly to Hans. "Now we shall have no end of arguments." His expression, however, betrayed more affection than dismay.

"Where have you been?" Aubrey eyed Robdan's riding clothes. "It must have been important to get you astride a horse."

Robdan bent down and slapped a few pieces of barnyard straw from his trousers. "I have been playing the part of tour guide."

"Robdan took me riding in the hills." Hans enjoyed the way Aubrey's lively blue eyes swung to meet his. "It was my idea."

Robdan nodded in agreement. "Neither old Gadfly here nor his old master much enjoyed the outing."

Hans fought a smile. For all the travel he seemed to do, Robdan made much of how little he liked to ride.

"Nonsense," said Aubrey. When Gadfly swung his head toward her chest, she gently scratched behind the horse's ear. "He's telling me he had fun."

"Don't you have a busy day ahead?" Robdan suggested.

"No," Aubrey replied. "My time is my own while I wait on a loom. I'll help you tend your horse, though."

Hans had given his horse over earlier to a man who would not dream of letting him tend it himself. Now only Robdan's horse remained to be stabled. Hans fell into step beside Aubrey as they walked with Robdan toward the barn where the Thegnkeld boarded their horses.

The weatherbeaten walls of the keep loomed a more cheerful shade of silver than the dull gray of the day before, and sunny skies had brought out a host of laundry to air like flocks of exotic birds above the rear courtyards, flapping their bright colors in the gentle breeze. Hans liked the way Aubrey's laughter seemed to belong up there among the linens, as light and airy as those fluttering sheets, far above the mud and dirt of the floor they walked upon. The muted colors she wore made her look lighter, softer, and prettier than when she had brought Dorilian as her captive.

"I understand you hail from Neuberland," Hans said. A trace of a frown, barely more than a wisp, touched Aubrey's smile. "Did I say something wrong?"

"No. But I've learned that when people ask about my homeland, they wish to talk of something else."

"The fighting."

"Usually."

"I've heard about that," Hans said. "But I really do want to know more about Neuberland."

Aubrey's gaze took Hans in and measured him against something behind her thoughts. They came to the stable, one of several solid, weathered buildings set against Rhodhur's western wall, where she looped shaggy Gadfly's halter to a stout post. "I can tell you all you need to know."

Robdan rubbed his old gelding's nose and frowned at Hans for having gotten Aubrey started.

"Neuberland is a beautiful green country, not as forested as Amallar but well watered and good for farming. The Staubauns had little use for it until we settled there. I was born in Saemoregh, the town my father founded just east of Bellan Toregh. Your grandfather, the old king, gave my father a large grant of land there for his service, which I now hold. Most of Saemoregh's people are settlers who have built a good economy in farming and wool. A hundred Kheld families live there and have fought for decades to hold their land. We have killed and died to defend our homes."

Aubrey's fierce expression let Hans know that anything he might say would sound self-serving, so he waited for her to continue.

"Fifteen years ago, soldiers hired by the Lord of Annech attacked our holding and my mother died defending it. Two years later they slew my father. Since then, my holders and I have been threatened and intimidated, but I still hold Amundhal and the people of Saemoregh remain in the fine town they have built. That's why I'm here, to speak for Saemoregh in choosing the site of the High Witan to be held once the harvest is in. Neuberland's Cruihcil wants it to convene at Bellan Toregh, not tucked deep in the woods so that leaders blinded by false hopes and fears need not see that their world is crashing down on them."

"Rhodhur's forests are safe, Lud's Sanctuary is near, and we are within a stone's throw of the Hill and its Moon Circle, where the power of the Mother is strongest." Robdan peered with reproval from the other side of his horse.

"And where old men feel safe to do nothing. It's the same with the Old Mothers." Aubrey jerked at the girth buckles. "Have you ever been to Neuberland? Do you even know what kind of people we are today or what we have been through? Why should the Witan be held where all but those who live deep in the forests must travel far to reach it, when more of us live in the river lowlands along the Brennan and Floh? Bellan Toregh is more central; it lies at the crossroads of our lands, and the Rill no longer causes the cold trees to shiver. If the future is what we are meeting to decide, what better place to sit beneath the stars to determine our course?"

"Perhaps the stars are not the same," Robdan ventured.

"They're the same," said Hans. "You have to go south quite a way before they change very much."

"See?" Aubrey said to her uncle.

"I knew as much," Robdan admitted. "But you cannot expect me to decide the place of the Witan."

"You have a voice. You sit among those who will decide."

"Then be kind to me, girl. It is morning yet."

Hans had to admit that what Aubrey said made sense. Rhodhur was Amallar's historical and cultural stronghold, to be sure, but Bellan Toregh straddled strategic highways both north to Dazunor-Rannuli and south to Leseos, as well as the east-west road between

Rhodhur and Kheld settlements in Neuberland. It had a navigable river that connected its trade to the Dazun. It would be a far better place from which to launch and supply a war effort.

And Bellan Toregh was Amallar's only known Rill node—albeit a nonfunctioning one.

"If I wanted to speak to the Witan, would I be allowed to do so?" he asked.

"I'd be surprised if they didn't insist on it," said Robdan.

Aubrey rolled her eyes. "Don't mislead him, Uncle." She turned to Hans. "Of course they will want you to speak, because they're trying to figure out what to do with you. But that doesn't mean they'll listen to what you say. If you're looking to negotiate a deal with Sordan, I can tell you right now it won't work."

"You don't know that it won't."

"It won't work." Stubbornness hardened Aubrey's rejection into something keenly revealing, cold and brilliant and filled with fire. "You've been away, Hans Thegn. And you've seen the enemy's soft side, the sleek, shining pelt of the beast. You've heard pretty words. Well, don't let the Sordaneon fool you. We have our soft side too. All people do. Except life isn't lived through pretty words; life is lived on the savage edge of the enemy's claws—and Dorilian's claws are sharp. I'm sure they're beautiful, and they glint in the sun like the towers of his City, but he will tear you to shreds. I know. I live beneath shadows cast by Sordan's armies as they lay waste the settlements of my people. I've had to flee from under the hoofs of their horses and escape the slashing of their knives. And if not Sordan itself, then the soldiers of Annech and Gobba, who they arm and mount to destroy us. That is the way my people have lived, and still do live, beneath the fast-falling shadow of the eagle's claws." Her mouth tightened. "And in all that time do you think no one tried to negotiate a stop to the fighting? Oh yes, there was talk and more talk, and a few agreements set to paper. And all of them were broken. No one wants to try again."

Hans noted the slight tremble at the corner of Aubrey's lips, the dry eyes that spoke a mixture of anger and pain. Was there any way to reach through so much bitterness? "I want to try." The ache he felt for her reached down into his heart. "Don't you see? The only way to stop this cycle is to end the fighting. This conflict is a dead end. You can't fight your way through it. There's nothing on the other side."

"There's hope."

"Hope only becomes real if people believe in it. Those negotiations, the ones that failed, they were made between parties convinced of their failure, maybe even invested in that failure. Sordan was slapped with penalties by Stefan's Archhalia, yes, but every time Stefan tried to end the war in Neuberland, he never included Sordan in the discussions."

"Because Dorilian Sordaneon wouldn't agree to discuss anything!"

"You're right. He wouldn't. Not with Stefan. But that doesn't mean he won't discuss things with me."

"You can't resolve our war against him. No one can." Aubrey slid the saddle from Gadfly's back and slung it across the fence. "Well-meaning words won't get Sordan's army out of Neuberland. Sordan has turned Gignastha into a garrison. Dorilian supports the Lords of Annech and Gobba. And Leseos… Leseos is his puppet. It's a Rill port and their Bas is afraid of him. Words won't root armies out of our land."

"What if *I* can?" Hans asked. "What if I can get Dorilian to pull his armies out?"

Narrow-eyed, Aubrey glanced back across her shoulder. "In return for what?"

"Free access for those armies to go into Essera to fight Nammuor."

That answer earned a sharp laugh. "Allow Dorilian Sordaneon to range free north of the Dazun? Then you're crazier than Robdan!"

Robdan sighed. Aubrey had the grace to wince and give a grimace of apology.

"I don't think Robdan's crazy," Hans said. "And I know *I'm* not."

Aubrey cupped her hand over the smooth pommel of the saddle. "After Sordan invaded Neuberland, Stefan tried to get Dorilian to leave. And failed. Stefan had all of Essera at his command; he had treasure and armies and he was King—he had power then that you may never have."

"Nammuor didn't have an army or fleet in Essera yet. He wasn't taking over and threatening Rill ports. Dorilian had nothing at stake. He didn't need Stefan—"

"And he doesn't need you. At least Stefan didn't give in."

At that moment Robdan interrupted. "Hans," he said, peering past Aubrey to a point over her shoulder.

Hans would have been happier to see Nalf Rhys. Herberth was laughing at something Dorilian had said to him and both men looked uncommonly relaxed. The two must have met up at the stable. Now, by the look of it, they might have been conversing on one of Dorilian's sunny terraces at Rhondda or among Herberth's warehouses in Ogarth. It didn't help one bit that both men were obviously foreigners. The Elector's well-tailored leathers bestowed his solid Estol frame with authority and Dorilian, even in the garb of an ordinary traveler, was exceptionally self-possessed.

At least he's limping. A little. It should have been more.

"And now our morning is complete." Herberth's mouth tightened upon seeing Aubrey, but he nodded pleasantly to Robdan.

Aubrey gave stocky Herberth a wry frown, but any retort died on her lips when she noticed his companion. Momentary surprise quickly gave way to a delicate coolness. Hans detected a warning as loud as any klaxon.

"Thron." Aubrey's response ignored Herberth altogether. "That is your name, if I remember."

"Of course."

Meaning that she remembers, Hans thought, catching the inflection.

"My kinswoman, Aubrey Amundda." Robdan's introduction interrupted what was almost certain to be a sharp rebuttal on his kinswoman's lips. "But then, you've already met."

Dorilian's gray gaze flicked over Aubrey with brittle appraisal. "I would not dignify that encounter as a 'meeting,' Master Aelfricson."

"No, it was an interrogation." Aubrey subjected Dorilian to a look just as scouring as he had given her. "I never did find out everything I wanted to know about you, Thron."

"Nor will you—in the middle of a Kheldish stable."

Hans knew that tone of voice too well not to act. It would hardly do to have Dorilian start acting Hierarchal. "Robdan, I think I should take"—Hans avoided names for the moment—"our friends to breakfast. Would you mind very much joining us when you're finished?"

"Of course. It would be a pleasure to continue our morning." Mostly, Robdan looked relieved.

Aubrey stepped forward to join them. Robdan placed a hand on her arm.

"Please stay and help your uncle with his tasks."

She could hardly refuse. Proper upbringing demanded that younger Khelds honor elder kin. Frustration apparent, Aubrey reached for a brush and joined Robdan in currying his old horse's coat. While walking away, Hans turned once to look behind him and saw her still staring at his back—or more likely Dorilian's, who never looked at all.

That was a good thing, because Aubrey looked like she wanted to throw a knife in that direction.

11

Most of those attending Marc Frederick's coronation
expected him to die when the Leur's Ring was slipped onto
his finger. When he did not die, alliances made in
anticipation of the event crumbled. Foremost of these were
those attached to placing the Sordaneons on the throne.
Labran Sordaneon found himself standing alone,
abandoned by Esseran Lords who had moments before
proposed to support him. Everything had hinged upon
removal of the rival.

PRINCESS PALAISTEA, *BEFORE THE STORM*

Mormantaloran standards hung from the ramparts at Trulo,
informing the populace that the Prince Regent hosted
Nammuor's chief baron, Coram Barzanes, and his foremost
general, Salkren Zel. Zel's army, in fact, had established its base at
the nearby town of Bogmuth, the smoke from their campfires
spreading in a haze to the west. Worse, Mormantaloran forces had
been seizing storehouses nearby and along the river.

Now, as Erenor rode through the town center, he sensed Trulo's
alarm. The people who watched his entrance did so in silence,
without cheers. Their stares asked a question their voices never
would.

They wondered who truly ruled this fractured land.

Erenor would have preferred to meet the Mormantalorans
somewhere other than in the Prince's Hall. It deserved better.
Faced with slabs of purest white marble and hung with tapestries
portraying the rich history of the Dazun River, the grand chamber
had been built during a time of peace, for the purpose of advancing
that peace. The tapestry dominating the long wall showed the Rill,

woven of silver thread, arriving at Dazunor-Rannuli. Carved and painted figures portraying a score of trades and occupations stood silent witness along the tops of the walls beneath a ceiling rendered like sky. Set against so tranquil a setting, the red-clothed emissary and his soldiers looked like bloodstains. Like all Nammuor's minions, Coram Barzanes was of pure Staubaun breeding, moon pale and fair haired, with dark eyes that drank in whatever light came near. Zel on the other hand looked feral, as golden and sleek as one of the great cats Mormantalorans hunted for sport. A Sorcerer's Star glinted upon the breast of his elegant leathers.

"Nammuor is unhappy." Coram slapped his riding gloves on the ancient table at which Stefan had once held court hearings. He appeared irritated, probably because he had ridden in with Zel instead of translocating as he preferred. "Not only has no one decisively located Dorilian, it appears your regency may be about to end."

Erenor scoffed, though something cold clutched at his gut. Did the message hint that Nammuor himself was thinking to unseat him? "What does he fear? I am more secure than ever. With Handurin out of play, even the cursed Khelds have ceased to challenge me." Erenor's most pressing problems of late came from the Seven Houses, their power diminished in restive Dazunor-Rannuli, where they sat atop vast supplies of grains and ores they could not move. *Damn the Rill! And damn the Seven Houses for having fostered our dependence on it. The heartland is paralyzed—and Nammuor straddles our supply lines by sea.*

"Oh? Do the Khelds support your regency, then?" Coram played with a ruby-tipped quirt, bending the shaft between his hands. "Over Handurin himself?"

"Handurin himself is in Sordan, in the hands of a villain the Khelds detest so thoroughly, they smile on any man who stands against him. I have but to invoke Dorilian Sordaneon's name and every Kheld within earshot ceases to think rationally." If there was one lesson Erenor had taken from Stefan, it was that. Erenor summoned a servant in blue livery to serve drinks to his guests.

"Handurin himself is in Rhodhur." Salkren Zel settled into a gilded chair. His frown caused the white scar upon his upper lip to bunch unpleasantly.

"Rhodhur? That's... impossible!" Fear sharpened Erenor's response. Without Rill communication, there had been no news from Sordan in weeks. The most recent relay message, sent from Stauberg by way of Askorras, said that Handurin was being held under close guard in Sordan's Citadel while Dorilian pursued secret meetings at the fortress sanctuary of the Initiates at Jharbala.

"The rumor is fresh," Zel told him, his soldier's voice indifferent. "It bubbled up from Amallar."

Coram stopped tapping his quirt long enough to add needed detail. "Zel's soldiers captured two Khelds on the river, spreading word. Handurin arrived at Rhodhur four days ago. He was in the company of Herberth of Trongor."

"Fuck!" Handurin was known to have met the Trongorian Elector in Sordan.

A cold smile accompanied Coram's response. "Never fear. Nammuor is planning something very unpleasant for Ogarth."

"Never mind that! Ogarth is inconsequential." Erenor cared not at all what happened to Trongor's paltry capital. Other threats filled his fears. Thoughts of Emyli writing phantom letters from Permephedon, misdirecting his attention. The Rill ceasing to run north of the Randpory. Amallar lurking just across the river with its barbarian horde. All directed at... what? Gaining Handurin a clear path to Essera?

"Nothing that challenges our Master is inconsequential."

Erenor detected the note of warning in Coram's delivery and decided to modify his approach. "Your Master can do what he wants with Ogarth. If it's true that Handurin is in Rhodhur in company with its Elector, then Trongor has committed an act of hostility against this regency. Yet I think the boy is naught but smoke which the Sordaneon blows in our eyes."

"We are aware of Sordan's troop movements," Coram informed him coldly. "That is why General Zel will be making a march to Dazunor-Rannuli. Aside from your personal forces, you are no longer to field an army in Dazunor but focus on defending Stauberg and dealing with Dannuth. You will also move your ruling seat to Stauberg. There are already insurgencies along the Dazun border. We believe Dorilian's next move will be to attempt to push through Neuberland toward Dazunor-Rannuli."

"And Nammuor thinks Handurin is a diversion for that?"

Coram paused before the window, looking out at the sweep of the Dazun. To the east, the richest city in Essera sat upon the river like a bloated, beached beast, swollen with vast stores of rotting grain. "Nammuor thinks Sordan's Hierarch is cleverer than the Seven Houses. Dorilian concealed his ability to manipulate the Rill until he could wield it to his greatest advantage. All know it galled him to have the Rill node at Dazunor-Rannuli used to our Master's benefit. The Seven Houses gambled that Dorilian could be held impotent, but the Rill is ever an asset to be weighed very carefully where a Sordaneon is concerned. One House or all Seven, the damned cartel may yet regret overplaying their hand."

Erenor recognized the brilliance of Dorilian's move. "They should have killed him while they had the chance. Now none of us dare assassinate him. We need him to restore the thing—and so do you."

With an eloquent shrug, Coram concurred. "What is it to Sordan if Dorilian throws Handurin back to the Khelds the way you or I would toss barking dogs a bone? He has no more intention of sitting Emyli's bastard brat on Essera's throne than he had of legitimizing Stefan's right to be there. His real game is self-protection. Who knows but he has allowed the boy to flee to Amallar just to create a focus of insurrection?" The hawk glance turned on Erenor again. "Such a diversion might suit any number of purposes. The Khelds are predictable. They will rally to Handurin's side—and by doing so create enough disarray within that country to allow Sordan's army to make its press through Neuberland to the Dazun. Or perhaps Handurin was persuaded in Sordan that he should send Stefan's Khelds against his Regent."

"Don't forget that Handurin could also set the Khelds against Sordan," Erenor pointed out. "We don't yet know what the boy—or the Khelds—will do." Or whether Handurin would prove able to do anything at all.

"All the more urgency, then, to find ways to be sure," Zel said. "Handurin Stauberg-Randolph will be no threat to us if he cannot raise the Khelds to war—and less so if he cannot lead them."

Erenor saw the implication and smiled. "And so we make sure they are focused elsewhere."

"Yes. On Sordan." Coram laid his quirt on the table, the ruby on the grip as baleful as a demon's eye. Erenor was reminded that in his own land, Teleg, Coram was from an ancient and powerful family.

It could be done, and easily. Sordan had been the Khelds' preferred enemy for decades.

"And what of Handurin?" Erenor asked. The question was to him more pressing than Nammuor's obsession with containing

Sordan. "I suffered him until now because I required legitimacy. I remain Regent. I could send men into Amallar after him."

"Do what you will," Coram said. He and Zel looked unconcerned. "However, I would warn you that Nammuor is mildly interested in this prince. Legitimate hope or Sordaneon cat's-paw, Handurin's possible uses are much to be pondered."

Erenor flushed at the rebuke. He feared that if Handurin proved tractable, Nammuor would promote dissolving the regency. Why nurse a beleaguered Erenor as figurehead when just as easily he could have Marc Frederick's grandson as his puppet king? All the more reason for Erenor to remove the boy. How close he had come to doing so in Sordan! Either Handurin had survived the attempt to poison him, or some other fate had intervened. All Essera had heeded the rumor that Handurin had attempted an escape and been taken by night to the Citadel, there to be imprisoned until the Hierarch's temper toward him improved. That the action might be protective in reaction to the poisoning attempt was something only Erenor suspected. That it might have become part of a deception designed to move Handurin secretly out of Sordan, he only now realized.

What does Dorilian want? Always it came to that, the question none could ever fully answer. *His Highborn mind spawns its own reality. He knew all along that he could stop the Rill, knew all along what doing so would accomplish. Cripple—and empower. We are all moving inside his vision of that event.*

"Something more." Salkren Zel sounded grave as he tossed a folded document onto the table between them. It lay there, a rectangle of crisp red, bearing words inscribed with golden ink. "Now that Handurin is in Amallar, it has become imprudent to tolerate Kheld settlements north of the Dazun."

Erenor's stomach turned at what he sensed was coming. He leaned over the table, toward them. "They're just farmers."

"They are Khelds. Their loyalties were fanatically with Stefan. Now that Handurin has joined their brethren in Amallar, they will be a breeding ground of rebels against you."

However true that was, Erenor found the conclusion too coldly expedient. It resounded the arguments used to reconcile him to the need to kill Stefan. "They hate Sordan no less than their brethren in Amallar do," Erenor pointed out. "If Dorilian intends to invade Essera, the Khelds living here are his natural foes."

Zel's icy gaze measured Erenor's opposition while weighing the reasons behind it. "Be that as it may, Nammuor has ordered me to secure the border with Amallar. I will begin by sending out soldiers pretending to be Sordan's agents. They will start the process by taking hostages in the villages along the river."

"In Sordan's name?"

"Of course."

All three men knew how ready the Khelds—any Khelds, even those in Essera—would be to believe the lie. Or that when Erenor's troops, or Nammuor's, freed some of the hostages, how quickly word of Sordan's perfidy would spread. It was, all told, a masterful deception. And if matters in Amallar took a turn Nammuor did not like, Erenor knew what would come next: the hostages would be but the first Khelds to be slaughtered.

Handurin was to be persuaded—if not to join with Nammuor, then of the cost of opposing him.

12

All who came to my father understood that he would not
oppress them with the crushing weight of an ancestral past.
He had left his past behind him. Marc Frederick Stauberg-
Randolph's greatest strength was his profound grounding
in the here and now.

EMYLI STAUBERG-RANDOLPH, *REFLECTIONS ON KINGSHIP*

"My mother says I have money now." Hans shared the
contents of a letter Robdan had passed to him just an
hour before. He conferred with both Robdan and
Herberth over a midday meal of tender simmered veal and spicy
brown noodles, eaten at a table tucked between the kitchen and a
rack of servers' aprons. Taking meals at odd hours and in less visible
locations had become Hans's best strategy for ensuring he might talk
with his companions while eating. "She says she's putting the money
to good use in Essera to help me."

He slid a sideways look toward Dorilian, seated at the other end
of the table like the common courier-soldier he was supposed to be.
If Dorilian had heard what Hans had said, he showed no reaction.
His frown seemed to be for whatever he was poking his spoon at on
his plate.

"How did you get a letter from your lady mother all the way
down here?" Herberth had yet to be convinced Amallar could
communicate effectively with the rest of the world. He stabbed a
chunk of tender veal. "This is truly delicious. Your cook is a
wonder."

"We have our ways with cookery and with letters," Robdan said.
He used a square of linen to dab some broth from his lip before

dipping his spoon again into his bowl. "The Princess has had great need to be cautious. She sends her correspondence by way of a network she has built over the years. It's made up of women she knows. Old Mothers. Young mothers. The mothers and daughters of friends. Women are skilled at exchanging information. Do not doubt them. It was a woman who handed it to me."

Hans recalled Asphalladra, neatly placed in Dorilian's court. Placed—and known about. Hans had yet to fully grasp whether Cullen's widow was some manner of spy or simply an accessible means of passing information.

Arne, seated across the table, had perked at hearing Hans's news. "Well money's a good change of luck! If you have coin, you can buy things!"

Until now, lack of funds had been an impediment. Even that Herberth was here in Amallar counted as a kind of loan from the Trongorian government. "My *mother* is buying things. She's arming some people and securing supplies in my name. In Merrydn."

Herberth lifted an eyebrow. "Smart woman. You will need more allies, preferably up *there*." He had agreed just that morning, after a few days of talks, to return to Trongor to advocate for an official alliance.

"Merrydn?" Arne protested. "Why not send the money here? To you! Then you could do your own buying of what you need."

Dorilian almost said something. Hans saw the restraint it took for him not to speak, though it was possible the scowl and the thought accompanying it were meant for the food. Unlike Hans, Herberth, and Robdan, the rest of the table—which included Dorilian, Farrl, and two of Herberth's other soldiers as well as Arne—ate from the common portion that was served to the Hall's guests each day. Dorilian's bowl held buttermash and stewed eel.

"The most likely reason for not sending money here is that Amallar has no means of holding or allocating the kinds of assets involved," said Herberth. "The Princess is most likely dealing with sophisticated financial instruments, perhaps even Rill portions or contracts, which Amallar is in no position to hold."

"We do have banks, you know. There's a big one in Eastmeary." Arne knew his hometown well enough.

Herberth nodded benignly. "Undoubtedly a very fine bank—for *farmers*."

Elbow on the table, Dorilian put his head in his hand.

Hans saw that he would have to get Dorilian out of here before he started setting *everyone* straight. Emyli had also told Hans the source of his windfall. There was no need for word to get out that most of whatever fortune Hans commanded was in *Sordan*.

When they rose to go back to their rooms, hoping to rest before yet another night of what was sure to be tedious introductions to yet more clan chieftains, Dorilian stood and stayed back, not leaving the table. Robdan and Hans, after discreetly signaling Herberth to leave and Arne to stand out of earshot, stayed with him. Hans braced himself for talk of banks and finances.

Dorilian pointed to the orange-tinged brothy remains of the veal and noodles Hans and the Elector had been eating. "What must I do to get a meal like that one?"

Robdan ducked his head and seemed to find the stitching on the lapel of his wool jacket fascinating.

"Gerd explained it," Hans said. "I'm a guest of the Thegnard, of Amallar. So is Herberth. Gerd cooks our meals himself as a matter of state hospitality. The rest of the food, the meals served to everyone else, he oversees those. He has a whole staff of cooks. It's perfectly good food!"

"It's... plentiful. If I wished to eat vast amounts of eel, mutton, and brown sops, I would do it nowhere else. The pea pottage is decent. But *that* food"—Dorilian pointed again—"is worthy of princes. The sauce—I took a swipe of it—is sublime. The rack of lamb last night was perfect: pink, tender, artfully herbed, and assertive."

"I should never have given you a cut of that," Hans grumbled.

"Spare me the common food. I want *that*."

Robdan held up both hands, palms raised and shoulders dropped in a plea for understanding. "Gerd has his rules. This Hall is his domain. He's strict about his rules because he must be. He couldn't possibly cook for every person here."

"He cooks for *you*." Dorilian was not above pointing that out.

To which Robdan could but nod, abashed. "We're old friends. And I *am* Amallar's Ambassador to the Archhalia. That's not much of a claim to importance anywhere else, but it does carry some weight here."

"And I do not."

Robdan's shoulders lowered further and he winced. "Not in your current occupation. And, frankly, maybe not in the other one."

Though Dorilian's eyes narrowed, he didn't contest that remark. Hans thought it might be best to mediate. "I could talk with Gerd, I suppose, but I'm just a guest here myself. I don't have a lot of pull with innkeepers or, well, anyone. At least not yet. And if word gets out that I'm asking for special treatment for one of Herberth's men—"

"No." Dorilian again frowned at the emptied bowls of veal and broth. "I will come up with something else."

As Handurin, Herberth, and Robdan went to meet with Nalf Rhys and his high-ranking chieftains for talk of... whatever Khelds talked about, Dorilian retired to Robdan's quarters. He did so as often as he could reasonably expect Khelds not to notice or question. For the most part, the barbarians paid him no mind. He kept his opinions to himself and his emotions tightly in grasp; consequently, his desire not to be noticed worked better here than it ever had anywhere else. As soon as Handurin and Robdan left the book-cluttered room, securing the door behind them, Dorilian was about as safe from discovery as it was possible for him to be in Amallar.

Such interludes were also useful. With quiet and concentration, he could contact and converse with Levyathan in secret. Sordan, at least, was informed of his whereabouts and well-being—and could provide certain kinds of assistance.

Dorilian picked up the book he had been reading, a rather battered and venerable treatise on beekeeping. Bees surely sat at the pinnacle of Leur's creations—orderly, productive, life-sustaining—and that the Kheld author of the tome interwove the lives of bees and human management of them to a vaguely Jharbalan philosophy was intriguing. Were beekeepers benevolent facilitators or did their actions warp what should be left to nature and the laws of Leur's Creation? Where did an individual life and its self-preservation end and group identity or protection achieve precedence? Honeybees sometimes killed their queens.

Seating himself in the chair with his sword at rest against the wall and his injured knee propped on a kind of cushioned stool, Dorilian had just placed the book on his lap when he heard a key in the lock. He looked up as the main chamber door edged open. He expected to see Robdan returning for some reason or other, but instead he faced Aubrey Amundda. Looking slightly surprised and with two books in arm, she forced a self-conscious smile.

"I thought you'd be out. I'm returning books." When met with only the silence of his disapproval, Aubrey tapped her belt and a ring holding several finger-length bits of iron. "I have a key. Robdan lets me borrow from his collection."

If that were true, Aubrey possessed more than the usual Kheld level of learning. Dorilian had listened to Robdan lament how few of his people took advantage of his painstakingly amassed library. With telling familiarity, Aubrey walked to where Robdan's books were shelved and deftly replaced the two books among volumes of poetry. From that same shelf, Aubrey selected a slender volume and took it into her hand. Noting that Dorilian continued to watch, she defiantly showed its apple-green cover.

"Myron," she said. "Do you know of him?"

"Yes." Not only did Dorilian know *of* Myron, he knew Myron. Now that Stefan had ceased to be an obstacle, Dorilian hoped to persuade the Esseran poet to grace Sordan's court.

"He's quite explicit sometimes—but I like that."

"His muse is Kheld." The unguarded way Aubrey's lips parted and eyes widened told Dorilian he had surprised her. Amused, he continued, "Verses from 'The Beloved Waiting' and other poems reveal it. *'His midnight hair upon the pillow, hyacinth morning in his eyes.'*" No need to mention that he had also met the muse.

"I wondered about that. Not that verse, but others. Something about the beauty of his lips being the shape of things forbidden." Aubrey ran the fingertips of one hand lightly across the embossed lettering of the book cover. "I like Myron. His poems are complex, full of layers, especially 'The Hills We Die On.' I'm not sure to whom—or about whom—he's speaking, which is part of the poet's genius. *'Your soul, which longs for all the World, confined in this decay.'*" She tucked the book in the crook of her arm and stepped toward him. "What are *you* reading?"

Dorilian displayed the cover.

"Beekeeping?"

"Philosophy."

A slight tilt of the head accompanied another parting of Aubrey's lips. Pretty. However the way Aubrey reined in her expression, curious at first, to something more deliberate felt sharply personal. She eyed the stool on which Dorilian had propped his knee.

"How's your leg? It seems improved. Did you get treatment?"

"Yes."

His curt answer alone should have dissuaded any woman, but in Aubrey's case it did not. Dorilian opened the book and prepared to resume reading. Instead of moving toward the door, Aubrey remained standing in front of him, looking far from satisfied. Rescue came when a voice hailed from the hall.

"Thegna Aubrey!" A girl, round-eyed and with her hair tucked into a cap, peered around the door. "Your people are here. Come with wagons and all else. They need to be guided. We've no room for them, not here at the Hall."

Dorilian trained his gaze on Aubrey's look of frustration. Understandable. She had only just begun to question him. "I expect you'd best see to that."

Aubrey's gaze narrowed. "Enjoy your book," she said on the way out. At least she had the presence of mind to lock the door behind her.

Visitorless again, Dorilian rose and wedged a chair against the door before resuming his seat. He would need to take better precautions in the future. Aubrey had wasted enough of his time that he must shorten his hoped-for communication with Levyathan. For that he needed solitude and quiet.

Fortunately, thought had but one dimension. He settled into the chair, leaned back his head, and opened to the Mind.

Dor! Levyathan felt sharp and bright. *Where are you?*

To know where a thought originated differed from knowing to whom it belonged. *Amallar. I told you—*

You told me you found Handurin. You told me you would leave—

I will leave when I have finished here.

Levyathan's worry surmounted platitudes. *I felt you get hurt! You were taken captive. You cannot stay in a situation so dangerous.*

Though Dorilian had communicated with Levyathan that first night during the briefest of stops while Aubrey and Wodd had debated how best to cross at the Fords, he had done so only one time since, soon after reaching Rhodhur.

I will be sending you a cylinder.

Hesitation. Levyathan's thought curled into a new shape. *You need more papers?*

No, ricina. Dorilian named a spice, rare and difficult to obtain. More silence, this time quizzical, before he added, *And more money. The damn seasons are changing. I need to buy a coat.*

Levyathan's acceptance was palpable, though his questions remained. *Handurin will not buy you a coat?*

He has even less access to coin than I do—but his Khelds at least care about whether he freezes to death. Among its many other shortcomings, Amallar was cold. A small amount of heat still radiated from the banked fire in Robdan's hearth but did little to banish the chill.

I will send what the cylinder can hold.

Krugs. Khelds accepted Trongorian currency.

Yes.

My absence is still secret?

For now. I have said nothing and Deleus is yet secluded in Jharbala. Correspondence and emissaries continue to accumulate, though. You will need to return soon.

Return… or come up with a new story. *Handurin needs more time.*

It is not Handurin who is running out of time.

Send me the thrice-cursed ricina.

13

The lands around Sarkuan are native to beasts large as
wolves but stouter of leg and porcine of appearance, with
noses that more resemble arms than snouts. They have
fierce teeth and foul tempers like boars. *Corpse pigs* they are
called, *myrti*, because they detect the least trace of any scent
and excel at carcasses, both the making and the finding.
The Lahgai of the south have domesticated them as guard
beasts and have also trained them to find the rare and
precious spiceroot of the Sansordan and Lahgaelan deserts.

AEBNER GETHEDSON, *TO THE MOUNTAIN OF FIRE*

"I would like you to cook for me."

In Dorilian's experience, the best path to a desired
outcome was to corral the person who held the power to
make the decision. To that end, he had gotten up with the milkers,
a time when most of Rhodhur Hall was asleep but Gerd the
innkeeper was awake and already in the kitchen.

Built behind the entire rear wall of Rhodhur Hall, the inn's kitchen
boasted several rooms, all with massive hearths ablaze day and night
for different kinds of cooking. There were baking ovens and cooking
ovens and ovens for meat and ovens only for roots. Other hearths
housed grills and spits and grates for pots big enough to cook whole
pigs. At points where the kitchen opened onto the yards, beyond the
cooking rooms and nearest the water sluices and spouts, were other
rooms devoted to the handling of yet-uncooked food and the washing
of dishes. Dorilian considered the kitchens at Rhodhur to be one of
the wonders of the World—not because they were engineering
catastrophes certain to cause disaster one day, but because amazingly
delicious dishes somehow appeared from such utter chaos.

He had cornered Gerd beside one of the kitchen's long, heavy, wooden tables, where a battalion of scullions and cooks were busy chopping and preparing the morning's common meal. Pans clattered. Spoons tapped. Someone shouted about waiting on eggs.

Taller than most of his staff and burlier, Gerd drew a long breath and folded his arms across his still-clean apron. Dark hair curled above his ears. "The Lord Elector agreed only himself would receive special meals. All his men would eat with our lads."

"Yes. And I have been. However I have seen that you will, sometimes, cook for a few of those lads." Over the four days of his stay so far, Dorilian had noticed that Gerd would occasionally serve up a platter to one or another of the regular patrons of the noisy hall.

Gerd nodded, though he did not unfold his arms. "If a lady or lad brings in some game to share with the Hall—maybe gives a goat or other beast to the kitchen—or brings in a load of produce to share, then yes, I'll prepare something special just for them. The best cut of goat or perhaps an apple and persimmon tart from those provided. Fair enough for having given to the common good."

The "common good" popped up often enough that Dorilian marked it as a prime Kheld bargaining point. Although he could not, for the moment, come up with goats or wagonloads of fruit, he had anticipated this argument. "What about *this*?"

He pulled a lumpy yellow pouch from his jacket and handed it to Gerd. The innkeeper gave Dorilian a baffled look but took the pouch in hand and rolled it in his fingers, feeling the hard shapes within. Gerd made a small grunt of curiosity, then he teased the drawstring open and tipped the pouch to spill several plump teardrop corms into his cupped palm. After a moment spent in study, Gerd set the corms and pouch on the table. He picked up the smallest corm and, using a bone-handled knife pulled from a sheath at his waistband, cut a tiny sliver from the hard brown shell, then sniffed. He touched the sliver to his tongue and his eyes snapped wide.

"*Ricina*? How in—?"

"I come from a trading nation. Spices, especially small amounts, are easy to carry—and trade."

"And worth more than gold! I'm surprised you would carry them around in hope of finding someone with coin enough to purchase a corm." Gerd sheathed his knife and, shaking his head, carefully transferred the *ricina* corms back into the pouch, which he offered back. "I can't afford even one of these."

Dorilian refused to take them. Having the goods in hand made a purchase more difficult to resist. "I will give them to you, all seven, in exchange for the privilege of your good cooking. You know the flavor they impart?"

"Yes," Gerd admitted. His fingers curled around the pouch's yellow leather as he gave it a glance of pure longing. "Nutty, a hint of pepper and lemon in the shell. And inside, that creamy center when just barely slivered"—eyes closed and nostrils aquiver, Gerd clearly envisioned an opened corm, its core scooped onto his board to be thinly sliced to succulent perfection—"there's no other taste like it."

"None. It's a pity *ricina* is so hard to get. The plant is almost impossible to see; it grows in the desert, under rocks." And required long-nosed, vicious creatures to find it.

"So I've heard. I knew a vendor in Essera—"

"You cooked in Essera?" Dorilian did not think he had ever met this man there, and now he hoped he had not. "I suspected, because of the quality of your dishes. Not all cooks know of this spice."

"Oh, I do! For a few years during King Stefan's reign, I cooked for an Enlad, one of our own lads, who was elevated to an Archon. The Archon of Heddros. He was the King's Trade Minister, an important man. I was with him for a time in Dazunor-Rannuli and prepared menus for his fancy dinners. Kheld food he wanted, and that was what I served. The best in the land! I made it my mission to impress. But I learned from Staubaun cookery too, whatever I could. So many new things! The world is full of meats and greens—and spices!"

So, Gerd had cooked for Cullen Brodheson. Cullen had often championed the merits of Kheld cooking at Gustan the year Dorilian was there.

Dorilian made another appeal, one he hoped would convince. "When fresh, as these are, *ricina* is so potent you would not need much of it. There may even be enough you could add a little to some of the common meals too."

Gerd's resolve visibly melted as he imagined that scenario. "I could!"

Dorilian would thank Levyathan later for being generous with the *ricina* corms. It also couldn't hurt to sweeten his offer. "I would, of course, provide whatever else I can. Some small game or fowl perhaps?" He was good at hunting; it might even relieve his boredom to bring in an occasional duck.

"Yes," said Gerd. Visibly snapping back from visions of a Hall full of happy diners, he smiled broadly and bounced the yellow pouch in hand. "Any contribution at all is of great help. This is already too much, but"—he hurried to reassure about his intent—"I will accept. I've had but one, maybe two corms of *ricina* since I last cooked in Essera, and those were so small and shriveled that they had barely any taste left at all. For this gift I'll cook for you gladly. I only ask that you not make it too obvious. Sit next to Hans Thegn if you can. I understand the Elector is leaving?"

"Yes. War, unfortunately, looms for all countries now."

"A pity. War did Stefan no good. None at all. I saw as much firsthand. It made him haggard! But you are staying?"

"Yes, for now. The captain and I and twenty men."

"Good, good," said Gerd. "A prince should have a guard, if he's to make any impression at all."

Dorilian and Gerd stepped aside as two bobs staggered past carrying a pan heaped with peeled potatoes. The pan banged against the table and nearly dumped its contents. Time to let the general get back to his troops.

"If any should ask, shall I tell how I got on your good side?"

Gerd laughed. "I'd prefer you don't. I have a reputation!"

As did Dorilian—as a Trongorian of modest means. He would set to work on procuring that duck.

"The Wheel spoke clearly. War is coming. We must prepare." Mother Ewlys was in grim form for early morning. "Don't dismiss our portents as doom-mongering. Gifu is a Rappeleye; her Wheels always prophesize true."

Aubrey turned her body aside to avoid bumping the herb basket on Ewlys's arm. Sprays of tartleaf, wisdom, sweet thyme, and mint overflowed the basket's sides, and it was important that they not spill. Aubrey's own basket held loose bunches of lavender, dill, and marchroot—all of which, along with those in Ewlys's basket, Aubrey had helped to gather at first light. The Old Mothers' kitchen garden at the Barrowwood provided Rhodhur Hall with most of its culinary herbs and quite a few of Gerd's favorite vegetables, many of which were not tempting enough for local farmers to grow. In exchange, the innkeeper sent over animal bones and fat and organ meats in ample supply, along with surplus fruits and vegetables for pickling and drying, and collections of seeds. And Gerd paid top barter for eggs from Mother Lilbe's chicken house. Aubrey carried a sturdy wooden basket of those with her free hand.

Being enlisted by Ewlys was Aubrey's reward for rising early and venturing to the Motherhome in hope of cider and a nibble.

Even from across the yard, sounds of food preparation broke the gray silk quiet of morning. Pots clanged in the kitchen and voices called instruction. Gerd's army of cooks and scullions were hard at work. He would soon join them. His usual habit was to meet Ewlys on the long, rear west porch of the kitchen, but today Gerd wasn't there.

Aubrey followed Ewlys up mounted wooden steps onto the broad porch, where they chose a sheltered spot near the cistern pumps to wait. The kitchen would be hot and its activity frenetic. Better to wait outside where the air was cool and only a kitchen scullion or two might disturb them.

Ewlys's questioning eyes studied Aubrey through the gloom. Plans stirred behind her blue gaze. "I trust we can count on Amundhal's barns?"

Barns were needed for the storage of supplies, for medicine and bandages which the Old Mothers would send Aubrey's way. Woundmoss grew abundantly only in the peaty lands of the Bogs, which meant the next request would be for wagons to transport.

"My barns and storehouses are always in the Mother's service. We house supplies for our defenders in Neuberland—and have done so for years."

"None better," Ewlys approved. Her expression softened. "We wouldn't overburden you or your holders. It's just that the coming war will be to the east of here, and north. We would have the supplies be nearer. I've sent messages also to our sisters in Eastmeary."

This war Gifu had prophesied would begin in Dazunor. So far, however, Hans had gotten nothing more from the chieftains than a few lukewarm agreements to "consider" his proposals. Aubrey was more convinced that if there were to be war at all, it would begin in Neuberland, where there was conflict already. It was premature to talk of war here—or in Essera.

Where was Gerd? Aubrey walked to the open kitchen door, peered inside, and saw why Gerd hadn't met them outside. He wasn't alone.

As unexpected as it was to find Thron in a kitchen, what surprised Aubrey more was that he looked so... different—less guarded, not like before, so walled off that he showed only swords and shields. This man talking to Gerd possessed the same fearless assurance, yet there was more ease about him, a warmth in the unforced way his smile reached his eyes, a glimpse of something beneath the armor. Aubrey already had so many questions she didn't know where to start—and now she wanted to see more of the man standing in the kitchen.

What would Thron have to talk about with an innkeeper? And why was Gerd smiling as if at a new friend?

Thron chose that moment to leave, giving Aubrey the pleasure of watching the retreat of his tall, well-made body. Aubrey noted that Thron moved smoothly, no limp at all. An uncommonly quick healer, then. Not a man who would play up his injury for sympathy. He exited through the doors into the dining hall, no doubt to meet Hans and the Trongorian Elector, and maybe Robdan who often joined them, for the day's early meal. Gerd, turning to look toward the porch door, saw Aubrey and waved before hustling over.

"Itse! Bano!" Gerd called for helpers to take the herbs and eggs.

"Sharing gossip with Trongorians?" Aubrey happily handed over her baskets, especially the eggs, which were heavy. Ewlys joined them and another scullion took the trove of herbs.

"Thron? An interesting man." Gerd's round face beamed at their offerings. "What fine herbs! And the eggs! I need more every day, every hour! News that Hans Thegn has come has spread and our rooms are overflowing. I have lads sleeping on the tables at night! Too many boots and not enough blankets."

"Ha!" Ewlys snorted. "We have women overnighting in Lilbe's chicken house. Can you tell me why any woman would sleep in a chicken house, even one as clean and fine as Lilbe's?"

Gerd's stunned expression was answer enough.

"They need baths, every one of them," Aubrey confirmed. "We're letting them bathe in our pond."

"So that's where all the men go after breakfast." Gerd looked over his shoulder as shouts broke out in the kitchen. "Speaking of which, I have a Hall full of people to send on their way. Trongor's Elector is leaving this morning."

Leaving? Was *that* what Gerd had been talking about with Thron? About departing?

"Was Thron making his goodbye?" Aubrey shouldn't have cared. Not at all. Yet she did.

"Oh no," Gerd said as he walked back into his now-chaotic kitchen. "The Elector is taking only half his men back to Trongor; he's leaving the *other* half to serve as Hans Thegn's personal guard. Thron is staying on."

Whether that news was good or bad, Aubrey wasn't in a position to say, but she was... glad.

14

The Entities challenge our definitions of immortality and life. If any system that ensures its own continuation by adapting and evolving is alive, then the Entities live. The living cells that vivified them persist throughout their structure. The real issue is consciousness. We do not know for certain the degree to which Entities are aware of and respond to their environment. How do they perceive the World? What do they feel?

EPIRADES, *PROGENITORS OF THE ESSERAN KINGDOM*

Sunlight set afire the russet leaves atop the hill yet barely warmed the morning air. Hans loitered around the tumbled remains of a long-abandoned homestead; with the toe of his boot he prodded stones scattered from vanished walls. Once home to a prosperous compound a short walk from the steep north wall of Rhodhur, the land had been given over to orchards. To every side apple trees marched in ranks of denuded, twisting trunks, their harvest spent. *The land pulls its life back underground,* Hans recognized. *But I cannot. I have to do something. Now that Herberth is gone.*

Though Herberth had toyed with the thought of staying longer, Hans and Dorilian both had agreed his extended presence might arouse too much attention. Because Dorilian had chosen to stay in Amallar rather than accompany him, Herberth had left behind half of the Trongorians, commanded by Farrl, both as a representative force in support of Hans and, if needed for such, the Hierarch of Sordan.

Dorilian sat nearby on a portion of half-fallen wall, the ruins of a former storeroom. Densely woven Kheld wool clothed his body and limbs, though sunlight rendered his looks foreign by teasing out the gold strands of his hair. They'd come here seeking a place away from roads and habitations, out of sight of Rhodhur's walls. A place to talk.

They needed to work through their impasse. Get into the open whatever was holding them back. Except it wasn't quite that simple. Dorilian knew Hans wanted to talk. But Dorilian wanted to talk about Nammuor and Essera and Hans wanted to talk about the Rill.

If Hans was sure of anything, it was that Dorilian was going to balk. Something about the Rill—maybe everything about it—was too close. Too secret. Too tied up with things Hans didn't yet fully grasp.

Hans steeled himself. "I can get you the alliance with Amallar."

But Dorilian had seen for himself the vehemence of Kheldish opposition to such a move. "I'm not convinced of that."

"I am. And you're going to help me do it. That is, if you still desire an alliance with Amallar."

Dorilian shrugged. "I don't desire alliance with Amallar, only with you. Indeed, an alliance between our nations might be difficult to maintain. Alliances imply reciprocity. A simple agreement to tolerate my armies in Essera will suffice."

"You won't get that. And you need more than a door that can be closed as soon as it's opened. What if the Khelds did allow you to take an army through Amallar into Essera, and then Nammuor approached them with a more palatable proposal? You know there are factions here that would like nothing better than to see you destroyed. You can't afford that risk. And neither can I." The thought of the man who had killed Marc Frederick and Stefan offering to seat Hans on Essera's throne chilled him to the very bone. Especially because he knew the Khelds, particularly the Stefanites who dominated the cruihcila, would find such an offer more acceptable than the prospect of Sordan's army in Essera. He perched on the wall near Dorilian. "If these clan chieftains try to join with Nammuor, I would jump this ship and leave them with an empty throne. They would cease to interest him then."

"Perhaps, for a time, until they become an obstacle to his plans."

"Which they would, eventually. That's why I need to do this right. Not halfway. I've studied history; I know that nations with cracked foundations crumble. It's full alliance, Sordan and Amallar, or nothing's to be gained from it."

"Perhaps so," Dorilian agreed grudgingly. "How like Amallar to present so intractable a problem." He rose to his feet. The wall was too cold and hard for long sitting.

"You knew this before you came here."

"True. Which is why it pleases me to hear you voice a similar opinion. It will make our eventual agreement that much easier to come by."

"So you still think we can agree?"

"As you have astutely pointed out, it is necessary that we do so."

Did Hans hear a trace of mockery there? A warning that no compromise could be pushed too far? That he would be expected to yield, having the most to gain and the most to lose? Even if they failed to reach an agreement, Dorilian would be free to return to Sordan, to sit out the storm, his position little changed from what it had been until Hans had suddenly appeared to give him another option. Free to negotiate with Nammuor from his own position of strength—although, knowing Dorilian, Hans didn't think that would ever happen.

And what if Dorilian was *not* free to leave Amallar? Hans might be able to force him to stay, but could he force him to compromise? And at what cost? Marenthro's assessment of what it would mean to have Dorilian as an enemy stopped such thoughts cold. *If so, he will be a terrible one.* And on the heels of that, Hans glimpsed something he had not seen earlier.

I cannot defeat him. If I do that, Nammuor wins by default.

That was the lesson Stefan had never learned.

"Amallar shows a few cracks in its leadership." Hans cut to the meat of what they needed to discuss. "It may be possible for me to assume that leadership, but any move I make will have to be decisive. Nalf Rhys doesn't appeal to everyone. Reasonable people like Robdan exist and have earned some ears. There are also the Old Mothers. They harken to the old religion, and women remain a force in this land."

"A rational force, I hope."

"I think so. They preserve the old ways." What that might mean for him, for either of them, Hans could not yet unravel. He learned new things every day. This World was a mosaic of which he, so far, had set only a few pieces into place. "There are so many moving parts. Times are hard and the people and their leaders crave more, much more, than the current situation can give them. They don't like the future they see and they want something better. Something they hope I can give them. Especially in Neuberland. I've been talking with Aubrey and a few others, and the sense I get is that frustrations there run deepest of all. If it wasn't for the fact that both the Amallar and Neuberland Khelds share a bond of long-suffering persecution, they'd have little else in common. As it is, they disagree on almost everything except that, as Khelds, they must stick together. They see themselves as surrounded by enemies, which is as good a glue as I've ever seen for holding people together. But Sordan is even more hated in Neuberland than in Amallar. It's a sticky problem."

"And do you think Khelds are less hated by those I must persuade to this confederation?" Dorilian grimaced. "You were in Sordan; you saw firsthand. As soon weld diamonds! The grievances are many and deep. My grandfather's murder, for one. And it was not even twenty years ago that the Princes of Leseos and Gignastha, both Highborn and, I might add, near kin of mine, were killed by Khelds. Those were heinous—and sacrilegious—acts. Gignastha's Princes were impaled alive. My grandfather was decapitated. So were the last Malyrdeons—on your brother's orders! Such brutality leaves an indelible mark, and my people have long memories. So do Essera's."

Hans winced, glimpsing more of a history that appalled him. "What about *your* memory?"

"I've been known to conveniently forget things."

"'Land where Highborn blood is spilled is Highborn land thereafter.'" The phrase leapt to Hans's lips before he'd fully thought to say it.

Dorilian looked at him sharply. "Where did you hear that?"

"Endelarin told me."

"The dim-witted knave. I'm surprised he recalls that old saying. Yet it is true, though interpretations vary. Take Gignastha. I could declare that 'Highborn land thereafter' to be as little as a spot of ground or as large as all Neuberland. Historically, it's possible to justify either position. Moreover, there are legal considerations. Sordan possesses hereditary suzerainty over Gignastha since the death of its Prince."

Hans remembered that part from his lessons. "Which makes you its ruler," he pointed out.

"Not in name. Although the domain is mine to bestow." Dorilian wryly acknowledged Hans's look of query. "It so happens I hold the only legal claim and, as the law is currently constituted, any change in Gignastha's status would require Sordaneon approval. We never gave it. I've not claimed the domain for myself because I want neither the land nor the grief that comes with it. Besides, Gignastha requires a lord in attendance. It is being administered through a regional magistrate. My man, currently. I recaptured the domain several years ago—a military move after Stefan... tried to kill me."

Another wince-worthy bit of history. "And before that?"

"Your grandfather included Gignastha with Neuberland and appointed a governor. Stefan appointed his own for a few years until I took over."

Hans smelled fresh opportunity. "Name me Bas of Gignastha," he said, obeying impulse.

But apparently Dorilian had anticipated him. "Don't be absurd. You're already Prince of Dazunor and heir presumptive to Tahlwent—not to mention Essera's Kingship. Besides which, you would not have the time to rule it. I said it needed a lord in attendance, not absentia. In addition," Dorilian added, with a look of warning, "you either never learned or have forgotten the full tale of that domain. Gignastha's Prince was slain, and his daughter raped, to install a Kheld as Lord in Neuberland."

"What?" Hans had encountered mostly vague angry silences in Sordan whenever Neuberland was mentioned, murmurs of deaths and atrocities, but never anything concrete. Even his tutors had skated around the origins of the Gignastha problem.

"A Kheld rebel named Howyce mounted the assault. He had help from within. He and his men took hostage the wedding guests and slew Emrys Gignastheon, then laid hold of the Prince of Leseos and his Heir, who was to have been the bridegroom. The Khelds impaled and tortured them. They lived three days, blinded and in agony, until some Kheld found the mercy to kill them. During that time, Howyce forcibly wed Veraisa and declared himself Lord of Gignastha."

"My history tutors weren't very good, then, because none of these names are familiar to me," Hans said. "When did this happen?"

"In the reign of your grandfather, before you were born. I was but eleven at the time, though I felt something of their torment and deaths. I learned the details later."

"So there have been atrocities on both sides." Hans saw no way to make any of it right.

"I haven't told you but half of it." With a look of disgust, Dorilian kicked at an apple some animal had gnawed and sent it rolling into nearby grass. "Howyce's Lordship didn't last but a fortnight. When his Staubaun peers didn't recognize him as quickly as he demanded, Howyce began killing hostages. A faction in his coalition opposed that move and Howyce was slain in the fighting. Somehow, Veraisa escaped and made her way to Leseos and the protection of her cousin, Ral, who had assumed leadership of the domain. She died later attempting to abort the child Howyce had forced her to conceive. Ral decided not to wait for a diplomatic resolution of the matter and set out with an army to besiege Gignastha and its new Lord, also a Kheld." Dorilian's frown was warning enough that the name would mean something to Hans. "Erwan Cedrecson, consort of the Royal Princess Emyli."

Stunned, Hans sagged beneath the weight of that revelation. "My *father*?"

"And your mother. She was one of the rebels. Your grandfather's family life was not always a tranquil one." Dorilian scowled. "I'm surprised your tutors didn't tell you this."

Hans tried to take it in, what it meant. The Kheld Wars in Neuberland were at the center of his family's claim to Amallar's loyalties—and also at the heart of the Staubaun hatred of the Khelds. No wonder people in Essera and Sordan could not separate their feelings about Neuberland from the fact of Stauberg-Randolph rule. Particularly Stefan's, and now Hans's. Their father had attempted to be named ruler of a domain taken by the murder of Highborn blood. His family was forever linked with that dark episode.

"But this explains so much!" Hans kept his voice low. Though they had not yet been disturbed or seen anyone else venture into the orchard, there remained a possibility. "Surely my grandfather never—"

"No. He was not behind it and he never did legitimize the Kheld presence in Gignastha. He vetoed and declared *nollo revivere* Erwan's petition to the Archhalia. He did, however, try to lift the siege being mounted by Lord Ral. Ral would have none of it."

Hans met that assessment grimly. The pieces were beginning to fit together—including why his tutors had avoided this matter. "And so the war in Neuberland began. The Sordaneons helped Ral, then."

Dorilian nodded. "My uncle Delos, my father's brother, destroyed the Vermillion Aqueduct—which released the water-powered locks on Gignastha's mighty gate and enabled Ral to enter the city. What else could we do? The Prince of Gignastha was Sordaneon, a few cousins removed. It did not matter to us if the Khelds hated us for that act. What difference there? Already they were killing us." His voice was as dead as the verdict.

"Nammuor had nothing to do with it?"

"That? No." Dorilian shook his head. "Not every evil in the World is Nammuor's doing. If only it were that simple." He sighed and looked out over the dying orchard. "How time changes things."

"I guess naming me Bas of Gignastha would be a bad idea." Hans managed a bitter half smile.

"A terrible idea. Even I could not make that work." But Dorilian returned a weak grin, a golden thread of understanding touching his expression.

Hans held his breath. The empathy that pierced his open emotions felt like sunlight, warm, filled with promise. Like a breeze on a day without wind, it stunned him simply by being. Then as abruptly as though a door had slammed, Dorilian drew a breath and looked away and the feeling died. The sun paled briefly beneath a sudden veil of clouds and the old orchard shivered with a chill wind.

Dorilian rose to walk away and Hans stood to follow.

"You don't need Gignastha to impress your Khelds. If you're so eager to be landed, look to Dazunor, which is yours by right," Dorilian said. "You are rightfully heir to Tahlwent as well. Had Stefan been more astute, he would have bestowed that title on his own brother, not on so worthless an ally as Erenor. Unfortunately, he knew only how to purchase people, and he did it mightily. I am not so inclined. What is vital to my interests, I keep near to hand. And Gignastha is not to be cast upon the bargaining table as an offering to soothe your barbarians."

"You'll have to give something."

"I will talk about a just solution. That is more than I have given any man."

"Talk is not enough!" Hans ducked beneath the branch of the apple tree beside them and swung about to face Dorilian. For the first time, he thought, they were getting to know each other. "The Khelds aren't going to believe that you want to bargain in good faith just because I say so. They'll toss me out of the Witan if I come to them with no more than that!"

Dorilian eyed him icily. "If you wanted more than that, you should have stayed in Sordan."

"But I didn't. And you know what? I'm glad I didn't. Because now I know where I stand with *my* people, not yours. I don't cling to any nice little dreams that Amallar or the Khelds are going to blindly follow me wherever I lead them. I know that I have to bring them more than what they've already got."

Dorilian leaned his weight upon the bole of the tree. It was a posture so natural to him that Hans could almost take seriously his pretense of contemplation. "And what do these Khelds not have that you would give them?"

"The Rill."

Dorilian fixed Hans with a piercing stare as brutal as an open assault. Hans reeled as something physical trapped his breath in his throat and squeezed, tightly, around his heart. Just as abruptly, the sensation let go. He staggered back a step as Dorilian lashed out at him, the word slashing across the silence in the same moment that it left Hans's mind.

"*No!*"

"Let me explain."

"Explain what? Your *lunacy*? Because that alone would explain why you might think I would concede the Rill to you at all—in any form, for any reason!"

"And you are overreacting! Just once, get your emotions out of it and hear what I have to say!" Tentatively, Hans took a step nearer, emphasizing not only his explanation but the sincerity of his belief. "You have everything to gain."

But Dorilian shook his head. "I do not command the Rill for gain."

"The hell you don't!" The admiration in Hans's voice was genuine. "You stopped it for gain. To gain time. To gain breathing space. To gain confusion among your enemies and an upper hand with the Epoptes. Well, now you can gain something even more valuable! The Rill can catapult *you* and your armies into Essera, and you can damn well name your own price for doing it. Short of the throne and their lands, Amallar might concede almost anything to the man they thought could give them the Rill."

"Would they grant me your head after?" Dorilian's words clipped tightly, a hopeful signal as he exerted control upon his temper.

But Hans detected that Dorilian's anger had been too quick and hot to burn long and was already cooling. They were on familiar ground now: their talk concerned the one subject every petitioner wanted, every friend and every enemy.

"It only makes sense," Hans hastened to explain. "Look around you. Amallar is huge, populated, potentially rich. All it needs is access. And there are Rill structures at Bellan Toregh. That means that the Rill can be made to stop there."

"That just shows how little you know. Mere corporeal structures mean *nothing*. Most are no more than vacant sentinels. For the Rill to stop or go, the corpus must be living, associated with an active node, and operational structures—pairings."

"Pairings?" The only image Hans had was a vision of Sordan's terminal, honey-combed and vast.

"Acceleration and deceleration rings. Twelve coming, twelve going. A sanctuary building, elevators, and a platform. Especially the rings and platform."

"Does Bellan Toregh have them?"

"Trestethion?" Dorilian gave the node its Aryati name. "How should I know?"

Hans stared at him. "You've ridden the Rill. You must have passed them."

With a grimace that barely overlaid his impatience, Dorilian explained, "And you've *never* ridden the Rill. But perhaps that wonderful Mentan education of yours can help you understand what happens to perception of light at very high rates of speed. Light... curves. Shapes blur, become color, and then not even that. A straight run from Sordan to Permephedon at full speed with no stops takes about as long as it has just taken me to talk about it."

"Full speed—"

"Is not reached when stops are made. But internode speeds are impressive. I have never even seen Trestethion."

"But if Bellan Toregh... Trestethion has these pairings—these... rings—could you activate the node?"

"Perhaps." Dorilian bent over to pick up an apple from the ground beside his foot, but it was small and soft, so he tossed it with careless aim at an old cistern. The thing splatted against stone. "But the Aryati will regain their thrones before I would attempt it."

Something had died in the orchard and even the birds fell silent. Hans refused to accept that he had failed. As long as Dorilian kept talking to him, Hans preferred to think there was still a chance.

"Who are you protecting? You opened the Rill into Teremar, didn't you?"

"Did I? Most people will tell you my grandfather did it."

"A dead man didn't stop the Rill three weeks ago. *You* did. Just like you did whatever happened in Teremar." Hans knew that he was right when Dorilian looked away.

"Hestya—was different."

"How was it different? It was a hostile act; everyone knows it. Essera never got over it. Quirin will never put it behind him. It was an act of rebellion, to pay back the Seven Houses. Tharos told me all about it. Oh, come on, Dorilian, don't get lily-white on me. I know you're not. Whose interests are you serving now? Not your own."

Dorilian glared a dark warning. "I liked you better in Sordan. Then, at least, you did not pretend to understand me."

"In Sordan you kept saying you *wanted* me to understand you. I tried, I'm still trying—and I'm a fool too by the looks of it. I honestly thought you'd be willing to compromise."

"We had not yet touched on any point that required compromise." A deep and unrelenting bitterness, memory of things gained and then lost, passed briefly across Dorilian's conflicted features. "You take the sacred and make it profane," he said at last, anger grinding an edge to his words. "How dare you speak to me of the Rill? You who know nothing of what it is—or what I am to it—you, with your child's understanding! What has Marenthro taught you—only words?"

"We never talked about the Rill."

He watched the way Dorilian's disbelief mingled with amazement by the extent of Hans's ignorance, then turned to frustration with having to correct it. "So I am to be your tutor in this as well? Your wizard chooses his tools by design—he goes to the source. Then know this, Handurin—what you ask is not simply a matter of dynamics, although dynamics alone may make the proposition impossible. The Rill is not just a machine upon which men have bestowed a kind of godhood. It is an Entity men have bound with the chains of their own ignorance. They've forgotten. In Sordan you heard that upon a time the Rill *was* a man."

"Derlon Sordaneon, one of the Three."

"You trotted that out quickly enough, but do you know what that *means*?"

"I know you claim kinship."

Dorilian smiled thinly. "You look at the thing but see only the skin. Look beneath it. Look at the blood, the history." He drew a breath. "Derlon owned a body at one time, an immortal, partly human one, before he transformed. And by that body he sired children. Sons. *My* ancestors. I don't *claim* kinship, Handurin, any more than I claim to be who I am. It does not matter how many people believe it or deny it—I *am* the same blood as that thing! The Rill *is* Sordaneon, something even Essera could not strip from us. My bloodline alone can ever commune with the Rill and inform its being. Quirin and his Epoptes will live and die and never touch the essence of their god. But I *do*. I am its guardian more than they ever will be. I am its future—if it is to ever have one. So now, knowing that, think about what you are asking of me. Am I to take my Entity-ancestor, a gift of Amynas and Leur—a living being, an Immortal and a god—and give it over to your Khelds as though it were a horse they now might ride?"

"No. Bring the Rill to them as what it is: a sacred trust and promise, an ally—a kinsman and a god, if you must—on whom you depend and whose abilities serve you well. I don't pretend to really understand your kinship with the Rill. I hope that someday I will. I know it's real and I don't think I dishonor either it *or* you to suggest that the Rill nonetheless presents us with an opportunity."

"You are dreaming. The repercussions of what you propose would negate the benefits to be reaped."

Steeling himself, Hans seized the opening. "Then you admit there might be benefits?"

"For your Khelds, certainly. And for you, oh yes. But I would be put in an impossible position. Nammuor, Essera, the Seven Houses to be sure—and Sordan as well—would fly into a rage. They would all as soon see me dead! I would be cutting my own throat."

"You can handle Sordan." Hans had never been more confident about saying anything in his life. "They're your people; you're their heart and their hope. Their living god. You own their minds as well as their hearts and you know it. They'll be stunned only as long as it takes for you to do something brilliant, and then they'll shout your praises so high that there can be no opposition. And what do you care about what Essera says, anyway? It won't be anything they haven't been saying for years." Dorilian looked away, and Hans knew that he had struck a nerve. "But what if the Rill could bring you a treaty with Amallar that gives you peace in Neuberland and a clear road to defeat Nammuor in Essera? Why let old hatreds hold you back from that?"

Dorilian turned on Hans, a feral gleam in his eye. "Oh, no, Handurin. Were I to put myself in such a position, it would be more than peace in Neuberland on the table. Far more. I would demand that the bond be equal to the risk! Your Khelds would pay a price no less exacting of their commitment!"

I've reached him! Hans struggled to keep a firm grip on his elation. *He's talking about it. Hypothetically—but he's talking about it. He can't resist the intellectual exercise of thinking through the possibilities.*

"What would it take?" Hans tried not to tip his hand by sounding eager.

But Dorilian let him wait, holding him at bay with a gaze like a steel-tipped arrow, glinting and dangerously close to being loosed. One false step was all it would take. Clearly Dorilian had sensed the tentacles of hope that reached out to him and had rearmed his defenses against further intrusions. Or perhaps he had realized that, indeed, there was something to be gained here—and behind that unreadable expression, he was retrenching his thoughts but not yet ready to admit it. Whatever the case, this time, for the first time, he had not outright refused.

"Think about it." In the face of indecision, Hans took the offensive. "You don't have to decide to do it, just say you'll consider it, and I can get Amallar to the table. They wouldn't sit down with you for anything less. And you don't have the time to waste trying to persuade Khelds otherwise. As a nation, they're too strong, and they're growing stronger, and when they eventually break out of Amallar, Essera is going to fall like a rotting giant. By withholding the Rill, you're not saving Essera. Nothing can save Essera. It can be Nammuor or it can be Amallar—or it can be me. You know which option serves you better. You can still influence where this goes."

In the warm sun that drenched the orchard, they breathed air heavy with an odor of apples decaying among fallen leaves, of summer's passage and the structure of the orchard crumbling back into the stuff of Creation. Essera, sifting down into essential elements, struggled toward a new order and would never again be as it was. The fruits of its glory had been consumed or lay spoiling in full ferment among the ruins of what had been. And Dorilian

Sordaneon refused to see it. He still saw Essera in terms of the Highborn Triempery of old, damaged but viable.

And yet....

He knows. He may not want to see it now, but he's been watching it die ever since he was born—and somewhere in that many-layered mind of his, he knows it's true. That ability to see beneath things is what allows Dorilian to change, to shift among alternatives, to move where others get trapped. It's his strength, and he doesn't even know it.

Now if only I can get him to fight as hard to change Essera as he is fighting to preserve it.

"Please, stop fighting me, Dorilian. We're on the same side."

Please, stop fighting me.

Hearing Handurin say those words awakened more than memory. Dorilian heard Marc again. *Felt* him. Not Marc's voice—Handurin's was too young and light for that—but Marc's sincerity and optimism and his thrice-cursed *hope* that the World could change. That it *would*, if only the pieces fell right and fulfilled the damned paradigm the Wall had placed on the World.

"We're on the same side," Handurin insisted. "We're fighting and we don't have to."

Dorilian closed his eyes. Stilled his mind. He could refuse to look at Handurin, refuse to hear him—but he could not block out the feelings. Those penetrated his every defense.

"Stop." Maybe by speaking, Dorilian could force a moment of peace.

Handurin immediately brought that hope to naught. "Why? Because what I'm saying is true?"

"True?" The word came out as a laugh. "What is true? Are you? Am I?"

"I believe I am. And I'm pretty damn sure you are."

"Are you?" Now that they were in this conversation, Dorilian recognized its inevitability. "Do you really think you know the truth of what I am? You don't grasp the truth of this miserable World at all, or of anything in it! These things we are talking about carry no meaning for you!" He laughed harshly, then shook his head. "You say you are a historian. So be one. Think about what you are asking. Think about what it would *do*."

"I know what it would do."

Sincerity again. It was time to cut into that meat. "You know what your Khelds would do. I'm not talking about Khelds. I'm not talking about Amallar. I am talking about Sordan and Essera and what our nations have been to each other." Dorilian sighed. "Three things have set the Triempery above all others: its Wall Lords, its *mythos*, and the Rill. It was not so long ago that *every* Staubaun land was Highborn-ruled. The Staubaun people were chosen by their gods, by the Three—the Sons of Amynas and Leur—to be their mortal form. The Wall Lords ruled from Mormantalorus and Essera to shape a society that would sustain the godborn, the Children of the Three. The Rill Lords in Sordan assured their might and prosperity. Ask yourself why.

"On the eve of the murders at Permephedon, more than fifty men of Highborn blood manifested in the Mind of Leur. Today, we stand on the verge of extinction and Essera is much diminished. Mormantalorus and Sordan are estranged from Essera and each other, and Essera is torn between a usurper's ambitions and the glories of their Highborn past. Its people are divided, their *mythos* of divine favor is shattered, and their Wall is silent. Staubaun society teeters blindly on the edge. But they still have the Rill."

Dorilian paused to let his words sink in, hoping to strike iron. He yearned for Handurin to hear the ringing of drawn swords. "What do you think they will *do* if I, Derlon's Heir and the Triempery's last remaining Highborn ruler, take the Rill from them—and give it to someone else? Will they stand quietly aside while I threaten to rescind all that my forbearers ever bestowed upon them? They will not embrace Khelds into their circle because of it, if that is what you are thinking. The threat, in their eyes, will be greater than ever."

"And maybe it should be." Though Handurin looked troubled, his jaw was tense. Stubborn. "Maybe it is time for something like this. Maybe it will make them finally move!"

"Move aside? Vacate the thrones of power? I don't think so, Handurin. Your brother tried that and look where it got him and his Khelds. Where it got *us!* Power is not something men yield. It must be wrested from them."

"You can do it, if anyone can—the yielding... or the wresting."

"I can also choose not to. In this matter, at least, I will have my way."

Handurin threw his hands wide, as if to embrace the old orchard and the World. "And that kind of thinking is a death grip. Can't you see that? It's a stranglehold. The Triempery isn't growing. It stopped growing generations ago and it's been tearing itself apart ever since!"

"It existed in strength for two thousand years."

"Two thousand years—and two hundred years too many. The Rill is the heart of the Triempery, yes, but it cannot revive a corpse!" Handurin looked around as if seeking something to force his point across. All he had at hand was the blue sky, a tangle of stone walls, and a few lengths of fallen wood. "All that history you hammered at me to learn? I learned it. I read the books and I requested source material. I know how the Triempery was born—and I know how it died. Endurin Malyrdeon, my great-something grandfather, the Wall Lord, was the Highborn Triempery's last flower, and then after he died it went to seed. That empire fathered a lot of petty states and a few great ones before it died. What will replace it is already growing. It's been growing for years in Sordan, which is less Staubaun today than it ever was. You see that, I know you do. *I* see it! And it's growing here in Amallar. And in Mormantalorus, where Nammuor is creating a society that feeds on desperation and fear. What are we feeding ours?"

"If you would get off your philosophical horse and down to real earth you might see that we could feed it stability!" Dorilian wielded the cold, razor edge of his temper, no longer caring if his emotions rose to the surface. "And what stability would follow were I to betray Essera, sell its primacy to a handful of Khelds, however much I gained by giving away the sacred trust that they and the Staubaun Triempery for centuries placed in the safekeeping of my ancestors? All they hold sacred and true would be torn from them. At the very moment they'd need leadership, they'd have none. They wouldn't follow me then—not if I were Amynas himself would they follow me! Not when Nammuor dangles promises of a new Staubaun empire anchored and shaped by his unholy power. And they sure as Mulsor's curse would not follow you!"

"I saw Mulsor," Handurin said.

Leur. When? Had it happened on the journey to Trongor by way of the Kolpos? Handurin could have seen the phantom City—destroyed and forever being destroyed—during a Rift storm. Seen it and survived. As the heat of their argument dissipated, Dorilian could almost feel hidden Wall machinations locking into place.

"That doesn't surprise you?" Handurin also appeared to have sensed the shift in direction.

"No. It should. But it doesn't. I, too, have seen Mulsor."

Dorilian had never told anyone. Only a few people knew—because they had been there that day.

"You know what that means, don't you?" Fearless of his own ignorance, Handurin dared to interpret Mulsor's meaning. "I read that book from Cibulitus, the one you lent me. You were right. It taught me a lot—and it all fits. The First Creation. The Second. We can neither completely be rid of the past nor escape it. The past gave birth to the present and the present will give birth to the future."

And with a voice more dead than living, Dorilian said, "The Past is but the Future that became, the Future but the Past that will be. And the Present is the child of hateful parents."

"What's that? Cibulitan philosophy?"

"Older still. The Leur said it, I think. I don't remember. But the Present is indeed the ground upon which great forces do battle. And we are the essential matter of that conflict. That's what mortality is. Leur's great invention. Change. We are doomed to change, to grow, to become something new. Do you know what the Leur said to the Deus Aryati just before he was killed himself?" Dorilian could almost feel the sun of distant Askorras on his skin and hair, recalling his childhood, when he had sat upon the steps with Legon to learn this lesson. "He said, 'Did you think it would last forever?'"

"Nothing does."

"There, that is Truth. If nothing ever changed, we would not be here."

"Even the Rill won't last forever," Handurin noted. "Not in its present form—which isn't its original form, because even its original purpose was destroyed by the Devastation. Entity or machine, the Rill is worshipped today because of how well it serves the society it created: it carries people or things from one place to another over great distances, at speeds people can barely comprehend."

"The Rill is more than that."

Handurin did not yet see the Rill for what it was—but Dorilian could also see that Handurin was trying. Trying so hard. Marc Frederick at least had understood what he was asking. Had understood how *much*.

"Then teach me," Handurin pleaded. There was that sincerity again, sawing at Dorilian's will. "All I know right now is that the ability for which men worship the Rill creates nations, and it creates powerful dependencies—and bonds. The people who founded the

Triempery knew that: they were able to settle vast expanses of territory using the Rill, and they used it to foster social and economic bonds across an entire continent and among diverse regions. That was Derlon's gift to them. The Rill *built* the Triempery, and it held it together when nothing else could. It's still doing that. The Rill *was* the Triempery, you know that. Well, I think it can generate another. A new society. What it can't do, on its own, is decide who plays a part. That's your role—the Sordaneon role—and you must see, you *need* to see, that Amallar can no longer be denied. Amallar is becoming *something*, maybe something powerful, and it's still for *us* to say what. We can forge an alliance of equals—that is all I ask."

"Equals." That the Rill might include and serve Amallar should have sounded impossible. It had sounded impossible the day Marc Frederick had first proposed this very thing. But now—

It does not. Because I have considered it before.

There was another reason also; there were several. The World had changed in ways Dorilian had only begun to grasp. It was more than just that Essera teetered on the verge of collapse. So did Trongor. So did Leseos if recent rumors had weight. If the Khelds rejected Handurin, threw their lot to Nammuor instead... the Rill might not matter at all in terms of logistics—or even politics. Dorilian's only recourse then would be to attempt *integration*. Risk losing everything.

"Don't you see?" Handurin continued to press his argument. "It's what *equal* really means. Equal access to the Rill. Equal access to the means of power. You wouldn't be taking the Rill away from anyone. You would be *giving* another people an opportunity they never had before. Set them on equal footing with the Staubauns in Essera, and they'll agree to let you move your armies. And they won't be any more dangerous because of it. They can't use the Rill as a weapon, even if they wanted to. Only you seem to be able to do that. And think of how useful Bellan Toregh could be against Nammuor. Leseos is bogged down with entrenched interests—the Seven Houses, right? and Esseran lords too—and you know you can't rely on Dazunor-Rannuli. Neither of us can. Just let the Khelds do as well as they are able. Whether they succeed or they fail will be up to them. No special privileges—the Epoptes will be needed to run operations, of course—"

"In case you haven't noticed, they are part of the problem."

"We can figure it out." Handurin used the pause to frame a new question. "Is there any reason, really, why Khelds can't use the Rill—or is that restriction just politics, rules made and enforced by men?"

Dorilian blew out a breath. "Both nature and politics. What Derlon abhors, the Rill will not abide. There is a breed in Essera that is proscribed from ever touching Rill corpus because doing so brings death to them. But Derlon never met a Kheld and has no knowledge of their kind. The decision was made by Dares I Sordaneon and the Epoptean Brotherhood to forbid Khelds based on... uncertainty."

"So you don't know."

"Of course I know. And so do you." It was amusing, in a way, to see the dawning realization on Handurin's face.

"My grandfather used it. So did Stefan."

Dorilian nodded. "So did Cullen Brodheson."

"This isn't the first time you've considered opening Bellan Toregh, is it?"

"I am not considering—"

"Rill access was part of the treaty that was to have been signed at Permephedon, wasn't it?" Handurin pressed nearer, circled Dorilian, boots pressing on fallen leaves and rotting fruit. "Marc Frederick wanted you to do it."

How could Handurin know that? Unless Marenthro had told him. Yet another betrayal by the thrice-cursed wizard.

"One of the treaty's provisions would have granted Khelds Rill privileges. Highborn Council approval would have overridden the Archhalia and Epoptean Brotherhood edicts." Dorilian forced the words between teeth and tongue. "We didn't know if it could be done. He wanted to try."

"So why won't you try now?"

"Don't press me." He did not want to explain this.

"What changed? You were going to attempt it once."

"Yes, once! Because I was young and a fool, and I did not know then what the Rill could *do* to me!"

Handurin stared at him. "*Do* to you?"

"Don't be dense! I'm bound to it! Contact with the Rill, even just being near it, causes me physical consequences. Pain, if I am lucky. Disintegration, if I am careless."

At long last Dorilian's words delivered enough pain—enough

reason—to stop the incessant questions. Slowly, never ceasing his stricken stare, Handurin sank to the ground and braced against the tree. "I'm sorry. I—"

"It wasn't that way at first, or even then." Dorilian sought to explain. Handurin's regret and distress only added to the confusion. "It happened after... after Permephedon, after everything. The Rill, when I tried to use it... it tore me apart. I demanded to return to Sordan. Just me, no *charys*. Naked. Exposed. I was half-mad to try it. I'm not completely certain how I survived but I... I can't trust it. I've trained myself in concealment from the thing. I can travel if I shield my presence using... certain techniques. But I haven't allowed living Rill corpus—or an active Rill field—to touch me skin to skin, or I it, since."

"Does that mean you can't—?"

"It means I don't know. I haven't run around trying to awaken new Rill nodes."

At least Handurin understood why he did not want to attempt it now. Visibly chastened, the boy looked up from his seat on the ground.

"This will work," Handurin persisted. "It may be the only thing that can work. I need to give the Khelds a reason to follow me—a better reason than that Stefan was my brother—and they'll fight to preserve what it means to them. Nammuor can court and dance until the floor falls through and they will not follow him if I can give them something they want *more* than a King in Essera."

More than a King—but also more than Dorilian wanted to give.

"I won't ask again, but will you think about what I've said?" Handurin sounded chastened. Subdued.

Which was a good thing, because Dorilian had reached the end of argument. "So be it," he agreed. "I will think about it, Handurin. That is all I will promise you."

Though Kheld men are boastful, fierce, and cunning, they worship a female deity alongside their male one and bestow great power upon their women. Kheld females alone own or inherit land, according to status and clan. Each child is accorded the clan and status of its mother. Women sit in judgment for all crimes or transgressions. Kheld women choose their own bedmates and decide whether to wed them. No man commands their property or decisions.

ELDHAN MALYRDEON, LETTER TO KING ERYDON

Aubrey bounced the burlap purse of coins in her hand and narrowed her eyes at the reddish bull in the pen. The animal was strong and in its prime, a proven sire of many milk-heavy daughters. To find a bull this fine for sale in Rhodhur before winter was surely a sign of the Mother's grace. Aubrey had examined the bull for stamina and signs of lameness and found none, tested its interest in two of the Hall's bulling cows, and assessed for herself the appearance and weight of its genitals.

"Mother's Milk, Thegna Amundda, I wouldn't sell a bad bull. You know my herd. You know my cows produce the most milk and the richest. This lad is my own breeding stock, and he's a good one." Otter Erdanson waved one hand toward the pen. "Only selling him because I got two more bull calves off his sire this spring, and I told you right up I could use the coin because Sunna and I got a son wants to wed."

"Please tell me he's building her a house."

"He is. Setting a foundation now. Stone, it is. Cut and laid by his own hand, as is proper. But her kilth are high clan."

Ah. The prospective bride or her kin wanted a large house with fine appointments. And who was Aubrey to stand in the way of a man wanting his son to marry well? "I only have so much coin, Otter. I just tossed half my croft's earnings at a fancy new loom. It's a hard choice right now to afford a beast of this quality."

Her compliment of his animal puffed Otter's cheeks and brought a smile to his eyes. "Won't find a better. And I came down on the coin, didn't I? Would be a boon to have my stock do well on your land. Make good my name in Saemoregh and those parts near the Toregh. A husbandman thrives on the reputation of his stock."

That was true enough. In all of Amallar and much of Neuberland, only women could own land. A Kheld man's prosperity depended on his skills at things other than land owning, like husbandry or farming or one of the crafts. Some, like Wodd, were soldiers. Otter did well for himself and his kilth because he was canny at breeding cattle—and honest at bartering them. What he said about it being to his advantage to have one of his prize bulls servicing Aubrey's herd was both true and smart business. Though Aubrey had come to Rhodhur for other purposes, she saw no reason not to pounce on an opportunity to purchase one of the region's famed dairy bulls.

She resumed studying the bull, admiring his heavy rear quarters. A quick light voice piped up at her side.

"Are you buying him?"

"Lark!" One surprise after another. Aubrey turned and embraced the newcomer.

Though no taller than Aubrey's shoulder, Lark commanded more eyes. Every person working or walking near the cattle pens openly stared. Long hair the deep black of raven wings swept in layers around a pale round face dominated by large eyes as blue and clear as the summer sky. A fine woolen cloak of midnight blue patterned with two shades of green and embroidered with purple fell lightly from Lark's shoulders. Fastened at the left shoulder was a great brooch of ornate concentric circles of copper, iron, and gold.

Upon seeing Lark, Otter immediately made the sign of the Mother and Oak. "Faetha Rappeleye." Respect deepened his voice and lowered his gaze.

"It's so good to see you!" Aubrey hadn't expected to meet with her childhood friend on this visit. Lark lived three days' ride on a good horse away. They had schooled together at Aurdollen starting the year they'd both turned nine, Aubrey fresh from having lost her father to a Staubaun raid and Lark having just seen her mother die of bog fever. Along with Nilla Lowenda, the girls had formed a triad that had lasted several years. "What are you doing here?"

"Old Grandmother's runes told us a man had come. A man who would change Amallar. So I came to see." Having answered the question, Lark placed both feet on the lowest pole of the fence and pulled herself up, arms folded on the top rail and chin resting upon them while she silently assessed Otter's bull. "Did you read him?"

Aubrey shook her head and braced for Lark's disapproval. "I left my stones at the cottage."

"You are endowed with every gift but that which the Mother gave a goose." Fixing a full stare on the bull, Lark reached into the gold leather pouch at her belt. Otter drew in a sharp breath and tensed when her hand emerged again holding a rounded stone of deep violet blue. Lark turned the stone and peered at it. Aubrey also found herself withholding breath as she, too, waited upon Lark's verdict. A Rappeleye woman's runes were regarded with as much respect as a warrior's steel.

"*Ban*. Bounty. This is a strong bull. The cows he sires will flow with good milk."

Otter relaxed and blew out his pent breath, while Aubrey envisioned meadows of cows producing rich profits for her dairy. Lark's readings were *never* false. Aubrey opened her purse and counted out five large gold coins and six silver.

"Mother's Blessing on your herd, Otter Erdanson."

"And Lud smile upon yours, Thegna Amundda." After taking the coins into his hand, Otter sealed the bargain by thrusting his profit into his purse. "Will you be sending a man for him?"

"Aye. My man Wodd will be returning to Saemoregh in a seven day."

After settling a few more details and seeing Otter untie the bull, which he would return to an enclosure more distant from the Hall's dairy barn, Aubrey embraced Lark again.

"I'm so glad you're here. Everything's in an uproar."

"As should be, if someone is changing Amallar." As she walked, Lark's rune pouch of golden leather swung at her hip, punctuating her stride. Even as a girl, Lark had been deemed strange. Men tended to call her frightening. She was also outspoken, loyal, and utterly fierce.

"Hans Thegn Erwanson, or rather Handurin Stauberg-Randolph." Aubrey decided she might as well catch Lark up on the news. "King Stefan's brother that was sent away. He showed up several days ago. Here."

"Trouble follows wherever kings set feet."

Communicating with Lark was unlike with anyone else. Lark spoke about things that touched a matter and seldom about the matter itself. Hans changing Amallar, for example. Hans hadn't changed anything yet. Not truly. Yet Lark was right about trouble following—though it was far from certain just what trouble she meant. It could be Nalf and his cadre of chieftains, or even some other threat.

"People already want things because Hans is here," Aubrey said.

"*Men* want things. Our men and foreign men."

"Ours will seek the Hand of Lud."

The War Hand. Lark had just raised the very issue about which Ewlys had warned. So had the Old Mothers' Wheel. Kheld men always turned to Lud, god of sky and war, for their wants—when they wanted power, when they wanted control, when they wanted to seize either of those things from the Mother.

If Amallar's men went to Lud to make Hans their king and arm him for war, the god would demand a price, and almost certainly a high one. If that were the case, there would be little the Mother could do to bring Hans under Her protection. The favors of deities came burdened with conditions. Hans's brother had suffered such a fate. Stefan, in choosing a bride, had looked past the Mother and sought only the counsel of Lud and men. To no one's surprise, war had followed.

So much for Kheld men. As for foreign men....

As she ever did, Lark read the direction of Aubrey's thoughts. She was good at that also. "Foreign men will seek their own gods."

And therein lay the trap. Essera's Highborn Princes, conduits to powerful gods, were dead—the last two slain by Stefan—which left only the abomination in Sordan. Dorilian. In that direction lay a great unknown. If what Hans claimed was true and he had *fled* Sordan, not been released, Sordan remained an enemy. And Hans had fled to Amallar. No one knew how to predict what might happen next. Would Essera's lofty Staubaun nobles follow Hans if Dorilian, the lone remaining Highborn Prince and link to their gods, stood in opposition?

"Whatever Hans brings us, you can be sure it is not of the Mother." Aubrey kicked at a cob of dried, mouse-eaten corn. It skittered toward a rain barrel. "He's intent on retaking his birthright. It will be men's work, destruction and ruin."

"All undertakings concern the Mother. She works within unfolding things."

"Well, things are unfolding for certain. I came here to tell the Rhodhur Cruihcil about what is happening in Neuberland. In Saemoregh. It's prime harvest season and there aren't any soldiers. The enemy is not attacking our villages, not burning our crops. Ever since summer the Staubaun bastards are holding back. Why? What are they planning?" From all Aubrey knew, to fight a winter war would be more difficult. Neither did it make sense to wait until spring, which would give the embattled villages opportunity to rearm and regain strength. "I rode to Bellan Toregh thinking I might find news there—thinking I would need to ride to Leseos—and that's where I learned that the Rill had stopped running. The Rill! Dead as stone. So what's going on with that thing? And what's happening in Essera or Leseos, or Gignastha for that matter, that none of us know? Nothing that will be good for our people."

"Except what already is."

Aubrey cocked her head at Lark, who answered with a shrug. "No burning. No killing. Trees murmur of new growth, fields overflow with food, rivers are filled with life and fat with trade. And the brother of King Stefan has returned to his people. The Old Mothers hold hope of an Awakening."

"You've been talking to your Oak again."

Lark didn't deny it. "My family's Oak is very old and wise, as befits a tree fed by the souls of a thousand Old Mothers."

The Rappeleye Oak had sprung from an acorn planted by One-Eyed Bess, the Mother-touched woman who had convinced Alm to lead the Kheld people through the Dread Door into this new World. That had been many hundred years ago and the tree had since grown so tall and thick with limbs that it resembled a small hill. Tales held that the Rappeleye Oak communed with all the forest between the Dazun and the Great Telarkans. Generations of the descendants of Old Bess and the Nine Hags—Bess's daughters and their daughters' daughters, and most of their daughters also—were buried where the Oak's roots could guard their spirits. Perhaps because of that, Rappeleye daughters were famed for having garnered uncanny knowledge from the family tree.

On more than one visit to the Rappeleye Motherhome near the

Bogs, Aubrey had lain upon the mossy ground beneath the Oak's mighty boughs and tried to converse with the tree. She'd heard only bird song and the secret languages of tiny crawling things. Nothing of portents or wisdom.

She and Lark reached the back of the Hall and walked along its series of rear porches, bypassing the laundry and dyeing rooms, ducking beneath ranks of drying sheets. They found an unused porch near the kitchen wing and sat on a weathered step, from which they could watch jens and bobs dart to and from open storerooms in preparation for the evening meal.

Lark sniffed the air. "Eel! I think I would like an eel pie. Gerd's pies surpass even my Gran's."

Eels and pies were just about the farthest things from Aubrey's thoughts. "I would like a strong, secure country not threatened by war."

"Death is strong. Life is war. Both carry the seeds of opportunity and disaster."

"Have your runes told you something of that too?"

"Only of change." An eloquent tilt of Lark's raven head told Aubrey her friend's opinion on that. "But is that not the same? What is youth but a time of change? Old age but looking death in the eye? We all lose the war against time—against change."

"But we're not fighting time. Or change! We're fighting Staubauns. People! Did you know the Enlad of Annech sent a message he would cease harassing Saemoregh and leave the surrounding villages in peace if I wed his bastard son?"

Lark's face scrunched. "The Mother doesn't know that word."

"Which word? Peace? Or bastard?"

"The last one."

Aubrey shrugged. "Maybe not. But Staubauns do. It was an insult, Lark. I'm not good enough for any noble's rightful heir. But my property? That's good enough for one's landless son, to give him a leg up. The Enlad's offer is nothing but a way to steal Amundhal from me and exert suzerainty over Saemoregh. I rubbed his ring on a pig's anus before I sent it back." *And then I rode to Bellan Toregh and Rhodhur.*

A man charged up on a thick-hocked pony, a courier's pack bouncing on his back. He dismounted in a hurry and dashed into the building by way of an unremarkable door. Aubrey knew the door led to stairs that would take the courier to Nalf's well-secured second-floor quarters. It galled Aubrey that there were plans afoot of which she was being kept in the dark. Nalf and his chieftains might respect Aubrey's standing—as high clan, holder of a valued cruihcil seat, and daughter of King Marc Frederick's Head Forester who'd left Aubrey a generous land grant even Staubauns must honor—but they included her only in plans to saddle her with their choice of a man.

"This change the Rappeleye Mothers saw," she asked, "what form will it take?"

"Leaving." Lark picked up a stick and used it to trace a rune in the dirt. "Blackthorn and holly. Wolf sign in the ashes. Powerful forces enter play."

"Perhaps the hunt is on. Wolves crowd our borders. Neuberland wolves. Sordan wolves. And Essera is home to even more wolves."

"We're not sheep." A smile teased Lark's mouth.

"No, we're not. We'll surprise them, I think."

Lark found her rune pouch again and cradled it with fingers orange-tinged from her work with proofing metals. "My laying of the Wheel foretold a different thing. Revelation. Revelation is the child of change, and Amallar will see great changes. Remember what the Crone foretold?"

Aubrey shuddered to remember the old woman. "We were lost in the Bogs. We were children! We were lucky to get out alive."

"She scared Nilla back into the womb. But not you. You stood with your fists balled at your sides and you faced her until she spoke." Lark paused and twined the ties of her rune pouch. "That's when she said she would not let us go until we had each chosen a stone and watched her lay the Wheel."

Aubrey snorted. "And you think that what happened to Nilla—"

"She married a king. That's exactly what the Crone said would happen: 'To one girl a king, to one a man, and to one—'"

"The cold trees. I remember."

"Well, Nilla wed a king."

"The Crone laughed when she gave us that reading. It was a *joke*. Or a riddle. A cruel and cutting riddle." Because a king was also a man, and any girl who grew up in the shadow of Bellan Toregh knew that the cold trees were Death.

Nilla had fulfilled all three.

"Nilla put herself outside the Mother's protection. She didn't choose her own man. The Crone's Wheel rolled her under because she let men choose for her."

"So what does that portend for us?" Aubrey disliked the cold confidence of Lark's pronouncement.

"Only that we must heed the portent. We must not do as she did. We must be instruments of the Mother, not of men." Or of Lud, the god of men.

A breeze lifted their hair and tangled the strands, a gentle binding that fell across their shoulders as they shared body heat and words. Movement at the edge of the pasture fences caught Aubrey's eye and she spied two men walking. Excited calls of recognition identified one of the men, as could be counted upon to happen whenever hope was present. Hans looked slightly embarrassed as he acknowledged the calls.

Lark leaned forward to peer at the pair. "So that is Hans Thegn?"

"In the flesh."

"People like him."

"He hasn't done anything yet to merit otherwise."

Lark's expression sharpened. "Who is the other one?"

"Thron. He says he's from Trongor."

"You don't believe him."

Aubrey tipped Lark a half smile. "I do. He *did* come up from Trongor. I'm just not sure he originated there."

"He wears secrets."

What was Lark doing? *Seeing* him... but not *reading*. Lark's hand continued to play with her pouch cords, her runes untouched.

"Yes," Aubrey agreed. "Thron has a great many secrets, I think. Hans likes him, though, from what I can tell. He trusts him. I'm... trying to."

"Why try?"

Because he's interesting. "I need to get near him, learn what he's about." Aubrey flushed. "I want to trap him in a lie."

"Let the Mother decide," Lark counseled. They rose to make their way to the Hall, where the midday meal was being laid and there might be eel pies to be had. "If you take this on yourself, who knows? Men also lay traps."

16

Though these newcomers are rustic, and most are
uneducated, their healers are quite knowledgeable in
medicinal plants and skilled in the art of treating many
bodily ills. The school at Aurdollen teaches anatomy and
bone setting, wound stitching and the preparation of
potions for sicknesses from itching to gout and cramping of
the gut or heart.

MERGAN STAUBAUN PAZOR, REPORT TO KING ESTEVAR

Dorilian tied a brace of pheasants to the rings at the front of
his saddle, securing them alongside a wood hen he had slung
there earlier. He then returned the weighted net to his gear.
His morning of sport had been damp and cold, but at least the addition
of game fowl to the menu would persuade Gerd to serve him
something other than eels. Last night's eel pies—seasoned with
ricina and served by Gerd with so much pride—had finished off
Dorilian's hope of an excellent dinner. Maybe today's meal would be
more satisfying.

At least the three birds would afford an adequate excuse for his
absence from the breakfast table.

Handurin would surely take a dim view of this excursion, as
would Robdan. Neither seemed to realize that to keep a man in
constant company was unnatural. Dorilian was not a child in need
of watching. All his life he had sought freedom from messy emotions
and expectations. He avoided strangers. Whenever possible, he
avoided *everyone*. As for mornings, it was his habit to start his day
before sunrise, which was hours before most of Rhodhur Hall so
much as stirred in their beds. After nearly two weeks among Khelds,

Dorilian knew that if Nammuor would ever attack Amallar, he would do so at dawn. With an ease he could not have managed just days ago, Dorilian swung astride his mount.

Autumn morning crisped the air. Fallen leaves lay sodden upon the ground, muting his horse's footfalls. Though birds broke the silence with song, they were fewer than before; most had heeded winter's call and flown to warmer climes. He followed a trail along the bank of a Frendel River wild and tumbling with rapids around large boulders, strangely carved sentinels knee-deep in churning white water. Finding a shallow spot where the bank was low, he dismounted to replenish his water skin and allow the horse to drink before he headed back to Rhodhur.

He let the gelding drink its fill, then tied it beside a break of small trees forming a thicket along the river bank. From there he wandered a short distance upstream along steep, often undercut, banks of gray slabs. Bare stone had always held a charm for him, if only because it so often revealed itself to be other than what it seemed. Those monolithic stones in the river... something had once stood there. A bridge? He stepped up onto one of the slabs, perhaps the body of an abutment, now fallen and eroded but bearing in its shape the traces of its former occupation. Kneeling, he touched a pocked surface as enduring as old bones.

Dorilian pondered it. Who had built this bridge in the elder days of the World? Who had crossed it? Once it had conveyed a road. Where had it led? The past wavered and then was gone. He did not have the Malyrdeon gift for such things. Only the anguish of inconstancy stayed with him, the terrible knowledge that nothing in the Universe was inviolate... that Handurin was right. And when things changed, what did they leave behind? Only ruins?

Perhaps. A thing that can only be what it is, and not change, becomes a ruin or a memory. Yes, he thought. He placed his hand into the clear cold water. The river swirled around his mortal flesh not very differently than it did the footing upon which he knelt. *This was a bridge, and now it is the ruin of a bridge.* But was the society of humans, or Highborn, made of similar stuff? Could someone isolate the structures of mortal existence and say this was the Triempery? And now it was... what? Simply the ruin of an empire? Could it not be the foundation of something else?

It had happened before.

The Aryati ruled the World before this one.

The starfaring Aryati had raised their cities and their civilization long before the seeds of the Highborn Triempery had even been conceived. Amynas and the Three stood heir not just to Leur but to what the Aryati left behind. *We are the last flower of the Aryati. We, the children of the Three who ended the reigns of the Hegemons and became gods themselves. Our Triempery grew out of the rootstock of the Aryati Hegeistate.*

Ruins surrounded Dorilian. Essera, and the Triempery, had died right out from under the Highborn—and the Sordaneons, at least, had not recognized its passing. Sordan, Mormantalorus, Amallar: all new and young and strong, all growing fast as weeds on the Triempery's fringes while Essera, that empire's foundation and heartwood, weakened and ceased to give rise to new growth.

The Malyrdeons, Dorilian was now certain, had foreseen this.

Marc Frederick knew. That realization hit him in the gut. *He knew, because he was trying to graft a new order onto the rootstock of the old.*

A new Highborn state, created on the foundations of the Triempery, but not dependent on a Staubaun society to give it shape. Why had Dorilian not seen it?

I was young, and Staubauns and my own kind were all I knew. He saw something else, too, in why Marenthro had chosen to raise Handurin apart, far away from both Essera and Amallar... and *Dorilian.*

Marenthro was beginning to surprise him. But what to do about it?

Aubrey stood on fading, tan-colored needles, surveying the river below. Lark was spending the day at the Barrowwood in consultation with a dozen Old Mothers, leaving Aubrey to devote the morning to her own oft-neglected service. These hills were home to elfshod, the deep-hued purple berries and berry pods healers coveted for their potent narcotic. Rhodhur's healers needed larger supplies than they currently possessed, especially if there was to be a winter war. Because Rhodhur's aged herb mistress suffered from old bones, Aubrey had offered to find some elfshod before the coming Witan. The large pouch of soft leather slung from her left shoulder was heavy with her gatherings of the thick-skinned berries and their thorny pods; enough, she thought, to satisfy her obligation. Although the meadow below looked promising, she already faced a long walk back to Rhodhur. She was about to turn back when she noticed a flash of color in the thickets lining the river.

Curious, she made her way down the slope, moving as she had learned during her Saemoregh childhood, stealing around trees and moss-covered rocks. At the bottom of the hill where the land flattened, Aubrey found a handsome roan, picketed to the stout main branch of a well-rooted bush. The bridle clacked occasionally as the horse tore at hummocks of tough grass. Its harness and gear were Trongorian, the saddle polished by use, low pommel and high cantle in the plains style, the fringed blanket boldly striped with red and blue, a ready means of identification across Trongor's empty land. Three freshly killed birds hung from the saddle rings.

Aubrey walked to the horse and ran her hand down its sleek shoulder. A good mount, and one she recognized. Thron would not be far from his horse. Not with his next meal hanging uncooked. His trail led to the river. Aubrey followed and when she reached the bank she looked down, then up, the boulder-strewn course of the rapids. Thron had gone only as far as the tumbled outcropping at the rapids' gate. Seated upon one of the great flat stones that jutted into the water at that point, he seemed to be engaged in flinging pebbles one at a time into the churning froth. And he was, as yet, oblivious to Aubrey's presence.

Aubrey hesitated. It was Hans Thegn she was supposed to engage, not this man. Only it wasn't Hans who wandered into her thoughts or awakened questions she could trace to their first meeting. She liked Hans, but Thron intrigued her.

Both Thron and Hans had rarely been alone of late. Hans, of course, might well have reason, with Nalf Rhys constantly issuing challenges. As the Witan drew near, Hans had yet to articulate his plan to bring Khelds to power again in Essera. And just this morning, according to Mother Idda, the faedu Wyver had declared that Hans Thegn, if he would be king over Amallar, must make a dedication to Lud. Nalf would no doubt inform Hans that he must ride to the Grove and the Faeduadan, the Seers of the Forest, to get himself a proper prophecy. Hans, yes, had reason to be preoccupied—but what would a Trongorian, not even their captain, be so thoughtful about?

Aubrey crept as near as she could before emerging from the thicket at the edge of the stones. Only then did Thron turn and let Aubrey know he'd seen her. Everyday clothing of plain wool and leather looked better on him than they would have on any other man. She doubted he could ever look truly rustic. Aubrey had heard comments around the Hall and in town from silly girls who thought Thron handsome but cold. *Cold enough to burn*, she reasoned, recalling their first meeting.

Indeed, the look he gave her was less than welcoming.

"If it isn't one of Amallar's lovelier weeds." Thron looked away after speaking.

Not certain whether she had been complimented or insulted, or both, Aubrey walked over to join him on the outcropping. "What does that mean?"

"No offense, lady. It seems I am also a weed."

"You certainly have thorns." When Aubrey moved to kneel beside him, Thron's mouth tightened in a frown, but he made no attempt to move away. She brushed back the hair from her face. "I don't suppose you're in a mood to talk."

"Now what would you and I have to talk about?"

"How about whatever you were thinking before I came?"

He shook his head. "I fear such thoughts would translate poorly. They were but private matters."

"A wife in Ogarth?" she suggested, then bit her tongue. Why had she asked that?

His gaze flicked to hers in sharp amusement. "No. A bridge in Amallar." He pointed to the huge rock formations in the river. "There lie the ruins of it."

How neatly he avoids the question. Aubrey decided to play along. "That doesn't make any sense. Who would've built a bridge here? And what for?"

"I didn't say it was recent. These ruins are ancient. And you do not know what that means."

"I do." Aubrey tried to think of what ancient might mean to a man like Thron, a man from Trongor or perhaps, as she was beginning to think, from one of the Staubaun domains. "The Malyrdeons built it, then—the Wall Lords of Essera—in the Golden Age of the Triempery."

"Is that what ancient means to you?"

Something in Thron's gaze mocked Aubrey. She bristled. "I suppose you have a better grasp of that than I do."

"You can be sure of it." He looked away again. "Do you know what a weed is, lady?"

"Of course, I do. A weed is a plant that grows where it shouldn't."

"You mean where it's not wanted?"

"Well, yes. What has this got to do with anything?" Though Thron was talking nonsense, his expression held an appealing, wistful quality that tugged her interest.

"You asked me," he said. "You wanted to know what I was thinking about."

"I thought it would be something of importance. Have you come up with a way to rid the world of weeds, or something as useful as that?"

"No, not so useful. And I think there shall always be weeds. The first conquerors of dry land were weeds. The first men to seek the stars might have been so regarded. The Highborn most certainly were and those who remain, I dare say, still are. All history has been patterned not only on the survival of the fittest, but also of the most desirable. Were there not farmers, weeds would rule the fields. But a weed of the right characteristics, planted in the proper soil, might emerge as a desirable species." He threw another pebble into the stream. "What this Triempery needs, lady, is not a king, but a gardener."

Uncertain where this conversation was leading, Aubrey took her lower lip between her teeth for a moment. "Let me guess—you think Hans would make a good gardener?"

"I think he has a head for cultivation. In a field of weeds, it's not easy to know which growth to preserve and which to destroy. He's done well thus far."

"That's because he hasn't preserved or destroyed anything yet!"

"There's his talent. A lesser man would have trampled the field."

Aubrey plucked a loose stone from those at hand and dropped it with a loud plop into the water. "It's nice to know you approve."

"To be frank, I had expected not to."

"I think a lot of people expect too little of him."

For better or worse, Aubrey's thoughts were flying in strange directions that had nothing at all to do with Hans. Thron was more than he presented himself to be. For one thing, he talked unlike any Trongorian she had ever met. Oh, his command of speech was perfect—except a Trongorian wouldn't be sitting on a riverbank pondering the nature of empires and weeds and drawing such strange conclusions. It was almost as suspect as his familiarity with the poet Myron, a verse from whom he had quoted the other day in Robdan's room, when he had claimed to be reading philosophy. Whether poetry or philosophy hardly mattered—both smacked of the Staubaun, something Aubrey had suspected of Thron from the first.

But *where*? Where had Hans picked him up? Trongor? Or was Thron a spy from Sordan or Essera? His features did not betray him. His face, half-turned away from her, showed a profile as bold and sharp as any Staubaun's—every bit as masculine and beautiful. Physically, judged by his height alone, Thron could be taken for one. Almost. His tawny hair and sun-touched skin were both too brown for a Staubaun to claim. And his eyes, silver as the dawn sky, were completely wrong. His blood, then, was mixed, as hers was.

"Why are you staring?" Thron's frown warned that he did not like to be studied.

I shouldn't wonder, she thought, if the man had something to hide. "You have Staubaun blood."

"Only that?"

"Isn't that enough?"

"Not enough for some. Here, I suppose it's too much."

Aubrey shrugged. "I have it too. My grandmother had an encounter with a Staubaun lord in Essera."

"My sympathies to your grandmother."

So, he understood about that. But she sensed no anger, no lingering bitterness about the predatory habits of Staubaun males. Thron's own parentage, then, was probably more conventional.

"I don't mind for the most part." Maybe if she talked about her family, he would talk about his. "Men dislike when I'm as tall as they, but I find it more of an advantage than not. And I'm Kheld enough in all the ways that matter. Clan right is bestowed through the mother, so I have that. And Thegn women have the gift."

"The gift?"

The sudden intensity of his attention pierced Aubrey, as though he might thread through her eyes and into her thoughts. Surprised, Aubrey pulled back and the feeling vanished. But the moment left her flustered, unsure of what she had encountered—Thron... or her own heightened awareness of him.

"Yes." She scooped up a handful of river-polished stones. After choosing several, she arranged them before her: smooth, round, dark, and light. "I have the gift of reading paths. I studied at Aurdollen, where I learned the Mother's Faces: Knowing, Life, and Home. For my first Calling I chose Knowing and spent two years studying the natures of woods and how to lay wands for the Wheel. Then by using runes"—she indicated the stones—"not these, but stones like these, which I don't have with me, I can discern What Is, see the path of an event or thing, even a person. Knowing What Is enables me to determine how best to heal, or provide clear guidance to those who face troubles."

Though Thron nodded, Aubrey could tell he was not impressed. Staubauns claimed to have higher magic. "Is this gift inborn or learned?"

"Both. Not all women possess an affinity with runestone. And of those who do, not all develop the skill to use them wisely. Knowing is the most difficult of the Mother's Faces, but I had a good teacher." Aubrey picked up the pebbles she had sorted and began lobbing them into the water. "The As'Faetha Ilfanwy visited me when I was still on my mother's knee. She said, 'This girl's life is written in the Stones.' After my parents died and I was sent to Aurdollen, I sought her out. She took me as a student and taught me to be a Knower of Ways."

A smile teased Thron's mouth. "And what ways do you know?"

He was her captive from the first day again, filled with casual arrogance.

"Knowledge, as I just told you. But I'm also a healer, which belongs to Life." Aubrey looked around the water's edges until she spied what she sought, growing among the rocks lining the bank. She got up and dashed to fetch a handful of the dainty purple blooms. She returned to the stone and sat beside Thron again, picking out one of the flowers. It hung like a teardrop on its stalk, its purple cap no bigger than the tip of her littlest finger. She held it out to him. "Go ahead," she told him. "You can eat it."

"Why should I?"

"Because it tastes good." Aubrey wrapped her lips around the blossom, taking it into her mouth, where the flower gave up its sharp, delightful essence. Plucking another, she repeated her offer. "Try it."

With a look at once dubious and amused, Thron angled his mouth toward Aubrey's fingers and took the flower from her. She felt the warm brush of his lips closing just short of her fingertips and knew the thrill of drawing a wild thing near. She barely resisted the urge to turn her hand, to feel the texture of his skin and heavy silk of his hair. This was not the type of man one touched on a whim.

"It freshens the breath," she said, then could have kicked herself for how that sounded. "And also the spirit."

Thron nodded, indicating that he'd found the experience not unpleasant. He took the next flower Aubrey handed him in his own fingers before eating it.

"This is a pretty spot," she observed. The entire length of the steep-walled valley was lined with rock formations that broke the river into musical rapids. "Do you come here often?"

"'Twas the first time only and, seeing as you now know of it, surely the last." Thron rose to his feet and strode across the rocks back onto the bank where he had left his horse tethered in the brush. Aubrey got to her feet and hurried after him, putting down two steps to his one.

When she caught up to him, he had already led his horse from its secluded thicket and was engaged in tightening the saddle straps he had loosened to let the animal drink and graze. Aubrey stood by, watching him.

"Where is your horse?" he asked.

"I didn't bring one."

He granted her an inquisitive turn of his head. "You walked all this way?"

Aubrey pulled at the neck of her bulging pouch and withdrew a yellowing, thorny pod sprouting stalks laden with purple, nearly black, berries. "Elfshod." She gave over the pod into his hand and watched his fingers, his face, as he turned it over, enjoying his look of curiosity. "In the hands of healers they yield a powerful narcotic. The drug is used to kill pain and bring sleep to the sick. This is the only season in which elfshod can be gathered in the wild. The snows are too deep later in the year and even now it is hard to find. A person on horseback would find their search unfruitful."

"Literally." Thron returned the specimen to Aubrey before he mounted his horse with the carefree ease of a man accustomed to riding. He then looked down at her, clearly pondering. After a moment he sighed and reached down a hand. "Come, lady. I will not have it said that I left a woman in the wild. You had best ride pillion."

That's where it shows, she thought. On horseback, Thron had the manner and bearing of an aristocrat. Arrogance and privilege gazed down at Aubrey without apology. She could play his game. Accepting his offer, Aubrey placed her hand in Thron's and welcomed his help. As he pulled her up, she swung her leg over.

Once seated, Aubrey tightened her arms about Thron's lower ribs. He smelled of leather and summer and wood warmed by the sun.

"Such a tall horse," she noted.

"That's why I chose it."

Just over the hill they came upon a rutted road barely less wild than the surrounding forest, little used because it serviced a few scattered farms belonging to less prosperous holders. The track left the trees from time to time to pass alongside fields planted with ripened grains or grasses. In one field men worked harvesting hay, long scythes arching in gleaming rhythm across the golden distance, bodies swaying as they pitched their gleanings onto an ox-drawn cart.

"The harvests are starting." Aubrey sought to continue their elusive communication. "It will be another phase before the farmers can leave their fields. Then we can hold the Witan. Hans will have seen the Faeduadan, of course, and then—"

"Faeduadan?"

"The Seers, followers of Lud. Knowers of the Sacrifice and Speakers of Omens."

"More 'knowing of ways'?"

"Men's ways. Only experienced Seers can deal with augury and portents. Before anything of consequence can happen, the Faeduadan must declare Hans acceptable to the god Lud."

"Acceptable to the god? I see." Thron sounded unconcerned, as if being acceptable to a god was not something he considered important.

"Don't you fear the gods? Or do they enjoy your insolence?" Even the Staubauns, Aubrey knew, feared their Highborn gods.

"I fear all gods, especially those that speak with human voices."

The crude earthen track they had been following left the woods for another path, wider and more trodden, which would wind along the valley until it reached the main road to Rhodhur. But Aubrey pointed out a shortcut she often used during her own forays into the woods. The trail led into a forested grove of old, tall trees still bearing the last of their brightly colored foliage. The floor was thick with leaves and autumn crocuses and the horse's head lifted, alert, spooked by its own muted footfalls.

"It's not quite what you're used to, is it?" Aubrey asked. Thron rode easily, with sure seat and hands, and was probably as plainsborn as his horse.

"Do you think I haven't seen forests before?"

"In Trongor?"

"Yes, in Trongor."

And that was all he had to say. Aubrey stared a hole in his back. She had hoped to uncover that he had seen other forests, in lands more familiar, maybe even those of Neuberland. Damn him, he was cagey. Every word he spoke was carefully chosen, free of unbidden responses.

"Is that where you met Hans?" She chose another tack.

Thron's knees relaxed away from the horse's sides, then tightened again. Hard. The animal leaped into a sudden gallop. Thron ducked beneath a tangle of overhanging branches. With a shriek, Aubrey tightened her arms, keeping her seat. Her cap, however, was snagged on a thorny twig and flew off her head. She twisted around to grasp at it unsuccessfully.

"Stop, Thron!" Aubrey clutched at him to keep from falling when the horse skittered again at her sudden movement.

"What do you think you're doing?" Legs clamped, he reined the animal to a halt.

"I lost something. Let me down."

Aubrey handed Thron her sack of elfshod and used his leg as an anchor to climb down so she could run back to retrieve her fallen cap from the damp forest floor. She picked it up and slapped it several times to dislodge a collection of leaves and debris. When she was satisfied with the results, Aubrey looked up to see him watching her with smug self-congratulation. *Got me off your back, didn't you?* She granted a thin smile of acknowledgment. Her boots pressed gently upon fallen leaves as she crossed the open space to the waiting horse and its rider.

She held up a hand. "Will you help me back up?"

Leather creaked as Thron shifted his weight securely. "I should leave you here. I trust you know your way home?"

"Aren't you the noble one?" Aubrey narrowed her gaze, certain he would not leave her. "There are people who make a practice of good manners, you know."

"Usually with more promising subjects." Thron's voice had resumed its familiar edge. "I was not aware you were versed in other than rudeness and confrontation. What manners you may possess you have not gone out of your way to employ in my presence."

"I could say the same for you." Once more she extended her hand for assistance. "Come on, Thron, help me up."

Thron's gaze stayed on hers and Aubrey's heart leaped beneath her ribs. He made her wait a few moments more before, with that smile she had so been hoping to see and a groan of reluctant laughter, he yielded and took the hand she offered. Again Aubrey accepted his strength pulling her easily onto the horse's broad back. But more than that, she accepted the concession of his smile and his laughter. She savored both as gifts, masculine and warm, and fleeting too, but hers alone. Suddenly, she liked this man.

They rode up to Rhodhur Hall accompanied by the carts and barrows of farmers and merchants arriving for the day. The stable yard was crowded and chaotic with activity. A large group of men, cloaked and huddled against the morning chill, milled like a flock of oversized birds near the enclosure reserved for the horses of the Hall's more prominent permanent residents. As a group, the men lifted their heads to take notice of the new arrivals. While Thron reined his horse to a halt at the stable posts, Aubrey noticed that Hans and Robdan both had already saddled their horses and were preparing to mount. Hans separated himself from the others and ran over to greet them, Nalf Rhys trotting behind.

"Thron." Instead of looking at him, though, Hans looked at Aubrey. When she searched his face, trying to read his thoughts about finding her and Thron together, Hans shifted his gaze back to the latter. "Robdan wondered where you'd gone this morning."

Thron nudged the feathered carcasses hanging from the saddle rings. "I'm earning my keep." He nodded toward the horses. "Where are you going?"

"To see the Faeduadan while the weather is good." Hans tried to laugh but sounded nervous. "I guess they need to see the stars to read them. Nalf thought I should go while the skies are yet clear."

"Aren't you a pair? Off that horse." Nalf Rhys stepped forward and reached for Aubrey. She swung down herself, shifting her elfshod-filled bag to her shoulder as she did so.

With a defiant thrust of her chin, Aubrey flashed a brilliant smile at her riding companion. "Thron was kind enough to let me ride with him."

Nalf Rhys stared at Thron, and his face clouded over. Whatever he intended to say was cut short by the approach of a robed faedu who bowed as he came to stand before them.

Ignoring Thron, the priest turned to Nalf, then Hans. "Daylight has its hours. None are allowed within the sanctuary after darkness falls."

"Oh, stop carping," Nalf Rhys grumbled. "The sun's barely up and you're talking nightfall."

"We must consult the god to discover the omens pertaining to Hans Thegn. For that, he must be present," the faedu insisted. "Only then can we decide the meeting place for the Witan."

"I'm coming," said Hans.

But Aubrey noticed how even after Hans had mounted and just before he rose away, he continued to look back at Thron. It seemed to her as if Hans did not want to leave, or wanted to say more, or hear what Thron had to say. Except that Thron said nothing beyond an exchange of looks Aubrey could not interpret. She watched as Thron dismounted and led his horse to the stable, alone, more closed off than ever he had been before.

17

Because the Highborn exist as beings in the Mind, they
can detect other thought and decipher its emotional
overtones or hues. The ability to exchange fully expressed
ideation is much rarer and limited to their own kind.

ZAMENES, *On the Nature of Gods and Men*

I n the day-long absence of Handurin and Robdan, Arne Anseldson
had singlehandedly taken on responsibility for Dorilian's welfare.
He followed from the courtyard and stood by while Dorilian
watered and fed and stabled his horse. He insisted on being at hand
when Farrl made the daily assignment of duties. He craned his neck
and counted the coins when Dorilian stopped by an old weaver's
stand to buy a pair of warm socks. Though Dorilian knew Arne's
sudden attachment stemmed more from concern for Handurin's
ultimate well-being than his own, he quickly found Arne's nannying
unbearable. At last, having maneuvered to the rear of the Hall and
the approach to the kitchen, into a corner where none would
overhear them, Dorilian used his greater size to back Arne against
the building wall.

"Let me be clear," he growled to the terrified Kheld, who he
knew beyond doubt had never overcome a deeply seated fear of him.
"I have not had a nursemaid since I last suckled mothers' milk. I do
not want your company and I am more than capable of looking after
myself in this termite nest your people call home."

"Hans told me to keep an eye on you."

"Then do it from across the yard!"

Though clearly blanching, Arne shook his head. "He told me to
stay with you if you got about."

Getting hold of the edge of his temper, Dorilian pulled it around to shape a different instrument. "You are the antithesis of secrecy. It is the goal of secrecy to make it appear nothing untoward is going on—not as though something is about to get out of the bag. Why don't you practice by keeping at least enough distance between us so you are not stumbling over my boots? If you can do that for the next hour, I can promise to make your ordeal a short one."

Predictably, Arne saw value in anything that would shorten having to be around Dorilian. "Do it your way, then," he muttered to his toes, scowling, "'cuz you will, no matter what I say. You're even stubborner than he is. Just remember I plan to keep you in sight—and in earshot, too!"

Dorilian said nothing but didn't prevent Arne from following him to the kitchen.

Gerd made his way over, wearing a flour-dusted apron and wiping his burly arms with a towel, having somehow noticed them despite what appeared to be flocks of cooks and helpers trotting between the preparation tables and the ovens. "Hullo, Arne! Thron! I hear Hans has been sent to meet the god. He should have told me. I would have packed him a good lunch!"

"Reckon he figures he'll be back by dinner," Arne replied from where he'd taken up position beside the nearest hearth.

"Even so, it's not good to meet the god on an empty stomach. The visions, I hear, go better with bread in the belly."

Dorilian handed over his three fowl. "My... contribution to the common table." He ignored Arne's eye roll.

"Excellent!" Gerd proclaimed. He hefted the birds with approval. "I'll prepare the fattest one especially for you. You won't have to pass in favor of the common plate as you did last night."

"That eel pie was a treat!" Arne exclaimed.

Dorilian loathed eel. To Gerd he said, "I respectfully prefer anything else."

Though Arne glared at that answer, Gerd chuckled. "Archon Cullen used to have guests like you. 'Anything else!' they said."

"Some folks don't know what's good for them." Arne sharply stated his opinion.

"Have you sweets available?" Dorilian ignored Arne's rudeness and moved to a more important matter. He was not here to negotiate his evening meal. "I wish to retire to my room."

"With sweets?" Gerd inquired.

"Yes. I—I have a craving for some." What moved Dorilian was more than a craving, though he saw no need to explain.

"Of course. Whatever suits." Though puzzled, Gerd appeared inclined to accommodate the request. "My best jen just made some puddings and jam. And the morning's sweet knots and rings are still warm from the ovens. I'll make you a plate."

The innkeeper hurried off on that mission. Arne turned on Dorilian and spread his hands, though he kept his voice down. "What are you doing? Just hold out and eat a normal midday like everyone else."

"What I will be doing is retreating from any further need to talk with you."

Minutes later, a big pewter plate laden with sweets in his hand, Dorilian led Arne from the kitchen and through the quiet, cavernous dining Hall to the stairs, and from there to Robdan's quarters. At the door, Dorilian made a point of not entering until Arne took the hint that his company was not wanted.

The young man rolled his eyes. "No way. If I stand out here the whole Hall will know something's up. I'm not going to leave you in there alone and not be nearby."

If there was anything in Amallar Dorilian could be certain of, it was that Arne would never fail at a task Handurin had assigned. Much as it irked Dorilian, he allowed Arne inside. This might even be for the best. The last time he had attempted a communication, he had been walked in on.

"I'm here to keep an eye on you, and that's it," Arne reiterated even as the door closed behind him.

"Do it from over there." Dorilian pointed to Robdan's favorite reading chair, surrounded by tables and books, as far as was possible from the door to the small bedchamber Dorilian occupied. Though Arne rolled his eyes, he didn't argue but sank into the chair and kicked out his legs.

"Read something. Prove your damn tutors weren't a waste of time or money."

Arne picked up the book about bees and made a show of opening it. Few things of late had pleased Dorilian more than closing the door between them.

The chamber Robdan had turned over to Dorilian's use was small but sufficiently comfortable. He placed his gathered sweets on the room's only chair and pulled the lone chest of his possessions to block the door, even though Arne, he was certain, would not intrude on him. He next targeted the window, which let in a distracting amount of light. Before untying the curtain, he took a moment to glance outside into a courtyard busy with Khelds. Dust and buckets. Carts and ponies and goats. Small people living small lives. Had Dorilian not ventured to this armpit of the Triempery, he would not know they existed.

Two spots of color and movement drew his notice. A pair of women strolled toward an archway covered with brilliant crimson vines. The archway provided passage through a high stone wall that separated the Hall's courtyard from the grounds of an adjacent compound. *The Barrowwood, where the women live*, Robdan had told Dorilian. The Old Mothers. But younger women stayed there when traveling or in Rhodhur on business.

Women like these two, Aubrey Amundda and another young female Dorilian had seen in her company. They wore full-length cloaks, one of dusky heather and the other of goldfinch yellow, and there was something cheerful too about the way they walked with each other, animated and quick. Both carried parcels probably bought at shops in the adjacent town. Dark hair caught up in woven bands, they angled their heads toward each other as they walked. At this moment, theirs was the only conversation in all Amallar that Dorilian would have liked to overhear. He pulled the draping over the window, blocking out that thought along with the remaining daylight.

With the room in shadow, he sat on the bed and pulled the compass from his jacket. From within its hidden chamber, he withdrew the Rill Stone and placed it on his finger. Even this far, with no known Rill node near, the stone glowed green.

Dorilian lay back on the soft feather tick of the narrow bed that had slept one or all of Robdan's three daughters and stared at the beams of ancient wood poking through the rough plasterwork of the ceiling. His rustic surroundings strangely echoed his mood. *Wild weeds, growing wild.* As in Sordan with its mosaic of not-Staubaun cultures, Amallar had evolved at odds with the richness and grandeur of the Triempery. As a people, the Khelds were not without promise. Their love of music and food, their energy, their laughter, their robust honesty and passionate loyalty to a cause— Dorilian appreciated all these things. As a nation, however, their backwardness was about as daunting as the Telarkan mountains and perhaps would prove as hard to scale.

All morning he had overheard whispers, muted voices tucked around corners and other places where they thought to speak in secret. Handurin's visit to the Sacred Grove aroused too much talk for it to be a simple presentation to the god. Any god. Dorilian had heard Aubrey arguing with that bearded uncle of hers, the Thegnard, voicing disapproval of Nalf's methods. But discussion of those methods had not ensued within Dorilian's earshot, and he had been left to his own conclusions. Those were bare at best.

It appeared something underhanded was in the offing, but to what end? All his life he had moved among the shadows of such plots until he had learned to see them clearly, webs strung to enmesh a man's fate so that no corner of his life was fully his own. Dorilian's very conception he could attribute to Labran's cold will, Sebbord's ambition, Dorilian's father's fear, and his mother's obedience to duty. Other wills had shaped Dorilian's earliest years. Some had even ruled over him for a time until at last, strand by strand, he had cut himself free—or so he had thought. Too late he had learned that the trick was not to escape but to master, to weave those other webs into his own.

That lesson once learned had served him well. What other people said of Dorilian was true: he often defeated enemies by turning their own plots against them. Few knew that he could literally see such webs before he came to them: structures of cognition and emotional intent twisting in the human ether of the Creation: deadly Time fragments littered with the husks of the unwary, seeking to ensnare *him*; other strands but wisps, fluttering harmlessly across his path, the ghosts of plots that had come to naught. But this one... this one Dorilian could not make out, though he perceived its shape uncoiling on the Mind's outer edges.

It is Handurin's, not mine.

But what touched Handurin touched Dorilian eventually. Had it not brought him here, to this drafty, book-lined sleeping chamber with its faded walls and primitive comforts? For what? Because he was still bound by a dead king's tattered web?

He was getting close to Essera again, getting close to testing a loss he had never quite banished. Visiting Marc in the Vault of Incorruption had not absolved Dorilian. Some ghosts refused to remain entombed. Sordan had not these changing seasons, these cycles of death and rebirth, to remind him. *Gustan ablaze with falling leaves, the surrounding hills clothed in scarlet. Flames leaping high upon a hill as he touched living stone and faced a man with yellow eyes. Handurin standing in the apple orchard. Marc Frederick before the fire, the same blue eyes, the same need—asking about the Rill.*

About death. About his son, Jon.

"What do you see with your Highborn eyes?"

"Your pain."

Dorilian ground his fists into his eyes, as if that would banish memory. Solitude but made matters worse. Here in Amallar there were too few others through whom he might drown out his conflict, drive it from him and into hiding as he had done before, so often and so well.

Now. *Now...*

Locating Levyathan took but a moment, a sideways turn of Dorilian's mind. Mountains were nothing, burning deserts but dreams of sand. Upon making contact, the distance between them vanished, to be replaced by a golden union.

Dor!

He had known Levyathan's touch from childhood. Part of his being—and sanity. Turning upon the bed, Dorilian closed his eyes and arranged his limbs. At this moment he wanted only comfort and peace. No longer alone, he breathed air warmed by an applewood fire and his mind walked the white *orcus* grove at the Serat's hidden center. Levyathan's thoughts pressed to his.

I sensed you in the orchard, your frustration and pain. For too many days you haven't allowed me to know your mind, Levyathan worried.

I should not allow you now.

You know why you do.

I'm trapped, Dorilian admitted. *I cannot escape it. Myself. The Rill. Handurin pries open old wounds.*

Wounds none can heal. Handurin will not try to persuade you again.

It is not Handurin who brings this burden upon me.

No, it is the promise.

Trestethion. Dorilian had tried to forget and bury as dead that promise to Marc Frederick. Forget the day he had made it. So much blood, so much death. So much lost. It had been easier to deny everything—love and trust and the sheer majesty of Marc's vision—rather than revisit a wound so great that it still bled at every touch. *Damn you, Marc! I loved you and you made me promise what I could not give! Couldn't you see that I was in pain, that I only did it because I wanted to save you?*

Instead I buried you.

And it had not stopped there. Dorilian had gone to meet Stefan at Permephedon, prepared to lay the Rill at his feet. Then, Dorilian had wanted to make whole his promise to Marc Frederick and, with it, his honor. To be able to say he had not let down the man who had placed in him such faith. But Stefan had betrayed that gesture. The shattered trust had never healed, and Dorilian had never forgiven Stefan, even though it drove more cruelly than ever the wedge between their nations. And yet... Dorilian had upheld the treaty, Marc Frederick's ideals, to the extent that he could. He had not sought to win the war in Neuberland or remove Stefan from Essera's throne; Dorilian had honored what no man could have forced him to honor. Few understood that, but he thought that maybe Handurin did.

Levyathan's quiet presence soothed, as might a heartbeat in the enclosed quiet of the womb. Thoughts twined like rare metals. Levyathan led Dorilian deeper. *This price is too high. Handurin was wrong to ask.*

If I could gain this enemy off my throat—

And Essera? Levyathan read too well the pattern.

Would not suffer such a thing in silence. The Seven Houses would cry Covenant and try to take it from me.

But Levyathan knew Dorilian better than any other person living. He had been there, with Dorilian, all along. *The Seven Houses! They broke with us long ago. Think of those they have killed! Sebbord's blood is on their hands. Our mother's! They flattered Stefan to disadvantage you. They corrupted the Epoptes. They have built a prison for you beneath their city and would gladly buy their machine with your blood! They are without conscience—they want only the Rill. They remind me of spiders!*

Dorilian could deny none of it. His very life had taught him well enough what the Seven Houses were. They had made his grandfather Labran hostage to their ambitions and later, when he had sought Labran out, they had treated him no better. They'd looked down on Dorilian for the taint of lesser blood, sought to trick him, trap him. For how many years had he endured them—not as Marc Frederick had, out of necessity, but because they had opposed Stefan?

They opposed you too, Levyathan reminded.

Dorilian mentally shrugged. *They fear my enemies as their own. If Nammuor would bring them the Rill, they would embrace him with the keys to their city.*

Do you realize what you just said?

Yes.

Dorilian had hoped, with Handurin as underpinning, the Kheld threat removed, that Essera could be salvaged. Now he saw it might not be possible. Handurin had correctly read the signs of a society too advanced in its decay to be resurrected.

Might it not be better to do what Handurin suggested, salvage what good remained and start anew? Dorilian pondered the possibility. Even without the Wall, hints of a future glimmered in that direction, surfaces and imperfections suggested as within a crystal yet uncut.

Dorilian added a key sequence. *Handurin would raise Amallar.*

Raise Amallar! In the unshielded closeness of the Mind link, Levyathan's excitement was difficult to distinguish from Dorilian's own. *Can he do it?*

With the Rill… if he has gauged them rightly. But that is asking too much.

Levyathan understood. Without knowing, Handurin had pushed Dorilian onto a path that led to the edge of an abyss. *Rill Lord.* To manifest that power fully, to find the shimmering edge of the Entity's immortality, to test powers that could—maybe should—sleep forever untested… to become what Dorilian's cells wanted him to become. So deep was Dorilian's dread of that path that he refused to examine the parts of it already manifest—in himself, in his actions.

Levyathan responded in the way only he could. *Let him know. Confide in him.*

So simple, an answer wrought by innocence—and the wisdom of two childhoods. *Levyathan, you do not see the World as it is.*

But Levyathan would not be dismissed. *Why should I? Why shouldn't we see the World as we want it to be? Why not a World as Handurin wants it to be? The World That Is is your prison! Others built it for you, belief by belief and stone by stone, then saw you born into it. Set yourself free and help to make another.*

Was that not what Dorilian had been doing? *How can we make another World without unmaking this one?* But the answer emerged from the question. *Nammuor is unmaking this one.*

Levyathan affirmed that conclusion. *Not obliteration, change. His vision—or yours.*

Or Handurin's.

The Khelds?

Perhaps. Dorilian examined the epistemology that would support such a change. To take that path would alter the Mind. *The Rill creates its own manner of blindness. Erenor and the Seven Houses see it stopped at Dazunor-Rannuli. And while it is stopped, they see that—only that. It has not occurred to Nammuor, to any of them, that there is another node I might employ.*

Trestethion. They think it is dead if they know of it at all. They all think it dead.

It may not be.

Marc Frederick's path.

The one I tried to forget.

Levyathan's insistent presence within Dorilian's mind entwined thought. *If you cannot forget, then remember. Emyli will make you remember. Stauberg will make you remember. Gustan will tear out your heart! Marc Frederick did not ask you to sacrifice your life upon his altar. He sacrificed his upon yours.*

It was after the midday. Dorilian opened his eyes to new shadows between the ceiling beams and light through the window onto his outstretched arm. In Sordan the *orcus* grove blazed in ranks of white, though he could not see that. It was, like all the World outside of his immediate senses, simply certain to be thus.

Does Handurin know what we are? Levyathan asked.

Why would I tell him, take that risk? Let others believe what they will. They lead narrow lives. They misunderstand everything.

Yet that blindness was also Dorilian's great opportunity to move through the currents of the World like a force of nature. It amused him that he could lay down a path for his enemies to travel. Here was his chance—perhaps his only chance—to gain the Khelds firmly in hand.

Mulsor! I am tired. All these years, and still I face nothing but battles.

Come home to Sordan, then. Your City will heal your spirit.

Soon. Nammuor must be beaten, that device of his destroyed. To that end, I must do all that lies within my power. Even if it means awakening this thing inside me. It may be the only way. With Levyathan hovering still on the edges of concern, Dorilian gave in to another worry no less deep-seated. *Handurin may require it. These Khelds are plotting to bind him to them. They set him against their god and are predicting his defeat. It may take another god to thwart them.*

Ours.

Dorilian heard the low snapping of coals collapsing in the grate, smelled the food—cold but sweet—from the pewter plate upon the chair. He was thirsty and hungry now. And tired, very tired. *Leave me*, he adjured. *I am at one with this.*

Are you sure? Levyathan sounded as though he did not want to go.

But Dorilian was sure. Already their contact suffered from his weariness, the communication drifting into his thoughts alone.

Such were his choices. He could not go back, for thus was the nature of Time. Nothing that had happened could be unmade. Neither could he stand still unless Time stood still. He must either go forward into what awaited, shape it as only he could—or die, and all his possibilities die with him.

Did you think it would last forever? The Leur's dying words hung like a jewel upon a failing legacy. Forever. Nothing was forever. Not even gods. Not even pain.

All things happen in the same moment. Destruction. Creation. Not one or the other but both, the same event. So what do I do? Hold the Rill to its original inception, its Staubaun-chained mystery and servitude, as my forefathers before me, and keep the skin by which the World has known it? Known us?

Or do I make the leap?

18

"Be wary of pigheaded men," the Leur cautioned Amynas.
"Not all of them are the work of sorcery. Some truly are
swine."

CIBULITUS, *ANNALS OF THE RETURN*

"I don't think Faedu Helmer likes me," Hans said.

A bony man wearing brown robes, the priest rode well ahead, leading the way but clearly not available for conversation. Robdan, riding at Hans's side, was better company.

"They're suspicious of outsiders."

Which Hans currently was and probably always would be. For all that he admired the Khelds and their robust passion for life, he had yet to fully immerse himself in their society. Part of it was the Khelds themselves, who treated him more like a visiting dignitary than one of their own. Nor did Hans like the way they'd sprung this sacrifice thing on him. He'd barely stirred from bed that morning before Nalf had cornered him and told him to go with the priest, that a sacrificial animal would be slaughtered and its entrails examined for portents of the future, its blood made into a drink that would enable a Seer to gaze upon the stars and then prophesize Hans's fate. Hans didn't believe in prophecy, but Khelds deemed the ritual important. An imperious Old Mother had even approached him before leaving, shaking a leather sack at him and insisting he draw a rune stone. At least she'd given him a blessing before leaving with her entourage of crones.

Hans had been given only an hour to prepare for the journey, and most of that time he had spent fretting about Dorilian's whereabouts. Seeing the Hierarch return with Aubrey riding pillion had been disconcerting, but at least Hans no longer feared that Dorilian had ditched him.

Only a day had passed since he'd spoken with Dorilian about the Rill, and already Hans felt Amallar slipping through his fingers. The more the Khelds realized he was not going to advance Stefan's agenda, giving out lands and titles, the less inclined they seemed to accept Hans as a possible leader.

"What frustrates me most," Hans complained to Robdan as they followed on horseback behind the priest and his mule, "is that I can't pretend Stefan never made mistakes."

"Yes. Well, our people are a stubborn lot, and we'd sooner suck on the seven curly tails of Madrock's swine than admit a failure. Never show the enemy your ass, we say."

Which explained some of what had happened. Stefan had been trapped between an Amallar that refused to see failure and an Essera that could see nothing else. And Sordan.

"What happened between Dorilian and Stefan?" The forest opened, allowing autumn sunlight to pour down upon the golden bowl of a grassy meadow. "I know they were enemies, but I don't understand it. Not completely." Not when he recalled hearing Dorilian's promise to Marc Frederick. *Look after my family.*

Robdan would not meet Hans's gaze. "Surely he could tell you better than I."

"He refuses to talk about Stefan."

"That's surprising, given the strength of his opinions."

"But you're not saying you don't know anything."

"No." Insect buzz rose from the grasses surrounding them. Something in Robdan's tone pleaded for patience and hinted at complexity. "You must understand that Stefan hated Dorilian. He hated Dorilian more, maybe, than he loved Amallar. I'm not sure why. They were both just boys when they first met, and later... I think it was in large part a carryover of the family quarrel. His grandfather and yours."

"Labran." Hans nodded. He and Dorilian had talked about that.

"And Stefan, well... his becoming King didn't remove the source of their contention. He had power, new power, but Dorilian had—still has—old power. Highborn, Sordaneon, Rill-given power—and Stefan feared it. He had watched that power threaten Marc Frederick's entire reign, and now it threatened his."

"Things didn't have to be that way." Hans was sure of that now.

"Probably not. Your grandfather opened another path. Or at least I think he tried to."

"And Dorilian never tried to know Khelds either."

"True, and his hatreds are well entrenched, from what I've heard." Something thoughtful touched Robdan's carefully chosen words. "However, he's an inoffensive houseguest."

"I was hoping for more than that." Hans caught Robdan's questioning look and sheepishly tried to explain. "I thought maybe you two would talk. I hoped he would loosen up, become less rigid in his views. See Khelds as people, good and bad."

"I think he will. It may be that he already does. He's difficult to read. I don't suppose he's very friendly with Staubauns either, and he's lived among them all his life."

Warmed by the sun and his uncle's clear-eyed sensibility, Hans relaxed. Without Robdan, he might have stumbled about in the forest, missing the vital point. "You're right, again." He recalled how seldom Dorilian seemed friendly with anyone at all, even in Sordan. "He's lived his whole life keeping people at arm's length. He may not know how to do anything else."

Robdan glanced around at the surrounding trees to make sure they were unobserved. The faedu rode far enough ahead not to hear them. "There's more. Something I think maybe you do not know. When Marc Frederick died," he confided in a lowered voice, "and most of the Highborn Princes of Essera died with him, Stefan was not alone in accusing Dorilian of the deed—but Stefan's voice was the loudest. In Amallar, Marc Frederick was forgotten as soon as he was dead. We had Stefan—a Kheld as King—the stuff of all our hopes."

Robdan shifted uncomfortably in the saddle and then continued. "Your grandfather's funeral was held two weeks after he died. Your Lady Mother and Stefan forbade Dorilian's attendance. And then when Dorilian didn't appear, talk grew that he had stayed away out of guilt for the deed."

He wanted to be there.

"They prevented him from mourning."

"Yes. Yet he consented to Marc Frederick being interred in Permephedon's Vault of Incorruption, among the Highborn Princes. It was a great concession. Quite unexpected."

To honor the deceased. To keep a promise. Dorilian honored Marc Frederick still, in ways Khelds could not imagine. "Is that where it went all wrong?"

"Not precisely, though it played a part. Stefan was not allowed inside the Vault to witness the great honor. Only the Highborn Princes attended—and *that* he resented. An obvious move to put him in his place, Stefan called it. It was a few weeks later, as Stefan prepared for coronation, that Dorilian came to see him." Robdan's face grew pensive, its creases more pronounced. "I was there, along with other of Stefan's kilth and kin from Amallar, and several of Essera's Staubaun lords were with him as well, men he had raised to his trust. Dorilian's appearance caught everyone off guard—it was right in the middle of a fitting and he just walked in. He was Hierarch by then.

"I witnessed with my own eyes and ears what happened next. Dorilian claimed Stefan had asked him to meet, which Stefan did not dispute, and then suggested that the two of them might be able to come to an accord of some kind."

"Stefan *wanted* to meet?"

"That's what I understood. It sounded hopeful."

So what had gone wrong? "Tell me the rest."

"Stefan would not listen. Instead, Stefan accused Dorilian again, in front of everyone, of having had a hand in the murders." Robdan peered with sadder eyes at the ranks of trees surrounding them, the peacefulness of the land through which they rode. "So many times I have thought back to that moment and wondered what would have happened had Stefan accepted that meeting, if they could have spoken. Or even had he simply let Dorilian withdraw in peace. He should have done that—if for no other reason than that Permephedon is neutral ground, sanctuary. But instead, Stefan attempted to have Dorilian arrested."

"I heard about that, from tutors," Hans admitted. Hearing it from Robdan somehow made it more real.

"It was a terrible thing to do," Robdan agreed. "Dorilian had all but said that he would attend Stefan's coronation because it was what Marc Frederick had wanted. The funny thing is I don't think anyone truly listened. And when someone, Goff Horvadson, I think, suggested taking Dorilian as a hostage and locking him up at Stauberg, just as Marc Frederick had done with Labran, Stefan leaped at the chance."

Hans could envision how the aftermath had unfolded. Anger. Words. More anger and more words. Stefan had committed an insult from which he had never recovered.

Of one thing Hans was certain: Dorilian had come to keep his promise.

"What happened after that?"

"To this day, I'm not really sure. Looking back, I can see that we dropped the vessel of Marc Frederick's new alliance and it shattered. Dorilian acted strangely, as though he was watching a troupe of performers playing out parts. I met his gaze—I remember thinking that he had wanted it to end differently." Robdan hesitated, then spoke quietly, as though he dared much to breach the subject. "Hans, do you think it's true, what people say, that the Highborn both see and create the future?"

"I don't know. I mean, I have yet to see any sign of that. Not in Dorilian, anyway. We all create the future, I think."

"But none of us see it ahead of getting there—and I think *he did*. I thought only Malyrdeons could do that, but the way Dorilian looked at Stefan that day—I don't know how to explain it, but I was suddenly afraid. I spoke up, but of course no one listened to me." A sudden quick wind skipped across the meadow, ruffling the grasses and the manes of the horses. "We never had a chance to stop what Dorilian did next. He grabbed Stefan and had a sword across his throat before we even realized he'd moved.

"He used Stefan as a shield, he and the men of his entourage. And then at the Rill, after he had reached it safely and had a *charys* ready to leave, Dorilian let Stefan go. Just let him go, though with many hard words. He could've slain him. Or taken Stefan with him to Sordan, done to Stefan what Stefan would've done to him. Everyone—even your mother, I think, for she was there also—thought Dorilian was going to do one or the other. I will never understand why he did neither."

"He may have thought it worse punishment to leave Stefan to face what he had done."

"Perhaps. It was almost like nothing changed. And yet everything did. Because all of us felt it. Oh, well." As Robdan looked away, across the meadow and into the shadowed bank of the forest, Hans thought he looked disappointed. "Maybe it is true after all that he set Stefan free for Marc Frederick's sake."

No wonder Stefan had hated Dorilian so relentlessly. Dorilian's continued existence reminded Stefan of that day, that humiliation. Stefan had chosen to do something dishonorable, and why? Because of his fear of appearing weak.

And he had gone on to do worse.

Robdan shook his head and patted his sturdy old horse on the neck. "I am one of the very few to say it, but Stefan was too much a Kheld and not enough a king. He never learned how to put aside his personal feelings to weave a political fabric. He lacked Marc Frederick's intuitive grasp of such things. All he knew how to do was try to change what was given him, try to stretch it to fit, cut holes where he thought they were needed—and he cut so many holes that the fabric began to unravel. He tried to force his Staubaun subjects to make room for us at their tables, and then raged when they didn't show up at the banquet. Marc Frederick did that too, but he also forced Staubauns *on us*. It wasn't pleasant to have ill-fitting shoes put on everyone's feet, but we all walked much more carefully then."

The trail had brought them to a stone marker, which Robdan leaned over to touch with a reverent hand. Many hands across many centuries had worn away the features from the stone face, and Hans asked to which god it was dedicated.

"To Lud," said Robdan, "whose name means Light."

They continued until they reached a wooden stockade, where Faedu Hellmer bade them dismount. Leaving their horses tied to posts beneath a ceiling of trees, they followed Hellmer's lead toward the stockade. A well-trodden trail cut across the leaf-covered forest floor. At the gate to the enclosure, Robdan rang a bell, the deep tones of which rolled through the stillness in a solemn knell. Within moments the gate swung open. Their guide led the way past stone dwellings and fragrant herb gardens tended by silent, brown-robed men. Some distance away, a paved area overlooked a sudden and surprising vale ringed by trees and bottoming out in a lovely silver lake. Students sat quietly on what looked like pelts, listening to the teachings of their master.

When they reached the edge of the vale, Faedu Hellmer bowed and then walked away, leaving Hans and Robdan alone to face the mighty pillars of the sacred oak grove. It was in this grove, Hans had been told during the journey, the god had planted a tree, the roots of which drank from the Well of Tears, the guardian waters of Amallar. While the Oracle Tree lived, so would the Kheld people.

Another figure appeared, framed by looming trees, and walked toward them.

"At least the bed is clear."

Lark bounced onto the mattress and assessed the general disorder of Aubrey's room. After leaving Nalf behind earlier, Aubrey had come upon Lark perched on a moss-stained barrel not far from the Common Well. After exchanging plans for the day, they'd walked to a handful of local shops to pick up the parcels Aubrey had bought days before and allow Lark to place orders of her own. The sun had just passed its height when they returned to the hallowed grove of the Barrowwood, where the great house of the Mothers stood shaded by the grove's Mother trees: the Thegn Oak and its many children.

Watched over by the Barrowwood, the Thegnkeld Motherhome was not as tall as Rhodhur Hall, but every bit as sprawling. Thegn women of all ages and callings found welcome here. Some sought shelter while traveling, some found healing or refuge, some stayed a short while to acquire training in a skill, and others resided as teachers or permanent residents. Aubrey paid an annual gift toward upkeep of a thatch-roofed cottage near the herb garden, one room of which was kept apart for her use. Two elderly Thegn sisters lived in the rest of the dwelling and maintained it in good repair.

Aubrey appreciated having a known place to stay on her visits and on this occasion was happy she could share her room with Lark. Regrettably, everything except the bed was covered by bolts of cloth, kegs of dried branroot, and boxes of shoes or books. Several large crates took up most of the room, and numerous smaller ones stood stacked under the room's lone window. Aubrey stashed her latest parcel in a gap between two of the crates.

Lark assessed the clutter. "Another successful year?"

"The Mother blesses industry. My crofters work hard and I see to their reward." Aubrey looked around at proof of Amundhal's prosperity. "So far, I've purchased and sent ahead a new loom for the weavers, five spinning wheels, and forty furs. You saw the bull for the dairy. And these goods are for the main house and loom croft: spindles and glass and yards of lace. And beads! Boxes of beads. Then there's that, for me." She watched as Lark ran a hand over a roll of soft woolen fabric Aubrey had chosen for a new skirt. The deep blue cloth shimmered in the gentle, ruddy light penetrating surrounding oaks. "It needs embroidery still. The sisters have agreed to do the work."

"New skirts have reasons."

"Good ones. I'll be standing for Saemoregh at the Witan. From the way Nalf is scheming, I think this one will be important."

Aubrey placed several late-season cuttings of cudweed and sweet trefoil from the garden onto the cloth and rolled it again before putting it atop her garment chest. She perched on the bed beside Lark. "I'm sending most of these parcels to Saemoregh in the morning with Wodd, along with the loom and my new bull." She was paying extra to send her goods and people by river, the better to travel with the beast.

"Wodd, your protection."

"Yes." Wodd had looked after Aubrey since she was a child. After her father's death, Wodd had organized the village to keep Aubrey safe and out of Staubaun hands. Since then, Aubrey had made Wodd captain of her men and appointed Hild, his wife, to be Amundhal's steward, with a portion of the estate to support their family. "I'm safe here, and it's where I need to be. Wodd can deliver everything and return, with more news, before I have reason to travel again."

"Others travel."

And what might that mean? Lark's cryptic half smile revealed nothing close to an answer.

Aubrey considered. "If you mean Hans, everyone knows he rode to the Grove this morning—and don't say you told me so." The Sacred Grove was sanctuary of the Faeduadan, adherents of Lud. Amallar's men had wasted no time going to their god.

Lark cocked her head, which caused a flight of embroidered birds to ripple across the fine scarf at her neckline. "Mother Aegdnis laid the Wheel."

A chill crept down Aubrey's spine. Aegdnis Breggeda was Rhodhur's most formidable matriarch, kilth to half the Thegnkeld. The ancient crone was revered for the exactitude of her readings. Women such as Aegdnis held power sufficient to wither men like Nalf Rhys at the knees.

"Did her Wheel reveal any portents worth knowing?"

"Travel. Conflict. Men on the move, making plans. Secrets and prophecies and events that they wish to conceal from the Mother."

"That's because they're planning war," Aubrey reasoned. "Men think the Mother stands in the way of that."

"They think too small. Wars are part of the Mother's Path; they do not supplant it."

Because the Mother's Path, unlike Lud's, was generative, time-spanning, and little concerned with human obsessions. Aubrey had spent enough hours with men to have learned that Lud's paths were easier to see and predict. "There's nothing small about war," she said. "You know what I think? I think the Mother might want to be less mysterious. Look around! Everywhere are signs of danger and hope—and yes, war. It's happening already. The powers of this world are thundering toward battle. Sordan and Mormantalorus, and Essera too, just like my cousin Cullen used to warn." Sadly, as far as Aubrey could recall, the world had never been otherwise. "There's something big going on. Great forces are on the move and not just in the northlands; they're at work *here*, in Amallar. We aren't going to be watching from the sidelines this time. We can't afford to. Our moment might well have arrived—so why doesn't the Wheel say something about *that*?"

Lark drew together her brows, thinking hard. "It does. Portents of change. Great change. Great movement. Changes create conflict and opportunity."

"Yes. Because we're all sleeping atop a woodpile of kindling." Aubrey wished more people would realize just what was going on. "This reading is about Hans. It *has* to be. Our chance to have another Kheld as Essera's King flies in the face of great forces."

Lark shook her head. "No, not him. Not Hans, not by any of his names. The Wise Mothers have long had knowledge of his rune—and this morning, just to be sure it had not changed, Aegdnis herself had Hans Thegn draw from her bag. When Aegdnis laid the Wheel, she placed his rune on a stave of ash. The portents were clear. Hans Thegn will gather men by the thousands to his cause. Handurin Stauberg-Randolph, too, is a name that will draw men to his side. By these names he will command a host and with them he will ride the Change as an otter rides the rapid. But he isn't the Change, neither as Hans Thegn nor as Handurin. He's Change's herald; he brings travel and battle, but he is not the Change."

Some of Lark's jumble of an argument followed what Aubrey knew. Hans wanted an army, and he wanted to take that army into Essera. But so far any change he might bring looked precisely like what Khelds wanted to begin with. "Then how is the Wheel not centered on Hans?"

"The Wheel reveals What Is. It cannot reveal what is Not Yet or Might Never Be. Here or then, Hans Thegn or Handurin Stauberg-Randolph, he already Is. The runes did not reveal the Change because it doesn't yet exist—only that which can bring it."

"Hans?"

Lark scrunched her face. "The Wise Mothers do not say."

"You tested Aegdnis' runes, I hope, before she laid this unhelpful Wheel."

Lark's blue gaze narrowed. "I would never allow anyone to lay a Wheel with corrupted runes."

No, of course not. No Rappeleye woman would. Aubrey ducked her head with apology. "I'm just so frustrated. My runes have told me nothing either, about Hans or anyone else. Would you test them?"

She pulled the velvet pouch from the sack of leather at her hip and spilled the runes onto the coverlet. Twenty-seven stones bluer than Lark's eyes glinted with flecks of midnight and silver: one stone for every day of a woman's course. Aubrey had been given them on the day she, Lark, and Nilla had met the Crone. From the moment Aubrey's fingertip had touched the stone bearing her runesign, she had known this set was meant for her. The ensuing years had revealed just how fine her stones were.

Lark slid Aubrey a cheeky grin. "Now you have a use for me."

"I will always have need of you. No one else here understands me at all."

"Wodd does."

"No other *woman.*" The difference mattered. Men never saw a woman clearly. The Mother always stood in their way.

"Hmm." Lark picked up one of the stones. "I remember when Grandmother gave these to you. Stones blessed by the Mother, she said, worthy of a girl portended by the Crone."

"As were you. Your stones are blue too."

"I'm a Rappeleye."

It was reason enough. Blue runestones, the rarest and truest kind, were found only beneath a single hill on Rappeleye land, which stood at the border of the otherworldly Bogs, a wilderness given to strange storms and tremors and other restless things. Rappeleye land possessed properties other land did not—mysterious powers of wood and stone, water and earth—and so did its women.

The oblong metallic sliver Lark fished from her pocket was lead-dull, homely, and vaguely human-shaped. Just by touching it to a rune, Lark would know if that rune's magic ran true or had gone sour. One by one, Lark tested the silver-flecked runes.

"All true." She tucked the nurse stone back into her pocket.

"Maybe I should lay my own Wheel tonight, seeing as the one laid by Aegdnis told us nothing." Aubrey gathered her stones.

"Only a fool lays a Wheel without clear purpose." A reading without apt questions was doomed to be false.

"I have purpose."

Dubious, Lark fixed Aubrey with an inquisitive look.

"I do." Since arriving at Rhodhur a week ago, Aubrey had

become a bundle of nothing *but* purpose. "I want to make sure my country and people don't do anything foolish. Will you be here for the Witan? Please tell me you will be."

Lark wrinkled her nose, then tumbled her runes onto the bedcover. Brilliant blue, they scattered the scant light. She plucked one and showed it. *Llalof. Llalof* meant "discord" and was Lark's runesign. Its secondary meanings were just as unfavorable.

"Even Old Mothers hold me at arm's length. They and a host of long-bearded chieftains forbid me from attending meetings attended by men."

"Because you told them the truth."

"And I would do so again. Because they are doing the same things, as if the results would be different this time." To Aubrey's questioning look, Lark cocked her head. "Look at the pattern. They presented Stefan with the women they wanted him to choose—with Nilla and me and you—rather than have a period of courtship so that a woman might choose him. Then, they wanted to follow Stefan as King, do as he wanted, more than they wanted to follow the Mother. Now, they are aflame with the idea of this Hans being King."

"And they are forcing him into their direction, just as they did Nilla," Aubrey realized. Rather than follow the Mother, Kheld men—and maybe the Old Mothers too—were trying to create a path of their own.

"We may be part of it." Lark's brow furrowed and she toyed with another of her stones. *Perhd.*

Aubrey gave a half frown to her runesign, drawn by the Crone that fateful day. Lark was not wrong that both their fates were still in motion. "Nalf thinks I should pursue Hans Thegn."

"Bed him. Wed him."

"Tie him down."

Lark swept back her hair with one hand and picked up her runestones again with the other. "The pattern repeats. A twisted path bent back upon itself."

"Doomed to fail."

"They do not see it."

But Aubrey and Lark saw it. And so would the Old Mothers, if they would but open their eyes to what was taking shape within the Wheel.

19

They believe they can see the future by drinking the blood
of slaughtered things.

Opareon, *On Khelds*

Hans watched the newest faedu approach and was glad to have Robdan with him. Even though everything about this day felt unsettled, this felt... different. The secretive figure's robes of deep red, the color of blood or of autumn oak leaves, swirled around a body that was tall for a Kheld. For that reason alone he would have been imposing. It bothered Hans more that the faedu's head was covered—and his face hidden—by a deep hood. Long sleeves did not cover the faedu's hands, however, which emerged, pale and strong, extended in the formal greeting of those consecrated to the god.

"Have you a token for the god?" The voice, light and cold, expressed only purpose.

"Do you know who I am?" Hans asked. Already, the feeling of ritual filled every space, every moment, every word being exchanged.

"Our late King Stefan had a brother. You are he."

"Then you know why I have come."

For a moment Hans detected an unpleasant firmness in the bare suggestion of a mouth above the beard, which alone of the faedu's face was not covered. "Wise rulers seek the advice of the oracle. Wiser still, those who are not rulers yet." The faedu again held out his hand, palm up. "Have you a token by which the god may know you?"

Because Robdan, Nalf, and a passel of Old Mothers had told him of the requirements of the ritual, Hans had prepared himself. He wore a white tunic beneath his travel cloak and had brought the knife for the sacrifice to be performed in his name: iron and gold, with a single red crystal embedded in the pommel. Nalf and his chieftains had pushed Hans to take it. He withdrew the ceremonial blade from his belt and handed it hilt first to the priest, who bowed over it.

"Do you dedicate yourself to the powers of earth and sky?"

"Yes."

The robed man turned to Robdan. "You are not needed." To Hans he said, "Come with me."

The Great Grove opened before Hans, an arching cathedral of intricately interwoven branches and rustling red leaves that would slowly brown but would not fall until spring arrived. Those who entered here walked upon sacred ground, beneath the gazes of giants. Deep within the grove, in a softly lit clearing surrounded by an impenetrable silence, Hans found himself facing a stone altar. Beside it, a young white horse stood between two posts. Chains around the horse's neck bound it to the iron rings of the posts. Above all this, peeking through the branches of the trees, the clear blue vault of the sky was bright, cloudless.

From the shadowy recesses of the altar, the faedu brought forth a shallow bowl and raised it to the heavens. Whispering the names of different gods and their many offices, he poured into the bowl the contents of a narrow-necked flask he had carried in his robes. When the incantation was done, he cradled the bowl in his hands and turned to Hans, holding it out to him to drink. The bowl burned to the touch. Every nerve in Hans's body begged him to drop the thing, to run from the clearing and this red-draped man whose unseen face withheld the secrets of Hans's fate. Even the liquid seemed murky and heavy, and it occurred to him that it might be blood.

I can't do this! The thought of drinking that unknown brew made his stomach rise. Worse, he could not contemplate the sacrifice of that beautiful animal without feeling a sickness take root in his soul. *I can't let them kill some poor animal for this hocus-pocus I don't even believe in!*

But the price would be heavy if he did not. Nalf and the chieftains had made clear that this ceremony was required of Hans, if ever he expected the Khelds to accept him as a leader. The Faedic Rituals were powerful and ancient remnants of the worship of a different World. A different Creation. He was among those people now, whose customs Hans had to observe and tribal gods honor, their sacrifices make. If he didn't permit the sacrifice, he would be declared a heretic, a man with a false heart.

They seek to bind me to them.

This is my rite of passage, he thought. *This makes me one of them. Is NalfRhys counting on me not doing it?*

In Sordan, mere months ago, Dorilian had asked Hans to take part in a mysterious ritual intended to bind them. It, too, had involved blood. That had worked out reasonably well. So far. Maybe this bizarre ceremony would prove worth doing also.

Hans raised the bowl and drank. The thick and clotted liquid tasted salty-sweet and coated his throat with a leaden, milky heaviness that refused to dissipate. Upon the altar, the bright flickering flames of the eternal fire began to burn within a brazier of horns.

An unfamiliar and fluid coldness settled over him, a strange disconnection from his limbs. Hans felt his body sway and struggled not to fall. The faedu's muttered incantations to the god became a droning litany that filled Hans's ears and flung his sight upward to the heavens.

I'm drugged, he realized. Overhead, the moon sang with a soulful warble. Its thin crescent wandered ghostlike through a gap in the towering branches of a mighty oak which, roots in earth, seemed to hold it captive. Earth and Sky. One was firmament and one was dust. But which, Hans wondered, was which? Before his eyes, Sordan rose in white splendor from its blue lake, the Rill streaming outward as currents of pure light. Permephedon towered in the distance—far, so far away—as the World shrank, retreating into shadow, the firmament opening....

Hans stood high above the sea and his wings closed the sky, his hand stretched out to calm waves beneath which Mulsor waited like a fulgent wound. A mighty battlement rose before him, white heights in motion upon cliffs above a blue sea, and he thought to move, that he might stand upon it. Upon the Wall and all that Was or Might Be or had ever Been.

Thaa placed their hand before his face. *This fate belongs to another.*

Hans turned aside to where the sea uncurled to show him a single bright tower piercing sea and sky. He reached out his hand and touched it with his fingertips. His vision exploded with light, carving the heavens like swords, beautiful and bright, and voices penetrated his dream.

...Five Cities built We under the Sky in the Ages Unremembered....

In a sudden, white-scattering penetration, Hans saw beyond this fragile, enclosed Creation, the precious sphere of his existence, and glimpsed the shimmering black silence of eternity, a billion blazing suns burning through space, crowding down upon this tiny speck of wonder.

And then the vault of the gods was gone, vanquished by the sky-blue veil of the Creation's dance with the Sun. The World reasserted; Hans watched as the faedu lowered the token knife into the water of a small stone well nestled among the tree roots upholding the altar. The faedu's hand withdrew the blade wet and running, precious millionfold molecules shattering into prism globes as they fell. The faedu then knelt and daubed the red crystal in the handle with a pinch of sacred earth scooped from the forest floor. This done, and with more invocations, this time to Bel who lived within the flame, the faedu plunged the golden blade deep into the eternal fire, where the moisture clinging to it crackled and the sizzle of escaping steam summoned an even more imposing silence.

"Bare to the god thy heart." The faedu's command transfixed Hans's will. With hands that obeyed but slowly, Hans unlaced his tunic and shirt to expose the skin of his chest.

"Lud, take his heart." The red-robed celebrant made a cut the length of the breastbone. Hans felt his skin open to release a bright trickle of blood and a dull, belated pain. "Bare to the god thy hands."

Again Hans obeyed, only vaguely aware of the blood running down his chest and into his shirt.

"Lud, take his deeds." The knife cut across Hans's palms between thumb and fingers, bringing forth more blood and more pain. "Bare to the god thy head."

The faedu grasped Hans by the hair and placed the knife against his right temple, where the tip pierced skin and the small blood vessels lying there in wait. "Lud, examine his soul."

Blood trickled down Hans's hair and onto his jaw, then neck.

With strong hands, guiding a man who was little more than captive through the motions of the ritual, the faedu led Hans to the horse. There Hans pressed his bleeding palms upon the animal's neck and again upon its belly, staining the flawless white coat with handprints of red. Hans savored the caress of warm, living skin, its vitality throbbing beneath his hands, and he willed it to live, but when he was pulled from its side, the sight of his blood upon the horse's hide glared like wounds already given.

The knife will kill.

The priest forced Hans to his knees before the altar. The knife was wiped in the blood still wet upon his chest, first one side of the blade, then the other. The knife was then laid upon the altar, where it glistened with a sickly red light as dappled sunlight filtered down upon the stone. Hans stared at that blade, trying to form thoughts and finding he was getting better at that. Intuitively, he knew that the knife had killed. But had it killed already, or was that yet to be? The Past had become the Future had become the tether of here and now. Immobilized by the motions of the ritual, he could but stand, not knowing what he did or what to expect. The faedu touched fingers to the blood oozing from Hans's head, then marked the four corners of the altar while intoning the protection of earth and water, wind and fire. After that, weaving a little from blood loss and pain, Hans followed some other faedu, maybe an acolyte, back to the clearing just outside of the grove, where Robdan sat upon a bench turning a small ball of something in his hands. Quickly tucking the ball inside his shirt, Robdan rose and darted to Hans's side.

"Hans, lad, are you all right?" Robdan reached an arm around Hans's ribs to support him. Something very akin to alarm showed on his pale face.

The faedu, now that Hans was in Robdan's care, turned and left.

Robdan tended to Hans beside a broad and shallow stone bowl into which ran the water of a sacred spring. Granite visages of gods as weathered as the one near the entrance to this place watched from the surrounding growth. Realizing that his ordeal was over, Hans knelt upon the damp and mossy ground next to Robdan, cupped his hand in the spring, and lifted water to his lips, wanting more than anything to wash the foul taste out of his mouth. The water tasted like iron. Not knowing what else to do, he sank back on his buttocks and took deep breaths, submitting to Robdan's ministrations as the Kheld dabbed a bit of cloth at wounds no longer bleeding.

"I feel weak, that's all. I didn't expect—" Hans drew away from Robdan's hand. "That asshole drugged me." He lifted fingers stiff with blood to explore the cut on his head. The wound felt rough, already crusting over.

For a long time Robdan said nothing. Using handfuls of grass and water from the sacred pool, he cleaned what blood he could from Hans's face, hands, and chest. At intervals, Robdan's gaze strayed to the pillared shadows of the Great Grove and its mysteries. The rites of the Faeduadan were secret to all but a handful of privileged guardians.

After a few more swipes at making Hans presentable, Robdan stepped away. He removed his jacket, then his shirt. He handed the latter to Hans. "Take yours off and give it to me. Put on this one." Shirtless, Robdan slipped back into his jacket and fastened every buckle and button to cover his torso.

Hans pulled off the bloodstained white tunic and gratefully donned Robdan's plain buff shirt. Other than the sleeves being short, it didn't fit too badly. "I suppose this is better. Thank you."

"Best not to raise questions." Robdan thrust the ruined tunic into his gear. He glanced up at the sky. "It's late, and we'd best be going."

"Wait." Hans stopped and looked toward the grove. "Shouldn't we find out what they say?" Something stronger, however, was urging him to leave. Now. Before someone would want him to slaughter his own sacrifice, or in some other way participate in what was to follow.

"There's no point, really. Unless you don't feel well enough—"

"I feel fine. A little lightheaded, maybe. I'm not used to having men bleed me."

"They usually don't." Robdan handed over a cloak, which he'd held along with the rest of Hans's items. "Your part is done, lad. The Faeduadan must now plot the omens and make the sacrifice. And they must make the drink before they can read the stars. It will take at least another week for them to interpret the portents. And we still have daylight enough to get back to Rhodhur."

Hard determination looked at him from Robdan's face, telling Hans they must get away from this place. That, as much as anything, persuaded Hans to go.

The sun had visibly lowered. They rode away in silence, Hans at every step listening for the scream of something being slain. The morning had begun with fear about Dorilian but now Hans felt only fear for himself. Nalf had said Hans must prove his Kheldish heart, that submission to this test would sway the Kheld people. Make Hans one with them and the land.

Instead, Hans couldn't shake the feeling that all the darkness in Amallar's heart had turned against him.

When they were well away and had reached the clearing where they had spoken earlier, Hans called a halt, though the day was growing late.

"Why were you so anxious to leave?"

Robdan looked down at his hands, neatly folded upon the horn of his old saddle. "I didn't like what they had put you through."

"Isn't that what we came to do? The sacrifice, the omens, and all that stuff?"

"It's—that." Robdan waved his hand vaguely, uncomfortably, at the traces of blood still visible on Hans's wounds. "And drugging you. You don't know what that means, but I do. I tell you truly, Hans, I thought it would be a simple sacrifice—a ram or perhaps a young goat. But they had you consecrate the horse this afternoon, didn't they?"

Hans stared at him. "What does *that* mean?" Dreamlike, in the clearing before him, Hans envisioned again the stone altar, the strong form of the young white horse shying away from the blood on his hands.

This time Robdan studied the fraying laces of his saddle rings. "Long ago, in our earliest home in an Age now legend," he confided, "our people often sought to discern the larger fate of our tribe through a practice we later outlawed, that of human sacrifice. One of the keld-chiefs would submit himself to the knife. Sometimes an important captive was used. The practice is very ancient and powerful. We... replaced it with this."

What seized Hans's throat felt like a clot. "You mean, the blood—*my* blood?"

With a ragged sigh, Robdan nodded. "Yes. The ritual consecrated the substitution of the horse's life and blood for yours in the actual sacrifice."

"Robdan—" Dry-mouthed, Hans stared in horror. "Is that what they were doing, back there? Symbolically *killing* me?" The pent-up nausea of his experience churned in his stomach, threatening to spill from him then and there.

"Not yet. That happens when they kill the horse. Hans, please, don't judge us by it." Robdan's distress was palpable and sincere. "I shouldn't even be telling you this. The rite is secret and seldom done. But I don't approve of trickery, and I think you should know. I think someone put them up to it."

Killing him. In symbolic form, at least, the Faeduadan were going to kill him tonight. Slashing the horse's throat would in their eyes be no different from slashing Hans's own. And when they took the steaming entrails from its belly—would they have rather had his? He had sent ahead word of his coming—who had decided that he should be made the sacrifice?

"Who ordered it? Nalf?" Something in Hans's tone caused Robdan to flinch.

"I don't dare guess." Overhead, the blue sky was rapidly fading to pinks and purples. "Once you consecrated the horse, you lost the privacy of your fate. The Faeduadan must declare the omens. Nor will they make these known until the High Witan meets in another full passing, when they will make the portents known to all. When your horse is sacrificed, the Faeduadan will be predicting not your fate, but the fate of all Amallar."

"And what if the Faeduadan say that the omens are not auspicious? Will that turn Amallar against me?"

"It could. More likely, you would be asked to put yourself right with the god. Oaths and trials, perhaps even a sacred marriage." Robdan shook his head. "Your fate now rests within the sacrifice. They have stolen it from you."

They reached Rhodhur later that night beneath a crescent moon ringed by frost, when the lights of the Hall cast golden patterns on the courtyard from its myriad doors and windows. Chimney smoke curled like guardian phantoms in the chilled night air. Hans saw Arne waiting in the lantern light of the entrance. Standing outside that light, a shadow painted by moonlight, was Dorilian. He walked forward and reached up to grasp the bridle of Hans's horse.

"I have thought about it," Dorilian said. "I will ride to Bellan Toregh."

20

The Wall and Rill played no part at all in shaping the First Creation. Their progenitors, the Three, were creations of the Second. The Jharbalan Initiates believe the Second Creation is ongoing and that the Entities are its architects. Leur's plan is revealed in the final words of Derlon to his sons: "It is in your natures to carry out acts of creation."

ZAMENES, *ON THE NATURES OF GODS AND MEN*

Pitar Kisthoda occupied space. So did all men, but it was the *way* Pitar claimed space that Chyralane found disconcerting. Pitar did not fill the Customhouse's grand reception hall with powerful or majestic presence, as did most people of rank; neither did he allow the marble and gold grandeur of his surroundings to diminish him in any way. The silver eagle aglow upon his forehead and the white metal horns upon his Circlet of Order imparted too much importance for diminishment. No. Pitar simply managed to be *present* in a way Chyralane found impossible to dismiss. Annoyed by Pitar's significance, Chyralane swept into the room with a flourish of ruby-dusted robes.

"Denizens." The subtlest of bows, barely a nod, accompanied Pitar's greeting.

"Archmage," Chyralane acknowledged. With a thrust of her chin, she indicated for the two men attending her—Iphithus Koillos and Geron Thoptis—to precede her and their guest to the more intimate seating of the Rillview Hemicycle at the opposite end of the chamber. The vaulted semicircular alcove was renowned as much for its beautiful architecture as for the view it framed. "I take it you have news."

"Little, other than that I am resuming my office in the city," said

Pitar. After the other Denizens had taken their seats, he too settled in a chair in front of the sweep of windows that looked out upon the Rill Mount and, behind it, the golden angles and massive domes of the currently uninhabited Rillhome. "The Psilant has chosen to remain at Permephedon. In addition to not wishing to undertake the long journey, he can monitor the Entity from Permephedon nearly as well as he could from Sordan."

"In the Entity's current state"—Chyralane gestured to the window and the Mount's unmoving arches and rings—"your office here is obsolete. Your presence in this city is pointless. Aside from presiding over the College, you have nothing to order and nothing to do. Unless you anticipate the Rill will resume function?"

Which of course Pitar did. Everyone anticipated that eventually, somehow, whether by choice or coercion, Dorilian would return the Rill to a working state. Chyralane closely attended the way Pitar's expression remained unrevealing. This man, then, knew nothing; neither would he offer false hopes. He crisply pointed to the window and the inert crown atop the Rill Mount.

"My office, though you despise it, is in service to that Entity. Its presence here is of great importance and so too, we believe, is its continuation. This stasis will resolve at some point. That resolution may involve changes and, if that is the case, I am to mediate the outcomes."

"Hah! Changes are afoot already. If you have not heard it is only because your journey here has rendered you deaf."

"Handurin?" Pitar inclined his head to show he listened, but did not reveal his thoughts. "You confirm the rumor?"

There was no point in denying what even the makers of chamber pots already knew. "Emyli's pup is in Amallar. The Khelds have been braying that news up and down the river. Every spy in every quarter of the Triempery knows where Handurin is to be found. Even Sordan has word of it. The communication array at Askorras still functions." Chyralane and all Essera cursed the destruction of the Sordan array in the immediate aftermath of Marc Frederick's contentious coronation. Fifty years and no replacement had been fashioned. But the Askorras array was not so far from Sordan as to be unuseful.

"And what do your sources make of Prince Handurin's appearance there?" Pitar queried.

What was there to say? Misdirection at this point would bear no fruit. Pitar was too potentially useful to be fed only dreck. "We believe Dorilian is aware of the situation—and has been aware of it all along. Either Handurin made his own way free of Sordan by way of help or Dorilian himself orchestrated it. What happened with the Rill is beyond clear: Dorilian stopped it to keep his enemies in the dark. Us, to be sure, but he has others. We have a report that Erenor sent an assassin to Sordan, a poisoner, to eliminate the Prince. The attempt happened—but it failed. That alone might have prompted Dorilian to play his pawn early rather than continue to hold him."

Pitar nodded, lips pressed. "And the Hierarch? Where do your sources place him?"

Chyralane smiled, though she tempered that expression. What the Seven Houses knew would not yet have reached Pitar's ears or those of the Order still at Permephedon. "We do not know where Dorilian is for certain. He was at Jharbala. Of that our sources are sure. Since his return from there, however..." She pondered how much to say. "The Rill still runs between Randpory to Hestya. Troop and supply movements to and from Hestya have increased, as have those to Randpory. Sordan has moved at least one army out of Gignastha and Neuberland, we believe into Merrydn. We do not know its ultimate destination." She gazed unhappily at the unmoving Entity looming above her confederation's city and fortunes.

"It is possible Dorilian is *with* that army," Iphithus said. "It is also possible he is still in Sordan. Unfortunately, the Serat has become impenetrable; our sources no longer hear anything out of there at all. We do get some word out of Askorras and Gignastha, though. Askorras does not place him in Hestya. Gignastha does not place him **there**. We have, however, been informed of activity and a display of the Hierarch's banners at the Tarlon Palace in Randpory, which is a possible indicator of his whereabouts."

"In Randpory."

By the way he said it, Chyralane could tell Pitar found the news intriguing. Two of the most important pieces in this emerging conflict were on the move. Whether Handurin and Dorilian moved together or in opposition was the vital question to be answered. Recent speculation had suggested the Rill stoppage too might have originated from Randpory.

That Dorilian might be preparing to make a long-anticipated move into Essera was only too clear. Princes didn't move armies without purpose. But which prince? And whose purpose?

"He would not leave the surety of the Rill's protection." Chyralane said the one thing about Dorilian of which she was certain. "Since the day of his birth we have studied that Sordaneon, waiting to see what he might become. The Demise all but crippled him— and the attacks that followed, betrayal then assassination, finished the job. The Rill is his sword but also his shield. This is a man afraid of being caught without his weapons. We saw that when he came to the Archhalia wearing the Coronal. He would not leave himself vulnerable. Dorilian Sordaneon is in Sordan—or he is in Randpory, armed with his Entity." Chyralane folded her hands upon her gold-sashed belly. "And he will not leave either place without an army at his back."

An army he would use hand in hand with the Rill to drive like a sword into Essera's heart.

Iphithus leaned forward. "The prevailing thought is that Handurin is a distraction," he counseled. Clearly, he feared that Pitar might not grasp a conclusion the Seven Houses had already embraced. "The Prince's possible whereabouts, whether true or untrue, whether Dorilian assisted him or not, excite Essera with rumors. Some factions favor the Prince; others do not. Erenor focuses on his imperiled regency, and not on the Hierarch."

"We would also have that be so." Pitar rubbed the gold bracelet on his right wrist. The Ring of Order on his left hand glinted in the chamber's filtered sunlight. "Please understand, the Order strives always to stand outside these politics. Our place is beside the Entity, never in opposition. None of us know Derlon's mind; it cannot be fathomed by mortals now—but we still have access to that of the Sordaneon. The Hierarch's well-being is paramount."

"For us also. Our highest goal is to protect the bloodline of Derlon."

Pitar's brief smile faded. His mouth folded into a frown as he gazed upon the tableau of the silent Mount framed by grand bridges and bright canals, splendid villas, and the Rillhome towers ablaze with the sinking rays of the sun. "Then let us hope, for all our sakes, the Hierarch remains where he is safest: in Sordan."

21

Their women start in gentle beauty and end as fearsome
hags.

OPAREON, *ON KHELDS*

"The Faeduadan did this?"

Hans winced as Aubrey sought to get a better look at his head wound by parting the hair at his temple. As she probed the cut, Hans flinched and dug his fingers even harder into the arms of the chair. Arne stood nearby with an oil lamp in hand, shifting from foot to foot and swathed in worry. Fetching Aubrey to look at Hans's wounds had been Arne's idea and Hans was going to have a few choice words with him later.

"Stop squirming," Aubrey complained.

"It hurts!" Hans snapped. "You keep pulling my hair."

She ceased poking and turned to Arne. "Bring the lamp over. I can barely see this."

"They shouldn't have done it," Arne said as he held the brightly burning lamp near enough to banish all hint of shadow. He met Hans's gaze of reproval with stubborn conviction. "Robdan said so when he was here. Going to the Grove don't usually mean they send people home bleeding."

"This barely qualifies" was Aubrey's reply. She dabbed at the cut with a cloth moistened with astringent. "All these wounds are crusted over. They're barely deep at all. You made it sound like he needed stitches."

"You should've seen him."

"Hey," Hans spoke up to remind them. "I'm right here."

Arne at least tried to look apologetic. "If Aubrey here says you're all right—"

"He's all right." Aubrey straightened and stepped back, assessing the cloth in her hand before tucking it into a pouch at her belt. "I'll put coverings on this cut and the one on his chest, along with a salve to ward off festering."

"Just the salve," Hans said. He noted their looks of surprise and explained, "Bandages draw attention. I don't want to run around with people asking what happened. I'll wear a hat. What about my hands?" He held them out.

"They should be fine. The cuts aren't deep. You can also easily explain them." Aubrey reached for the large leather bag she'd brought with her. "Just say you made a bond with the god."

A claim Khelds would believe, given it was also true. Probably. Hans decided it was time he put a moratorium on blood bonds with gods. "Right. Yeah."

Arne's snort likely meant he knew what Hans was thinking, but it was surprising to see Aubrey, wide eyes weighing Hans with sympathy, look like she understood. She chose a small jar from the collection in her roomy healer's case. The jar was one of several shallow, wide-mouthed pots made of what looked like porcelain. Each white pot bore a different design in its glaze. The one in Aubrey's hand yielded a brownish ointment that smelled like pine sap and honey, strong but not so much that it would alert the entire Hall to Hans's approach.

"They shouldn't have touched you, not with a weapon." Aubrey spoke carefully, perhaps because she was not—as a woman—certain of Lud's rituals. Frustration laced her conviction. Her touch, however, remained light and gentle.

"Damn right," said Arne.

Hans shot his friend a look of warning. Earlier, when Hans had retired with Robdan and Dorilian to this room and they had gotten a look at Hans's bloodied state, Arne had threatened to run out and give a good thrashing to the nearest faedu. Only confronting Dorilian standing in front of the door, barring the way, had kept Arne from barging down into the Hall and making a scene.

Dorilian's response to Hans's blood and dishevelment, on the other hand, had been withering. Something about Hans wandering into things like a mindless goat. Few reliefs had ever felt more merciful than watching Dorilian and Robdan leave some minutes later to prepare for their journey to Bellan Toregh.

He's taking Robdan with him. At least I got him to agree to that.

It was a triumph of sorts for Hans to have that weight off his shoulders. He should've felt more joy in his success. Just getting Dorilian to agree to... anything should have felt more monumental. At least Aubrey had finished with her ministrations and would also soon depart. Hans wanted to be alone with his failure for a while. Redolent with pine balm, Hans groaned and, elbows on his thighs, placed his chin on the knuckles of his gashed, ointmented hands.

"I've been doing this all wrong." His own voice startled him. He hadn't meant to speak those words aloud.

"You still are," Arne said, still planted with his arms crossed upon his chest, "if you let them get away with that."

Aubrey closed her leather pack, into which she'd replaced the pot of salve, along with her many bags and boxes of powders and herbs. "You've been away too long," she told Arne, "if you think he was given a choice."

"There's always a choice. He"—Arne pointed his chin at Hans— "keeps telling me that, every time he makes me decide my own course. And he does that a lot."

Hans sighed and spoke up before Aubrey could. "He's not wrong. I did face a choice. I didn't have to drink the potion. I could have left, turned my back on all of this. I thought about it." He met and held Aubrey's wondering gaze. "I chose Amallar."

Aubrey's mouth softened. She understood what he had done. To judge by the way he uncrossed his arms and gave Aubrey a slow nod, so did Arne. Together they watched Aubrey stand and lift her healer's pack to her shoulder.

"I hope the chieftains and Old Mothers take heart from your choice," she said. "Our gods are not gentle; they don't exist only to bestow grace or hand out blessings. Lud is a god of war and sacrifice. I hope our people don't pay too high a price for using you to get what they want."

With a tense nod, Aubrey left and closed the door quietly behind her.

Arne cut Hans a look. "What she just said—do **you** know what they want?"

Hans frowned. "Not exactly." That bit about sacrifice bothered him.

He watched Arne relax a bit more and was glad of it. He was even gladder when Arne strode to the chair and knelt beside it to give

Hans an apologetic head tilt. "Better you tell me what you think you're doing all wrong, because maybe that's not quite what's going on."

Maybe.

"Dorilian's here for the same reason I am. You realize that, don't you?"

Arne took a deep breath. "I'm not the one to ask, not about him and not if you want any kind of answer. Whole time you were away, we hardly exchanged five words. He hasn't killed any Khelds yet, which I count as good news."

The cut on Hans's chest burned slightly as he laughed for the first time since the Grove. Weariness enfolded him. He was so damn tired he might just sleep here in this chair. His eyes had closed already.

"I'm going to beat my naysayers," he said. "They've got me all wrong. The more they look for Stefan, the less they're going to find."

22

Leur counseled that all parts of Vllyr be destroyed. It is the
nature of a god that every part of it be divine—even so little
as an eyelash or tooth.

CIBULITUS, *ANNALS OF THE RETURN: THE FALL*

Deep beneath Aral, in the Halasseon Palace's tallest tower, the
Undying Crown hungered.

Nammuor had experienced its craving for well over a
decade: the way its voice filled his thought, the way its power
swelled, becoming ever more transcendent. He called it his Diadem,
as had the Aryati during Exile, and treasured knowing that the
immortal core of the device possessed power beyond the dreams of
mortal sorcery. Power irresistible. A jagged longing sharp as teeth
gnawed at the Diadem's fulgent core. Agony by agony, Nammuor
had awakened to its hideous purpose, had watched the crown reveal
itself to be a ravenous maw that would bore through the very
firmament to devour the singular prey that would make it whole.

Nammuor saw because he had helped his Diadem find that prey,
had brought it to the godborn's nest. Had aided in the slaying. The
taking. Had brought the Diadem to the brink of all Vllyr desired.

Had sought to sate it—complete it—and failed.

Now the malignancy within his Diadem clamored and clamored
and would not be silenced. Its prey had fled to safety and put itself
out of reach. And now the Diadem's hunger, unsated, tormented
Nammuor's every hour—asleep or awake, he hungered.

Like now. Nammuor sat draped upon the Halasseon throne and
gazed upon the device as it burned its desires into his hands. He wore
it often, for as long as he could bear its weight. It had been heavy

before—before he had added life crystals to feed it. Now twelve large crystals bristled in attendance of the Diadem's eyelike core. One of those crimson lifeforces held the immortal blood and brilliant power of the Prince who had sat on this very throne.

I sit here now, Elegiros. I, not your daughters or even their bastard get. Not one drop of your cursed bloodline remains.

The Diadem, Nammuor could tell, relished the extinction. In blunt, often crude, ways it had begun to communicate with him.

"Master?"

The reedy voice disrupted his attention. Nammuor glanced down the dais steps to the kneeling form of Bamatu, recently become Archmage at Aral. Although *lr* crystals could not be manufactured outside the Cities, with their magic harnessing power sources, Nammuor was able to import enough crystals to enable Bamatu and a few midlevel mages to craft simple devices.

"Yes?" Nammuor acknowledged.

"The linkage placement in Sordan's Serat failed. The device was detected and destroyed. The shield mirror—"

Bamatu cut off the rest of the report as Nammuor's hands tensed on the Diadem. "And was our agent captured?"

"We do not know. She and the crystal might have perished together."

"Try again."

Bamatu bowed. The silken edge of his red mage hood dipped forward to conceal his bright hair. "At once, Master."

"I am receiving far too many rumors from Sordan—and not enough verification. I'm not content with unconfirmed sightings or reports of reports. Is Dorilian in the City, or is he not? The man has advisors! Servants! Are there none who will verify, or testify, to have seen him? He's not an Initiate! He hasn't resigned his godborn body to a cell in penitence for evil deeds!"

Bamatu's bow became a prostration. "We will find him, Master."

Nammuor's attention snapped back to the Diadem in his hands as a frisson of something—impatience, perhaps—crackled across the Diadem's crimson facets and stabbed Nammuor's fingers with greed. The hunger never stopped.

As Nammuor watched Bamatu's form recede down the long, azure corridor of the throne hall, understanding took cold root. He had not moved quickly enough.

Vllyr's craving for Highborn blood and power had always

stemmed from something far more terrible. An immortal lifeforce would make for itself—if it could—an immortal body. The kind of body Nammuor's could not yet be. Lifting the beautiful monster so he might look into its single ravenous eye, Nammuor frowned.

I will give them to you, he vowed. *The last of Leur's children. Even the immortals. But I will do so on my terms. You were made a slave and will remain one.*

Mine.

The Rill runs only between Sordan and Permephedon,
making stops between those great Cities at the new young
towns of Leseos and Dazunor-Rannuli. However, the Rill's
existence before Exile can be found in other places.
Stauberg is crowned by the Wall, but a Rill mount
commands the center of its great harbor. Folk gaze upon
the arches and reflect upon the beauty of the City of the
Malyrdeons. But the Rill there is silent and still, a promise
yet to be fulfilled.

PATROLOCUS, *JOURNEYS TO MANY LANDS*

T hree days on the road brought Dorilian and Robdan to
Eastmeary Brenna, a teeming city less hemmed by hills than
Rhodhur. The town had been settled at the place where the
river Brennan left behind its hills to become a wider, well-behaved
waterway blessed to drain a prosperous land dotted with farms and
mills. Famed for bountiful crops, fat herds, and rolling hills planted
with branroot, Eastmeary Brenna was second in trade only to Skairen
on the Dazun River. Even Bellan Toregh, which straddled heavily
traveled highways to Leseos and Neuberland, held less importance.

Bringing Robdan had not been Dorilian's idea. He had wanted
to travel to Bellan Toregh without encumbrances, human or
otherwise. If he determined the Trestethion node could be made
operable, awakening the Rill was a dangerous process he didn't care
to demonstrate. Handurin, however, still feared that Dorilian might
encounter a Kheld who would recognize him or that he might need
help of some other kind, and for those reasons had insisted that either
Farrl or Robdan travel with him.

As things stood, Robdan provided a ready explanation for their absence. He'd only to express a wish to visit his daughters who lived outside of Eastmeary Brenna on properties inherited from their mother. To further embellish the tale, Robdan rented a pack mule and loaded it with a mountain of gifts for his veritable tribe of grandchildren. That Robdan would want a companion was understandable, so too that he might choose his Trongorian boarder.

Dorilian had gone along with the pretense solely because the story was a good one, even if it meant an overnight stop to be rid of the excess baggage.

"What is he? A mercenary?" Ressany lifted a porcelain cup, salvaged from a set she had purchased when she'd briefly lived in Tahlwent with her now-deceased husband. She eyed Dorilian with suspicion.

"He is… an emissary," Robdan explained to his eldest daughter. "From the Electorate of Trongor, here to observe and report on our preparedness to become allies."

"Well, whatever he is, the children like him."

That was good because there were quite a few. Robdan didn't see his grandchildren often and until this afternoon had not laid eyes on the youngest one at all. From the porch on which he and Ressany sat, he looked out at a bit of lawn upon which more than a dozen children, Ressany's and Trella's and those of their holders, played a game of ring toss with the Hierarch of Sordan. Each ring that successfully fell over the stake was announced by happy squeals and lifts high into the air. That Dorilian looked so at ease playing with children surprised Rodan; it pointed up how little he really knew about the man.

Robdan's middle daughter, Trella—mother of three of the children—sat on a bench amongst the fallen leaves of a nearby tree, reading a book to a toddler much as Robdan had once done with his daughters. Meanwhile, Ressany's youngest, little Ebbert, born after his father's demise, napped in the crook of Ressany's arm.

"I'm happy to see them enjoying the game." Robdan had purchased the ring toss in Rhodhur. The pine stakes were crafted with heads like those of geese and the rings were fashioned from sturdy red rope.

"Trella and I are happy to see *you*," Ressany said. "You're always away."

"You know why."

"Yes. I just wish there was someone else."

Only a year ago there had been. Bren Forbasson, who had been Ebbert's father. Goff. Lowen. Cullen. Men Stefan had ennobled, and all better suited than Robdan for the job of Archhalial ambassador. Though he was high clan and well educated, a scholar of modest repute, Roban was too little known in either Amallar or Essera to be of much influence.

"I don't expect I will be good for anything else with what's coming," he offered. "I'm not much of a fighter and there will be war with Essera before spring."

"Never fight a winter war—isn't that what all the old warriors say?"

"Yes. And with great wisdom." Robdan put aside his cup. He enjoyed a fine nog and Ressany had sufficient wealth to afford a good cook for her holding. "Hans Thegn trusts me and might seek to make me part of his war council. If so, I'll decline. My heart would not be in it. My expertise lies in finding reasons *not* to fight!"

"Even you can find reasons to fight Erenor Tholeros!" Ressany's voice hardened. "What he did to our lads! He sent back the heads and the bodies, but what of their lands? What of their names? The lands he stole and the names he dragged through the mud!" Her bitterness had strong roots: her husband had been one of the men hunting with Stefan that day and who Erenor had ordered killed.

"Hans is aware of these offenses. People remind him of them daily."

"Then he'd best do something about it."

The cook called from the rear porch of the house, announcing the meal. Trella put down her book. The children on the lawn abandoned their game and raced for the table at the back of the yard. Ressany rose in a flurry of mantle and skirt and, babe in arm, hurried toward the growing confusion as the household converged on food-laden tables. Robdan followed and had just rounded the corner when he remembered his companion and that he'd just left behind the Hierarch of Sordan.

Embarrassed, he turned back. Robdan stopped when he saw that Dorilian stood unmoving at the edge of the grass.

Dorilian had picked up the rings from the game and held all six red circles in one hand. He stood still as an indrawn breath, as still as stone. As still as the space between heartbeats. When he moved, his body flowed—a bend of the knees, a turn of the torso, one leg straightening from the hip and power racing upward into a sweep of the arm and opening of the hand. The six red rings spun into the air. Robdan followed their scarlet trajectory, the perfect arc as each ring appeared to overlap the other, not touching at all as they crested… then descended. One by one they landed neatly, red ring atop red ring as they stacked onto the grass, encircling the goosehead stake. Dorilian's arm had dropped back to his side, his body's energy no longer coiled, his neck bent as though in thought.

What had Robdan just seen? He had never witnessed even two rings thrown at once with success, though he had heard rumors. But six? Dorilian had tossed six in one throw and seen them fall, as if commanded, onto the stake. What ability produced such unnatural accuracy? Extraordinary command of the body and mathematics? Or some Highborn mastery of Leur gifts? Though but a ring toss, some such as Nalf would call it dark arts. Unsure of what to think, Robdan turned back toward his busy daughters and the laughing children. Back to food and familiar, wholly human things.

"Mealtime?" Robdan called out.

As he'd planned, Dorilian immediately joined him for a walk to the back of the house. It had been a two-day ride to get to Eastmeary, with stops at reasonably good inns. Robdan had chosen their accommodations with attention to the reputation of their kitchens. About Ressany's cook, he had no anxiety. The woman was superb.

"You warned them?" Dorilian prompted as the group came into view.

"No eels," Robdan confirmed.

Ressany and Trella had saved seating for them at the better end of the long table, the better end being more completely shaded by the heavy-crowned Mother oak of their great-grandmothers. Robdan sat beside Trella and Dorilian sat beside Robdan. Remi, Trella's eldest and Robdan's oldest grandson, won the battle to sit at the other side of their guest.

"That capon you're eating, I made him. Did it myself with a spoon. Grew him too," Remi proclaimed. His round face glowed with pride. It took many weeks to produce a fine plump capon.

"How excellent! Caponizing is a fine skill," Robdan praised the lad's work. Dorilian contributed an appreciative nod, then returned to enjoying his joint of capon, which had been stewed in milk and served with a delicious side of creamed leeks.

"Rem has his own flock," Trella added brightly. "Sells them around town. He'll always have work."

Puffed up with pride, Remi queried their guest. "What do you do?"

Robdan paused.

Dorilian took a moment to answer. "When not eating *excellent* food such as this, I like to boss people around."

The cook beamed. So did Ressany and Trella and Remi. Robdan relaxed.

"Does it work?" one of Ressany's wide-eyed daughters asked.

"Most of the time. I will demonstrate." Dorilian turned to the cook. "The bread, if you would."

The cook passed a basket of savory bread. The meal proceeded in good spirits, with happy children, a happy cook, and Robdan feeling as though he and his family had passed a test of some kind.

The morning following the visit, leading a mule laden only with their gear, Dorilian and Robdan rode across the Brennan Bridge into a land of low rolling hills and dense softwood forests, now leafless and gray. Two days later they crested a rise to glimpse the crown of Bellan Toregh.

Set upon a naked crag of storm-colored rock, the dormant Rill mount presented an otherworldly remoteness. Its pale inflorescent structures rose high above the trees, stately limbs spread and frozen above unmoving arches, a god trapped in eternal stasis. Afternoon sunlight, full and bright, added no warmth to structures that gave Bellan Toregh the same cold, surreal beauty as sister mounts in Leseos, Randpory, and Dazunor-Rannuli—except that those nodes were active and, in the case of Randpory, had limbs and rings engaged in motion.

As with other Rill nodes, a town had sprung up and crowded the foot of the hill. Bellan Toregh formed the crossroads of three vital highways: the Neuberland Road that connected Amallar to the turbulent settlements of Saemoregh and Anwithal; the King's Pike that traveled north to Dazunor-Rannuli and south to Leseos; and the River Floh. A prosperous community of farmers and herdsmen lived within sight of Bellan Toregh's mount, along with a burgeoning population of merchants and tradesmen. The latter prospered on light industry, Neuberland traffic, and a steady stream of the curious come to witness the silver passage of the Rill. But the

Rill no longer threaded the hilltop and so the curious had dwindled, and approaching winter was fast paring the numbers of travelers on the roads and river.

Dorilian felt a pang of regret as he gazed upon the dormant Rill node. Whether known as Trestethion or Bellan Toregh, it was but a footnote, all but unremembered. If there had ever been plans to vitalize this node, those plans had been abandoned long ago upon the ceding of Amallar by King Erydon. The village at the foot of the hill differed little from any other Kheld town. But different it was—and the sight of the Rill's immense limbs stretching above timber and stone buildings brought home to Dorilian the reality of his actions in Randpory.

Were he to go to Dazunor-Rannuli, Permephedon, or Leseos, this would be what he saw: the Rill motionless, frozen, and silent.

"It ain't there, yod."

The speaker wrenched Dorilian out of his thoughts. He glanced down from his horse at a disreputable-looking man in tattered clothes who leaned against a stone wall. The fool regarded Dorilian and Robdan with the mocking sneer of a village know-it-all.

"I think we should be on our way. It will take some time to purchase supplies," Robdan said.

The man moved to bar their way.

"Wastin' yer eyes, looking for it. The god-thing's dead, see. It don't *fly* no more." The annoyance hooked his thumbs in his armpits and flapped his elbows. "See there?" He jerked his head at the high tor. "Right through them tall ring-rocks Lud's spear used to fly, thrown by the god, faster'n you could see. Stand on the top and only sharp eyes'd see it coming, little piece of light, like... just that big, I tell you." He showed the tiniest space between his fingers. "Had to know where to look or you'd miss it, you would, and then it would hit the Toregh and if you got caught between the cold trees you'd be gone, just that fast, all or part of you." He spat in the road. "We test a man's courage that way. Make him stand in the cold trees until the god spear comes."

Dorilian was aware that sometimes lives were lost to the Rill from accident or ignorance, but to know that people made a game of it appalled him. Rill rings generated a clearing field to facilitate a nonstopping *charys's* passage, activating as it went, so that any spatial disruption created by the vessel was negated. The field effectively vaporized anything *not*-Rill. He doubted that many of the poor bastards whose bravery was proved by that method got out of the way in time.

Though the man offered to show them the Toregh, Dorilian declined. He would not waste time visiting the hilltop until he had first determined that the rings were in good order. It was a pleasure to leave the grinning yokel behind. It took little time to locate a market and purchase a small supply of food before heading again out of town.

"There will be twelve." Dorilian directed Robdan's gaze to the graceful arc of a ring that bracketed the northmost edge. "That is the twelfth." He lifted his arm to point across an open field to another structure that rose to the same height. "And that is the eleventh, with the tenth far behind. The others will be farther apart."

He was only mildly surprised to detect the rings as he rode along the course of the approach, the dance of Rill presence near enough that his senses picked up its fine vibrations. He had always done so near other manifestations of corpus but had not been certain he would feel it here. Although promising, the sensations were not the proof he sought.

Hours later, long after nightfall, they located the towering mass of the first approach bracket. Dorilian had not attempted to probe those nearer the town, using them only to mark the path to this one. If this structure could not do its job, if it could not generate a null field to halve the *charys's* initial speed, then the others would not matter: the *charys* would have sufficient velocity when it reached Bellan Toregh to break away from the containment field and enter the acceleration coils on the other side. There would be no stopping it.

Even though night was near and the sun only a glowing memory crowding the west, Dorilian swung down from his horse. He climbed an earthen mound built up over many centuries around the structure's massive base. The containment ring looked as if two colossal branches, wind-smoothed and twisted, had been thrust into the ground by opposing titans. Halfway to their ultimate height they bent again toward each other, towering above the trees, as graceful as cupped hands. Dorilian approached and laid his palm upon the silent structure. The surface was cold to his touch, so smooth his fingers tingled with the unnatural absence of tactile stimulation. *Cold trees.* He overrode the sensation while Robdan, who had also dismounted, clambered up the low incline to watch wide-eyed, expecting to see something miraculous.

"Can you tell?" Robdan prompted.

"Not yet." Dorilian resisted an urge to snap at the interruption. Robdan didn't know what Dorilian had been about to do or understand the concentration required to do it. "I need quiet. The only way to tell if Rill substrate is functional is to sound it. I have not done this for many years."

In truth he had never done it at all. Not by himself. Sebbord had assisted this work at Hestya.

"What do you need from me?"

"What I would appreciate most from you is silence."

"Yes, of course." Robdan looked visibly cowed. "I'll tend to the horses." He turned to go back down the slope. "I'll... set up camp."

When Robdan had gone, Dorilian took the Rill Stone from its secret place in the back casing of his compass and placed the ring on his finger. Itself a device, the Rill Stone was not magic, though not far from it: the genetic signature of Derlon's Eye, the central green gem, identified Dorilian to Rill corpus; the combination of immortal Sordaneon tissue and allelotropic metals embedded in the setting bridged resonant sequences within living Rill matrix. Dorilian pondered what he was about to do.

His affinity for the Rill was not what any of them imagined.

Handurin had assessed accurately: Dorilian had awakened the node at Hestya to proclaim Sordan's rebirth, to strike the one blow that would sever Essera's iron control of his birthright and remind them what the Sordaneon bloodline could be. From that one act, the rewards had been such that Dorilian had not needed to repeat the deed. He was powerful enough through their fear of him—of what he might be capable, what he might do... what he might *become*. They didn't know he feared the same thing they did. Even he did not know what would happen if ever he picked up the powers hidden within him.

He only knew why he had not done it.

I do not want to become their god. To set foot upon that road would be madness. Human was all Dorilian wanted to be. What he knew how to be, what he *needed* to be. For Levyathan and Fahme. For Sordan. Even for Essera. What he was attempting to do here in Amallar could set him on another path. Stopping the Rill at Randpory had cost him nothing. He had merely used his unique affinity to bespeak his ancestor, had set an operational limit, and embedded a restore sequence. He had touched nothing more than the Overlay's sheathing. But to bring a new node into Derlon's awareness demanded that Dorilian link with the corpus itself, allow the Entity to make incursions into his neurons, synapses, and blood.

Contact with the Entity changed him, however minutely, every time. Altered senses. Heightened acuity. Greater thresholds of summoned energy. Ultimately, the Rill would change Dorilian far more than he would ever change it.

Here, as he contemplated the Rill, even as he felt its hidden energies seeking pathways into his being, Dorilian knew himself enlarged. Nammuor was nothing to this. The Triempery was but a thing in passing, Dorilian's cherished flesh but an avatar, a conduit between realities—and between beings.

He touched the Rill Stone to the surface.

Robdan unsaddled the horses. He looked back only once to remind himself he would not be needed. Not for *that*. Truth be told, as a traveling companion Robdan was far from optimal. For one thing, he had never set up a camp before. He had always found an inn to stay in on his way or traveling companions who preferred to bypass his ineptness. He and Dorilian had enjoyed inns and the hospitality of Robdan's kilth all the journey so far.

When Hans had spoken of this plan right after their arrival back from the Sacred Grove, Robdan had felt a surge of excitement. He had just as quickly banished that exhilaration. It was too great a hope to imagine that the Rill could be brought to Amallar—or that Dorilian would even consider the matter. It was like something from the histories Robdan so loved to read, a thing at once compellingly real and the stuff of distant legend. Everything about the Rill had the remoteness of Highborn magic, lodged in Essera's romantic past, too powerful to be conjured in the familiar daylight of the Amallar Robdan knew. Awe kept drawing his gaze back to the massive structure that dwarfed Dorilian, who stood before it with such sure and perfect silence.

That was another unbelievable thing, that Robdan should be traveling in the company of a Sordaneon. Dorilian was the stuff of legend. Of Highborn myths and ancient Promises. Even more so, a creature of Kheld fears. Robdan had been at the Archhalia the day Dorilian had illuminated all three of the Thrones of Light and set aglow the Triemperal Seal of the Three. He had done so with but a touch. So what was a man armed with that kind of magic and power doing here? And why? Not just now, with the Rill, but with *everything*?

Hans had brought more into Amallar than just a claim to Essera's throne.

To clear his mind from such thoughts, Robdan set about making a fire, the one task at which he could claim some proficiency. The roots of any Rill structure spread wide and deep and the ground near those arches was always clear of trees. Fortunately, there were dry branches and other fuel to be found at the fringe of the nearby woodland. He had just gotten a nice flame going and put some meat pies to warm on the grate when he heard footsteps and turned to see Dorilian cross the low growth at the edge of their campsite.

"It worked?" Robdan could not read his companion's face.

"Yes." Dorilian scanned the meager comforts of the camp and appeared to find it acceptable. He lowered himself to sit on one of the blankets Robdan had placed near the fire. "Rill energy permeates it."

"And the others?"

"The first is always the most critical. Sounding the others will go more quickly. If they are functional, then I will be able to proceed."

"To awaken the Rill?"

Dorilian simply slid Robdan a look that asked what other purpose there might be.

Robdan resolved to make better inquiries. "Will that be difficult?"

Dorilian frowned, a sure sign he was irritated. "I won't know until I attempt it."

Curiosity compelled another question. "How do you do it? Did you study wizardry at Permephedon to be able to talk to Rill trees?"

Dorilian did not answer. Instead, he took a deep drink from his water skin and began eating one of the meat pies. Robdan wondered if he had offended him. There was about his companion a reserve he could not penetrate, though at Rhodhur of late it had seemed to fade. They had talked one night about books and poets, learning that they shared a love of Issahan. Dorilian had helped Robdan with a better translation into Kheldish of a verse from *Seven Springs in Agalor*. And then, quite abruptly, the distance between that Dorilian and the mask he showed the world had returned as they had set out for Bellan Toregh. With a sigh, Robdan conceded he must accept their new terms. He pulled his ball of string from his pocket and began to add to it from threads he had collected while in Eastmeary.

"What are you doing?"

Surprised by the display of interest, Robdan looked up. "This? Oh, it's nothing really. An old habit of mine handed down from my grandfather. I take pieces of string I find and tie them together and wrap them, you see, around sharp objects I keep in my pocket. There's a fishhook, or maybe two, in here. And a needle. And a nail. Useful things. And string, well… I have a fishing line if I need one, or can mend my cloak, or pry a stone from Gadfly's hoof. It's terribly frugal, I know."

"Your people have often had need to be frugal." Dorilian appeared to appreciate the practical aspect of Robdan's habit.

Robdan wound a blue thread salvaged from his eldest granddaughter's scarf fringe about the multicolored mass. "My grandfather said it was a wise man who kept a well-wound ball of string in his pocket. He used to keep a coin or two in the center of his, should he find himself in need of a copper. But the Mother has provided for me well enough that I have fallen by the wayside of that habit."

His curiosity satisfied, Dorilian finished eating the meat pie, then turned away, seeking darkness and sleep. Robdan pursued his own sleep soon after.

The next day was dismal and overcast, with a wind that left Robdan huddled in the saddle, too miserable to do anything more than watch from horseback as Dorilian proved Rill tree after Rill tree to be functional. They bypassed Bellan Toregh and the final two structures on the northern approach and rode south along the Run. It would be just as important for the furthermost Rill structure on the south to be capable. As the sun dwindled and a fine drizzle began to fall, the first Rill tree on that approach answered to Dorilian's touch. That success inspired him to quickly prove the others sound. Though rain fell in dull patters on the musty leaves of the forest bed, Dorilian pushed forward, testing two more arms in darkness before Robdan begged him to halt and make camp. But morning, though it dawned gray and cold, found Dorilian pressing for an early start.

By afternoon they had made their way back to the rain-drenched town of Bellan Toregh and the looming promise of its silent mount, now crowned by towering storms. The clouds thundering overhead made Robdan shiver with more than autumn's icy chill through his waterlogged clothes. Nine days had passed since they had left Rhodhur, with maybe several more until they would return.

At one of Bellan Toregh's less-favored inns, they purchased a room in which to dry and wait for night. The final rings approaching the Rill mount were very near the town and to sound them in broad daylight would draw unwanted attention, even if Robdan and Dorilian's acts could be explained by simple curiosity. The mount itself would need to be approached in absolute secrecy as well.

For Robdan, the inn was a blessed relief. The pace Dorilian had demanded so far had been grueling. Though he had not complained, or even let Dorilian know he had them, Robdan's saddle blisters were near to killing him with pain. Because of the weather and the hour, the inn's tables had been full, making it necessary to postpone their meal. Their room, though barely more than a closet, was private and had two cots—and adjoined a bath not yet in use. Robdan gave in to his misery and spent the little bit of money he had kept aside hoping to give to his daughter Wytha on their return journey. A bath of warm water, with an extra coin spent for a lump of soap, was the purest luxury in the world. The modest inn with its dry room, clean linens, and warm bath was as close to the Mother's promised Hearth of Blessed Souls as Robdan had ever dared to hope for.

By the light of a second candle he had paid yet another copper to obtain, Robdan washed away the grime and sour sweat of travel, after which he soaked his aching muscles and saddle-abused bottom in the tub. Whatever Dorilian was doing in their room, separated from the bath by a wall and a door to the common hall, Robdan could put from his mind. He could, finally, *relax.*

A soft but impatient rap on the door proved him wrong.

As Robdan tugged a wash rag across his submerged lap, Dorilian entered. After he'd closed the door behind him, he crouched beside the bath, notes balanced upon his knees. "We must be sure of the date. The impact will be greatest if Handurin can maneuver the Witan to be held *here* and we can all be present for the occasion—him especially."

"Yes, of course. It's just—"

"You *do* know when the Witan will be held?"

They had been over it three times already. The Kheld calendar and the Staubaun one differed sufficiently to make guesswork out of setting a date for anything. Robdan often worked with Staubaun calendars during Archhalia sessions, but a Kheld calendar marked the year by the moon's phases and the mysteries of women's courses. Days were simply night and day, termed barren if the moon was dark or a sliver, for such were the days a woman could not conceive, or fertile while the Mother's sister goddess waxed. A Kheld might say he would be by on the next barren moon or promise to complete a project when the moon finished her course. Staubauns, on the other hand, numbered their days meticulously and assigned a name to each, filling the month with syllables.

"The Witan will meet at Sameth," Robdan answered. "When the moon preceding that of the solstice waxes full." Robdan glanced nervously at the closed door. "Would you mind doing this later?"

"Why?" Gray eyes, uncomfortably near, looked directly into his.

"Keep your voice down at least. People might think we're bathing together."

With a slight lift of his chin and lowering of his eyes, Dorilian indicated he understood. Or at least wanted Robdan to think he did. Dorilian shoved the calendar he had been working on in front of Robdan and proceeded to speak less loudly. "I can pin down the solstice. And the moon's phases. Would you hazard a guess as to which *day* I should address?"

Because nothing but an answer would prompt Dorilian to leave, Robdan pondered the series of circles and numerals. The phases of the moon were neatly marked, traced beside each date when they were known to occur. Faeduadan and Old Mothers used such systems.

Robdan pointed to the fully drawn circles. "The Witan will commence on the day the moon first shows," he said. "But a Faedic ceremony requires a moon at its fullest and most fertile. That would be several days later. This one"—he pointed to the middlemost circle—"is the most sacred. The Mother Moon."

"Here?" Dorilian's finger tapped that circle.

"Yes. I think so. I'm a little wet or I would look at these more closely."

Dorilian gathered his notes and rose. "Meet me in the room." A phantom would have made more sound upon leaving.

Robdan dried and dressed. He stepped out only after looking around the doorframe at the empty hall. As he entered their room, he ran a hand through his damp hair. His head of curls was gray now and thinner than in his youth, but he still combed his locks back out of habit. He padded over to the cot where Dorilian sat peering at notes scattered over the coverlet.

"I understand Staubauns base much on calendars. If this is for the Rill, however, couldn't you call it when it is needed?" Though Robdan had never ridden the Rill himself, he had overheard people say the Sordaneon Hierarch could call a *charys* at will.

"Trust me, Master Aelfricson, I do know what I'm doing."

"Of course." Robdan flushed. "I just thought that was how you would do it."

Dorilian frowned. "I could do that—if I wanted to stash a month's supplies in the sanctuary and hole up inside there like a rabbit while wondering what in the Creation is going on with Handurin in Rhodhur. As things stand now, we don't know where any of us might be. Or even how Handurin's proposal will be received. Under such circumstances, I must guess on when—and whether—to make a suitable demonstration of goodwill. It may even be that I cannot. All our efforts will mean nothing if I cannot cause the Rill to see this node." Again, Dorilian pondered his calendar.

Robdan resolved to be more helpful, even if he couldn't speak with authority. He pointed again to the first of the two circles of the moon's showing. "This day will be the grand meeting, the High Witan. Hans will almost certainly be asked to speak and submit to questions from the elders and chieftains. It'll be the day for him to make his proposal."

"And the day they will accept it? Provided they do?"

"Perhaps. Maybe it will take two days, or three."

"But he could get them to agree to talk? And, on that understanding, send word?"

"Yes. That day would be the soonest."

"So the soonest I would know"—Dorilian carried forward the proposal's timing, tapping two half moons five days out—"would be here." He granted a thin smile. "Handurin could use the interim to make an event of it."

Robdan felt only unease. "He will meet opposition. It'll seem like a lie, a smoke dream. The Faeduadan and chieftains will not believe in it and, even so, may move to counter the event. The Witan is where the Red Priests will declare the omens from Hans's horse. This momentous announcement they can keep even to the last day."

"The Mother Moon."

"Yes."

When first told of what had happened to Hans at the Grove, Dorilian had called the sacrifice and its intentions insidious. Robdan had not disagreed. He was mortified enough that the entrapment had happened and understood why Hans wanted to hold the Witan where he would make his plea for the Sordan alliance: at Bellan Toregh—far from the Grove and in view of what all Khelds stood to gain.

Even so, Robdan had a bad feeling about having Dorilian summon his own god amid another deity's ritual.

Before the kitchen closed, they went downstairs for their meal. The late hour ensured fewer patrons crowded the tables but also resulted in a poorer selection of food. Taking pains not to be mysterious, they secured a small table with but stools to sit on, tucked into an odd corner near the stairs. Dorilian obscured his head and features with a hood and, given how rough he looked, was unlikely to be recognized. The types of men who might have seen Sordan's Hierarch in the flesh didn't travel to Amallar. Neither did they frequent third-rate inns.

A trencher of bread and roasted roots with one shank of goat was the best to be had. The drafty room offered pools of dim light from tallow bowls and was warmed by a single hearth. From their table, Robdan and Dorilian listened to talk of strange goings-on in the world. Not only had the Rill stopped running, disrupting the lives of the locals through diminished trade from Dazunor-Rannuli and Leseos, but the latest rumors from Neuberland could not place one of Sordan's two armies.

"Holed up for the winter in Gignastha, most like," said one of the men discussing the matter.

"Fran Gorseddson says no, says no way a stinking army could've snuck past his lads back into Lower Neuberland." The bearded speaker put down his mug with a heavy hand. "And if the Bane Hound took his horse soldiers into the Geroe Valley, there ain't no one that's seen them. Mother be kind, but there's settlements in the Geroe ten to a tree."

Someone laughed. "Hells, maybe the damned Bane is headed here."

"Don't joke. Could be!"

"They found somewhere tidy to hole up," the first man said. "Mark my words." And talk then drifted to one man's problems with keeping his cattle out of his neighbor's cornfield.

But Robdan noted Dorilian's quickly averted smile and wondered. How much else was going on that no one knew? The corner of a tapestry but hinted at marvelous patterns woven through the whole. Hidden behind the mindful steadiness of Dorilian's gaze lurked a vaster world than that of Amallar, a world where armies could be moved as easily as pieces on a board and the marvelous Rill changed at the whim of princes. Dorilian might need an alliance with Amallar to gain his ends, but already he spun entire empires about his designs.

Robdan suspected that soon the Hierarch would show he could spin Amallar as well.

Dorilian watched doubt creep into Robdan's gaze and wondered if the man guessed the story behind Sordan's unfindable army. Handurin would hear an explanation of the situation upon Dorilian's return. But for Robdan to have misgivings about armies or Sordan's politics could prove disastrous. Suddenly, violently, Dorilian wished he had not allowed Robdan to accompany him, that he had left the Kheld with his passel of grandchildren on the outskirts of Eastmeary Brenna. More, he wished that he had never come to Amallar or encountered the brutish ignorance of its unwashed horde. All he had ever distrusted about Khelds—their delusional aspirations, stubborn hatreds, and love of violence—welled up to fill his pores.

He should not even be here.

Across the table, Robdan's face paled. Seeing this, Dorilian clamped his flare of resentment. He hadn't intended to cause pain. He just wished Robdan would go away.

He wished being with people other than his own kind was less... complicated.

"Are you angry?" Hearing Robdan speak was a surprise. Most people who experienced Dorilian's emotional surges felt sufficiently threatened to stay silent. "You're not having second thoughts, I hope."

Now he wished more than ever that Robdan would go away. "No." Dorilian lifted his gaze. "You are."

Robdan's swallow was as telling as a nod. "Of course. You felt my doubts. I—I apologize. I'm not accustomed—"

"I don't read thoughts."

"I know that. I mean—" The man insisted on being understood. "The old king explained it once, the difference. Marc Frederick—"

"I know who the old king was."

"Yes, of course. He said your kind pick up on feelings and radiate them also. Powerfully sometimes. And you especially."

"*Me?*"

Robdan broke the gaze and ducked his head. "I'm sorry. I'm being familiar."

True as that was, this lapse begged exploration. Dorilian restrained a degree of satisfaction with Robdan's discomfort. "Continue. I want to hear what he had to say. The old king."

It carried enough force to compel a response. Robdan softly spoke about having sat in on a meeting between his brother Cedrec and the king at Gustan. Fourteen years past. Winter. Robdan had overheard Cedrec counsel Marc Frederick about handling two difficult teens. About young men, and pride, and the wisdom of enlisting time as an ally.

Dorilian did not think it necessary to let Robdan know he was imparting a gift beyond price: insight into the heart and mind of the one person Dorilian would, to this day, give anything in his power to resurrect.

What is good and what is evil can be the same thing. Even
a volcano's nature is defined by its consequences—and on
whom those consequences are visited.

LEVYATHAN II SORDANEON, *REFLECTIONS ON PHILOSOPHICAL FOOTNOTES*

"And so you are telling me... what? That Dorilian is not at
Sordan?" Nammuor placed the decanter of spirits back
into its rack and studied the goblet cradled in his hand,
the way the amber fluid within swirled from side to side.

"He *may* not be in Sordan. There's some... disagreement about
that." Coram Barzanes, unlike the contents of the goblet, looked a
little green. Robed and miserable, he hunched on one of the cabin's
two benches. Though the ship they were on, the flagship of
Nammuor's fleet, handled the rough sea of the Kolpos as well as any
vessel could, it still rocked.

"But no one has *seen* him."

"Therein is the source of disagreement. Dorilian has been *seen*
but not spoken with. No meetings. No visits to any agency or
person—for any reason—since his return from Jharbala."

Yes, Jharbala. Nammuor frowned at mention of that inaccessible
redoubt, warded by the Initiates against *Ir* devices and effects.
Though he might possibly succeed in attacking Jharbala using his
Diadem, the outcome was far from assured. In addition to its
formidable wardings, Jharbala sat atop a dormant Rill node.
Dorilian was nearly as safe there as he was in Sordan.

"But he did leave Jharbala. So if he *is* in Sordan, why not show
himself?" Nammuor finished off the spirits and put aside the goblet.

His already foul mood darkened. Dorilian was up to something. Not one bit of surprise in that, but the possibility the Sordaneon annoyance had slipped his leash added a dangerous element to Nammuor's current venture.

Coram arched an eyebrow. "Consider what we know already. Reports place Handurin in Amallar. Might that be part of some larger plan? The Seven Houses posit Dorilian has consolidated his armies at Gignastha and is preparing to push through Neuberland into Essera's underbelly, counting on Handurin to neutralize the Khelds. The Epoptes, in yet another twist of the knife, speculate Dorilian could already *be* in Essera."

"Unlikely, with the Rill in stasis. Even if he had traveled ahead—even if he could do so in secret—he would not have cut off his own escape."

"Well, there's always the third possibility: that he is taking advantage of *your* absence from Mormantalorus, and is with his army in Teremar to make a push against *us*."

A possibility no sane person would dismiss. "If that is the case, he will discover to his great undoing that I am ready for him."

"Do you think he would personally direct his troops against ours? In Suddekar?"

"No."

Nammuor strode out the cabin door and up the stair to the main deck. As sails billowed overhead, sailors scattered at Nammuor's approach, scurrying into the rigging and belowdecks. Red-robed mages and yellow-clothed acolytes backed away to let him pass. Coram scurried in Nammuor's wake.

Nammuor stopped when he came to the foredeck. His gaze raked the nearing coastline and the stone buildings of a city emerging into view, its bay guarded on the west by a fortress-crowned hill and the whitewashed palaces of merchant lords. Buildings just as grand ringed the impressive harbor. That Nammuor's fleet had gotten this close to Ogarth without being seen was proof enough of where Dorilian was *not*.

Nammuor signaled with his hand and a bright-haired mage wearing a circlet of golden *lr* gems stepped forward. Eyes so wide-pupiled they were nearly black met his.

"Drop the illusion."

Where but minutes before the watchers at the city or fortress, or on nearby ships, would have seen only a single ship with a friendly flag, now a dozen warships bearing Mormantaloran banners sailed into the harbor. Within moments, though already too late, alarm klaxons from the doomed city reached Nammuor's ears.

Trongor's warships were either berthed or at sea. Only a few would be on patrol. Ogarth's defenses stood unwarned. None could oppose what was to come.

Two heavy bolts slammed hard into the metal-sheathed hull of the first warship to enter Ogarth's harbor. The next bolt tore into the prow at the waterline.

Nammuor allowed the Trongorians their brief success. The ships had been tasked as shields to his own.

Crowned by power and blood, Nammuor stood at the bow of his black-hulled ship, two battle mages to each side of him. He stretched out his hands. Plasm, the firmament's aether, flowed toward him, to be collected... to be shaped... to be deployed as arcane energy.

Ten immortal blood crystals, and two merely mortal, instilled the Diadem with the raw capacity to summon and contain such vast power. To perform this shaping. To direct it as Nammuor willed. His mages, mere puppets, could but aspire to wield the raw energy Nammuor commanded. The terror he might unleash. And Ogarth did not yet suspect.

Change.

Through a captive sliver crafted from the stolen omnificence of ten Diadem-enslaved Leur lifeforces, Nammuor focused. The aether he gathered changed, as did the air and water with which it communed. Initially crackling and blue, the energy expanded and thinned into a sphere that drew in the ordered elements and arranged them into an immense ball of yellow mist. With a push of his hands, Nammuor ignored the hilltop fortress and sent his creation directly into the harbor. Into whatever ships had raised sail or were at anchor. Lahgaelan. Ardaenan. Sordani. Trongor's anchored warships. Each ship when touched wavered, lost shape, and collapsed, their outlines sliding unnaturally into amorphous slime. An oily, sulphureous green sheen rode the waves.

The cloud rolled toward the city, a wave from the sea. A towering wall of thick yellow surged into the wharfs and billowed into warehouses, enveloping all it touched. Its ochre fog rolled over trees and pushed into houses that, even as Nammuor and his mages watched, dissolved to sludge before their eyes. As it moved inland, his spell also devoured Ogarth's people, and Nammuor smiled as he envisioned their screams. Living flesh turned to soup and life dripped from dissolving bones.

If only it did not feel as if something just as malignant gnawed at the roots of his brain. Nammuor clenched his jaw and focused to keep his breathing even. Blinding pain behind his eyes threatened to smudge the brightness from his victory. Though it caused him agony, power swelled with a fierce, savage joy within him. This was the stuff of gods. Triumphant, Nammuor watched as his mages, having witnessed their Master's work, unleashed their own devices.

The mages stationed on the two ships that sailed near the harbor entrance slammed incendiary bolts into the high-walled fortress atop the hill. Brilliant webs of blue energy laced the mighty battlements. Though more conventional, the magic unleashed by Nammuor's minions was no less deadly. The fortress's foundations and then its walls crumbled, sliding down the hillside in avalanches of stone. Part of the World itself fell toward the sea, crushing Ogarth's defenseworks and troops in their path. Three other ships, unmanned and propelled by currents Nammuor's companion mages had been generating all this while, drove onto the rocks beneath the now ruined fortress. Their wooden hulls violently rended and broke open.

From the gaping wounds of those broken holds emerged new horrors. Giant beasts—ravenous and clawed, many-legged and many-armed, slavering with poison—climbed from those shattered prisons and leaped free. They rolled and clambered over water, rocks, and sand. Upon gaining the shore, they pursued all that moved. They had been unfed for many days and now hungered to devour any living thing they might capture.

"You have excelled." Nammuor delivered the first praise his mages would receive. They would receive other rewards they craved far more, later, delivered by way of crystals lodged in their temporal bones. "Domains will turn from Essera's Prince now before they back him. They will *run*."

They would flee from Handurin—and Dorilian too. No sane people would wish to earn Nammuor's displeasure. From this day forth, they had only to look upon what had happened to Trongor.

Ogarth was gone. Not one ship sat upon the slime-covered waters of its famed harbor. No discernible structure, of any kind, graced that once formidable hilltop or prosperous shore. Nothing moved at all but collapsing ruins and the vague, hulking shapes of monsters that would haunt and hunt the land for years.

Had the citizens of Ogarth appreciated the elegance of their demise? The quickness? Or had they registered only the brutal cost of the alignment their leaders had foisted upon them?

Nammuor hardly cared. He had just rendered Trongor worthless—as an ally, as a source of aid or succor. Even as a conquest.

"Come about!" he ordered his captain, then strode away from the bow. The world to every side of Nammuor had taken on the texture and color of blood-stained gauze, rust-tinged, drained by the energy and light cast by his blazing crown. Pain ripped at his brain. Every step it would take to reach the privacy of his cabin, in the seclusion of which he could remove the Diadem away from the scrutiny of his mages, was a step too far.

Once there, he removed the device and placed it in its deathstone box. He needed rest. Perhaps overnight. It might take him that long to recover sufficiently to use a lesser device. Maybe in the morning he would translocate to a more critical location—one where he could safely replenish a body he had let his Diadem drain to the bone.

"Resume the illusion. We sail to Stauberg."

Gongs tolled across Rhodhur, deep full-bellied tones from the Hall Tower, rolling above pastures and fields, calling those yet at work to come in for early meals. Ducking his head as he made his way down a lane, Hans tugged his collar to hide more of his face. Arne hurried alongside as they shouldered past laughing, boisterous people going the other way. The last thing Hans wanted was to be recognized. It had been more than a week since his visit to the Grove, and the betrayal by the Faeduadan still stung.

His emotions swung wildly between knowing he needed the Khelds for troops and supplies and feeling so damn trapped he wanted to leave. More than anything else he felt bruised. Daily meetings with Nalf and other chieftains eager to talk about his prospects and their futures did nothing to improve Hans's mood.

He still doubted whether he could be their king. *Anyone's* king.

A turn at the bottom of the lane took him and Arne away from the street and its bustle. Rhodhur's training barn, sometimes used in winter for working with horses or conducting sales of livestock, at other times provided a good space for practice with weapons. Despite the many demands placed on his time, Hans had kept up his training. Dorilian had insisted on it, saying that any invasion of Essera would certainly involve blades, so Hans should at the very least aspire to look like he knew how to use one.

"I'm not as good as Farrl, not even close." Arne pointed out this truth for the seventh time since they'd left Rhodhur Hall. Farrl had taken up the task of being Hans's sparring partner after Dorilian had set out for Bellan Toregh, but today Farrl was somewhere else, training his own men.

"You're getting better."

"I reckon."

"You don't have to be the best swordsman in Amallar. I just want to get in a little practice."

"If that's the case, you should have come with me to the Hill. There's things other than blades you need practice doing."

Arne had hounded Hans to come with him on a visit to the Mother's sanctuary, a place called the Hill. A two-day ride from Rhodhur, the Hill at Aurdollen was steeped in mystery—a temple complex with sacred pools and trees, and also underground chambers wherein men and women coupled anonymously to attain the Mother's greatest blessing. After his experience at the Grove, Hans had about as much interest in exploring more Kheldic mystery as he had in jumping off a cliff, even though Arne assured Hans the offering involved would be a pleasant one. According to Arne, Priestesses of the Mother paired the celebrants, who met and did the act in darkness without ever knowing the identity of their partner.

"You said sex under the Hill was a gift to the Mother," Hans said. "That makes it a sacred act, not practice."

"So you practice doing something sacred."

"Your view of what constitutes a sacrament needs work."

Arne ducked under a branch when he moved off the path to avoid a cart. "Having a good time is the Mother's own nature. She tells all of us, men and women both, to give of our bodies with joy and purpose. Sex under the Hill is just a sacred way to do it."

"And the women who go there? How do they feel about it?" It was a question Hans should have asked someone else.

"Joyful. Every one of them," Arne asserted. "At least, I think they must be. No one makes them do it that I know of. But the woman I served a few days ago seemed happy enough. It was only a little bit awkward because it's not like I do it much."

And Hans had never done it at all. His sexual inexperience would be a sore point if it ever got out, but he didn't want his first time to be under a hill with a stranger.

The door to the long, thatched training barn was propped open, probably to allow a pleasant breeze to pass through. Loud clacks and rubs, along with grunts and yells, reached Hans's and Arne's ears even before they entered. Inside they found an open space brightened by hazy light filtered through unshuttered windows on the long sides of the building. Hay bales and wooden crates were stacked near the door along with an array of practice weapons. Two people wearing light practice armor faced off in the arena, exchanging blows with heavy wasters. Hans recognized Brec even before Arne's elbow dug into his side. It took a second look for Hans to realize who Brec was fighting.

Aubrey?

She'd tucked her hair into a knit cap and a vest of fawn leather protected her torso, while plain leather breeches clothed her legs with a subtle sheen. She sidestepped and turned, crossed blades, moved close, then back again and—in a move surprising only for the quickness with which it happened—lifted one leg to plant the sole of a well-fitted boot in Brec's stomach, sending him backward onto the sawdust.

"Hey!" With that loud shout, Arne rushed to his brother's aid. Brec, however, laughed aloud and didn't appear to be hurt. He rolled to one side and pushed himself back onto his feet.

"Wench said she'd put me down—and darn did it."

"Only 'cuz she fought dirty."

Aubrey smirked at Arne's narrow-eyed glare. She whipped off the cap holding her hair. "Dirty? He lost focus when I got close."

Brec didn't deny it. He winked at Hans. "There's truth. Every good sense fumbled when I looked down her blouse."

Really? Hans glanced in that direction. So did Arne. Aubrey, however, had turned her back and walked toward a pile of what were probably her belongings, including a real blade with a gold-chased belt and scabbard. Hans watched as she buckled the short sword at her hip like it belonged there.

"You got no sense at all," Arne upbraided his brother. "Don't you know to fight a woman brings the worst kind of luck? Get the Old Mothers on you for that. But to lose to one...."

Brec put an arm over his brother's shoulder. "Arne-lad, two things. One, losing to a woman is something a man learns at his mother's knee. And two, this was all good for both her and me, and the Mother would approve. A woman should be trained up so she can take down a man, if that's what needs to be done."

"I fought off my first man when I was nine. And two years ago I fought off another." Aubrey faced them again. She'd wrapped a yard of calf-length Thegn plaid about her hips to look like a skirt, obscuring her sword. "I just want to be prepared should I need to do it again."

Arne frowned. "Aw, our men know better than to do that."

"I never said they were Kheld men."

Staubaun men, then. Neuberland's circumstances were different from Amallar's and much more dangerous. The town where Aubrey lived had been subjected for years to raids from Annech and Gobba. Hans had been studying up on that conflict from the Kheld perspective, and it wasn't pretty.

Brec took in Hans's sword belt. "You here to practice? I can't stay, but Aubrey here might take you on." Brec turned to give her a grin.

Oh, hell no. Hans couldn't even begin to count the pitfalls inherent in that invitation. At minimum, Aubrey would make him look inept. He needed a way out of this. His gaze met Aubrey's, and she smiled.

"Was that early meals we just heard?" she quipped. The gongs. She was giving him a way to save face.

"Yes. I—"

Aubrey turned to Brec. "I'll catch up with you and bring along that remedy for Egdith."

"Darn me, I near forgot. She'll appreciate it greatly if your remedy can drive out her cough. See you at meals!" Brec appeared to know she wouldn't be joining him and hurried out the door.

To the question with which Hans and Arne regarded her, Aubrey shrugged. "A little weapons work in exchange for a remedy. It's a fair trade."

"Do you practice often?" Hans asked. To make small talk seemed the polite thing to do after she'd spared his ass.

"Every day I can. Wodd—my man—told me when I was a girl that the way to become good with a blade was to practice until I could slay men in my sleep."

"Have you done that? Slain anyone in your sleep?" Hans removed his jacket and hung it from a nearby post. Arne did the same.

Aubrey shook her head and the smile in her eyes joined that on her lips. Late afternoon sunlight traced fiery glints in the tumbled waves of her hair. "No. But I tell every man who shares my bed that I plan to someday."

Hans couldn't decide if that was a good plan or a horrible one. After removing his sword belt, he grasped one of the sword-shaped wooden wasters propped against the wall and tossed it to Arne, then picked one for himself.

As he performed a warm-up swing with his waster, Arne shot a frown at Aubrey. "You're not planning to hang around, are you?"

"Maybe I should." Impudently, Aubrey perched atop one of the hay bales. Mock poleaxes stood against the wall behind her. "You might need an arbiter."

"Keep your fancy words," Arne said. "I fight just fine."

What was she about, staying to watch, wearing a half smile as she studied them both? Hans hadn't yet figured out whether Aubrey reported to Nalf or was working through some agenda of her own. Seeing her with Dorilian just last week... she'd been playful and teasing, but also wickedly pleased about Nalf's displeasure with her choice of companions. Often when Hans talked with Aubrey, he couldn't decide if she was fishing for information or simply being inquisitive.

"Let's do the whacking pole," Hans said. Arne looked visibly relieved to walk over to the padded pole, man-tall and thick, that stood in the middle of the training ground. Striking at it would provide them both with less chance of exposing ineptitude.

Soon Hans and Arne were working through footwork repetitions and arm exercises they'd acquired in Sordan. It wasn't necessary to hit the pole with any great strength; it existed to provide a target for their approaches and retreats, as well as the different repetitions for their swings. Wide. Close. Direct thrust. Backhand. Upward. Downward. Blocking. Overhead. Each set worked different muscles. Perhaps, if they kept at it long enough, Aubrey would get bored and leave.

No such luck. She watched Hans and Arne the whole time until they tired themselves and a small crowd of curious onlookers had gathered to watch their future King's display of battle-readiness... or lack of same. Hans was breathing hard when he walked back to the hay bales to reclaim his jacket. While he cooled down and caught his breath, he sat on one of the crates facing Aubrey. Gasping even harder, Arne plunked onto another of the bales. Onlookers continued to hang by the wide door, none quite brave enough to approach. When it became clear that Hans would provide no further entertainment, they drifted back to their own business.

He had just mopped a trickle of sweat from his neck when the second call to meals sounded through the walls.

"You're not bad with a sword." Aubrey's perusal stayed on Hans when he stood, retrieved his sword, and buckled it again at his hip. "You may even be good. It's hard to tell most times. Your usual sparring partner is so much better than you."

That she'd noticed didn't surprise Hans. Aubrey was often among those who gathered to watch his practices—and it wasn't so she could report back to Nalf about Hans's skill level. Swordplay was one of Dorilian's best-honed talents, right up there with the art of appearances. As a sparring partner, Dorilian pushed Hans, tested him, and tired him out, yet those attacks for all their elegance and expertise were clearly exercises. Training. Hans inevitably came out looking as though he'd performed better than he actually had. A few Khelds, Aubrey among them, perhaps realized what they were watching, but most didn't, and word had gotten about that Hans was good with a sword. Of course, word had also gotten out that Thron was better, which was not a bad thing.

"There's an advantage to learning from warriors," he said.

"Thron's not a warrior. He told me himself. He does 'administrative work.' I thought that to mean he reads and writes."

"Neither of which rules out also using a sword."

"No, I suppose not."

Hans recalled Nalf's boast that Aubrey's father had given her a Staubaunish education, hiring tutors and using books gifted by Marc Frederick from Gustan's library. Hans already knew from talking with the Old Mothers that Kheld women were taught to read Kheldic script; fewer learned the scripts of Stauba or Esta. That Aubrey could read and write in all three languages was useful enough to keep in mind.

Hans caught Arne's gaze and recognized a plea to get moving before Aubrey asked something more dangerous. He slipped on his jacket. "I think it's time we head to meals. People get testy if I don't show up."

"So why come here at meals?" Aubrey had stood and clearly meant to join them.

"Because when everyone's at meals there are fewer people. I—I miss privacy the most. I like having time for my own thoughts. For things I want to do, for myself, not to please everyone else. I never really understood how much of myself I would give up by coming back here."

They exited the training barn to a sky already faded to mauve. A stiff breeze out of the west penetrated their clothing and chilled sweat-dewed skin. Aubrey looked thoughtful as she trudged beside Hans and Arne, boots pressing fallen leaves underfoot.

"Why?" Her voice had lost its lighthearted edge. "Why did you come back? You make it sound like you didn't have to."

"From Mena'tantaureus, you mean?"

"Yes."

"I didn't have to. I mean, no one forced me. Marenthro—" Answering the question was proving more difficult than Hans had thought it would be. "Once I remembered my childhood and life here again, once I realized I didn't have anything left there, not really, not like what I would have here"—he sighed—"it mattered. Because there, in that World, *I didn't* matter. I was inconsequential in Mena'tantaureus, and I mean that in every possible way. No family, no people I really cared about or who cared about me—not after my moms died. Once they were gone I had no meaningful history there, no true connection to a single person or place. I often felt like I didn't matter to anyone or exist for any reason other than my own pursuits. I couldn't even change anything, not for better or worse. Not at all. But here I *do* matter—and I *can* change things for the better."

So many things about him mattered here. His birth mother, Emyli, struggling to preserve what was left of her father's and Stefan's legacy. The Khelds, yearning to hold onto a vision given them by men now dead. And Dorilian, risking everything to defeat an enemy whose malevolence Hans had witnessed but barely understood. All he knew for certain was that Nammuor and his Diadem would try to destroy them.

And not just them, but the World. This World. All worlds. The Creation of Leur. More and more Hans saw that he was part of something bigger. Something fragile. Threatened.

"I wonder if you understand how much you matter." Something wistful resided in Aubrey's words.

Arne shot Hans an inquisitive look. Hans shrugged. "How much I matter depends on who I talk to these days."

Aubrey snorted and nearly bumped him. "You matter because

you can keep Essera from sinking its teeth into our necks the way Sordan already does. We can't afford to have *all* the war-thirsty Staubauns in the world set against us."

"You know, Sordan may not be as against Kheldfolk as people think."

She frowned. "We've had this conversation."

Yes, they had. Hans sighed. "Well, what about this one: did you know Cullen Brodheson?"

Aubrey stopped walking, so Hans pulled up short and so did Arne, who rolled his eyes and shook his head. She narrowed her gaze. "My *cousin* Cullen?"

Her cousin? Hans must have looked bewildered because Aubrey laughed and explained.

"His grandfather, my grandmother." She held up and waggled two fingers. "Brother and sister."

"Are you related to *everyone?*"

Both Aubrey and Arne broke out in snickers. "No," she said. "But you were talking about Cullen."

"I met his wife."

Every trace of levity vanished. "I was hoping she was dead."

Was she serious? "Asphalladra's nice! She tried to help me."

"She's a coldhearted status seeker who married well and tried to profit by it. After Cullen was murdered, Asphalladra sought to succeed to his title, his property, and when that didn't work, she ran off to Sordan." Anger ground a sharp edge to Aubrey's words. "Some people say she became Dorilian Sordaneon's mistress. That would make sense of why Cullen's children disappeared. I'd bet a bushel of gold that man killed them."

Since coming to Amallar, Hans had heard a few tales about the fate of Cullen Brodheson's family. All so far were wrong. "All right."

"What?"

"I'll take the bet."

Aubrey looked to Arne, who waved his hands. "Will you hold me to that?" she asked.

Hans glared at Arne. "I should."

"No, you shouldn't," Arne said. He dug the toe of his boot into the dirt of the path. "Even if she's good for it—and she is—it's not a fair bet."

Now it was Aubrey's eyes that narrowed to blue slits as her expression turned wary. "Why? What do you know?"

Hans indicated Arne and himself. "We met them in Sordan."

"Who? Cullen's *children?* They're in Sordan? Alive?" Aubrey's surprise was genuine. She looked hard at Arne, who nodded.

"Wulf and Allysa." Arne ticked off the names on two fingers and grinned. "Allysa's hair curls and Wulf has freckles."

Hans was glad to put yet another ugly rumor to rest. "Asphalladra told me she sought refuge in Sordan because Erenor—*my* regent—was in league with her own family. They were forcing her to wed some man she didn't want, a man named Bragord, who wanted to take over Cullen's estates. Who did take them over from what I hear. Asphalladra was afraid what Bragord might do and not just to her—to the children, to Cullen's legal heirs. Essera wasn't safe for them."

For a moment Aubrey took one corner of her lower lip between her teeth as she looked toward the looming stone and timber shape of the Hall. "So many men. Every ennobled Kheld to whom Stefan gave lands, all of those lands were taken away, their holders driven off or murdered. But she, Asphalladra... people saw her with Dorilian. At Permephedon. Saw her leave with him—"

"I guess some prefer to believe the worst about people they already don't like." Seeing Aubrey look down at the ground and wince, Hans knew what nerve he'd struck and was glad of it. "That's probably when she asked for asylum. Erenor was moving quickly. He completely removed Khelds from the hereditary landholdings Stefan had given them. Erenor did it in *my* name and gave those lands to his cronies. Do you wonder that I can never trust my regent—no matter what he promises?"

Hans's defense earned an acknowledging head tilt of agreement from Aubrey. "Staubauns are made of lies. So tell me—you're certain you met Phalla? Not some pretender?" Her scrutiny passed from Hans to Arne.

"Yes," Hans said and was glad for Arne's nod of affirmation. "She lives at the Sordaneon Serat, the safest place in the City—the place where the Hierarch lives, which may be why some people got the wrong idea. But the Serat isn't a house, it's an imperial residence. Asphalladra passes information about Sordan to my mother. And she isn't Dorilian's mistress."

"You're sure?"

"Yes."

They resumed walking.

"It's a relief to hear that, and that Cullen's children are alive and safe. I... he was my favorite cousin growing up. He sent me books. Everyone was saying...." She sighed. "This changes things. Wulf and Alyssa might be my heirs someday." Aubrey's brows drew together. "Unless they've been turned into Sordan-loving brats."

So much for bridging that chasm. With every passing conversation in Amallar, Hans grew more certain that nothing less than the Rill itself could possibly overcome the way Khelds looked at Sordan.

The cold trees shed a soft light over the town, part of the
reason our folk built there. That, and the river, because you
need good water and lots of it if you're to brew large
quantities of ale. The Highborn Kings built a road from
Dazunor and Merrydn down to Leseos, and the light from
those cold trees made travelers and merchants feel safe, so
Bellan Toregh grew there, in the shadow of the Rill.

ABLE ORRSON, *GUIDE TO AMALLARAN ROADS AND INNS*

I t was deep night when Dorilian ascended the mount of Bellan
Toregh, through sapling woods upon a path thick with weeds and
grass, beneath the stark watch of forgotten elevators and a cloud-
heavy sky devoid of moon or stars. He noted how Robdan followed
in his footsteps with a curious, hard faith. The opportunity to
witness a Rill summoning might well persuade a man to put aside
his misgivings. Robdan moved like a man who, although he did not
swim, was grimly determined to find out what awaited at the
headwaters of a river.

A canopy of Rill arches presided over the hilltop and its ghostly
sanctuary, their otherworldly shapes the only things unmoving in a
landscape lashed by a bitter west wind. Dorilian and Robdan made
their way through patches of rank growth that had claimed the
fringes of the station. Each step crushed frost-bruised tall grass
underfoot. The musty sweetness of autumn felt appropriate for the
lonely white building and the platform's windswept desolation. The
mount greeted them in darkness, its surfaces fading into the night.
A faint fog rose from the platform and the sunken channel of its single
run.

Dorilian turned to let his companion catch up. Dwarfed by the looming structures overhead, Robdan looked insignificant and out of place. Briefly, Dorilian glimpsed Bellan Toregh through Kheld eyes: ghostly planes and black shadows, angles piercing the night like knives, brighter than moonlight and promising death. For all that it occupied the human realm, the Rill was ultimately alien. He waited until Robdan stood beside him, a shivering huddle in an old woolen coat, trying to be brave.

"What do we do now?" Robdan's lowered voice quavered.

"You do nothing. You stay here and, should anyone come, say you had a sudden urge to look for moonlight."

Robdan stared, visibly shaken. When Dorilian moved in the direction of the mist-shrouded white structure at the platform edge, Robdan trotted after, his footsteps hollow echoes in the darkness.

"But you said you don't know how long it could take." Robdan peered at the darkness in alarm. "I could be out here all night!"

Dorilian placed his hand on the sealed entrance. Cold. Unlike the living Rill corpus that made up the rings and arches, and underlaid a portion of the platform, the stuff of the sanctuary and platform surface was inorganic and assumed ambient temperature.

"What if something goes wrong?" Robdan persisted. "Why did you bring me, if not to assist you?"

"As you may recall, I did not wish to bring you."

"Except tonight. You insisted."

Dorilian *had* insisted; he feared Robdan would become anxious about the progress of his mission and by some behavior arouse suspicion or, in an even worse scenario, attempt to learn more news about the armies and draw attention in that way. Best to have the Kheld at hand. But Dorilian had not thought through completely what to do with him.

Emboldened by Dorilian's silence, Robdan pleaded his case. "I won't bother you. I won't get in your way—" Though he cut off his appeal, Robdan acknowledged Dorilian's look of disdain. "I know I'm an annoyance even just standing here, but... I want to learn. I've never seen anything of the Rill before, only the Mount at Dazunor-Rannuli, and that from across the great canal. Even at Permephedon I'm not allowed to set foot past the first colonnade. Staubauns don't let Khelds near the Rill, not ever. This, right now, is the closest I've ever been." Robdan squared his shoulders and lifted his chin. "I'll do whatever you say. And, if you don't want me to, I will never say a word to anyone of what I see. Not even to Hans. I promise you that, and I am a man of my word. I just don't want to come so close and see nothing."

Except that for Robdan to see *nothing* was exactly what Dorilian preferred. "Whatever you might see, you will not understand."

"Then let me be amazed. Please," Robdan beseeched again. "I have never asked for anything from you."

Dorilian weighed this complication. While he was convinced to attempt to awaken the node, his ability to do so was less certain. Though he had read and committed to memory his grandfather's entire library of books, the Aryati technology within the sanctuary might yet prove mysterious—only the Rill itself was not. There remained an element of risk.

And yet he felt kindly toward Robdan, who during the last few weeks had assisted Dorilian in many ways, obliging his needs while keeping his identity secret. Dorilian knew his presence as a guest must have been trying. He was often moody and remote—this night more than ever. Yet Robdan had gone to extraordinary lengths to accommodate his temper. A gust of rain-laden wind pierced Dorilian's skin with a thousand tiny needles, deciding the matter. He wanted to keep Robdan close for secrecy's sake, and the weather was too cold and harsh to leave him outside, even could he be sure of the man. Furthermore, it might not be so bad if there was *one* Kheld in Amallar who knew that the Rill was not a monster.

"You may accompany me inside. I but pray I can open the door." That would be the first challenge. Dorilian had never *opened* a dormant Rill sanctuary before. Sebbord had done so at Hestya.

As he had each day for testing the approach rings, Dorilian placed the Rill Stone on his finger. The stone blazed green. Robdan's wide eyes reflected the glow. The door looked seamless, but when Dorilian pressed the hand bearing the Rill Stone to its surface, a cartouche appeared, framing a module crisscrossed by ornate glowing lines. While Robdan watched, Dorilian turned the ring on his finger as he had seen Sebbord do with the Ring of Order at Hestya, then placed his hand over the device so that the Rill Stone fit against a thumb-sized depression at the top. Derlon's resonance bridged the range the Aryati key in the Ring of Order would have filled.

With a silent inhalation, the thick door slid to one side and into the wall. Air rushed to fill the void within. That violent wind threatened to suck Dorilian and Robdan into the abyss that yawned before them, blacker than night and unguarded. But rather than struggle against that force, Dorilian grasped Robdan by the arm and drew him into the chamber. Moments later, the door just as silently slid shut, performing its age-old function of safeguarding the Rill's Aryati components.

With the door sealed, the chamber seemed a void. No light at all. No sound but their own breathing. Robdan clutched Dorilian's arm as if convinced there would be no floor. But there was a floor, as perfectly solid as was the wall against which they stood, and soon Robdan loosened his grip. In Sordan, Robdan would have been punished, harshly—perhaps even beheaded—for latching onto Dorilian so violently. Here, in Amallar, it did not matter.

Dorilian groped for and found his compass again. Made in Gweroyen at a time when Aryati arts still flowered, at the dawn of the Second Creation, the compass served a multitude of needs and was a minor treasure of the Sordaneon arsenal of devices. Flipping open the lid, Dorilian activated the precious power source and directed the resulting light around the room. He had other means of creating light at his disposal, but none so bright or far-reaching. To his relief, the sanctuary interior appeared typical enough.

"Your hand glows!" Robdan spoke reverently.

Dorilian showed him the device. "I came prepared. This building has lain dormant for tens of thousands of years. Did you truly expect to find a light within?"

"I—I don't know. I think maybe I did."

"If possible, I shall soon provide one."

Using the compass to light their way, Dorilian crossed a floor as black as darkness itself. The sanctuary revealed its configuration in planes and curves, sweeps of smooth surfaces cut with crystalline patterns. A curving wall at the center of the structure took shape, and Dorilian followed the spiral passageway downward, not bothering to examine its dimensions. All sanctuaries were constructed along the same pattern. Before long he stopped in front of another portal. It, too, was sealed.

"This time, we stand out of the way."

He pulled Robdan behind him, well to one side of the door. The room behind this door was not the sort one wanted to fly into. When pressed to the portal's barrier, the Rill Stone matched resonance easily, and again the door sighed as it slid open. Though the inflow of air was less forceful than that of the first ingress, Robdan clutched at his ears and gasped for breath. Dorilian too felt the sudden decompression and realized what had happened. The air he had let into the ancient building upon entering now must fill this chamber as well. He had thought of the vacuum but not of its consequences on their air supply.

He had erred dangerously.

But what choice had there been? Only leaving the Rill Stone in the doorlock would have kept the passage open, and to do that would have been both unwise and counterproductive. Neither his nor Robdan's life was in immediate danger. If Dorilian could not activate the power source, they could simply leave the station. Still, there was need to move decisively. He half dragged Robdan into the vast, high-ceilinged room he had opened.

"Stay here." Dorilian pushed Robdan down along a wall. It took more breath to force the words than he would have liked.

"Bad air." Robdan coughed and struggled to speak.

"No, just not enough of it. Don't talk. There's enough to live on if we save it for breathing."

Dorilian turned and flashed his light over a host of metallic shapes and devices until he found what he sought: an array of sleek black tubes in the hub of the chamber, their darkness infinite, swallowing every luminous reflection that ventured near.

There, he thought, *that is the cursed thing I must move.* He played his light along the railing that divided the platform he and Robdan inhabited from the edge of the service pit. A ladder descended from the platform, its metallic rungs disappearing into the pit below. Powerful as the light was, its beam found no bottom. But he knew what waited there, not that far down.

The platform reached by the ladder was a service walk, suspended in the free space that plunged deep into the station's core. It placed him in reach of the core array. He raised his light to play upon the intricate collection of metallic spires and rods, the underside of the black tubes. In the thin light cast by the tiny compass, the array appeared as a series of shifting reflections.

Srava-Aryati. The device-sorcery of the ancient race, metallic and cold and gleaming, breathtaking even to one who had breath, heart-stopping to any who did not. Even now, bound to its eternal silence, it seemed poised to destroy. Dorilian reached out his hand until his fingers were parallel with the massive power rods that glittered blacker than the void below, looming in the surrounding dark like arcane jewels. No sooner did his skin approach the glistening tip of the nearest spire than the Rill Stone sang a burning kiss of warning. He snatched his hand back, recalling the oft-told tale of how the fourth son of Derlon had touched the power core of the Leseos node and collapsed screaming in the pit, dead before any could reach him.

Not just the Rill endangered Dorilian here. He staggered back. This Aryati thing of metal and madness—filled with captive, forgotten power—could destroy him just as easily. Why was he doing this, risking his life? Because he was trapped by the charred remains of promises made and not kept?

Damn you, Marc!

Dorilian had given that promise in desperation. In hope, pushing aside all questions of peril.

I thought you would take my hand. But you didn't... you didn't even try. Yet Dorilian had done all he could to honor his word. Isolated. Surrounded by hostility. He had sought ways to keep the treaty alive. Or perhaps it was Marc Frederick he wanted to keep alive, if only in memory of having been true to the singular legacy of a singular man.

Dorilian might have done it, had it been anyone but Stefan.

For a moment Dorilian wavered, convinced of his old enmity, unwilling to yield. Great as the gift was, Handurin and the Khelds did not need it. *No*, another thought slid sideways.

I do.

True power flowed not from ability but from the willingness to use it. *Levyathan is right. My chains are made not of their hatreds but of mine. I must break myself before I can move.*

Stefan had been spited enough. It was time to bury the bastard once and for all—declare himself as Sordaneon and Rill Lord, fulfill the promise.

Reaching up, Dorilian laid hold of two of the many insulated handles on one side of the device. It had taken six men to bring down the core ignitor at Hestya, six powerful men chosen for their strength, straining with all their might on every handle and with a full atmosphere to breathe. The Aryati had crafted machines to do this work, lurking within the pit walls at Dorilian's back, activated by power sources long vanished with the cities that had fed them. They had also allowed for manual emergency measures—for the enhancer-strengthened, the slave commanders. Dorilian had neither resource at hand. Though he hauled with all his strength, the inertia of the thing defeated him, refusing to be moved. Gasping for air that could not be replenished unless he made the node and its ventilation system operational, Dorilian released the handles.

The device itself seemed to mock him. But the core array was not the only presence here.

Sordaneon. Dorilian stood back and battled his own laughter for breath.

Derlon himself was at hand. Here beneath this hill, the body of a god stood with Dorilian.

Anticipating contact, Dorilian armed his flesh to ward off an immortal's appropriation. This time, if he assessed his ability correctly—if lessons from his ancestors' ancient notes and his endless hours spent summoning and containing Rill energy proved worthwhile—he would do the appropriating. A simple act of will bid kinetic shielding to slide over nerves and sheathe muscle, organs, and bone, leaving only skin. Skin was enough, if it bore his blood.

With his right hand, Dorilian grasped one handle again, this time to steady himself. He did not know what would take place next, if his will would be enough to contain the Entity's incursion or direct its purpose. Already the corpus blossomed overhead on filaments of plasm. When he opened the aperture in his shielding....

He extended his left hand toward the corpus and a blue-green tendril of Rill energy snaked to the Rill Stone and from there webbed his fingers, then his hand. That light climbed down his arm and he winced at the sudden burn.

See me, Father. The echo of your lost humanity. For what Dorilian was, Derlon had been. And what Derlon was, Dorilian could become, though if ever he fully did so, the Rill might overpower all memory of this incarnation.

From the edge of awareness, Dorilian guessed that Robdan was seeing this. That the Kheld watched as cyan strands emerged from the walls to wrap around Dorilian's arm, flow over it like another skin. Robdan could not see through clothing or the way those searing tendrils swept over Dorilian's shoulder and sought to hook into his spine.

No. Dorilian directed Rill energy away from his core, into his limbs and extracorporeal vessels he had not known he had, something vivid and utterly alien seeking ingress—

No! The touch was stronger now. Dorilian fought the Entity for control. Derlon was not, had never been, a passive being. *And neither am I.* You *will not consume* me!

He focused as Sebbord and old scrolls had taught him—on constructs, persons, memories that were his alone, neural imprints Derlon did not yet know and could not incorporate. Remotely, Dorilian felt Levyathan, aware and alarmed—*You should have forewarned me that you were with it!*—then Levyathan too waited focused and steady on the edge of awareness. With cold precision, Dorilian filled his mind with images and presences he controlled, contained within boundaries he was certain were his own. Steadily, the primacy of his being reasserted. He curled his fingers and found himself able to move, power at his command.

This time when he held both grips on the array, his body's strength multiplied manifold through the larger being to which he was symbiont.

Slowly, very slowly, the massive, many-tipped device eased from its long sleep, turning on its pivot, graceful and deadly as it overcame the inertia of ten thousand years. Once its descent had begun, the core ignitor lowered easily, following a pathway unused for millennia, metal rods and spires gliding down into a cylindrical housing set into the crystal floor of the pit. As those gleaming spires slid silently into place, a blinding pulse of energy shot upward through the core tubes, a glimpse of glory darkened as Dorilian slammed down the shields and secured the safety covers that would hold the power core fast.

He glanced up at the platform and saw Robdan slumped near the railing, possibly unconscious. How much had Robdan seen?

More than Marc Frederick ever had.

What is it like, to have the Rill in your blood?

When Marc had asked that question, Dorilian had not known the answer. It had taken the horrors of Permephedon to open his eyes, and years after that to discipline his body and mind so he might attain the necessary degree of control. To bring himself to the point where he might safely attempt it again.

It is like this, he told the ghost residing so vividly in his mind. With blue-laced hands, Dorilian locked the massive clamps and activated the seals. *It is the edge of annihilation.*

From within the bowels of the node, deep beneath the shielded core of the hill, a power no Kheld had ever imagined surged into hidden linkages beneath floors and within walls. Fresh air flooded the room and he filled his lungs.

It is this: to invite assimilation to visit me while I deliver on promises.

For years Dorilian had known he might be able to direct Rill power. The only wonder was that he had first fully called upon it in Amallar. Leaning against the warm metal railing of the platform, he looked up at the snaking plasm overhead. Before he shed this skin, and while his contact with Levyathan remained steady, he had but one thing left to do. He raised his left hand a second time, watching as the Rill Stone, blazing bright as a sun, attracted vermiform filaments of green.

"See me," Dorilian commanded. He no longer had need of hidden control consoles. Through the tiniest of neural irises he allowed the Rill's being to make contact with his own—the barest moment, because a moment would be enough. Two would be too much.

Trestethion.

The World opened to every side of him. Sordan. Permephedon. Mountains of ice and lakes of fire. And now Bellan Toregh was there, too, a shining hill above a dark and empty land.

Dorilian closed his fist, silencing the visions and the Rill, snapping threads of pain as he broke contact. The azure filaments lacing his skin bled away, leaving him purely mortal again.

Weakened and retching, he sank to the floor. *Lev?*

Dor! So distant, that contact. So far away. *What did you do? You need me with you.*

You are with me. But I also needed you to be there. Separate. Not Dorilian and not Derlon. Someone to reach for should he fail.

You did it? We did? Wakened Trestethion?

Yes. I— Wearily, Dorilian was seized by another bout of nausea.

You need Tutto's malt! Do you have any left?

All of it. During his entire adventure so far, Dorilian had not drunk so much as a drop of the brew. *I will drink it now. Put your mind at ease and tell Tiflan what we have done. Go.*

The mental contact had sapped his remaining strength. With trembling fingers, Dorilian fumbled at his jacket to pull out and uncap the flask of restorative. Disgusting as the stuff tasted, he drank it all, then took several minutes to catch his breath and recover. Rill contact always drained him, and this time had taxed him to the limit.

Gazing up beyond the platform, he glimpsed the dimly lit corridor to the sanctuary's operations node. His work was but half-finished.

When Dorilian climbed the ladder to the platform again, he found Robdan had sagged to the floor. Dropping to his knees, he turned Robdan over, relieved to find him still breathing. There would be time later to find out what the man had witnessed before succumbing to the chamber's poor air. He lifted Robdan into his arms. "Let's get you warmed."

By the time Robdan woke, slumped in a suspension chair in the control room, Dorilian had finished. From his chair beside the faintly glowing boards and lustrous panels of the node's main console, he watched as Robdan stirred, then tensed at finding himself in incomprehensible surroundings. Wide portals no person standing outside the building could suspect existed looked out upon a seamless, smooth platform gleaming palest rose in the first light of dawn. Beyond, mists swirled upward from the shadowy hills and forests of Amallar.

"Bellan Toregh is awakened," Dorilian told him. "All my promises are kept."

"I saw—"

"Don't tell me. I'd rather not know. But whatever you saw, I will also hold you to your promise to tell no one." It eased Dorilian's mind only a little to know that promises made to a Highborn Prince were, by their very nature, difficult to break.

Robdan nodded, then swallowed hard... and stared out the window at an Amallar not yet aware that it was profoundly changed. The time had not yet come to light up Bellan Toregh as though it were Sordan in full blaze and moonlight.

For now, the hill remained as it had been. Silent. Waiting.

A god wrapped in shadows.

26

Staubauns do not cook their food. They fuss over it as if it were a woman on her day to wed. More attention is given to the garnish than the meat, the plate than the meal. A man could starve waiting for dinner.

Tobold Forbasson, *A North Country Primer*

The messenger from the Seers arrived on the first dark moon after the sacrifice. Hans noted the arrival. For nearly two phases, the Faeduadan had deliberated the meanings of his omens before reaching their conclusion. The priest bearing the news had made the journey on foot, predicated on the belief that a fully sanctified Faeduadin would neither eat nor in any way abuse their fellow creatures. *Except for humans. You cut me up well enough. And I'm pretty damn sure if you had a prophecy, that means you killed the horse.* Hans continued to be angry about the deception worked upon him, though Dorilian had correctly stated that it was no less than what Hans had set himself up for.

"If you learn one lesson from this, let it be that you must decide your own destiny, not allow others to do it for you. You walked into that ritual like a mindless goat!"

And Hans had. He had, and he knew it, and the sheer humiliation of that blunder worked within him like a bitter stew. Fortunately, the lesson was all the more powerful because it smarted. Only cold resolve restrained Hans to merely watch as the gathered leaders of Amallar, Nalf Rhys at their head, welcomed the messenger. The Thegnard's meeting chamber was packed to the walls with Old Mothers, local elders and keld chieftains, and a few people like Hans and Aubrey who held standing in other ways.

The priest bowed deeply—not to the men before whom he stood, but in deference to the god whose judgment he conveyed. "The god has spoken through the Horse. The place most auspicious for the Witan shall be the mount of Lud's Spear, the High Rock of Bellan Toregh."

"What the holy—" Nalf Rhys barely contained his outburst. His gaze flashed from one side of the crowded room to the other as he tempered his response. "Is that so?" He thrust his chin at the priest. "And what if we say otherwise? What if we choose to hold it here?"

"The god Lud was consulted. The holy sacrifice performed. Thus fell the omens. Hans Thegn's fate waits upon Bellan Toregh."

All eyes turned to Hans. For his part, he eyed the brown-robed priest with some surprise. How could the Faeduadan have known? Sacrifice or no sacrifice, even Hans had not known until he had returned to Rhodhur that very night that Dorilian would agree to attempt to awaken the Rill node at Bellan Toregh. To *attempt* it. Did this verdict mean that Dorilian had succeeded? Or that he had failed? Either way, the portents seemed apt.

Hans spread his hands. "I submit to the will of the god." It seemed the right thing to say.

Nalf Rhys glared. It was no secret that he had expected the Witan to be held at Rhodhur, the ancient significance of Bellan Toregh notwithstanding. Aubrey had told Hans that when the Khelds first came to Amallar, Bellan Toregh had awed them with its mysterious power, and they had believed the High Rock to be the place where Lud tested the mettle of those who would lead his people. The test of Lud's Spear had dropped by the wayside when the Khelds acquired greater knowledge of the Staubaun Rill and its passage through their land. Nonetheless, the site retained its importance and was still the focus of powerful local legends.

The priest's hood hid all but his mirthless smile. "The god has spoken. And Hans Thegn has spoken. If the matter is to include them, you had best pay heed."

"This needs talking, faedu," Nalf growled. "I want a word with you later."

At that, the priest bowed again and departed.

Hans pulled Aubrey aside as the gathering dissolved into raised voices and dispute. "Why did the Seers decide that the Witan should be held at Bellan Toregh?"

Aubrey shook her head, showing that she too was puzzled by the unexpected announcement. "I didn't think they would. They prefer to hold Witans at Rhodhur so they can be near their Sacred Grove and have the blessings of the Old Mothers."

When she turned to look back over her shoulder at the gesticulating elders, Hans tugged at Aubrey's sleeve. "Let's go. Before people start asking questions of *me*."

The longer Hans stayed in the room, the greater chance someone would interrupt his chance to talk with Aubrey. With Robdan's absence, Aubrey had become Hans's primary source of information on Kheld ways and mores, and this conversation was laden with both.

"I still can't believe it." Aubrey continued to express her doubts as she and Hans descended the stairs to the outer hall. "Why? The Rill doesn't even run there anymore!"

"I thought you wanted the Witan to be at Bellan Toregh."

"I do want the Witan to be at Bellan Toregh." Aubrey slid a cutting glare his way, warning Hans not to mistake her feelings on the matter. "I think it's wonderful that the Priesthood agrees. I just think the timing on their part makes no sense. At least if the Rill were running, they could appeal to old tales, arrange everything around the Rill's appearances, maybe sacrifice an especially good-looking goat, and make themselves look wonderful. They have more to gain by holding the Witan here and conjuring the moon than coping with an absent Rill and all the talk *that* topic is sure to stir up in their faces. Unless—" Aubrey's expression changed as she stepped aside to let a pair of Old Mothers step off the stairs and onto the landing. "It may have something to do with your prophecy."

"The priest said my fate waits atop Bellan Toregh. They want me *there* when they reveal it."

"But who wants you there? The god—or the priests?"

The note of suspicion in Aubrey's voice told Hans that she was on his side. Until recently, he had wondered. Her attention had initially appealed to him because he found talking with her both informative and pertinent, punctuated by observant humor. Aubrey didn't have to pretend that Hans's opinions interested her. They did. And he did, though not in the way others were prone to believe. Even Arne had taken to snickers whenever he caught the two of them together. Hans, however, had noted that Aubrey's interest in that direction was more firmly fixed elsewhere. It was too bad Nalf Rhys had not.

"What's this?" True to form, Nalf looked pleased to find Hans and Aubrey together. "Stealing kisses of victory?"

Along with a host of other people, Nalf Rhys had filed from the meeting room onto the wide balcony overlooking the main hall. Now Hans stood tensely while Nalf trod heavily down the first stairs to join him. Most of the crowd hung back, muttering comments of discontent and scowling in the manner of their leader. They recognized that Hans stood in full favor of the Priesthood's decision but were uncertain how wise it would be to oppose him. Kingships and prophecies had more power to move Khelds than the preferences of clan leaders. And the priest had said that the fate of not just Hans but Amallar *itself* waited upon Bellan Toregh. The Khelds could not afford to go against both their god and their king, if indeed Hans was to be one. Even Nalf and his followers would not attempt to force the hand of the Priesthood.

"Bet you're pleased about it." Nalf Rhys spoke to the defiance he saw in both Hans and Aubrey. "Damn Rill won't even put on a show and we're traipsing half across the land to see it. And to make a bad idea worse, word has it that Sordan's pocketed an army, sent it somewhere deep in Neuberland." To Aubrey's look of surprise, he snapped peevishly. "Gods below, girl, what do you think I'm talking about? Bersyas and his bunch!" Nalf ground his back teeth with obvious rage. "Sordan's moving like a tiger, sneaking in the bushes somewhere, and we're mucking about with the stars on top of Bellan Toregh!"

Aubrey turned to Hans, waiting for his answer along with every other person in the crowded passageway.

"That's news to me." Hans didn't see what else he could or was supposed to say. Whatever the movement of Sordan's army meant, he was sure beyond sure it was something Dorilian had set into motion before leaving Sordan. But for what purpose? Or was that why Dorilian had gone to Bellan Toregh? Not to open the Rill, but to rejoin his army? The possibility was so real the chill of it filled even Hans's throat. "If an army is on the move, that doesn't necessarily mean it's coming after *us*. You haven't heard it's attacking anything, have you? I'm sure there's a good explanation."

"Explanation! I can think of a dozen, and all of them stink to the highest mountaintops!" Nalf looked ready to attack something himself. "Between the priests and Sordan you've got a fine lot on your tail." His small eyes, shrewd and piercingly ice blue, narrowed.

"You still want to deal with Sordan, knowing what you do? And about this?"

"Yes." Hans was not about to be backed into any corner he had not yet investigated. "Until I know more, I will deal with Sordan."

"Know *more*?" Aubrey demanded. "What more do you need to know? This is about armies!"

"I don't have all the facts yet."

"And from where will you get those? Your good friends in Sordan?"

A loud thump sounded from the deep coathook-lined vestibule near the bottom of the staircase as something heavy hit the floor. "Can't I ever leave this Hall for a few days without returning to find it in uproar?"

All heads turned to look past Hans and Aubrey to the Hall's wood-beamed entrance, where Robdan, travel-rumpled and stoop-shouldered, weighed down by his bags and with his head covered by a battered hat, stepped out of the shadows. Behind him stood the taller form of his traveling companion.

Dorilian came back! Hans experienced a relief that bordered on exultation. That feeling extinguished all flickering doubts. *It wasn't just a ruse to join his army.* Hans tried to catch Dorilian's attention, hoping to learn the answer to a question he had to restrain himself from shouting. Dorilian, though, had read the situation, and kept his silence as he met Hans's gaze with wry appreciation.

See? Hans could almost hear Dorilian say. *I told you they'd be troublesome.*

"Well?" Robdan removed his hat, dropped another bag to the floor, and stepped forward. "What is all this about?"

Faced with a man who always opposed him in matters of policy, Nalf Rhys snorted. "Seems the Priesthood has decided that the Witan is to be held at Bellan Toregh."

Robdan's plain face brightened. "Really?" He glanced at Hans to gauge the temper of that news. "That's... unexpected."

"Sure as bird's crap," said another man.

"Well, should my opinion be of interest here, I happen to agree with the choice of location." Robdan looked tired and probably wanted nothing more than his own room, a warm bath, and a good hot meal.

"You and Hans Thegn here." Nalf Rhys spat in disgust, clearly too angered to yield the offensive. "He's got Sordan up his nose."

With equal disgust, Hans turned away and met Dorilian's smooth curiosity with an aggravated frown.

Robdan tucked his hat into his jacket and, with a shrug, shifted his backpack from one shoulder into his hand. "Maybe you should listen to him, Nalf. Maybe we all should. We could do with a fresh start."

"Aye, and you egging him to it, I'm sure. You and this mongrel outlander you've taken up with, thick as pet cousins." Nalf Rhys glared at the pair with undisguised disapproval. "Thron," he redirected, "you don't say much, but I saw the Elector give you his ear often enough. Even Gerd thinks you worth listening to. So what say you to this: that Sordan's army under Bersyas, an army fifteen thousand strong, has left Neuberland?"

Robdan's jaw dropped open, though he closed it again quickly.

Dorilian, however, set his travel bag on the floor and removed his gloves. "I would say it is old news. Robdan and I heard as much five days ago outside of Eastmeary Brenna."

Nalf Rhys stiffened as his followers looked to him, aware now that he must have known for days as well—and that he had withheld the information. Aubrey whipped about, fury in her glare at her uncle. "Is that so?" Nalf blustered. "Heard it ahead, did you? Well then where the seven hells do you think they've gone?"

Hans thought about jumping in and saying something to get Dorilian off the hook. He never got the chance because Dorilian spoke first.

"Do you actually want me to answer that?"

"Yes, damn you."

"Then I would say they have gone north. To Essera."

"Essera!" The packed balcony seethed with Nalf's rage and the furious mutters of angry Khelds. "The hell you say! Essera!" Nalf's face flushed red as he bristled at the notion. He marched down to the landing. "Out to conquer them next, is he, now that Stefan's cold in his grave? Get a jump on Hans Thegn here and cross our lands to do it? I'll skewer his balls, the bastard, if he tries!"

Now that he and Nalf were face to face, Hans needed to take this problem back where it belonged: on himself. "And if you're smart, you'll let Sordan do the dirty work for us! Instead of standing here arguing, we should be fighting in Essera too—and at the side of that army, not against it. That army goes against Nammuor, not Essera and not Amallar. And not *me*! It rode *past* Amallar. To Merrydn, maybe." To the sudden sharp looks people gave him, questioning his choice of geography, he threw up his hands. "I don't know! But when I was in Sordan, I learned that Merrydn had asked for military aid, and Lacenedon too."

"So they can turn it against us."

"No, not us. Against Nammuor and my two-faced regent, Erenor. If Nammuor is not beaten this winter, he may not be beatable at all. The domains of Essera, the ones who stand against Erenor and want to preserve their kingdom—you know, those who want *me* to sit on their throne—know this too."

With the suddenness of a striking viper, Nalf's hand shot out and grabbed Hans by the arm, fingers digging into his flesh. "Will you get it into your head, boy! Nammuor the Mormantaloran is not the enemy! Not ours. Not yours and probably not theirs either. He's a dirty sorcerer, they say, and I don't like him, but Nammuor has sent us a proposal that should set you up for good and for life! Set you up and us with you! Promises you'll be King, he does, with all Essera to be yours and his army to support you!"

"Like hell he would!" Hans tore free from Nalf's determined grip and pushed the man away, shoving him toward the crowded stairs and balcony with more muscle than he had meant to use. Nalf stumbled back into the supporting arms of his followers, who stared at Hans in alarm. "Nammour's proposals are death warrants! He would use every man under his command to control me! I'm not signing on for that. Accept his proposal and I am done with you! Done with you and done with Amallar!" Breaking from the crowd, Hans turned his back on all of them, and stormed to the handful of steps leading from the landing to the Main Hall, where it seemed half of Rhodhur was listening to them argue.

Nalf Rhys stomped in pursuit, too heated to allow an advantage to cool. "And where would you go? Who'd have you, you little snot-nosed brat? Sordan?"

"I don't know!" Hans shouted from the bottom step. As he had thought, the main hall was packed with silent, intensely interested Khelds waiting to hear the outcome of the argument. The Old Mothers who had not left before the fighting broke out clustered in their orange cloaks near Robdan in the entry. "But if you side with Nammuor and think you'll have some say in Essera, you'd be fighting *me*. Not Dorilian Sordaneon. Me! Because I'm not going to step out of the way." Hans smiled and was glad to see that expression freeze the anger not only on Nalf Rhys's but a hundred other tongues. "But Nammuor won't want you, then, will he, if I'm not part of the bargain? He doesn't want an alliance with Amallar. Why would he? He wants Essera for himself! He bought it piece by piece, noble name by noble name, right out from under Stefan's nose. By the time Nammuor made that alliance with Stefan, he owned Essera already. He had his puppets in place, doing his bidding—all he needed from Stefan was an excuse to move in after he died. And like an idiot, Stefan gave it to him."

Nalf Rhys barreled down the steps, Stefanites and cruihcil members hard on his heels. With the rough grasp of an outraged bear, he shoved Hans against the balustrade. "You should be ashamed of yourself. Stefan was your brother, damn it! Your own gods-damned brother! You can't talk of him that way! He *stood* for us when he signed that alliance!"

"Alliance—what alliance? Where is it? *Where are your allies,* Nalf? They've gone back into the woodwork, to their luxuries and plots of domination, now that they don't need you anymore!" It felt good to shove back, to give Nalf a broadside of what Hans had been thinking for weeks. On the entry landing above, behind the others who crowded near, Dorilian and Robdan hung back, attending every word but refraining from taking part. They were letting Hans fight his own battle. "The only thing Stefan signed was his death warrant! He was dead the moment he signed the edict making Erenor Tholeros regent to his Heirs. I demanded to see proof and I saw it. Archhalial copies. Correspondence from witnesses, including our mother! Stefan signed away Essera and everything in it for a handful of lies. He signed *me* into that man's power. He made it so easy, I'm surprised Nammuor waited as long as he did to kill him!"

"Why you little—" Nalf Rhys launched a blow that never landed.

Hans ducked to the side and the blow brushed past his ear in a rush of sleeve. Was he in a fistfight? A brawl? Was that what this had turned into? If so, no holds would be barred. Whether moved by calculated risk or heat of anger, Nalf Rhys had just staked his own leadership on the outcome of public combat with his rival. *Back off!* Hans's good sense demanded. But how could he? To do so would brand him a coward, a weakling, and he would lose all hope of influence among men who would use this confrontation as a measure of his true fighting spirit.

Sensing Nalf momentarily off-balance, surprised by striking only air, Hans struck back with a fist to the jaw. It sent Nalf reeling sideways, down the steps from the landing to sprawl across the floor of the Hall. Nalf pushed himself to his feet, licking at a trickle of blood from his mouth. The blow had done little damage, except perhaps to Nalf's pride at being caught off-guard. With an enraged growl, he lowered his head and charged up the steps again. *Defend yourself*, Hans thought, *just defend yourself. Play fair. You might need him later.*

As Nalf Rhys bore upon him, Hans sidestepped and threw his shoulder behind another punch, this one a sharp, quick uppercut that snapped the bearded man's head back as though it had been jerked and dropped him to the landing in a limp, undignified heap.

Wincing, Hans clutched his hand. *Damn*, that had hurt. It had taken less than a minute and no skill—Nalf Rhys had obviously not believed Hans capable of fighting back.

Arne rushed to Hans and embraced him briskly. Others ran up with congratulations, arms clapping Hans on the shoulders as voices shouted offers of ale in his honor. Though Hans wanted to see to Nalf's wellbeing, he was too crowded by people to act. He caught a brief glimpse of Aubrey and several others on the landing kneeling at Nalf's side, and Nalf swiping at them. Apparently, he had suffered no ill consequences. It was entirely possible that Hans, with his throbbing right hand, was hurt worse. Only when Nalf had been taken to his residence, to recover from his bruises and injured dignity, did Hans think to look for Robdan and Dorilian. But the two were nowhere to be seen.

I need to talk to them. I need to know if I will have anything to offer at Bellan Toregh.

By then, however, his supporters had inflated Hans's two well-delivered blows to the status of a good thrashing. Hans could hardly afford to refuse the resulting celebration. Already Arne, ale mug in hand, was demonstrating a Kheld talent for exaggeration.

"What'd I tell you?" Arne shouted, raising high his cup and spilling ale down his sleeve. "Hans here don't let nobody push him to the wall. Nobody—not even in Sordan—no one ever did! Not even the Sordaneon himself!"

And at that moment, at least, the entire Hall believed it and burst forth in cheers and laughter, clashing mugs and spilling as much ale as they drank. Beer flowed as thickly as tall tales. It was a good round of drinks later that Hans felt a hand upon his arm.

Aubrey smiled at him. "Not bad," she assessed, "for a fellow no one thought knew how to fight." It was a congratulation Hans valued above all the others.

"I don't make a practice of it." He recalled his last fight, with Dorilian on the beach at Rhondda, and ducked his head. "I got caught off-guard by a punch myself once, and I wasn't going to let it happen again. I don't like getting hit."

"Who does?"

Hans showed Aubrey his swollen hand. "I also don't like hitting people."

She took the hand and gently turned it. "Gerd can get you some ice for this. It's not displaced but it may be broken."

"I don't think so. Everything moves the way it should. It just hurts."

"You still need ice." Aubrey called over a passing jen and made that request. "Nalf likes to settle his fights with his fists, but he's not getting any younger—someone needed to show him that it's time to stop." She grinned and added, "And maybe to start acting like a grown man for a change."

Hans tempered his own feelings of satisfaction. "You know what I like least? It didn't end the argument. All it did was postpone it. Everything Nalf said is still out there, needing to be resolved. And I figure it'll fall on me to resolve it. How is he?"

"Thegnard still. He says you pack quite a wallop for such an unfinished runt." Aubrey drew Hans over to a nearby table that had become unoccupied and pulled him to sit on the bench alongside her. Arne took a seat on the other side. "But you're right about the argument. It isn't over. That offer he talked about, the one on the table—"

"You mean the offer no one told me about?"

"It's not like anyone told me about it either," she countered. Arne simply shook his head and quaffed another mouthful of ale.

"Don't you think if something involves me—things like, say, making promises in my name or putting me on a throne—I should be part of the negotiation?" Kheld chieftains engaging in these sorts of things felt uncomfortably close to what Hans had gone through in Sordan: treading a path dark with suspicion and doubt. It had eventually led to his escape, and he didn't want to go through that kind of thing again.

"I think they should involve you, yes." Aubrey met his

accusatory regard with a look that begged him to accept that she, at least, felt sympathy. "It's the Mother's Law that any person, not just women, cannot be forced into false relationships. That means weddings and beddings, but also contracts. The proposal from Nammuor was made to *Amallar*, which means our chieftains. Maybe they just... hadn't finished discussing it yet before they would have presented it to you."

"Or maybe they just thought they could slip it on him like some collar all of them together could yank and haul for whatever they wanted," Arne snapped. A few cups of ale had him speaking freely. "The damn Hierarch was a bastard but he didn't try to sell Hans to the highest bidder."

Aubrey squirmed and lowered her voice. "I too think it interesting that this Nammuor person didn't approach Hans directly. Maybe he doesn't know how. Not everyone has contacts here who can get messages through. But that doesn't mean the proposal is a bad one. It's very tempting."

Hans grimaced. If Nammuor's offer existed at all, Khelds would take it in one easy swallow and never see it for what it was. He made a stab at adapting one of Robdan's metaphors. "Didn't your mother warn you about temptation? You have to look it in the teeth, not the eye."

"Have you looked in Sordan's teeth?"

"I put my hand in them. They're sharp, but they didn't bite me."

Aubrey shook her head in disbelief. "And you still think you can trust him?"

"Sooner than I'd trust Nammuor. Of that, I'm certain. I wish people would listen to me. Nammuor's not doing me any favors with his offer. When, while he was establishing himself in Essera, did Nammuor ever approach Amallar for anything or to offer support for me as King when Stefan died? Did Nammuor ever say that he would welcome me to return and claim the throne? Over Erenor? I'm not exactly a secret." At this point Hans was an established fact—and threat.

The bowl of chopped ice had arrived. Aubrey covered the pieces with a thin cloth, then placed Hans's hand so the swelling would chill. He decided he might as well continue his argument.

"I wish people would understand that Nammuor is playing games too. I was no danger to anyone as long as Erenor and his Archhalia stooges could keep me suspended in an impotent regency that never raised a finger or even a voice to oppose him. And while Nammuor thought I was a prisoner in Sordan, he was content enough to sit back and watch the show. If he'd wanted to, Nammuor could have pressed his Esseran puppets to speak up, but he didn't. He also didn't speak up himself. Did anyone but me notice that? The only reason Nammuor came forward with this proposal of his now is to prevent something else he likes less."

"Your talks with Sordan?" Aubrey guessed.

"That's what I think. He knows where I am now. Everyone knows. What he's trying to prevent are any agreements that would give me a stronger coalition—and especially any that would allow Sordan to move against him."

"Sordan never said they wanted you on the throne, neither," said one of the younger keld chieftains. He'd wandered over along with several other of the Hall's revelers.

"Chalk up one for Sordan." Hans welcomed the opportunity to answer. "At least they never pretended otherwise. The Sordaneons are the last of the Highborn Princes, the founders of the Triempery. The legitimate rulers. I've studied this and it's true. There's not a Staubaun alive who can say that Dorilian Sordaneon doesn't hold a valid claim to Essera's throne. Even Nammuor would own to it."

"That's a lot of bull!" one of the men challenged.

"That's what I said too," Arne offered. "But he'd rather believe books."

"Because I know how to check out what's true. That claim is cold hard *fact*. Stefan knew it and it scared him to death. Ask around. It's written in their law. My family has Essera's throne through a Malyrdeon adoption and a Wall Lord's exception. The Triempery split over that exception. And if you doubt what I say, Robdan has books about it. The Sordaneon claim scares Nammuor too, because if Dorilian supports *me*, that would unite Essera."

"I don't think you should hold your breath waiting," Aubrey muttered. "It's not likely to happen."

Hans wondered if it were possible to loosen a few entrenched hatreds. Not eradicate them, certainly, but if he was skillful, maybe he could nudge reconsideration. "I haven't been just waiting around looking for things to happen, you know. The man who will not court a maid seldom marries." Around the table rose a chorus of congenial chuckles. One woman elbowed the man next to her. Even Aubrey relaxed enough to smile as Hans continued with fresh vigor.

"The truth is I went to Sordan on a double dare. Dorilian dared Marenthro to put me in his path, and Marenthro did. Then Marenthro dared Dorilian to do something about it. And Dorilian did. And, as you can see, here I am. Marenthro's gamble paid off. I'm in the middle, talking to both sides—exactly where I need to be. And while I was in Sordan, I did my share of courting."

"Say, Hans." The younger man who'd been elbowed spoke up while others looked uncomfortably into their cups. "All this talk of Sordan, you know we don't like it. And it ain't like we need to. If you have it to go against this Nammuor, you don't need to go to Sordan for a hand on it. We can take him on. We don't need the help."

"That sort of thinking plays right into Nammuor's hands. That is just what he wants us, you and me, to think. I'd go so far as to say he feeds our fears and fans our hatreds. After all, what better way to defeat both Sordan *and* the Khelds than to keep us from joining forces? That's what he fears. He'd rather see us fight each other."

"And we do it gladly!" a woman countered to cheers all around.

"You say this is true? This Sorcerer fears us too?" Another woman, a silver-haired Old Mother who had stayed behind, spoke up. "Set those who might stand against him against each other, that would be clever." Perhaps she had less difficulty seeing the conflict as part of the plans of other, vaguer interests. Old Mothers studied patterns and pitting one enemy against another made sense.

"Ask Robdan if you doubt me. He's been saying as much for years, but no one would listen." Hans shifted his hand atop the ice, finding more cold—and relief. The pain was less and the swelling had gone down.

"Say, where is old Robdan anyway?" Arne scanned the room. "He didn't come back down with the others."

"Probably tired." A nearby keld chieftain wiped his mouth on his sleeve. "Bit of a jaunt he just took, him and that Thron character. Who knows but the young fellow rode him hard in a hurry to get back?" He guffawed and nudged the woman seated beside him. "You don't think old Rob has a mind to get his Ressany with a new husband, do you?"

The woman barked with laughter. "A sell-sword outlander? She can do better!"

Another man blew a breath out his nose. "No man like that is gonna take on no woman with seven kids, even if she does hold the best crop land in Eastmeary!"

"Quiet, hey. Here he comes."

Dorilian had taken time to change and wash away the dirt of travel. His hair was still damp and looked darker for that, and he smelled of whatever soap Robdan kept on hand. Hans saw that a few of the Kheld men wrinkled their noses and snickered in observance of the largely male-held wisdom that bathing was for smelling sweet and softening the skin and therefore natural only for women. But Hans had also noticed that they had yet to taunt Dorilian for it. When he slid onto the bench, those same men made room for him. He'd just made a point of resting his long Trongorian sword against the wall behind their table.

Hans rolled his hand atop the ice, hoping to mask his intense interest. Dorilian only rarely sought Khelds for company. Mostly when he did so, it was with Gerd. The only possible reason Dorilian would seat himself with a mass of Khelds was to let Hans know about the Rill.

"So, did Robdan show you the sights?" Aubrey asked before Hans could speak.

Dorilian caught the double meaning and parried it for the benefit of grinning onlookers. "He showed me his *grandchildren*—and little else. The man is a doting grandfather of twelve, he tells me, and those but to start with." He grimaced and said to Hans in all sincerity, "If all Kheld men contribute so well to the next generation, I foresee no future shortage of Khelds. Nor grandfathers to spoil them."

A chorus of appreciative laughter broke loose around the table. Kheld grandfathers were fabled for their indulgences, and they were glad to have that tradition recognized. Aubrey's smile deepened as she leaned across the table. "Surely grandfathers are the same all over?"

Dorilian's expression became more guarded. "Not that I've witnessed."

"Oh, come now, Thron. Surely your grandfather doted on you."

Dorilian held Aubrey's gaze. "My maternal grandsire did his part, I suppose, in his fashion, but I did not see my paternal grandfather at all until I was nearly a man. And neither of them *doted*."

A bare arching of Aubrey's eyebrow indicated an interest in the answer. Somehow, Hans knew, she was fitting her new discovery into place, fashioning a simulacrum from bits and pieces. What kind of picture was she forming? Dorilian's answers were so general as to yield little information at all. Nonetheless, Hans moved to stop the conversation where it stood.

"Then you enjoyed your trip?" Hans presented the question with all the casualness he could muster, even though he intended to pounce upon the first word or nuance flung into his path.

"Yes." Dorilian turned to thank Gerd for the cup being offered, and Hans caught the heady waft of sweetened branroot. "All told, the journey proved equally as fruitful as Robdan's bountiful daughters."

Hans laughed, unable to restrain his relief and glad he could treat the comment as a jibe. Dorilian had done it! Whether the Hierarch had wielded knowledge or power, whether doing so had cost him much or nothing, Hans would learn later. Tonight if possible. For now, it was enough to know that whatever else Hans was going to face at Bellan Toregh, he was going to give the Khelds a damn gift from the gods. He raised his ale cup in tribute, in the jesting manner Khelds loved best. "Then I don't suppose you will mind too much that we will be riding to Bellan Toregh. The Witan might hold a few surprises this year."

"But will they be good ones?" Aubrey's smile suggested she spoke only half in jest. She loosened something from her belt, then placed on the table a pouch of gold-hued, embroidered leather. The stones within it rattled. "Shall we see what your runes say?"

"Aw, faetha Aubrey," Gerd interrupted, frowning sternly as he stood over those seated at the table. "You know I don't hold with soothsaying at my tables."

"Hey, Gerd, let her!" Arne for one looked eager to see what the runes might say. One of the first things he'd done on getting back to Amallar had been to seek out a faetha to read his stones. Several other patrons also called for Gerd to let Aubrey lay her runes.

"I won't be soothsaying," Aubrey promised the offended innkeeper. "I'll do simple readings. One rune per pick. Here." She retrieved the pouch and held it out to Gerd. "You pick first!"

To the laughs and grins of his patrons, Gerd relented and thrust his hand into the pouch. Coming up with one of the smooth, shimmering blue stones, he handed it to Aubrey, who examined the symbol imbedded within it by the stone's natural veins and coloration.

"*Tycleth*." She named the symbol, which she proceeded to interpret. "Strength, home, love on all sides. You are a beloved innkeeper, Gerd."

The rotund man laughed, knowing he'd been had. "All right, give each their due," he told Aubrey, "but no soothsaying!" He made his way back to the kitchens to check on his pots.

"I'm next!" Arne insisted. He pulled out a stone and set it before him hopefully. Aubrey traced the sign with her finger.

"*Hraesa.* Stability, perseverance, unwavering defense—you apparently are not about to change your role soon." She retrieved the stone and shook her pouch, holding it out to Hans. "Let's see what yours says."

Intrigued, Hans reached his uninjured hand into the soft leather bag and felt the polished stones within, identical to his touch. Closing his eyes, he isolated one, took it out and set it in front of him as Arne had done.

Aubrey tapped a finger on her lower lip. "*Menhir.*" She pronounced the Old Kheldic word for 'raised pillars.' "Unity with self and others, partnerships of all kinds. Perhaps you really shall unite them."

Hans grinned at such an auspicious reading. "It's a shame you're not really soothsaying tonight. I like that one." The Khelds around him laughed.

"The runes don't lie." Again, Aubrey retrieved the rune and shifted the stones in the bag, then held it out to Dorilian. "Your turn," she said. The challenge was in the way she said it.

Dorilian hesitated, then drew a stone, balancing it in his fingers briefly before handing it back. Feigned indifference didn't conceal Aubrey's sharp focus as she took the stone in her palm and studied the marking. "*Lahd,*" she identified the ancient symbol. "It represents a journey, discovery, and self-healing."

"Looks like he already did the journey part, faetha Aubrey," one of the men said, causing his fellows to break out in snickers once more.

"But what did he discover?" Aubrey wondered aloud.

Everyone laughed and one of the women at the table clamored for a reading. Hans noticed that Aubrey put the rune back into the bag, but reluctantly, as though it held secrets she meant still to pry from the stone.

Aubrey laid each person's rune before her, focusing on keeping her voice light and her readings true. Rune reading deserved respect, even when done for entertainment. Except it hadn't all been for fun. She noted the way Thron continued to watch her as she picked up the stone he'd chosen and placed it back in the bag. Every time she looked his way, his gaze locked onto hers and her blood quickened.

He knew what she was doing.

She had been trying to see him in her runes for weeks without success. Many nights, she'd taken out her wands of sacred woods, gathered and polished by her own hand as a girl at Aurdollen, where the Aged Mothers had taught her the reading of portents. This man's were deep. When Aubrey had first laid the Wheel for him, focusing with all her skill, asking careful questions as she laid her runes upon flattened spokes of hazel and rowan, alder and yew, she had sought to learn anything she could. The stones had told her only that Thron had no wife, had fathered no child, and in some manner possessed a fortune. He had killed but never stolen, loved but never given a woman his heart. Even laying the stones upon strands of his hair, garnered in stealth from his pillow in Robdan's chambers, had yielded little more than that Thron's actions toward Hans were true. The runes revealed bits of truth, but they could not tell Aubrey what she most wanted to know.

Who was this man? No matter how she framed that question, all the runes would ever reveal to her was one word.

Sordan.

27

One of Stefan Stauberg-Randolph's great failings was that
he was not open to uncertainty. He refused to act other
than upon conclusions he had already reached.

PRINCESS PALAISTEA, *BEFORE THE STORM*

"Visitation!" Nalf Rhys scowled at the priest, who stood
between the Thegnard's chair and the hearth and because
of that looked even darker than was usual for his order.
"What in Madrock's hells does that mean: visitation? Are you trying
to tell me that the god came down from the trees, said a few words,
or what?"

It was the last straw. First, the damned priests had decided to cast
for holding the Witan at Bellan Toregh, then Hans Thegn had
played a fast card and turned out to be a fighter, of all things. And
now the priest was telling Nalf that the Witan had to be held at
Bellan Toregh because of a *visitation*. It wasn't the sort of thing
Kheldish gods were prone to do. Staubaun gods made visitations,
showed themselves at dawn on the Third Day or some such thing;
but Kheldish gods were a quieter lot, dwelled in the heartwood of
trees, or the moving waters of rivers, or in the clouds or the faces of
the moon. They weren't likely to pop up and have conversations.
That the Faeduadan truly believed Lud had paid his servants a visit
could not be dismissed as the usual mystical gibberish.

Nalf looked about his room, regretting his own half-dressed state
and wondering where he'd tossed his robe. He liked to keep one in
this room, near the fire. Priests and prophecies had him not thinking
straight.

"Thegnard, I was there." Faedu Wyver bowed so that his hood concealed his features. "The god came beneath the Daughter Moon while the sacrifice yet burned upon the altar."

"Came, heh. Showed up right there beside you, did he?" Nalf barely attempted to conceal his incredulity. "How did he come, eh? Can you tell me that?"

Wyver paced, lost in rapture. "I can see it still! He came when summoned for the sacrifice. 'Lud!' we called and set our bloodied knives into the holy ground. 'Lud!' we cried, and he roared with the voice of fire. And then we saw him stir within the flames, man-shaped but lacking substance, the form of the god who comes to earth. Even so did he appear to Alm, his magnificence too great to be looked upon, with his hair of flame and the light of the sky in his eyes. And the Spear in his hand! Ah! Never have I seen such a sight! The sacrifice burned afresh and was consumed before our very eyes as Lud spoke through the flame. Truly, Thegnard, it was a visitation."

"And the Groddi Wiccena, did he see it? What does he have to say?"

"He was there. It was he who declared the apparition to be Lud."

"Did he now? And what about our little agreement?" Nalf Rhys rose to his feet, but slowly. He was feeling quite stiff and sore after his battle with Hans Thegn. *Teach you to land on your back, you old fool!*

Wyver looked uncomfortable. "It is understood that your request will be honored insofar as it meets with the will of the god."

"It ought to be the will of the god that Hans Thegn be made to prove himself a proper Kheld. Get him a wife and a proper scare, that's what he needs! He's got Sordan on the brain, he does," Nalf tapped a finger to his forehead. "Marc Frederick's disease, thinking he can do something with that lot. We've got to set him where we want him—and fast. He's not letting the dust settle on his feet, not by the All-Giving Mother—and we can't afford to let it settle on ours!"

Wyver's fire-brightened gaze didn't falter. "Lud has spoken, and though his instructions are cryptic, they must be obeyed. The god himself said Hans Thegn's fate would be decided upon Bellan Toregh, before the High Place. Those are powerful words. The Groddi Wiccena cannot ignore them."

"Nah, damn the man. And neither can I. Wish I could, the bother of it!"

"Do not blaspheme the god's will."

"God's will? Hans Thegn's will, might as well be." Nalf found the woolen house robe fallen behind the chair and pulled it from hiding. Slipping his arms into the sleeves, he tugged the garment firmly across his shoulders, concealing his bruises and the salves upon them. "Seems to me the Faeduadan would do the god one better to settle the matter here at Rhodhur. I don't like it that Dorilian Sordaneon has an army out there that we can't find—and Bellan Toregh is damn near the border with Neuberland. Not only that, but Hans Thegn's got some sort of Sordan alliance in his head, and he's been open about wanting the Witan at the High Rock. I hope to hell the god knows what he's doing!"

A knock sounded at the door and Aubrey entered, still wearing the fawn overdress and embroidered girdle she had worn for the assembly meeting with the priest that afternoon. She hadn't gone back to her room, then, like she had said she would when she'd left Nalf earlier, leaving him in the hands of old Ewlys. Nalf might have taken a hard fall, but he was no fool; he knew Aubrey had gone back to the main Hall. He also knew why, and it wasn't just so she could give young Hans Thegn an approving punch on the arm. Nalf had put Rannuf to spy on her and the report had confirmed Nalf's suspicions.

He gestured to Wyver, who came forward to accept the letter Nalf Rhys pressed into his hand. "Godspeed, Faedu Wyver," Nalf told the priest. "Now let the Groddi Wiccena know my feelings on this."

"I will, Thegnard." With a sweep of dark robes, Wyver bowed in Aubrey's direction. "Faetha Amundda, the Mother's gifts are fleeting. Do not withhold their purpose."

"She does, doesn't she?" Nalf muttered. He glared after Wyver until the door had closed behind him. "Well, there you got it," he groused to Aubrey as she, too, frowned after the departed man. "Can't argue with a bunch of damned faeduan who think they've seen their god. An apparition, he said! Right there in the fire! All I wanted was a simple sacred sacrifice, and what do I get? Gods!"

Aubrey gave a small shrug. "Maybe they really did see Lud."

"Of course they did!" Nalf stomped over to the fire, where his chair waited and a good hot drink. "I'd be seeing gods in my dreams too if I drank that nasty potion they mix up from the sacrifice. Drink enough of that, add a little smoke, and—begoe! Lud of the flaming hair!"

He studied Aubrey as she stood before him in the fluid glow of firelight, her beauty softened by amber shadows: a young, ripe, desirable woman who had yet to take a man as her own. The priest was right. "Damn it, girl," Nalf swore aloud. "What are you waiting for?"

Aubrey's eyes, goldened by the glow of the fire, widened. "What are you talking about?"

"Hans Thegn. You haven't bedded him yet."

"Of course not." The words blistered. "Hans hasn't shown the least bit of interest in bedding me! Neither have I sought to tempt him. I'm a woman, not a beguiler; neither am I an exploiter of young men's lusts. And I don't throw myself into men's beds out of desperation."

"Desperation!" Nalf Rhys blustered.

"Isn't that what you're coming to? Pushing me to pursue poor Hans in the only way men like you can understand? Well sorry, Uncle. He's taken me into his confidence somewhat, but not into his bed."

"And do you know why not?" Even Nalf's teeth ached with anger now. "Because *his* bed's not where you want to be! He'd fall like a stone apple if you'd throw your beauty at him the way you toss it around for that no account, half-blood Trongorian you've taken your eyes to! I haven't been a man all these years not to know *that* look when I see it!"

"Uncle, you're mad."

"Oh, am I now? At least *that* man's been gone a good fortnight, so I know you haven't bedded *him*. Who knows but maybe he doesn't want it, eh? And even if he does, what do you stand to gain from his like, a man who sells his sword to the highest bidder?" Nalf expelled a heavy sigh. "Damn you, Aubrey Amundda, Hans Thegn is no small catch! He'll have wellborn women giving him eyes as soon as he steps north! A woman should jump at the chance of having a king in her bed, a man who can put princes in her belly."

"That's for me to choose." Aubrey's voice turned cold.

Nalf heeded the warning. "Well, then, choose with an eye to the crop." He picked up a poker and stabbed at the logs in the hearth until they burned brighter. Even the poker reminded him of his body's aches as he put the heavy iron aside. "A woman like you can do better for herself than most. You have Thegn clan right! You have land—a king's grant, even—and an income. Amund saw to it you can read and write better than our scholars and he hired tutors to teach you the Mother knows what else! Why, there's hardly a man in Amallar with fortune or balls enough to court you. And Hans Thegn needs a wife, more now than ever, to bring him into line. He's getting more vocal about wanting to make a deal with Sordan, saying he'll get out if we cross his spear."

"I was there, Uncle," Aubrey reminded him. "And I can tell you he means it."

"Well, see there! We need to get an anchor on him!" With a grunt, Nalf dropped heavily into his chair and rubbed his hand along his swollen jaw. Gingerly, he nudged a couple of wobbling teeth with his tongue, hoping he would not lose them. "Boy's willing to fight for what he believes. That's good! But I don't want him fighting *us*."

"That's what this is about, isn't it?" Aubrey walked across to the nearby cabinet, from which she took up Nalf's favorite flask and cup and set these on the table beside him. "You can't get your King in hand. He won't back down and you don't know what he is going to do—or want, or try—next, and now your worries are making you act like a fool. If simply bedding Hans was the answer, you wouldn't have wasted your time with me. There are women enough here at Rhodhur willing to do it. If that was the way to handle him, they'd have done it in Sordan."

Nalf eyed Aubrey with fresh appreciation. The lass had a keen mind even his best counselors were hard put to match. The lot he had couldn't see the two sides of a coin! "Then what'd they do to him down there, that he's so fired to take them at their word?"

Aubrey sat on the footstool and faced him squarely. "I wish I knew. Hans has this strange admiration for Sordan—its wealth, its power—you would never guess he had been the Sordaneon's prisoner. And isn't it odd that he almost never talks about Dorilian? He spent months in his company, yet it's as if Dorilian doesn't exist. Seems to me, Hans is unwilling to awaken our feelings about that monster, probably because there's something there that will harm his cause, so he goes to great pains not to mention him. And if Dorilian's name does come up, he chases the conversation aside. Perhaps if he doesn't allow our grievances to become personal, he believes we'll more likely consider his plans for alliance. There are many who begin to think like him."

"How's that, girl?" Nalf Rhys poured a pain-killing dose into his cup. "You've got the ears on him. What's going on that I should know about?" He downed the fiery liquid in one swallow. It burned its way down his throat, bringing a film of tears to his eyes.

"People are tired of fighting." Aubrey leaned forward, elbows on knees. The pensiveness of her gesture reminded Nalf of other gifts she failed to use to advantage. "Our people want progress. They have dreams they yearn to touch, communities they hope to build. Hans is offering them a way to reach those dreams and build those communities. New hopes may eventually override old fears."

"We can't let him do that. He's not a proper Kheld, talking like that—thinking like a goddamned Staubaun. Stefan wouldn't have done it. Damn! But if I didn't think the boy's heart was Kheld!"

Aubrey's deep sigh punctuated her wistful expression. "I think he has more than a Kheld heart. He has a Kheld mind, also, in so many ways. Good ways. He wants this alliance for *our* sakes, not just his own. Why he is so keen to fight the Mormantaloran, I can't tell you. He won't talk about the reason—but it's very close to him, I think. And he's not of a Staubaun mind at all; he's quite different. Hans doesn't just talk about wanting us to be held as equals with the Staubauns or Estols or any other people. He sees us in that place already; he sees it as *natural*. A Staubaun would never think that. Everything Hans says to us, he believes. Heart *and* soul. All these weeks I've been with him have convinced me he's the sincerest person I have ever met."

Nalf watched her from between narrowed lids. "Looks like you've grown a soft spot for the boy after all."

"I think he can serve well for Amallar if we can wean him from Sordan."

"And how do we do that? You're the one with the ideas. Out with them."

Aubrey looked to the ceiling and shook her head. A dark sweep of hair swung down across her left shoulder to cover her golden clan brooch. "I don't know. I haven't figured out yet what ties bind him to Sordan. But forcing him in any way, especially a ploy as crude as putting a woman in bed with him, won't do it. Whatever Sordan's hold on him, you can be sure it will withstand such simple wiles. He's not Stefan."

"Stefan was ours, heart and marrow. It took no wiles to trap him! You spend too much time with that cursed Rappeleye witch."

"And you know I speak the truth. You were there that day too. Our chiefs presented Stefan with three young girls as if showing him heifers at the market—and he chose one. He chose, not her! No one ever asked Nilla, or Lark or *me*, if we wanted him!" Aubrey's raised gaze dared Nalf to contest her words, but he couldn't. What she said was true.

"That doesn't excuse what she did. Casting a curse—"

"It was men who thrust that curse upon them. They broke the Mother's cardinal commandment. Women must not be forced to bear like the land beneath the plow, or the beasts of men's husbandry. A union created by an evil act doesn't have the Mother's Blessing. This is to prevent evil from entering the world."

Damn her. Nalf grimaced, but Aubrey continued.

"Lark tried to save Nilla, keep us from offending the Mother. She tried to save *you* from making a mistake. You—and Stefan too. He probably should have married a daughter of one of the Esseran Lords who still stood by him—a Highborn Princess even! Doing so would have strengthened his position there, and ours right along with it." Aubrey shook her head and her gaze strayed to the warm coals of the hearth. "We bound him in every way we could. Stefan even moved his capital to Trulo, away from the Staubauns we feared and closer to us. And that's what you're proposing to do to Hans. Except he's not Stefan, and he doesn't see us as his only people—or option. Maybe, just maybe, he'll tear himself free of all our traps and bindings, and we'll wish upon the Mother's holy earth that we had tied ourselves to him instead of trying to tie him to us!"

Nalf could barely contain himself. "And who are you to talk at your betters like that?" He pushed himself out of his chair and stood over Aubrey. He had the mass to look imposing, especially over a seated lass. "So he's won you over, has he? Sordan talk and all, he's won you over! Got you to thinking it's all well and good, setting us up to be stabbed in the backs by the damned Highborn and their tricks. He's a boy, damn it—a fresh-faced, wet-nosed, big-headed boy who wouldn't know a bad dog if it bit him in the ass!"

"I don't like his flirtation with Sordan, either! I don't understand it," she snapped. "You know I loathe Sordan as much as you. As much as anyone. But Sordan is the unknown factor here. Hans is clearly aligned with Dorilian somehow. We need to learn what it is that Hans finds so worth having. Gold? Noble allies? Any attempt to force him away from Sordan without knowing what that something is could result in no Hans, no kingship, and no hope of claiming our rightful place in Essera. And if there is need or good reason for an alliance, we might as well know that too."

Little as Nalf liked it, Aubrey spoke sense. "But you're not close to finding that out, now, are you?"

"I can't tell you everything, Uncle, only that I have my suspicions." Aubrey absently fingered the leather of her bag of runestones, her gaze drifting into smoky blue thought. "I think I see a pattern, but I haven't quite put the pieces together."

Nalf combed his beard with his fingers. "This has to do with your Trongorian, doesn't it?"

"Maybe. In part."

What a woman, Nalf thought. *The Mother would have done us better to make a few more like her.* Damn, but how would Aubrey ever find a man worthy of her choosing? Other lasses might be willing to choose Hans Thegn—perhaps younger women, perhaps sillier—and Nalf wasn't sure he liked that possibility.

He laughed at the questioning look Aubrey shot him. "Lass, I'm on Hans Thegn's side, whether or not it seems that way. I want him to be our King, and I want it bad. But I don't want him if he belongs to Sordan first and Amallar second. If the Sordaneon is calling the tune, I'll be damned if I let Hans Thegn dance with Amallar. I'd cut his feet off first! Better no King in Essera at all than Sordan's creature. Get me proof of that, and he's a dead man."

28

Erydon Malyrdeon was a Wall Lord, great in wisdom and
farseeing. When the Kheld barbarians first walked out of
the Bogs to claim lands in Tahlwent and the Glainoi, they
were soon defeated. Erydon, however, spared the lives of all
he could. "These are a strong and determined people," he
said. "Our history is not yet done and theirs is just
beginning. We will have need of them."

PALLIDEMON STAMIDES, *HISTORY OF THE MALYRDEONS*

"They *what*? Make people stand in it? Down there?" Hans
stood at the edge of the concave channel that bisected the
Rill platform and peered down into... what had Dorilian
called it? A slip? A run? Whatever it was called, the seamless
depression that ran the length of the platform atop Bellan Toregh's
dawn-kissed hilltop wasn't especially deep, maybe chest high, but it
was wide.

Hans had planned his escape from the throng—also making the
pilgrimage to the Witan—by arranging ahead with his guard. They'd
left the encampment west of the town in the dead of night and made
good time. Only Dorilian, Robdan, and of course Arne accompanied
him. Hans had wanted to visit Bellan Toregh's famed hill and its Rill
structures without being followed.

Had Hans never seen Sordan, he would have felt more awe, but
as it was the sight of the hill before dawn had shattered reality.
Strange, faintly luminescent structures lifted above the brown and
dormant woodlands like a crown of alabaster lilies, incongruously
out of place and utterly beautiful. No wonder the earliest Khelds had
thought the tor an otherworldly place, frequented perhaps by gods
but not intended for mere humans.

"The locals boast of the practice," Dorilian said. "In keeping with that colorful tradition, Khelds in this town also use the Rill to execute people convicted of crimes." He frowned. "Which explains why Bellan Toregh has not executed even one wrongdoer since the Rill stopped running."

Was Dorilian suggesting the practice might resume? If so, Hans was going to have to adjust the wording he'd been working on for the Rill treaty. Following Dorilian's return to Rhodhur, Hans had spent as much time with him as possible during shared early mornings. With each solitary conversation, Hans pieced together more understanding of the Rill's unmovable place at the heart of the Triempery. They talked of the god-machine's potentials, consequences, alliances, and myths. Now Hans had a chance to learn the rest, what it was like to actually stand upon a Rill surface. Touch it.

Since their arrival earlier, Farrl and his rangers guarded the approaches to the platform. Hans and his party had the Rill to themselves.

But an armlength away, Arne stood stupefied and looked around in amazement. All of this—the sweep of the platform and towering grace of the Entity's arches and rings, the sheer size and how incongruous it all was—had to be as alien to him as it was to Hans. Only the white sanctuary building, though featureless and unnerving, was of human scale. Only Dorilian looked completely at ease as he toed the platform and peered to the south.

"Please try not to blame them. The people who do these things are ignorant," Robdan said in the town's defense. Hans had been so caught in wonder he'd forgotten Robdan was there. Hans gave a look that invited further explanation, which Robdan readily provided. "It's efficient, you see. As methods of killing a person go, the Rill is very neat and... well, no one dirties their own hands. None of them know what the Rill is, not really. They know only that people who stand in its path tend to... vanish."

Dorilian still looked disgusted. "Making executions easy on the executioners is a dangerous road : either they punish too liberally—or pervert understanding of the means." He pointed to the massive channel at their feet. "*Anything* caught in a run during Rill transit will be vaporized. Boulders. Trees. Animals. Mountains. The Rill can carve mountains. So don't put anything in there you want to remain in one piece. Ever. Not on a bet and not on a dare. However, seeing as we are going to be standing upon this platform with a horde of lunatics...."

Dorilian jumped into the shallow depression. Landing securely on his feet, he stood, his body commanding, surrounded by surreal elements and framed against the paling sky to the east.

"What are you doing?" Hans cried. Dorilian had just told them not to do this! But in the next moment, Hans remembered: the Rill was stopped, the sanctuary behind them silent. Dorilian had told them that the *Entity* had awakened to the node but the Rill's operational centers had yet to do so. No one standing on the platform, or in the run, was in danger, at least for now. Not even in danger of being watched, except by birds.

"I'm doing what no one else has bothered to do for you," Dorilian said. "I am teaching you how to stay alive."

He positioned himself at the center of the depression and faced east, his back to Hans and the others, and pointed to the south.

"Sordan." He then pointed north. "Permephedon." He looked over his shoulder at Hans. "Remember which is which."

"Will it matter? I mean, I know—"

"It might. Knowledge serves for either defense or offense. This... could be both. Follow me." Dorilian walked to the right—to the south, Hans noted—toward the ring arrays at that end. Accompanied by Arne and Robdan, Hans followed, striding parallel, staying on the platform.

By the time Dorilian stopped walking, they had passed the midpoint of the slip. Rings and arches bracketed both north and south, casting long shadows to the west. The forested hills surrounding them, none as high as this one, presented a carpet of muted mauves and blues.

Dorilian gestured to Hans. "Join me."

Arne grabbed Hans by the forearm. "Don't!" he urged, practically hissing under his breath. "Might be a trick!"

"Seriously? He's in there too!"

With a roll of his eyes, Arne let go. "Reckon so. But I don't trust that thing! Or... those!" He pointed up to where the rings rose in elegant white curves, painted pink by dawn.

"I'll be fine."

Hans tried to leap into the slip as deftly as Dorilian had done. His boot heels struck first and skidded out from under him so that he landed on his ass at Dorilian's feet. He looked up.

"Next time, land flat-footed."

Hans accepted the hand Dorilian extended and the easy strength that pulled him to his feet. He grinned back at Arne and Robdan, who looked concerned, and said, "Only thing wounded is my royal dignity."

The view from the slip was otherworldly. The huge rings at the far end of the run, toward Permephedon, stood barely diminished and framed a distant, vivid landscape. But the rings at his back, so much nearer... Hans gazed up in wonder at concave undersides etched with glyphs and marks, curves traced with translucence and lines filled with flat, nonreflective patterns.

"Wow."

"That's not what I want to show you."

Who cared? Hans stood on one of the wonders of the World. He waved a hand in a circle to include the slip, the rings.

"Do you understand *any* of this?"

Dorilian squinted up at the rings. "A lot. Probably not enough." He waited while Hans continued to marvel at the massive structure.

"This is amazing. It's just... I've never seen the Rill up close like this—but I've also never seen it... well, not *moving*. In Sordan, I liked to watch it shift and flow, and it was like music in motion, something unreal."

"It's very real—and will move at the time ordained. Which is why I am showing you this. Look at my feet." Dorilian turned, facing north, and moved his left foot a step back.

Only then did Hans notice: the color inside the slip was not uniform. The wide section upon which Dorilian's right boot rested, slightly forward of his left, looked different. White still, but faintly translucent. Glassy. A demarcation as wide as a man was tall.

"What am I looking at?"

"The brake." Dorilian granted Hans a wry affirmation. "Should your Khelds or anyone ever seek to finish you by pushing you into a Rill slip, remember these rules: If you ever find yourself in an active run with a *charys* in transit, you are already dead. If you ever find yourself in a slip with an outgoing *charys* ready to travel, you will be considered debris and be removed when the Rill clears the run—which also means you are dead. If you ever find yourself in a slip with an *incoming charys* and cannot get out of its way, you will be crushed beneath it—unless you stand *here*." He moved his right foot back. Now both he and Hans stood fully behind the translucent portion of the slip, facing the rings at the far end. "This is the point at which the *charys* will stop. There is a brake at each end. It helps if you know the direction it is coming."

The advice seemed awfully specific. Hans turned to Dorilian. "Have you actually done this?"

Dorilian looked off into the distance, to the south. "Once. In Hestya. My grandfather was with me. He had done so in his youth also. A Sordaneon tradition."

That lesson, an almost cozy familiarity with the Rill, had to have come before the day Dorilian had experienced it tearing him apart.

Arne reached down to help pull Hans out of the slip. Dorilian was able to extract himself; he started at the far side of the slip, ran, and leaped to seat himself on the edge. He did so easily. He just as smoothly swung his legs up onto the platform and stood. There was something in Dorilian's stance atop this platform that had not been there before. Not the brittle arrogance Hans had seen in Sordan but something newly confident. Bolder. In it Hans glimpsed the enormity of what Dorilian had set in motion. By visiting Bellan Toregh, Dorilian had thrown the Rill into the wind and himself with it. Sordan and Amallar, Marc Frederick and Stefan, Marenthro and Handurin, and Dorilian's own consuming reality—all now shifting and changing, an entire world of constructs and beliefs, some fixed and others unfixed, if only in Dorilian's mind. And Hans had learned that Dorilian's mind could give birth to some very surprising creations.

Just make this real, Hans wanted to urge him. *Help me give these people a dream they never dared to dream.*

A Trongorian trotted up. "Your Royal Highness," he began. "A large party of people—they look like priests—are coming up the road. Do you wish us to stop them?"

Priests meant the Faeduadan, Hans guessed. The Brothers of the Grove arriving early, to see the top of the Rill mount, perhaps secure it, in advance of making their public announcement of Hans's oracle at the Witan. Hans had correctly guessed that he would have to come here first. Once the priests arrived and the Rill became a topic of discussion among Khelds, this hilltop would be anything but private.

"No," Hans said. "We're finished here." He looked to Dorilian, who nodded, though not without slight hesitation. Did he dislike that Amallar's priests were about to get near his Entity?

The Rill meant many things to Sordan's Hierarch, but Hans was pretty sure Dorilian didn't fear for the Rill's safety from the priests of the Grove.

29

Amynas once asked the Leur, "Are you a god?" To which
the Leur answered, "Does that matter? Because if it does, I
will refuse to answer."

CIBULITUS, *ANNALS OF THE RETURN*

The village of Bellan Toregh burgeoned with the coming
Witan. Streets were swept and every house appeared to have
been washed or painted. Tents sprang up in the fields like
towns of linen hung out to dry. Homes converted overnight to inns.
Merchants from as far away as Rhodhur and Leseos catered to a
flourishing demand for good food and drink and the finer things
required for a horde of keld-chieftains and important folk from all of
Amallar and Neuberland.

Hans had taken the advice of people more experienced than he
and arrived in plenty of time for those gatherings he needed to
attend. The richest and most important man in Bellan Toregh had,
to a great deal of fanfare and the admiration of his neighbors, given
over his entire compound to Hans and his party. The party included
Robdan and Arne and the twenty Trongorians who served as Hans's
bodyguard—an entourage that impressed the Khelds to no end. The
mere presence of bodyguards gave him status beyond measure.

"Maybe you should tell 'em you don't pay all these men," said
Arne on the day they were to go to the full gathering of the cruihcila.
"Maybe that way they won't think you're rich and ask you to pay
for this house when all's over." The house was on the edge of town
and huge, and Arne was sure that the owner had to be a scoundrel
to have gotten it.

"When this is all over," Hans answered, "I intend to have an alliance with Sordan." He chuckled at another thought. "Hey, maybe then I can tap Dorilian for a loan. Or my mother." As Herberth had predicted, no money had yet come their way from Emyli.

Arne scowled. "I can just imagine what that bastard would make you do for it."

Along with Robdan and Hans, Arne had sat in on some of the discussion about Dorilian's terms. The Rill would awaken to Amallar, but the price of keeping it would be high. A signed alliance with Sordan was but a prelude. If Amallar and the Khelds wanted the Rill, they would have to accept the Sordaneons into the bargain. Especially in the matter of Essera. If Hans died without an Heir, the Khelds—and Dorilian—would acknowledge Emyli as Essera's rightful ruler. This Dorilian would do in memory of Marc Frederick. If Emyli provided no heirs for Essera, however, the kingship would return to the Highborn. That meant Dorilian's Heirs—though not Dorilian himself—would become the next rulers not only of Sordan but of Essera as well.

Amallar, if it wished, could become an autonomous domain like Trongor or Leseos. And it could keep the Rill.

Hans didn't know if he could get the Khelds to agree to those provisions. No arrangement had been proposed to include the reverse, to name Hans Heir to Dorilian's domains and titles. Sordan was not on the table, its leadership not in dispute. What *was* on the table was Amallar's future role in the resurrected Triempery and the need to place a ruler on the Esseran throne—and, of course, the unparalleled gift of the Rill.

"I can hardly believe any of this is happening," Arne said, looking around him. They walked across the stone court of the big meeting place that dominated the center of the town, a huge and cavernous hall where the cruihcila would meet when night fell. Already it was dusk and the weather had turned sharply colder. "It seems impossible he's set it up to make the damn thing run again." Arne so seldom used Dorilian's name, refusing even to call him Thron, that Hans had long since concluded his friend feared invoking something evil.

"Don't you believe it?"

"I reckon I do. I just don't know what to expect."

Hans pulled Arne around to face him. Arne had taken to shaving his beard again after several weeks of letting it grow, leaving a pale shadow along his jaw and an almost boyish face that reminded Hans very acutely of the young man he had saved months ago in Ben Aranath. "Listen, Arne. Don't repeat that to anyone. I mean it. I'm going to talk to the cruihcila tonight, and I don't want to be fielding questions on that before I get to anything else. The alliance with Sordan has to be worked out from the ground up—that's a lot of hard work, a lot of hard talk. The Rill won't even come into the conversation until I've tried everything else."

"Why?"

"Because I don't think any of this is going to be easy, and before I present the idea of the Rill to them, I want them to be chewing on the rest of what I have to say. Do you understand?"

"Not really. But I trust you. I won't say a thing, not to anyone, not if it's important to you that I don't."

"I wouldn't ask if it wasn't."

The great room of the meeting house could easily seat two hundred people. It held twice that now. Scores shouted greetings when Hans and Arne walked into the room. A sea of metal-studded jerkins and buckled leggings, a style most of the Kheld men preferred, glinted with reflected light as the deepening dusk outside the door gave way to flickering lamplight within. Rich cloaks and mantles clasped with gold added color to the room. Although Hans knew few of these men and women, he understood them to be leaders in their respective cruihcila, people whose voices had influenced Stefan's policies and who wanted that influence restored. These leaders, along with the Council of Elders and the Old Mothers—several of whom had traveled from Rhodhur to be in attendance—could bring Amallar into an alliance with Sordan or, if they chose, dash that hope forever.

Although the culminating meeting of the Witan would take place a week from this one, the meeting tonight could prove far more important.

Looking more dignified than usual, Robdan walked over to join Hans. His somber dark tunic and neatly draped mantle were relieved by a bright dash of blue, green, and maroon Thegn plaid pinned by an ornate iron clasp.

"You'll find yourself by far the most sought-after man in this room." Robdan's observation was apt. Hans had already noted a few persons making the decision to approach. "As I am kin to you, I shall stand to make the introductions. Oh, and I think I should warn you"—Robdan's cheerfulness cracked to reveal a dismal apology— "I could not dissuade him."

"Here?" How could Robdan have let Dorilian appear at this meeting? "Of all the people in Amallar and Neuberland, these are the ones most likely to have met him!"

Helpless in his frustration, Robdan managed a shrug. "He says not. I tell you, Hans, I tried, but I don't intimidate him. And, well—have you ever tried to argue with the man?"

Arne tried not to look thoroughly disgusted as Hans clasped Robdan's shoulder with lukewarm reassurance. "Where is he?"

"Mingling. He's very good at it."

"He's mingled the Triempery inside and out for years, that's for sure," muttered Arne. "Seems to me he could be mingling for secrets."

Hans frowned him into silence. "There are precious few secrets in Amallar. The only secret I'm worried about right now is his!"

Having spied a splash of rich sapphire blue among the browns and greens and rusts of the men, Hans watched the approach of Aubrey Amundda. She was smiling and confident, her skirt of fine wool embroidered with gold-threaded deer and hawks, her cream silk blouse tucked into a wide girdle of gold-hued brocade. A brooch of gold and garnets pinned her sash of Thegn plaid, and a brass ring heavy with keys and pendants swung from her belt, identifying her as a woman of property. She propelled a tall man along by way of her hand on his elbow. At first glance, Hans feared she had cornered Dorilian again. As the pair drew near, however, Hans saw Aubrey's companion was Kheld, despite his height and the streaks of gold in his brown hair. That, and a few bare traces of beard, spoke of more than a little Staubaun in the man's family tree.

"Hans Thegn Erwanson." Aubrey took over this introduction from Robdan. "I want you to meet my countryman, Franwelf Vesl Gorseddson."

A pained grimace crossed Franwelf's face. "I answer to Fran. I feel like I should bow to you or something." He had a clear, strong voice.

Fran Gorseddson? The Neuberlander rebel and hero? The man who had captured a Gignasthi lord and traded him for the lord's daughter? Perfect.

Hans forced a smile to cover his thoughts. "Probably. But it's too confusing. I've heard of you."

Fran laughed but his hazel gaze sharply weighed the greeting. "And I've heard of you. But last I heard, you were imprisoned in Sordan. How did you get here?"

"It's not hard to leave Sordan. Arne and I used a boat."

"Is it hard to get there?"

"That depends. We used a boat for that too."

Fran appeared to note the careful response. He motioned with his head to a point behind Hans's shoulder. "Your answer rings true. When I asked about invading the island, the Trongorian there told me to study the making of small boats. Said big ones would be too hard to carry across the desert."

Hans had but to turn his head to see the man in question. Dorilian was talking with a graybeard from the Torthui cruihcil and a red-cloaked Old Mother, his attention fixed upon some point being made. Though he sought to blend in by wearing ordinary garments of deep burgundy wool with but a plain leather belt and boots, there was no hiding Dorilian's height or sun-bronzed looks. Just the confidence of his bearing and the intensity with which he listened was out of place. And for some, that was enough. Hans knew where Aubrey's eyes lingered. And why. *Put those two in a jar*, he thought, *and not even Marenthro would dare to shake it.*

But there was little time for such musings as other introductions intruded on Hans's attention. The meeting convened with a call to the great oaken slab with its dozen narrow-backed chairs carved with animistic figures, set before a roaring hearth. The table dominated the high-ceilinged room. The night outside might be blowing cold with a wind out of the north, but those who sat at the head table would be warm. Hans sat there by right of rank. He was high clan by birth—through both his father and his mother—but his standing as Stefan's brother and Heir mattered more. He embodied their hope to regain the Esseran kingship.

To Hans's left, Nalf Rhys, dressed in his best threads and having groomed his eyebrows and whiskers to full glory, presided for the Thegnkeld. The heads of Amallar's six cruihcila and Neuberland's two, along with two fully invested Old Mothers—Aegdnis and Lavrel—took the other seats around the table. Facing the table on benches set in a line across the floor sat representatives grouped by cruihcil who held the right to speak when matters rose for discussion. Robdan took his place at the front of the Frendeli group, which boasted a spindly table for his papers and writing implements. He served also as scribe and would take notes of their meeting for later use in the Archhalia. Aubrey sat with the Neuberland Cruihcil, her presence dignified by the sash of Thegn plaid that drifted from one shoulder and tucked with intentional authority into her ornate golden girdle. Other women and men wore their clan sashes as boldly, displays of family ties.

Hans had decided not to wear keld colors, hoping to emphasize his standing apart from the kelds. He wondered now if he would not have done better to point up his Thegn ties. But it was too late to think of such things.

"We've got here several problems before us." Nalf Rhys spoke loudly to the assembly after he had pounded the staff for silence and achieved an acceptable amount of it. "For you who've been living in a cave these last few wanings, this man here is Hans Thegn Erwanson. Some call him Stauberg-Randolph, but the Kheld name's his and he answers to it."

"Did he answer to it in Sordan?" a man shouted from the crowd.

"A name is a name, for godsake!" Nalf stared down the man. "What do you want to make of it, eh, at a time like this? Damn Staubauns wouldn't know what to make of him, he comes in with a Kheld name like Erwanson. Ain't never heard of 'im, they'd say, and toss him in the trash faster than you could spit. And who ever heard of a Thegn in Sordan, I ask you now? Nobody, that's who. But throw Stauberg-Randolph at them—well, that makes a difference. Besides which, it's his mother's name, so as much his name by our law as the other one."

That matter settled, Nalf cleared his throat and consulted his notes, perhaps making a point that he could read. "Now while in Rhodhur I've heard Hans Thegn's tale for more times than I can count. I've heard it over breakfast, and I've heard it over the midmeal, and I damn well got an earful at supper too! And what he didn't tell me I got from young Arne Anseldson there." Nalf nodded to where Arne stood along the wall with the other nonspeaking onlookers. "You all know Arne and his kilth, and it was his own brother Brec who picked up their trail when they came out of Trongor."

"Nobody the hell cares about Trongor!" Fran Gorseddson spoke up from his place at Aubrey's side. His clear gaze, brightened by suspicion and defiance, met Hans's across the table that separated them. "No offense to these fine Trongorians among us. We think real well of them and all, but I don't need to hear about how Hans

Thegn has friends in Trongor. Seems to me he should tell us what happened in Sordan."

What happened in Sordan. Hans had been telling them for weeks, in bits and pieces, leaving most of it out but for his heroic adventure. Now they wanted to know the rest. Sensing that the time had come to tell them, Hans rose to his feet, though he brushed his sweating palms upon his trousers first. With a directness he hoped would be taken as confidence, he faced the assembled clan leaders.

"I will tell you whatever you wish to know," he said.

For a long moment he stared at them while they stared back. Finally, the long-bearded head of the Cothesci Cruihcil spoke. "I think we all have one great question that bears asking: were you indeed the Sordaneon's prisoner in Sordan?"

In the press of the room, as the milling bodies crowded closer to the front to hear, Hans could not find the one man he sought.

"I thought I was," he answered.

"What does that mean?" Nalf Rhys growled. "These folks aren't faeduan or wizards, you know. You got to speak in plain language, not riddles."

"I mean that I thought I was a prisoner—at least at first. But I gradually came to see that I wasn't a prisoner at all."

"And how do you figure that?"

"The education I received more befitted a prince than a prisoner. I was taught Triemperal law and history, languages, strategic economics—and how to use a sword. It was not always obvious what my lessons were. But mostly it's that I now see the ruse. Rumor had me being held prisoner there long after I was gone. Some of you only learned of my freedom days ago. It was a ploy," Hans explained, "a game of bluff without which I probably would not have made it to Amallar. It was easy for me to make my way here when my enemies thought I was being held captive in Sordan."

"Enemies!" The old man nearest Hans curled his lip. "Sordan is your enemy. What other enemies have you?"

"More than I ever dreamed. And for every enemy I thought I had in Sordan, I have three in Essera." It was important to lay out the connecting facts. "My supposed regent Erenor sits proud on lands that are mine by right, wearing my titles and spending my treasury. If I return, he no longer rules. He signed and still holds orders for my mother's arrest. His next move will be to order mine."

Hans ticked off one finger and moved to the next. "How about

Nammuor the Mormantaloran? He doesn't want to lose his footholds in Aral and Stauberg and Dazunor-Rannuli. He's got designs we don't even understand! Or the Epoptes who order the Rill"—Hans continued ticking off fingers—"they've conspired to keep me at arms' length from their god-machine and the power they hold over it. I saw that for myself in Sordan. And how the Seven Houses fear I will reclaim lucrative Rill contracts or disrupt an economy that has filled their coffers for a hundred generations. Even the pirates of Merced fear I will banish their ships from Essera's harbors or arm a fleet to send against them. I can't turn around without running into enemies. And if Sordan was filled only with enemies, then how did I escape so easily? Once Sordan knew I had gone, why didn't they try to bring me back?"

"Perhaps they did try and failed," the old Cothesci chieftain said.

Nalf Rhys concurred. "Arne here told us how you were too damn wily for the Sordaneon, that's why!"

"That's right. I did escape. I fled Sordan—Arne and I both—but the fact of the matter is we were *not* pursued." Hans spoke to every person in the room, even the one he knew could verify or refute every word. But more than that, he wished that Arne had had the sense to keep his mouth shut! What else had he blurted out over his beer? "Do you think Sordan is a backhills blockhouse? You ascribe to the Sordaneon every conceivable deviousness, but you think him incapable of patrolling his own courtyard? Yes, I escaped. I might even go so far as to say that I surprised him. But by the time Arne and I reached Trongor, it was clearer than daylight itself that once we had made good that escape, the Sordaneon had decided *not* to send pursuit. No warships chased me and Arne down the Sorand'ruil. No word ever filtered into the towns along the way. They have ways to do that. Instead, Sordan continued the charade and pretended I was still prisoner. I'll bet half of Essera is still not sure whether I am or not! That ploy bought me time to reach Amallar before any of my *real* enemies knew I was gone. With the Rill not running to any of its cities or allies, Essera is deaf to news from Sordan. It takes weeks for ships from Sordan to reach Esseran ports, and longer for news to cross by land. Did it ever occur to you that there might be a reason for the Rill stopping?"

"Yes!" Fran Gorseddson slammed his fist upon the table, then gestured to the room, asking consideration. "Invasion!"

As the general outcry responded loudly to that declaration, Hans held his tongue and waited for the outcry to die down before speaking. "Invasion of who? Amallar? Neuberland? We're a waning from winter and there's no sign of an invasion that I can see."

"He's stockpiled troops and supplies in Gignastha. And the Rill still goes to Randpory!"

"That's true. But then why did Sordan pull its army out of Neuberland and send it north? Away from us?" Word had since reached Bellan Toregh that Sordan's army had in fact crossed into Merrydn.

"To attack us across the Dazun. Staubauns hold the bridges, don't they?" Fran seethed. To him, past infractions loomed all too near, as did the current threat. "And lest we forget it, Sordan has *another* army in Neuberland, just as big, waiting to drive at Gosdagga! Lud's Spear, Hans Thegn, the bastard's been fighting us for years—low, hard, and dirty. He isn't going to stop now just because you asked him to!"

"I didn't ask him to."

"What?" Fran snarled and rose to full height. The room about him buzzed with conjecture as much as outrage. "I don't suppose you had the balls to *tell* him to!"

Nalf Rhys pounded with his staff to bring the room once more to order. This time, however, when silence fell it gripped the throats of those gathered with the cold bite of shackles. "Hans Thegn here wants us to make our peace with Sordan, Fran." Nalf made a point of that reminder. "You've heard it. We all have. And while we don't like it, it's what he wants to say. Seems to me we might as well let him get it out of his blood. That's what we have these damned Witans for, now ain't it—to air these things out?" He gave another sharp and unenthusiastic nod to Hans. "Go to the task, lad. Say what you came here to say."

Alone, standing upon his own merits before the quiet cavern of an unreceptive assembly, Hans froze. Nothing he could say would convince these stubborn, angry people.

I don't have to convince them, he reminded himself. Lessons he had absorbed over the last few months buttressed him. *I just have to create two things: doubt and opportunity.* Wasn't that what he had done before?

He looked at their hard faces, knowing that whatever words he said now would remain upon him forever. He had their ears, and it was time to tell them who he was. "I am a rightful Prince in Essera. This is true; but I also know it will not be enough. All I have is a name and a few alliances that still cling to that name. You want me to take power in Essera? I can do that, but I also know that I can only make that power work if I have the kelds behind me. That's why I'm here. I wanted to meet my brother's people, and I wanted to find out if you could be my people too." He swallowed and stood straighter. "Now you're asking if I can be what *you* need. So if you want to know why I went to Sordan, I'll tell you. It's because there were things in Sordan I needed to learn for myself. Important things. Legitimacy and stewardship may be just words to many of you—but they're not just words to me. They are what I must be if I'm to champion what my family has always stood for, what we have been. Not just Kings, but protectors. I wasn't sure if I could do that, if I should return. But Marenthro Dru'vida told me that I would find what I sought in the city of the Sordaneons." Hans looked over at Robdan, whose nod beseeched him to continue. If only Hans could interest them in what he had to say! Force them, somehow, to experience even a little of what he had learned....

So he told them. Told them what had happened, starting with that day Marenthro had found Hans among the Mentans where he had been hidden, his reawakened awareness of who he was—all those years he had forgotten! He left out the parts they didn't need to know, might not understand. *Permephedon, the violence and the promises made, witnessed through eyes they would never believe, in an agony they could never imagine.* He didn't want Dorilian to hear of it here, in this place. *So much exposed....* He told them how he had left Mena'tantaureus, his indecision, and then his resolve. It was best to tell them the beginning. He briefly described the Gate between Worlds and Thaa giving him a dagger he didn't know how to use, a *deiknya* he didn't understand, and a purse he didn't have for very long. He put more meat on his journey up the Sorand'ruil and his spending the purse to free Arne in Ben-Aranath. How they'd worked their passage on a salt barge.

And Sordan. Sordan refused to be described, but Hans did his best, though facts often gave way to feelings, finding that certain episodes shone through: the fires in the Dekkora and his first encounter with Dorilian Sordaneon; Hans's and Arne's rescue from the Haliasts; Tiflan of Teremar and the King of Ardaen; the Illumination and the godhood upon which Sordan rested; Asphalladra; Rhondda; the Rill; those final few weeks before he had decided to leave.

"What I found in Sordan was not evil," he found himself saying at the end. "What I encountered, I didn't always like, but the rest I can live with. I learned so much there, so much more than I can tell you. Mostly I learned that Marenthro was right, that Sordan is an ally I must have, not an enemy I need to destroy."

"But they tried to destroy you, didn't they?" A graybeard from the Combroggi Cruihcil just north of Bellan Toregh piped his challenge. "Or is it false that Sordan put poison in your drink?"

Curse you, Arne Thegn Anseldson, when I get my hands on you! You had to go and blab that to every old fool in Amallar too! To recover from his surprise, Hans offered the only explanation he could. "I don't know who put the poison in my drink," he said. "I most suspect Erenor, my regent, ordered the deed."

"Him's that the most likely—"

"Ain't not always the one what does something about it!" This time Arne stepped forward from his place on the fringes of the assembly, his face flushed and jaw tense. "I'm sorry, Hans, that this got about. Shows you can't trust people talking. I've got a big old bucket mouth and not enough sense to know when not to spill it out. But I got to say something, even if it's out of turn." Arne stepped to the front and faced the staring, cold-faced elders at the head of the chamber. "I don't think it was the Sordaneon that wanted us dead. In fact, I'd stake my life on that now. Because if he had wanted to get us done and out of the way, he had more than enough chances to make it look like he didn't do it. It doesn't make sense that he'd want to make it look like he did! And he sure as hells wouldn't let us get away so's we could live to talk about it, stir up more trouble for him than he's got. I've heard enough men what agree with that. Herberth of Trongor said it, and Endelarin, him what's King of Ardaen, said it too!"

"Herberth the Trongorian," Nalf Rhys mused aloud. "And Endelarin of Ardaen too! Well, who are we to argue with high folk, eh? It still doesn't sit right!"

Agreement rumbled across the room in accordance with that verdict.

"Maybe the dead man doesn't always know his murderer," Hans countered, "but you'd take a victim's word for it if you had it!" He had more to say while he was at it. "I went through hell in Sordan. I arrived there knowing next to nothing and maybe that's a good thing, because I had no choice but to listen and learn and find out the truth for myself. People told me what they believed or wanted me to believe, but I had to make up my own mind about all of it, and that includes here." As he looked at the sea of faces, he saw eye rolls and snarls but also some nods and lowered chins from a silent few who appraised him anew.

"Marenthro told me I was returning to make something right again, to save a kingdom. To save a World!" Snorts of derision broke from the crowd, followed by snickers and laughter. Hans remembered how absurd it had sounded to him the first time. "I know how it sounds. Really, I do! It's hard to imagine dangerous things like magic and threats when life all around you is normal. But there are dangers out there, things people have heard about—things people have seen!"

A few elders and others grimly nodded and Nalf stopped another man at the table from raising protest.

Hans took a breath and forged ahead with the rest of his argument. "Marenthro said the World, our World, hangs in the balance of what happens here, tonight, and in the days to come. Well, I don't know if I can save *anything*," he admitted. "But I'm willing to try, and in Sordan I learned more about what it will take to save Essera than I could have learned under any other hand! Essera doesn't exist in isolation. Neither do *we*. Enemies surround us, and they may not be who you think they are. You think Amallar is Sordan's grand obsession, even as Sordan is yours—but we're not. The world is too big for that. People who look at the world and see only themselves are looking in a mirror!"

"Mirror!" Several cruihcil leaders sputtered in chorus.

Hans knew he'd struck a nerve. It must be something they had heard before, or else already knew to be true. "Yes, a mirror. Look at us! We're so wrapped up with ourselves and our problems that we spend all our time assigning our ills. If we would *just once* open the door and stop worrying about Sordan coming to visit, we would see that some very nasty characters have moved into our own backyards."

"We know who you mean. You speak of the Mormantaloran." The man who spoke, Orem Darm, headed the Ekkuna Cruihcil. He was bearded, as were most Kheld men, but his beard was close and neat and not yet gray. His gaze for some while had been among the less hostile in the room. The Ekkun coalition of river towns, strung along the Dazun and Floh rivers, harbored a more pragmatic breed of Kheldmen.

"Yes." Hans welcomed the opening and counted Orem as a friend for having given it to him. "Mormantalorus. Erenor has given Nammuor access to Essera's ports and let him bring troops. Between them they control almost all of Essera except for Lacenedon and Merrydn. Sordan stopped the Rill because Erenor granted the Mormantalorans access to the mount at Dazunor-Rannuli. Mormantalorus was using the Rill to supply their troops."

Fran Gorseddson loudly scoffed. "Of course Sordan stopped it. Dorilian can't like seeing the Mormantalorans ready to stand by us, well armed to keep him out from stealing Stefan's throne! And he knows that the Southlanders send some of their weapons down our way, to use against him in Neuberland. The man's the devil's own, but he's no fool."

"Those weapons aren't gifts. They're bribes. The Staubauns send you a few weapons so that you can stir up trouble."

"Trouble Sordan started!"

"And we could rehash that conflict for a hundred years. You should hear them in Sordan—they're just as bad. It's that sort of thinking that stands in the way of doing anything about it."

"We don't want to do anything about it except kick Dorilian's ass," Fran told Hans. "He's had his way for years; now let him stew."

"So Sordan stews now and we'll stew later." If he was in an argument, Hans figured he might as well make his points. "Neuberland is a border war, Franwelf Gorseddson—it's bloody and it's messy, but that's all it is. What's worse is that it's keeping us from seeing something far more dangerous and frightening waiting just across the river. Because while we squabble with Sordan over Neuberland and old injuries, a far worse enemy is stealing away Essera. And when that enemy has Essera, what makes you think that he will be content with Khelds living in the lands he'll want next?"

"The Mormantaloran never said he wanted Amallar. He can't do it." That reminder from Nalf Rhys brought chortles of agreement. "Even Staubauns know that Amallar is Kheld lands."

"And why would that matter to Nammuor?" Hans recalled something from a history he had read, something forced on him by one of his tutors at Rhondda. "He never gave lands to you and he never promised not to invade them. The Highborn Kings of Essera did that, hundreds of years ago. To revoke that grant, Nammuor need only say that the Oath of Erydon doesn't bind him."

Nalf Rhys colored purple. Growling a curse, he turned to the one Kheld in the assembly who might have knowledge of such a thing. "Robdan Aelfricson!" he called. "You're a scholar, such as we have. You know the damned gold-hairs and their Law. Is what he says true?"

Robdan stood to address the table. His face was ashen and grim. "I think it could be."

"You mean the Oath of Erydon the Gift-Giver doesn't bind them forking Southlanders?"

"As I recall, it binds only the Highborn."

"No one else?" Nalf's booming voice sounded off the ceiling beams.

Robdan's shoulders dropped, and he blinked with thought as his mind worked through what he knew. He laid down his pen and began to explain. "Well, yes and no—it's part of how their law is ordered. The rulers of Essera—of all the Triempery, really—were Highborn. Essera's Kings were the descendants of Ergeiron Malyrdeon, who created the Wall, who they say *is* the Wall. Marc Frederick was the first king who was *not* Highborn. Even the Staubauns consider the Highborn distinct from other races of men. You see, all the Highborn trace their ancestry to the god Amynas, and...." Robdan hesitated. Hans understood why. Dorilian's presence. It was enough to make any scholar doubt his adequacy.

Robdan, however, clearly knew quite a bit. "Well, it happens that all Highborn Princes regard themselves as manifestations of the original god. Equal. Brothers, if you will. They hold—and create—the Mind of Leur, which is to say the Order of the World. That is why the sworn word of *one* is binding on *all*. Their race memory is very deep. They remember these Promises, and they honor them." Robdan took a moment to outline the problem. "While the Highborn first established the Triempery, and while they ruled it, this is how they made their treaties. There is no recorded instance, in all that time, of any Highborn treaty made by this manner ever having been broken. This is considering that there were always Highborn rulers to remember and uphold those treaties, or non-Highborn rulers like Marc Frederick who were *willing* to uphold them. But now"—Robdan looked Nalf in the eye—"it is conceivable that Essera's ruling nobles or the Mormantalorans or the Seven Houses—or anyone else— because they are *not* Highborn, may say that these treaties do not bind them, that these are Highborn treaties and bind the Highborn only."

"Are you saying that damned devil in Sordan can be held to the Oath of Erydon, to leave us our lands—but that Essera or the Mormantalorans can't?" Nalf Rhys roared.

"I'm not sure they've thought of it yet, but I think the answer is... yes."

Looking across the room even as Robdan spoke, Hans located Dorilian standing at the far wall, his back resting against one of the massive oak pillars that supported the high ceiling beams. As if they stood but feet apart, Hans could read the gently twisted half frown of a point well made.

"Ain't that the holy bull!" Nalf threw up his hands in disgust. "Can't trust one and can't trust the other. It's a two-headed beast of a world, and we're damn well caught on the horns of it too!"

Again, Fran Gorseddson rose to speak. "I still say we should consider the Mormantaloran's proposal. He's never done a thing against us."

"He killed Stefan," Hans pointed out.

"He did not!" someone shouted. "Sordan did it!" Many cried out the same, entering argument when other voices rose to tell them to let Hans speak. It took Nalf rising to his feet and bellowing, all the while pounding the floor with his great gold-headed oak staff, for order to be restored.

"Sit down, the lot of you!" Nalf directed. "And let this man finish."

Hans gave Nalf a nod of thanks.

"Think of the way Stefan died. Really think about it. I read more reports than any of you ever will. Stefan was butchered by his *friends*. I saw it in a dream given by an old woman in Mena'tantaureus. She gave me a potion and said it would show me the lie. And that's what I dreamed: Stefan as a stag. And Nammuor turning him into one."

The room had fallen silent. At the back of the room, Dorilian had dropped his head back to stare at the ceiling, mouth open in realization. Hans met Arne's stunned gaze but didn't regret not having told him before this. Magic. Visions. Who would believe such things? Hans hadn't, not completely, until he'd read those reports.

"I'll provide the reports to you when I am able, but my mother confirms them. There are even people here in Amallar who say that's what they heard. And the Highborn don't create illusions. They can't. It's completely counter to their nature."

But Hans could see he had not yet convinced them.

"Please hear me out," he said to the silenced crowd. Most, even those who scowled the darkest, appeared to be listening. "I've told you my reasons. Well, there's more, but it all leads to this: the only reason Nammuor hasn't invaded is because he's been having us fight his next battle for him. He doesn't need us much longer. Just long enough to see himself well entrenched in Essera. Maybe long enough to destroy Sordan, as long as he's got us fooled. Then he could step in and murder me like he did Stefan." As expected, more grumbling arose, though this time the voices were fewer.

Fran Gorseddson stepped forward to speak. "You got it wrong. We fight Sordan because we want to. Because we have to! We'd have made a proper war of it years ago had there not been skirts on the old men who voted us down. War! That's what Stefan wanted us to do. And it was Stefan who asked the Mormantaloran to help him do it! Stefan got the Mormantaloran to send Southlander soldiers in to help keep holds on Essera. And ain't that what those soldiers are doing? This Nammuor could be making a fair proposal, for all we know."

"But how can we know?" Orem Darm asked. He too stood up, his voice taking the other side. "Hans Thegn is right to remind us that Staubauns are full of lies. And the Mormantaloran is Staubaun. He's a Purist and an outsider—and he's a sorcerer too, and so are the people he has brought with him. Rumor on the river runs thick with such talk. Stefan may have done us a bad turn to have brought that lot into our midst."

"I don't trust him." Hans crossed his arms. If people were taking stands, that was his. "And I won't agree to any proposal he presents."

"Better listen," Nalf Rhys said, "or he's like to take you on!" A ripple of laughter from the Frendeli group lightened the mood of the assembled leaders. "But what you're asking ain't any better," he told Hans bluntly. "You don't want the Mormantaloran, think he killed your brother, well fine—we don't want Sordan. We both got baskets but there ain't no eggs."

Now's the time....

Hans drew a deep breath, then took the plunge. "Not even if I can get Amallar the Rill?"

Every chieftain and Old Mother, every person at the table stared at him, mouths agape, not trusting what they had heard. Only Robdan and Arne stared at Hans anxiously. The silence in the meeting hall became so complete, so seemingly solid, it had texture.

"The *what?*" Nalf Rhys repeated, as if he might have misunderstood.

"*The Rill.*" Hans paced his next words carefully. "What if I could get the Sordaneon to have the Rill stop in Amallar? There's a node right here, at Bellan Toregh. It's sleeping but it's *here*. Have him awaken it as part of an alliance. Could that prod our Kheldish hen to lay a few eggs for my basket?"

"Don't start making a fool's promises." Nalf's face had hardened, along with his eyes. "Khelds can't even ride the thing! The god-monsters of the Staubauns decreed it long ago—we're not allowed near it! It won't take us and it won't take our goods."

"Because the mounts are controlled by men who make those distinctions!" Hans pressed forth his argument.

"Stefan rode it," Orem Darm pointed out, to a rumble of agreement.

"A fucking King," said Fran. "The Stauberg-Randolphs are... special."

"Not that special," Hans asserted. "Khelds are barred from Rill mounts by *people*, and it's people that make rules about who can use it. Maybe we're being fed stories to scare us away. But what if we have our own mount, a Kheld port on Kheld soil? What if I can get Sordan to agree to give us that?"

"In return for what?" Nalf asked suspiciously.

"I don't know. But isn't it worth discussing?"

Fran shot Hans a freezing stare. "It's a trick! The Sordaneon wouldn't really do it!"

"But what if he *would?*" Hans repeated the seductive promise. In the core of his gut, he knew: he had lodged the hook. Already murmurs from the crowd rose to his ears, words not of anger and not only of doubt. There was also hope—and yearning.

Nalf Rhys scratched his chin and pondered Hans with a calculating glint in his eye. "And what if he would? It's not like we have reason to think it. Yet you say the Sordaneon is willing to talk Rill this time? And give you no grief in Essera?"

Hans caught wind of a possible shift in Nalf Rhys's stance. It might be for gain, not conviction, but if it got Hans the alliance he wanted, he'd take that. "Dorilian will talk. He's promised me that, remember, in the letter he sent. Half of Rhodhur saw that letter before you tore it up. And we talked in Sordan—we talked a lot—and that's why I believe that if I assure him the north without Amallar rising against him, he will not contest me for the throne of Essera."

Nalf Rhys drew his head up, sniffed deeply the woodsmoke-laden air, and rubbed his fingers thoughtfully along his bearded jaw. "You think. You believe, lad," he noted thoughtfully, then muttered, "Stefan never had that." Nalf's gaze moved to the other folk at the table, from Fran Gorseddson's rebellious, troubled face to the even less certain expressions of the Old Mothers and bearded clan leaders. Sordan to them was little more than a name, though it was a name they were most often moved to condemn. But they had not lived north of the Dazun, as Nalf and Robdan and some of the others had, nor as Fran did on the edge of Staubaun countries. The Rill was wrapped in such mystery that most Khelds didn't know what access to it might bring—or even what it meant if the Sordaneons agreed to hold back on their claim to Essera's throne.

For Khelds, Hans's offer of the Rill dangled like a shining pearl of dew upon a spider's hidden web.

"Even if you get this agreement to get the Rill, what's to say he can do it?" Fran Gorseddson's open suspicion gave voice to the doubt that clouded many Kheld faces. "The Rill's stopped running."

Hans shrugged. "I believe he stopped it. Let him start it up again."

"Just like that?"

But Nalf Rhys said, more to the point, "And have him stop it on us too, again, as soon as he's got it going? What's to stop him from doing *that*? Or turn on you once he gets across the Dazun?"

Hans, however, had already considered that argument. "Have him swear an oath." He smiled as Nalf's eyes narrowed in understanding.

"Is that so?" Nalf's gaze flicked across the benches crowding the room, the startled, disbelieving, hopeful faces of the people who looked to him—and to Hans now as well—to lead them. "You're the Mother's red-haired son to tempt us to your side. The gods-damned Rill! Staubauns say it can't be done, but Orem here is right: they're full of lies. I wouldn't put it past them to have kept it from us. And someone did wake the thing in Teremar, didn't he? The old king always said he thought he knew who. Cullen Brodheson too." Nalf was thinking out loud, putting pieces together.

"And that could be a lie as well," Fran said. "So could the part about the oath."

"Lies cannot sustain over time. Truth, not a lie, has kept us safe these many years," said the red-cloaked Old Mother from the Combroggi Cruihcil.

Nalf's shrewd eyes raked the crowd. "We got us some other folk here," he growled to his fellow cruihcil leaders. "The damned Trongorians always got bits and pieces put by. Deal with Sordan, they do, and Essera too. Had their Elector at Rhodhur for a bit and he's well traveled. Thron! And Farrl, you too. The both of you. Come forward, let us hear what you have to say!"

Hans forced himself to remain expressionless as Dorilian approached the table, as conspicuous as a gold coin among coppers. Farrl, not as tall, looked tense and was probably unhappy with being weaponless. What was needed here was composure, but Hans felt only fear. So many eyes... so very many. What if Dorilian was recognized? Was it truly possible that all these important and influential Kheld leaders, men and women who had known Stefan, had never met Sordan's Hierarch? Never *seen* him? Remembering the isolation Dorilian had lived in even in Sordan, it soothed Hans somewhat that Robdan looked concerned but not sharply worried.

Nalf Rhys drew a careful breath before he spoke. "Let me be plain. I think between the two of you, you know some things—and probably a hell of a lot more than you let on. Maybe heard a fair share of lofty talk on your travels. So tell me, what do high folk say about the Rill? Can that bastard Dorilian Sordaneon get it running again?"

Farrl cleared his throat. "I would not know, Thegnard. Trongor trades with Sordan, and I have accompanied the Elector there, but... I know nearly nothing about the Rill."

Nalf looked unsurprised. He redirected to Dorilian. "Back to you, then, as I figured this would. Gerd tells me you've knocked about, seen a thing or two. So what say you, Thron Estol Bevvan: can the Sordaneon make the damn Rill run again?"

Hans carefully watched Dorilian's hesitation. How much would a Trongorian, even if well traveled or a confidant of the Elector, know about the Rill and its Highborn origin? Too much of an answer would be more dangerous than none at all. And yet an answer could work to advantage. The consideration, therefore, was brief.

"Yes. I believe he could."

"You *believe*. Sure of that, eh?" Nalf snorted. "And this Highborn stuff and nonsense, about oaths and all—would an oath like that hold him?"

"It would—if you could get him to make it. As has been so eloquently pointed out, no Highborn oath has ever been broken."

"Not yet, you mean. He's not the kind to be shy about being the first, now, is he?" Nalf groused in frustration. "Damn it! If it wasn't the Rill on the table!"

"But is it?" Aubrey rose from the Neuberland benches and stepped forward. Her gaze at Thron was disturbingly direct, filled with questions and opposition. When she stood in the open area before the table she turned to Hans. "Or is that just what you would have us think?"

"I wouldn't offer anything I didn't think I could produce," Hans told her.

"Then produce it."

Caught off guard, Hans could only stare at Aubrey in shock. Did she expect Hans to produce it in this room? The entire congregation of taut, anxious Khelds, their minds boggled by the conversation, dissolved into gales of laughter that rang off of the ceiling in endless peals. They suddenly realized what it was they were supposed to think could be brought to pass and how ridiculous it was that Hans could somehow give them what generations of kings had not been able to pry loose from Sordaneon hands.

The Rill might as well have been the sun or the moon.

"You can't, can you?" Aubrey said. She looked more disillusioned than triumphant. Hans saw what she was doing. Aubrey didn't believe him about the Rill. Rather than see her people make fools of themselves, she'd called Hans's bluff. "You don't have it on paper, do you? You don't have it at all! *He* has it! Dorilian Sordaneon has the Rill—and the last thing in the world he's going to do is give it to you! Or us. He'll let you believe anything—have *us* believe anything—just to get what he wants. But don't expect him to make good on it. He never does!"

Dorilian blurted, "What did he ever promise *you*?"

Aubrey turned on Dorilian like a wildcat ready to pounce. Hans stepped between them, bringing her attention sharply on him again.

"I'll bring the Rill to Amallar!" he announced as triumphantly as she had denounced him but a moment before. He and Dorilian, and Robdan too, had talked about this; they'd planned it meticulously. "I will need Dorilian's agreement to bring the Rill as a show of good faith. I will need time to communicate with him. I ask only that you give me seven days' time. Seven days to get word to him. And on the seventh day, when the sun is high, the Rill will come to Bellan Toregh!"

"*You'll* bring it?"

"It will come!"

"On whose word?"

Mine!

No one had spoken. Hans detected the word in his thoughts, maybe all their thoughts, but it had never vibrated through air. *My God*, he thought. *I know he's an empath, but can he do that?*

Hans caught his wits and gazed back into Aubrey's startled stare.

"Mine," he repeated. It was the word Dorilian had given him, and it would be on Hans's word no less than Dorilian's that the Rill would appear in Amallar. A glance around at the faces of those who watched showed that they now thought Hans had sent that word into their minds. Their near awe had a force that struck at the soul of what he intended. "My word. His promise."

Aubrey's face was stark and pale at that revelation. "He gave it to you?"

"He will. And if I'm wrong, I will no longer press for an accord." Looking at her, and not at the man into whose hands he had just put the fate of his Kheld leadership, Hans added, "And once the Rill awakens at the top of that hill, upon my honor as Thegn, we'll talk our way to an alliance."

30

The ordering of society begins with its assumptions of
itself. It is not enough to give people something to believe
in. We must give them the right things to believe in.

Epirrhemos Aethes, opinion paper to the Royal College of Standards

Aubrey thought the wind raging at the windows sounded
mournful, ominous, not joyous at all. If anything, the wind
promised a storm and presaged change. *Change.* The very
thing the Rappeleye Old Mothers had read in their Wheel.

Six days had passed since Hans Thegn had spoken to the Witan—
six days since the message sent by bird to Leseos; six days of
meetings and arguments and high emotions—and everything had
changed. Word had come from Sordan: the Rill would appear on
the morrow.

Every Kheld since Alm had been told that, for the Kheld people,
the Rill could not change. The Rill never changed. Except when it
did.

That prospect now filled Aubrey with foreboding. If the Rill
altered, if it did so *here*, for any reason, so would Amallar, in ways
she could not even begin to imagine.

The evening's special assembly of cruihcila elders and leaders had
just broken up. Hans had been called into a private session to confer
with Nalf Rhys and his advisory council. Now that Hans had
produced an agreement that promised to deliver the Rill, they wanted
more details. And they didn't want him addressing the entire assembly
about it—many elders feared their people would believe in Hans's
proposal before their leaders could find a way to turn an advantage.

The Faeduadan, in opposition, had moved their ceremony to that day. Not only that, but so many people had flooded to Bellan Toregh in hope of witnessing the event that encampments ringed the city. Thanks to exuberance and the town's storehouses of ale, there were fights every hour of the day and twice as many each night.

As she stood near the head table, watching the assembly break into smaller groups, Aubrey barely listened to Old Mother Gyffa speaking at her side, issuing an invitation to the local Vesl Motherhouse for a laying of the Great Wheel. Aubrey should attend that session. Saemoregh's fate, as well as Amundhal's, might well reside among what the runes revealed. But she felt in her bones there was another thread of this fabric yet to be unraveled.

"I will attend if I am able, Mother." Even as she spoke the words, Aubrey knew they were empty. She hoped Mother Gyffa would attribute the flush in Aubrey's cheek to the warmth of the overfilled room. Or even, as many believed, that she had once again begun to encourage the attentions of Fran Gorseddson. Turning away, she was glad to see that her real target had not left.

Aubrey thought it interesting the way Thron watched so intently when Hans walked away with Nalf Rhys and the others. Usually Thron masked his interest in Hans's activities. This time his look struck her as too openly hopeful of a favorable outcome. Others hoped for the Rill. Thron hoped for Hans to *convince* them of it.

Suddenly, Aubrey was sure. She walked toward Thron.

He noticed her perusal and immediately became unreadable again.

"Don't you find it even a little disturbing that Hans should have that thing in his pocket?" Aubrey took a seat on the oak bench beside which Thron stood. She liked looking up at him and the way he looked down at her, as if doing so were the most natural posture in the world.

He frowned. "What thing?"

"The Rill."

"Ah. *That* thing."

"What else?"

"The alliance, perhaps. Or maybe the prophecy? If I were Handurin, I would worry at least as much about that." Others had overlooked that impending event—but not him.

"Some might think this is his way of trying to circumvent it."

Thron shook his head. "Prophecies, in my experience, are difficult to outmaneuver. They can dog one's footsteps to the end."

"Your experience? What prophecies dog you?"

He laughed, a low sound that acknowledged Aubrey's interest. "I would be a fool to answer such a question. Why should I provide you with conversation from which—I am certain—you would concoct an absurdity?"

"You talk with others. Why not me?"

"They are not forever laying traps with their questions."

"Maybe I'm just interested in you."

Thron gave Aubrey a ghost of a smile, then looked away again. She laughed. "Is that so unbelievable?"

"No. It is undoubtedly part of the truth. Just not enough of it."

Was it possible he could read her? Before he could turn away to seek more privacy in the crowd, Aubrey placed her hand upon Thron's arm. He stopped. When his gaze delved into hers, she removed her hand. "I would do nothing to cast a shadow on Hans or imperil his leadership, but I fear what he is doing. People will use it against him."

"What people?"

"The Faeduadan."

"If he can bring the Rill, Handurin will have little to fear from priests spouting hoary prophecies."

Aubrey fit her answer alongside his. "Prophecies can be self-fulfilling. You said yourself that they're difficult to outmaneuver."

"And you think this one will be?"

"I'm Nalf's niece, close to him. I was in his room when the priest explained something unusual about the prophecy." Aubrey tried to discern the emotion that looked back at her. Curiosity. Guardedness. Always guardedness. Part of it, she thought, was that they were observed. Arne, for one. He was seated out of earshot but watching closely, with a scowl that fairly shouted across the tables. "We can't talk here," Aubrey said, because it was true. "Too many eyes, too many ears."

Thron looked unconvinced. Whatever else he was thinking or feeling, he suspected her intentions. Persuading him rested on another trait Aubrey's runes had confirmed—that he was watchful of Hans, protective even. It was more convincing to have Thron think she raised this matter of the Faeduadan and some hidden pitfall as a means of warning Hans through him.

Thron leaned nearer. "So, lady, do you propose we should find a more private situation?"

Aubrey noted the insinuation. He had detected that too. Her heart beat faster.

"Yes. Unless you're afraid to be alone with me?"

Thron's gaze betrayed no fear of that. Something else made him uncertain. Arne had risen and was walking their way. *Damn.*

"Across the way, behind the Bridge and Chimney." Aubrey leaned her face close to Thron's, close enough to smell the warm, faint spice of his skin. "They'll toll a bell to change the watch. Meet me then."

Arne stepped up and if frowns could kill, his would have. Aubrey noticed Arne looked only at her, even when he spoke to Thron.

"Robdan's asking for you. Said the cook's fixed up a dinner."

Apparently, the news pleased Thron because he smiled and drew away. "Next time, lady, offer a meal," he said.

As the men walked away, he looked back. Aubrey knew then that he'd said those words to throw off Arne. Thron too would be listening for the bell.

31

Upon the eve of Devastation, the Leur went to his friend
and said, "They know the peril, yet the Hegemons persist
in wielding the things of Vllyr. Don't they care what lies at
Mulsor's heart or what will be unleashed upon the World
should it be broken?" To which Amynas replied, "The
Undying Crown has consumed them, so that destruction is
all they care to unleash upon the World." To which the
Leur sighed. "It's going to be a long night."

CIBULITUS, *ANNALS OF THE RETURN*

"He sure isn't the next Stefan." Fran Gorseddson's angry
gaze scanned the other tables and what was taking place
there. The Black Goose Inn was overheated and
crowded with loud, exuberant patrons.

Aubrey had met Fran outside the meeting hall. Now they shared
this table in a cold corner to wait out the elders' deliberations. As far
as anyone could tell, the damn special meeting had dragged on into
late hours with heated discussions serving no purpose but to
underscore their divisiveness.

"No, he isn't, is he?" Aubrey sent a smile Fran's way. Their table
was littered with the remains of a meal. She picked at the chicken
carcass on the trencher. "Hans fools people. He lulls us into thinking
he's easily influenced, then like a mule he pulls his own way. He
drove Nalf Rhys mad at Rhodhur."

"Well, I don't like the way he's pulling."

"Neither do I."

"He's got us all in an uproar." Fran sighed, then frowned. "If it's
true that Hans Thegn can get us the Rill—"

"You don't believe that do you?"

Fran was a few years older and for a time when she was a girl, Aubrey had idolized him. For her coming of age, she had chosen Fran to be her first man. He had pleased her well enough until she'd learned he was also enjoying the beds of Wodd's daughter and two other holders' lasses. Fran's casual enjoyment of women and complete lack of interest in, or support for, the children they got from him was reason enough for Aubrey to stop inviting him to her bed. Fran disliked her decision but not enough to put aside their acquaintance.

Fran put down his empty cup and signaled for a bob to refill it. "Well, Hans would be crazy to say something like that if he didn't think he could bring it off. I don't think he's crazy. So unlikely as it sounds, that upstart of a lad thinks he has the Rill in his pocket."

"Except that you and I know the Sordaneon isn't giving it away." The only thing Aubrey was truly sure of was that there was more to be learned. "And that being the case, I'd really like to know what Hans will have to give up to get it from him. Or what we'll have to give up."

"I think that depends on what the Sordaneon wants."

"We've got to find out what that is. Because if the Rill does show up tomorrow, once it's here and people see it, once it's *real*, the Sordaneon can ask for just about anything he wants—and probably get it." Aubrey frowned into the brown depths of her cup. She'd seen the Rill a few times in her life. Memory burned brightly of silver *charysi* gleaming in transit through the surreal rings atop the mount at Leseos. The image gave her shivers. "Maybe Hans has been blinded by it already."

"Ah, Aubrey lass, you don't see the sheep for the wool." Fran smiled at her reflectively. "Dorilian Sordaneon's up to something. And I think he's using Hans as a way to get it." He looked around the smoky confines of the main room in which they sat, and his smile faded to a troubled scowl. Each time the main door opened, a fierce wind blew handfuls of swirling white to briefly glisten upon the floor. "Doesn't it seem just a little bit odd that we've been told Bellan Toregh was a dead mount all these years—a hundred years... no, two hundred and more, our whole history of it—and all of a sudden now it isn't?"

"Something new?"

"Or nothing changed."

"Are you saying that it's still dead?"

Aubrey tried to read Fran's face. She had learned to respect his instincts, just as he had learned to respect hers. Another blast of cold air filled the room as more patrons departed and she tugged at the heavy woolen cloak which had fallen behind her, pulling it up across her shoulders. Its warm weight was welcome relief from the chill.

"I don't know that much about the Rill," Fran conceded. "And I don't know any man who does. But I'm saying that if it's to come on the morrow, it sure came alive awfully fast. I'm also saying it doesn't look any different to me. The crown atop Leseos glows lots brighter than this one."

As did the structures atop the even larger mount at Dazunor-Rannuli, a city Aubrey had only glimpsed from afar. She swallowed. "If Bellan Toregh really is dead, and the Rill doesn't run, or it just passes by—then Hans will look like a fool."

Fran nodded.

Aubrey regarded him fiercely. "Well, we can't just sit here and hope for the best. Maybe we should try to find something out before tomorrow."

"Great idea. You tell me how. Hans sure is keeping his mouth shut about it." Fran studied her anew. "You can't get to him, Aubrey lass, even if you have wheedled into his bed the way the graybeards are saying." He laughed at her glare. "Don't look at me like that. You know I'm for it."

"You and too many other men."

"Don't think harshly of us. We have a kingdom at stake." Fran straightened, chin high. "Hans needs men behind him. Strong men. Men good at arms and willing to use them. Men worthy of trust. You and the Mothers will harvest the future, but only if men succeed in keeping our royal prince there alive."

"Men are doing that already, have been doing that. Even in Sordan. Hans is dead right about one thing he said at the Witan: Dorilian *let* him escape."

"So what of *that*? It would be just like that bastard to send a rival to his doom."

"As we know. So why this way? Why dangle the Rill? What's doomed about that?"

"We're back to the first question," Fran noted. "*Is* he dangling the Rill?"

"Thron."

Fran cocked his head and squinted at her. "Thron?"

"You met him six days ago, the day of the Witan. Tall, well dressed, strong opinions about boats and deserts." She smirked. "Handsome, with a dash of self-importance."

"I remember." Fran frowned at her description. "The Trongorian."

"Maybe not."

"Maybe not what?" Fran's voice lowered to nearly a growl. A server came to clear the trenchers and plates, leaving behind a pot of branroot and two cups, courtesy of the innkeeper, who knew Aubrey and Fran from frequent stays. It helped that Aubrey had taken a room at the Black Goose, and Fran still took most of his meals there even though he was boarding with other Neuberlanders at a farm outside of town.

"He may not be Trongorian. He's more than a little Staubaun, for starters."

"I wouldn't make too much of that." Fran's pointed reprimand, punctuated by a hard stare from hazel eyes flecked with gold, reminded Aubrey that he too had an unknown Staubaun father.

"You know I don't. It's other things that've been sticking pins and needles in me every time I look at him." Aubrey explained her first meeting with Thron, adding, "Ever since then, folk have been very closed-mouthed about him. He doesn't talk about himself, and I found out that the other Trongorians don't know any more about him than we do."

"So he's a sell-sword."

"Maybe. People are saying that. It's other things, little things, like how for a while at Rhodhur he never even went to meals alone. And then, just before last waning, he and Robdan set out from Rhodhur, supposedly to visit Robdan's daughters who live on their kilth's big holding near Eastmeary Brenna."

"So?"

"So I talked to Wytha Robdansda on my way here. Robdan and Thron only stayed one night at her place. And I don't think anyone who owns a right mind would stay a week with Ressany and her brood. Wytha also said that Thron seemed in a hurry and pressed to not stay even another night. I think they may have made a little side trip to Bellan Toregh."

Like a hound picking up the scent, Fran's nostrils flared slightly, the skin across his cheekbones drawn taut as he clenched his lightly bearded jaw. "Robdan? And Thron?"

"I think Robdan was just along for the ride. But what was Thron doing here?"

"Be sure, girl," Fran said hoarsely. "We can't afford false moves. *Was* he here?"

Aubrey flicked a glance at the innkeeper. "I inquired at every inn. This one's not certain. He remembers a tall stranger who came in with an older man, and that they stayed one night and were gone the next morning."

"Right before the announcement of the Witan." Fran caught his lower lip between his teeth and sucked on it. It meant he was thinking. Just as she was.

"And it was not long after they got back to Rhodhur that Hans really started pushing this alliance of his. I tell you, Fran, I'd stake my life that Thron is more than just some sell-sword."

"All right, you've made it clear you've got a spider in your hair. What would you say he is?"

"Sordani, maybe?"

Fran stopped short, stunned. "Dammit, Aubrey! You'd better know what you're saying! We can't go making accusations like that on a stab in the dark!"

"You're right. Maybe he's Esseran. Hans has friends *and* enemies there, and his mother might have sent someone. That's possible. Thron's accent is one I can't quite place. What I *can* tell you is that Thron is too exceptional. He speaks Khelda too well to have just picked it up on the side, and he listens too intently to be a casual observer. He is far, far too skilled at evasion. You've seen him but a few hours altogether. I've studied him for weeks—he forgets nothing, his ideas range too far afield. He quotes poetry! No common man of anywhere does that or knows the things he knows. And men follow his lead without even knowing they're doing it. Watch him long enough and you'll see it. People sense his ability. If breeding tells, as the Staubauns like to say, then his shouts of higher places than Trongor."

Fran nodded, warming to her idea. "So you think he's the go-between?"

Pressing her hands upon the table, Aubrey leaned closer. "I think that when Dorilian Sordaneon realized that Hans had made good his escape, that he would go to Amallar, he sent someone after him to try to recoup something from the loss. Who knows what he was thinking? Maybe an alliance is better than nothing at all. He could always renege on it later." Aubrey frowned and looked at the hide-covered window. "I'm almost certain Hans knew from the start who Thron was. Maybe he'd met him in Sordan. And I think Thron came to Bellan Toregh because he had to talk with his damned Hierarch. Maybe a messenger, or maybe the Rill. You know yourself that's one way the Staubauns use it."

"But this one? Dead as stone?"

"Or maybe not. Do we really know? I just find it odd that Thron was here for one night and *only* one night. Then he came back to Rhodhur with Dorilian's 'offer.'"

"Which Hans swallowed feather and claw!"

"And once Hans got us to agree, he sent his acceptance." After a moment, Aubrey sighed. "The real problem is that there may be something to be gained in the offer. Hans isn't stupid. Nalf Rhys has been pushing me at him, and I've learned that much. And the Rill isn't something the Sordaneons have ever dangled to anyone. *Ever.* Either Dorilian doesn't mean it, never meant it even for a moment, can't even do it—or he *can* do it, and really would go through with it if Hans can offer something he wants in exchange."

"Like what?" Fran waited on Aubrey's thoughts, gaze shadowed with some of his own. He rapped his knuckles in turn upon the scarred planks of the table.

"Maybe the Rill is just the bait to get us to the table."

"But we're not there yet."

"Neither is it—yet." Aubrey pondered the other possibility, then said it. "Maybe what's happening already is what he wants. Maybe he *wants* us to follow Hans."

"And he'll dangle his precious Rill to see that we do—it's a gods' damned bribe!"

Aubrey sank back in her chair, newly thoughtful. "Yes. But why? What stake would Sordan have in Hans?"

"Treachery, that's what." Fran slammed his fist on the table, knocking his carved cup to the floor, where it clattered dully across the wooden planks. It was a good thing for their conversation that the late hour had seen the inn's common room emptied and there were few left to be startled. "I'll send my men, get that Thron fellow in hand. Then I'll fetch the cruihcila—"

"No, Fran!" Aubrey grasped Fran's wrist, holding him as she hissed an urgent whisper. "Hans watches him like a hawk! Do it that way, and we risk losing it all! Hans, Essera's throne, the Rill—

everything we may yet stand to gain! What if it *is* there for us? I don't want us to be the ones who threw it away!"

"What then? We move under the table?"

"Yes, for tonight. We don't yet know anything! Accusations would just make it necessary for Hans to defend himself. The stakes could not be higher. We can't afford to blow this bag open until we know what's in it. And that is what I can find out for us, what I *will* find out for us. But you must leave Thron to me."

"Aubrey." Fran spoke with real concern. "If that man is what you think he is, he could be very dangerous. We've met Sordani agents in Neuberland, and the more they know and the more they got to lose, the harder they are to crack. They think that Hierarch of theirs is some kind of god. They don't betray him even if you start shaving the flesh from their bones. You aren't going to get through."

"I already have. We've talked several times now. He's familiar with me and less guarded. Unguarded enough to have given me glimpses of what he might be. More than that, I'm Hans's cousin and tied to the powers of this land. Thron has reasons to trust me."

Disapproval darkened the shadows that underscored Fran's frown. "Dammit, Aubrey! I've seen the way you look at him. You're playing games of your own."

"Yes. But I'm good at them." This game, especially. Aubrey had shown Fran over the years that she was no fool when dealing with men. He was himself a prime example. "I've arranged a meeting on the dock at the Four Boars Inn. I've got him wondering what I'm after, and curiosity loosens tongues. By the time he knows, it will be too late. And I promise you, if he doesn't come up with any good answers to my questions, you can have him in the morning."

32

It is imperative to place the godborn above common
politics and see that they are exposed only to the best we
have to offer: the best women and men; the best characters;
the best minds. The creative powers of the Highborn will
be thus directed. It would be folly to bombard them with
the raw, confused stuff of human existence.

SEVEN HOUSES COMMUNICATION TO THE PSILANT KERBASIOS

Aubrey leaned against the wall of the Bridge and Chimney
Inn, glad for its extended eaves. The overhang provided
some shelter from a snowfall that had become heavier as the
night had deepened. The bridge over the canal had seen little traffic
since the closing of the inn's public room. Even the looming town
hall's three floors of windows had gone dark. The streets of Bellan
Toregh stood white and empty. It had been a short while since the
bell had tolled the change of watch.

Hearing muffled footfalls, she turned and saw Thron enter the
yard alone. He approached when he saw her.

"I hope you have a warmer place in mind for our conversation."
He squinted at the snow. "We shall be buried if we stand here for
long."

From the far end of the street at the bridge emerged a wagon on
runners, the first of the season, drawn by a brace of sturdy horses
that seemed to pull several drunken men in its wake. The few
remaining lights in the inn went out.

"This way." The path angled uphill, around the corner toward
the inn's squat outbuildings, tucked between the river and the hill.
Although the town guard had been strengthened, they weren't
exactly prowling the streets. Fran's men, even had he decided to

interfere, were safely downriver. Far above the town hall and its dormers stood the towering, portent-crowned shape of the Toregh.

Aubrey took the short path to the fallback blacksmith's shed, used only when there was an overflow of smith work, such as now with the Witan in town. She had chosen the secluded place earlier, knowing it would be deserted because the smith had stumbled home drunk from the Witan. It was unlikely he would return. Leading the way inside, she searched for the lantern she'd placed near the door. Soon its low light showed an open space dominated by the blackened, stony mouth of the forge. Within it, the banked coals for the next day's fire still gave off considerable heat. Aubrey walked over to warm her hands, leaving her companion to shut the door. The rasp of the bar being lowered soon followed.

Thron faced her and removed his leather gloves. "Are you very cold from waiting?" His gaze swept the room, possibly indicating a distrust of closed places.

Aubrey removed her snow-wet cloak and took Thron's from the table where he had discarded it. That cloak was heavy, made of good leather and lined with wool. A few steps away were two anvils, as good a place as any for two garments to be hung to dry. "It wasn't so very long. Besides, I'm used to this weather. I'm glad you decided to meet me."

"I was detained by the need to come in secrecy." He walked across the shed to lift the hide curtain from the single small window, beckoning her to look out upon the yard's deepening drifts. "And then I took some time to watch the snow fall."

That he could take pleasure in the sight struck Aubrey like a physical blow. "Do you like snow?"

"Only to look at. In every other way, I despise it." The heavy curtain dropped, concealing the view. Thron walked toward the hearth and its promise of warmth. Even ordinary movement on his part was fluid and sure, never a hint of awkwardness.

"Snow doesn't come often to your homeland, I imagine."

"No, not often."

Being with him felt easy tonight, alarmingly real, no longer tinged by imaginings or schemes. Aubrey didn't think Thron had agreed to meet her merely to procure information. She sensed the Mother's hand running like a current through her words and his, attraction and opportunity. If Thron was even half as aware of her as she was of him.... Even more than words, things unspoken ruled this night.

Wanting distance, she approached the door, its rough planks smoky from the everyday fires of the forge, and placed her hand on the bar that ensured their privacy.

"I was speaking of Sordan, Thron."

Alertness replaced friendly expectation. Thron's neck bowed for a moment and his shoulders tensed as he reached some conclusion. When he faced her again, Aubrey saw a man she did not know—one utterly free of useless emotion, whose calculating gaze openly weighed her assertion. More, she saw that her runes had read true.

"You're Sordan's agent. I... I recognize the training." The last part was a lie, but worth the gamble if the accusation proved true.

Something, mockery or acknowledgement, traced the slow curve of his mouth.

After these many weeks of observation, Aubrey had known she would find Sordan somewhere behind Thron. Now she wanted him to... what? Deny the accusation? Say it didn't matter? She still hoped to force an admission—either of his identity or of his imminent peril.

"We need to talk," she insisted. It was important that Thron listen and not attempt to leave. If he did that, Fran might find him first. She walked forward, placed her hand on his chest. Her fingers found and caressed thick smooth leather over hard muscle sheathed in wool and skin.

His silence broke. "No. I don't think so."

"I'm trying to help you."

"This conversation is at an end."

Snake-quick, he clamped his hand over her wrist and took a step toward the door, dragging her with him.

"Thron!" Aubrey pulled back with all that was in her, only to find the smith's worktable at her back, barring her way. She yanked again, harder. "What are you doing?"

"I'm taking you to Handurin."

They were in this together. Of course. But how deep did it go? So deep Hans would just disregard her every warning? And Thron... about him she still knew nothing except that if he wanted to kill her, he would do it here—out of sight—and not out in the snow.

Aubrey groped her free hand across the table's rough surface, finding and closing her fingers over a length of wood. Sanded, heavy, long, and thick—a haft meant for a pickax but not yet joined to its iron head. She lifted it and, with an accuracy Wodd would have approved of, brought the rounded end hard against Thron's skull.

He dropped as neatly as any beast at slaughter.

His head hurt like all hells had been poured into it. A persistent, pounding pain spread hot fingers along the margins of Dorilian's skull and stabbed into his eyeballs, blurring his vision. With the pain came nausea, but he battled that too, forcing consciousness. Light flickered in shadows nearby, nothing quite distinct, his surroundings unrecognizable. He sensed the Rill and that it lurked nearby, pulsing beneath his buttocks and legs, behind his back, much as it did in Sordan. No... more like at Stauberg or Simelon, some dormant place. But he wasn't anywhere so civilized.

When he tried to move to gain his bearings, Dorilian discovered he was braced against some hard, large object and his wrists were lashed. *What?*

Unable to believe it, he tugged again. Astonishment, then alarm, ran cold through his viscera.

Ignoring the pain in his head, he shifted as best he could to sitting fully upright. A wet cloth that had been touching his forehead pulled away and he turned to look. Aubrey knelt on the earthen floor beside him. Worry smudged her inquisitive gaze.

"Oh, thank the Mother! I was afraid I'd killed you!" The relief in her voice and face were real and flooded Dorilian's nerves.

"You almost did!"

Aubrey winced and looked contrite. "Not on purpose! I didn't bring you here to hurt you."

"That's not reassuring." Only because Dorilian was Highborn had he recovered this well. His propensity to heal had quickly repaired the bleed in his brain. The neurosystem always healed first. As the swelling resolved, he was regaining function. Rapidly.

"I understand why you're unhappy."

"Unhappy? Unhappy does not begin to describe—"

"I was just trying to keep from being dragged off!"

Dorilian remembered that. Vaguely. Now that he looked around again, he recognized the forge. Aubrey had moved him only as far as one of the heavy anvil and tool-bearing tables. She had, however, loosened his clothing and removed his weapons. He twisted away from her attempt to put the wet cloth to his head.

"Stop fighting. I'm trying to help."

"It's not helping." He said it as much to himself as to her.

"I'm not going to hand you over." Aubrey ducked her head and a sweep of hair curtained her face. The low light barely revealed her features, but her sincerity shone through with every tight, pain-filled word. "I could have done that, based on my suspicions, but I didn't. I'm trying to protect people." Her blue eyes, newly defiant, lifted to his. "Including you."

She meant it, however strangely that sentiment fit with her actions. When Aubrey lifted her hand again to reapply the damp and mercifully cool cloth to the bump throbbing on his skull, Dorilian ceased to struggle. Encouraging her to tend his injury might purchase time to think.

"Does Hans know who you serve?" Aubrey asked. On not receiving an answer, she set her jaw and sighed. She pulled the cloth away to assess if the bleeding had stopped. "I think he does know. I also think he should let everyone in on just how closely he has been working with a monster. Those things Hans said to the cruihcila, those high-minded words so calculated to bring us into this alliance, the things *you* said—whose words were they, really? Dorilian Sordaneon's?"

A careful answer was needed here. "Handurin chooses his own words."

Aubrey dipped the cloth again in a nearby pan of half-melted snow and wrung it out. "Your words. His words. It makes little difference. I suppose you speak as the villain tells you to speak; you act as he tells you to act. And for what? So he can spread his vile influence even further? Don't you care what comes of it? You've eaten at our tables, slept in our homes, played with our children! Yet you think so little of us that you would put us in the hands of a man who wants to destroy us?"

"You know nothing of what I think—or of what he would do." It was best to add that last part.

"But I will. Once we've finished our conversation."

"Oh, that is finished. Stop dabbing at my head and release me." Dorilian spoke as though to a child. "Handurin will not find this nearly as amusing as I do."

Aubrey rolled her eyes and dabbed harder. "I wonder if your disappearance would really harm Hans now," she reflected. "He has most of Amallar eating from his hand tonight. He no longer needs you to keep him to Sordan's path or make sure he does not oppose his dubious benefactors there. He might even be relieved come morning to find you suddenly, conveniently, gone. Hans Thegn's need for you is over, even if your inhuman master's isn't, and I doubt very much that the removal of Sordan's spy would distress either of them enough to make an issue of it. You might want to reconsider your situation, Thron."

Dorilian had been doing exactly that. "What do you want?"

"Answers."

Aubrey set aside her cloth and stood, arms crossed, looking down at him. "Who are you? I mean *really*? Not who you pretend to be. Not Thron Estol Bevvan. That's a handy identity, but I don't believe it's your own. I suspect you can claim a better name in your own country."

"Please, don't flatter me." Dorilian tugged again at the ropes. All that did was tell him that Aubrey tied a strong knot.

"I wouldn't dream of it." As she had done before just bare weeks past, Aubrey reached her hand into the leather pouch of her belt and brought forth something metal and shiny. His compass glinted with brassy lights in the cup of her palm. "While you were communing with the Mother, I took the liberty of looking you over good. Much better than I did by the Fords." Her smile wore an intimacy that struck at the pit of his stomach. "I found a couple of very interesting things among your possessions. This one, to start."

Aubrey handled the compass adroitly, pried at its casing, and loosened a medallion from beneath the rim of the cover. She bent to one knee beside him. Dorilian flinched as she pressed the *deiknya* to the bare skin where his opened tunic had fallen away from his collarbone. He needed only to watch her eyes to see in them the warm colors that flooded the metal as its heraldic achievement blossomed into view.

"Interesting, isn't it?" Aubrey studied the design, turning it in her fingers. When she pulled it away, the image faded. "Hans told us these things serve to identify the bearer. Only, I don't think a common spy would own one of these. Not one like this. The eagle, the sword, the design and colors spell Sordan, but I've never seen one quite like it." Her lips curved, too clearly enjoying her advantage as her gaze delved into his again. "Did your Staubaun daddy give this to you? Or did your pretty Staubaun mother bed a man who was beneath her?"

Dorilian couldn't look away. Let her think him some nobleman's bastard if that kept her at bay.

"Damn you, Thron." Irritation frayed the words. "I don't know the identity of this symbol yet, but I brought one of my Uncle Robdan's books with me from Rhodhur. It's in my room right now. I'm going to have your name by morning."

She would too. That *deiknya* told all if the book was what he thought it was.

"And while I'm at it, I'm going to track down *this*." From another compartment in the compass's rear casing, Aubrey brought forth a gleaming, star-gilded object. This she displayed pointedly, held lightly between her thumb and forefinger.

All smugness left Dorilian when he saw the Rill Stone in her hand, its emerald matrix slumbering with subtle sparks.

If Aubrey knew what *that* was, what it *meant*.... Had she placed the ring on his finger while he was unconscious? Touched it to skin? If so, she had seen the device ablaze with power.

Dorilian tried to strip the truth from Aubrey's features and then, tentatively, the surface emotions of her mind. He sensed only simple pleasure at trapping him in range of discovery. Anger, yes, mated with suspicion—but no hatred. None. Only a hint of triumph and something else that yet lingered between them, unexplored. He regretted that.

"A ring like this one is no small trinket." She turned the ring in her hand, studying it, then Dorilian. "Your Hierarch favors you much, I think."

"Point taken."

Faced again with no answer, Aubrey frowned and dropped the ring back into her belt pouch.

"You must be brought to heel, Thron-whoever-you-are. It's one thing to deal with mysterious Trongorians, and quite another when the Trongorian turns out to be Sordan's spy. I know you came to Bellan Toregh ahead of the call for the Witan. But what did you do here?"

"You know much already."

"The Rill?" Scorn dripped from the word. "Do you expect me to believe, like those simpleminded fools on the Witan, that Dorilian Sordaneon really means to send it? That bastard would sooner see Sordan gripped by plague than have the Rill stop within these lands. My people petitioned for Rill shipping access—just a chance to be *allowed* to include our goods as cargo—after he was crowned, and we never received so much as a hearing! Stefan begged him for it, and Marc Frederick before him. Our pleas for passage rights

Dorilian rejected by calling us lower than animals, unfit to so much as even step upon a platform!"

That last remark had been delivered by Dorilian's father, but now was not the time to correct the point.

"All the world clamors for the Rill," Aubrey continued, "and Dorilian laughs. He pisses on the mighty and sends arms and food to our enemies. He smirks when Staubauns exclude us from every market because they, not we, fill his treasury! He went out of his way to spite Stefan at every turn. He invaded Gignastha just to hurt Stefan—and rejoiced in hurting us too. So why should he favor Hans, when Hans is Stefan's brother and seeks to win Essera from him? What is it that he wants? It cannot be to our advantage. I have questions but no answers—and I think you have those."

Dorilian stayed silent. He had come closer to his death, but never—save once—with so little room to maneuver. Or so much. For all Aubrey thought she knew, she was blinder than any of them.

"Don't do it, Thron." Aubrey's softly spoken plea was surprisingly earnest, with a sincerity so bright and clear that it could only be absorbed as true. Her skirt of russet wool mounded on the floor as she knelt before him. "Don't stand on pride. Don't make me give you over. Fran Gorseddson has suspicions too, because I talked with him first—but I sent him on a false trail. Why? Because he would hurt you to make you talk. I thought this way would be better. That I could get to the truth. But I can't just let you go." In her words, Dorilian heard a depth of fear for him. "Don't you see? You can't look to Hans or Robdan to help you anymore. Hans has no power of his own, just ours if we care to give it to him. And the men and women on the Witan may be old, but they're not gentle with Sordan's spies. Do you think they can't break you? You're flesh and blood. They'll let Fran do it. They'll tell him to blind you or cripple you. They may even impale you to send a message! That's the common punishment for spies. And what's left won't be much good to any man—or woman."

So... it came to that. Aubrey cared for him—his well-being, his opinion—in ways that surpassed expectations. Dorilian had wondered.

In the flickering lantern light, her candor took on a beauty all its own. "Tell me what you know," she entreated. "It's the only thing that might save your life."

Not the only thing. But he was not yet ready to resort to that. Time yet remained an ally.

"I fail to see—"

"Must I lay it out for you? You're intelligent enough to see for yourself that whatever it is you and Hans are up to will be destroyed the moment I turn you over. To Fran or the Witan or even the Old Mothers, it hardly matters—every Kheld in every part of Amallar and Neuberland will reject that plan *and* Hans the moment they learn they've been deceived. And you and Hans, both of you, will be as good as dead."

Damn the woman, but she was probably right.

"I don't see how answering your questions would improve that outcome." To keep talking was Dorilian's best tactic. To free himself, he needed time. Time to do what was needed to break the knots.

"You would gain me as an ally. I would withhold all my accusations."

And would then hold them in reserve as threats—along with whatever answers he gave. He managed not to laugh. "I fear the price might be too high."

Warmth broke through the cool of Aubrey's smile and she leaned nearer. "It might be fun to see how much I can make you pay."

"For my life? A great deal."

"Perhaps, for answers, I too would give a great deal." Her voice held a throaty vibrato Dorilian wished to explore.

How strange. He usually found the shunting aside of sexual impulses—his or those of others—to be far easier. It was also true that Aubrey's attraction to him comprised one of his few weapons.

"What are you offering?" he suggested. "I don't really need land."

"Or coin?"

"Don't insult me." He met and held the spark of heightened, and amused, interest in her gaze.

"Perhaps a less insulting gesture will get us to a better bargain," Aubrey said. Boldly, she bent forward and pressed her lips to his.

Stunned by the move, Dorilian allowed it, this gesture that answered all his questions. What seared his senses was pure, living, and true. He should be affronted, jerk his head away, but he didn't. Instead he allowed the soft fullness of Aubrey's mouth to linger on his, tasting the vivid allure of sex. All these weeks he *had* wondered—though he had fought that impulse. How not? Aubrey was every bit as dangerous as she was beautiful. Dorilian's body overpowered restraint, rising quickly.

That much, he could not allow. Already the situation was perilous. He couldn't tell whose emotions he was feeling—Aubrey's desire, drawn from her alone... or emotions that *he*, as a projective empath, had compelled within her. His desire, his carnality, reflected and amplified and thrown back upon him. Hesitation would have been less confusing, less confounding, than what Dorilian felt now.

"I think you have your answer to that question," he said when their lips had parted. He looked up into the satisfied gleam of her eyes.

Aubrey's smile deepened. "One answer is better than none. Maybe I will simply extract answers kiss by kiss."

When her mouth sought his again, Dorilian yielded. He opened to the gentle play of velvet tongue against his teeth, a sharp nip on his lip, a woman's soft enveloping heat. Desire this honest sang along his nerves—a purity of motive he had not known since Palimia. Aubrey's hunger was primal and real—but it was also misshapen, directed at a man he both was and was not. Worse, her proximity and body overpowered all resolve to remain unmoved.

Weakened by his own urges, he closed his eyes rather than look upon Aubrey's satisfaction at his response. His body would get him out of his predicament yet, but not like *this*. Yet how? Though Dorilian possessed the skill needed to translocate, he had trained that ability through the Sordan Coronal—a device far from his possession. And the one device he *had* brought, Aubrey had placed in her pouch and out of reach.

All he had left was the Rill.

Aubrey brushed at strands of hair that had fallen across his forehead, traced her thumb along his jaw.

"I've thought all along you and I would make for an interesting match," she said.

"Perhaps you should have told me before this."

"I'm glad I didn't. I've been foolish, mooning like a besotted girl and not thinking like a woman about the consequences." With a sigh, Aubrey pushed herself away. Abruptly, Dorilian missed her heat, the skin-intense experience of their contact. "I should have discerned first if you were friend or foe—and remembered that I have higher obligations. I'm going to find out who you are and where your allegiance lies. Shortly, I will return to ask you better questions—and maybe you'll feel more like talking."

Cold air filled the space Aubrey left behind when she rose to her feet and reached to undo the sash from around her hips. It didn't matter what she meant to do with it—Dorilian was reminded of his precarious circumstances. This Kheld woman's game and his unexpected response had postponed thoughts of escape—but escape he must, and now, in full sight of her if need be. He could not let Aubrey leave with the Rill Stone and his *deiknya*. There were folk enough even here in Amallar who would guess what the devices were.

Aubrey had tied her ropes well, but no rope made by mortals could long hold a Sordaneon body-bound to the Rill. Just as in any other town with an empowered mount, Rill energy pulsed thick beneath and around Bellan Toregh. This shed was built into the side of the hill, its rear wall in proximity to the mount's ancient core. So near, the energy was easily tapped.

Never taking his eyes off Aubrey as she knotted her pretty sash into a wad with which to gag him, Dorilian located the Rill vein beneath the cold dirt floor. Even without the Rill Stone, his Entity-bound flesh could summon a trickle of power. As he had within this very mount but weeks before, he unshielded just a fingertip on each hand. Immediately he felt the burn of the Entity seeking to join with his cells. His hands were behind him, hidden, but the invading energy would be blue. Glad his clothing concealed it, he allowed the incursion to climb the sheathing of his arms to his elbows and, as he had before, fashioned a second skin. This second skin he pushed outward, away from the supple flesh that encased his bones.

Energy could be soft as water or hard as rock, dull as stone or sharp as razors. Subjected to his attack, the rope frayed and fell away. Not even a heartbeat later, Dorilian had closed the fistuli he had opened, severing the contact so that the energy upon him dissipated, harmlessly.

When Aubrey knelt beside him, sash in hand, Dorilian was ready.

Aubrey's first inkling of her captive's freedom came when Thron's hand shot out to grab her wrist. When she twisted in surprise, he pulled her down, then forced her backward. Off-balance. Aubrey felt her head and shoulders hit the floor, the hooded cloak she had donned mercifully softening her fall. She fought like an animal, arching violently under the weight of Thron's larger, heavier body. Pain shot through her shoulders as his hands pinned her wrists to the floor.

Aubrey had fought men before, but never like this. This was a man in whose company she had never felt unsafe. It was that knowledge that allowed her to look upon Thron's face, so familiar now, so known, to watch what he meant to do. He must want to kill her. She had hurt and endangered him, and Thron had killed before. Of that, she was certain.

"I should slay you." The words escaped his throat as if torn from it, betraying a man at war with himself.

"But you won't." How Aubrey knew this, she could not say, only that it felt true.

His stare of torment was the only answer she needed. Breathing hard, he continued to hold her beneath him. "Damn you! Why? Why now? Do you think I want any of this? You don't know what you've done!"

"Because you won't tell me!"

"Stop!"

He was trying to think of a way out. From what? From killing her? Something else? Aubrey sensed only that she had gained a toehold of ground. "Please. Let me help you."

"Help me?" That bark of disbelief offered no hope.

"I won't let anyone harm you! Believe me. I won't lead you falsely. The Mother forbids it."

Again that stare, pain so visible that it cut deeply into the very heart of truth itself. Thron's conflict was clear: he was struggling to understand, grasping at what to believe—about everything, about her, about what to do. She had threatened this man with talk of torture and death. He needed to know if he released Aubrey, he would not pay a terrible price.

"I promise, I will tell no one," she whispered and meant it with all her soul. "Give you to no one. I want you in too many other ways."

This was what it felt like for a woman to choose a man fully before the Mother. Aubrey lifted her face, her body, toward Thron, to let him know, to take this chance at bringing the world back to the way it should have been and could still be. For only a moment she wondered if he would succumb to rage and fear—or yield to life and hope, to the Mother? *To her?* "Please," she whispered.

At last he spoke, words ragged. "I cannot be false. I cannot... You promise?"

"Yes."

Thron hesitated, then released his grip, freeing Aubrey's wrists. "I wish—"

Giving him no chance to say more, Aubrey reached up, pulled him near, and their lips met. A deep note of something, frustration or surrender, entered his groan.

As it had before, hunger met hunger. Bracing on his arms, Thron moved his body above hers, accepting the invitation of her parted knees. The cloak beneath her did little to cushion the hard floor, but she didn't care any more than he did.

"Is this what you want?" Thron's weight shifted as he tugged with one hand at his trousers. "Is it?"

"Yes." Aubrey clutched his shoulders, locked her legs around his hips, willing him to do it. Her choice or the Mother's, no man had ever made her feel like this.

He mounted her surely, more conqueror than lover and yet somehow both. An inarticulate moan of pleasure escaped from Aubrey's throat as he found entrance. Each thrust but proved her choice. *Dear Mother, yes...!* This was the man she had yearned to know, not closed off and cold, but unlocked, body as heated and raw as his emotions. Now at last she and Thron were as the Mother intended: woman and man. Aubrey accepted and yielded and begged for more. Her cries crested and a sweet spasm went through her—but when she looked up at Thron's face she could not read his features at all. Just tension and pride and pleasure too until she won his shudder of surrender, the easing of his hardness, and she drew him down into her arms.

Afterward, Thron lay across her body, breathing hard, his skin sticking to hers through the fabric of his shirt and the disorder of her garments. She felt as though she was still floating, flattened by his weight yet finding it less than she would have thought for a man his size.

Aubrey could barely breathe, but she did not care to breathe, or even to think. If she did, she would ruin the fragile moment. She wanted to feel Thron's body covering hers, his masculine scent heavy upon her skin. He smelled like summer and sex and her. She pressed her mouth to the hard line of his collarbone, surprised to find his skin not salty but sweet. That caress was a mistake, for it roused him. Thron left her, abruptly, pushing himself from Aubrey as though eager to get away. The absence of his body left the perspiration of their coupling to chill in the winter air.

She watched him pull together his clothing, take up his cloak.

"I hate him, your Hierarch," she said. "I hate everything he's ever done. And I hate that he owns you."

Thron bent his neck, and she saw again the man she knew. He picked up the dagger she had taken from him and slid it once more into its housing, then buckled the sword again at his waist. "You and I are going to pay dearly for what has taken place between us. It would be better if we had never met. Just remember your part in this night."

It was clemency, Aubrey knew. The cold aftermath of their choices. He was angry and she was a traitor to her own convictions. Thron's hand brushed her belly and thigh as he retrieved his ring from her belt pouch and closed his fingers over it. "A family heirloom," he told Aubrey. "I would not like to lose it." He retrieved his other items also and, with an owner's deftness, fit the ring and the strange medallion back into the compass from which she had taken them. Just before he left, he spoke again, his voice raw with bitterness and regret. "You have lost your chance to kill me, lady. You will soon hate me so well—you will wish you had used your knife and not your wiles."

"And you didn't kill me."

He shot her a sardonic grimace. "And for that you're going to hate yourself."

The door closed with a rasp of splintered wood, leaving Aubrey to shiver in the gust of incoming cold that he left in his wake. She lay motionless for a long time, thinking of what had just taken place, that she had let him walk out that door, all questions but one unanswered. She had not asked him to stay, knowing that he would not, that now he feared for his life and would flee Bellan Toregh. If he stayed, Fran would see the Witan take him. No, Thron was gone and better so.

Aubrey didn't know how much time passed before she realized that dawn would soon bring others to this shed, others who must never know what had happened here. No one must ever know what she had done—or what she had failed to do.

At the foot of the post where she had thought Thron so securely tied, she found what was left of the rope with which she had bound him. The frazzled strands crumbled at her touch. How had he worn them so without her knowing? Absently placing the fragments in her pouch, Aubrey blew out the lantern and wrapped her cloak about her shoulders, stepping into the cold blast of winter. Thron's footprints were already gone, erased by blowing snow. Cold flakes melted upon her skin as she tilted her face to the night. High above the inn, Bellan Toregh was cast in blue and white shapes seen through a snowy veil.

Just before she reached her own inn, Aubrey glimpsed shadows flitting across the shrouded fields on the other side of the river. Men on horseback. Had there not been so many, she might have thought of Thron. But Thron, Aubrey knew, would leave Amallar as he had come, alone and in secret.

Hans heard his bedchamber door open. Only briefly did he
wonder who it was. At this time of night, there were few
people the Trongorian guard would let pass and, at the
moment, Hans would have been glad to see any of them. As it was,
he had paced the varnish off the floors. The Rill was to arrive the next
day—and no book, no menial task, no diversion he could find, had
the power to dull his all-consuming excitement. It was long after
midnight before he realized he was keeping others up with him and
finally sent Arne and Robdan to their beds. The thought of seeking
his own bed never entered Hans's mind. The rush of his success was
too heady and near. He wanted to run through the village shouting
from high places.

From tomorrow forward, Khelds would say how Hans Thegn
had brought the Rill to Amallar.

He had just started to ponder the idea of sleep when the sight of
Dorilian put off that thought entirely. Darkly clad in riding leathers

and heavy garments suited only for winter travel, the Hierarch walked into Hans's room with a commanding briskness that bespoke urgency.

"What's going on?" Hans felt his heart sink before he knew anything at all. What he saw before him was enough.

"I'm leaving."

"Now? Tonight?"

It was nearly morning. Hans knew that Dorilian had planned on taking the Rill back to Sordan at the first opportunity, ostensibly as the Trongorian emissary. To abandon such a clear plan on short notice spoke of something gone terribly wrong.

"Where are you going?"

"Merath, to start."

"But you can't!" Hans stared. Dorilian was clearly agitated, but he couldn't be thinking of going north. Going to Essera—alone—was crazy!

"I can. And count yourself fortunate that I didn't leave without telling you! I am pushing my luck by coming here at all."

"But why? You could take the Rill back to Sordan tomorrow!"

Taut as a caged cat, Dorilian walked to the window, where he furtively moved aside a corner of the window hanging, peering for a long moment into the darkness outside before turning back. "I dare not chance waiting. As it is, I require men for an escort. Unless, of course, we care to tempt our fates and Mulsor's curse itself by my going unattended."

"Tempt the fates too far and Nammuor will thank us for it. Take as many men as you need."

Dorilian nodded. He'd gotten the answer he wanted. "Herberth left you twenty," he said. "I shall take ten."

"No," Hans told him. "Take them all. I don't need them. You may."

Dorilian shook his head. "You're a prince. If you ever want to be a king, keep a bodyguard. Ten."

Hans sighed but Dorilian was right. Hans turned to the Trongorian guard who, having followed Dorilian into the room and not been dismissed, had listened to the exchange. "Summon your captain. Get horses and gear for an escort for this man. You will be one of those going. Also, I want Robdan Aelfricson to go with you. Tell him to pack whatever he needs for a long journey. Quickly!"

The man nodded curtly and left.

Dorilian had already started to say something when Hans forestalled him.

"Why?" he demanded again, now that the guard had left and they were alone. "What happened?" The oil lamps in the room were less than adequate and the low light cast as many shadows as it banished. But Dorilian's face, though he turned aside, for once betrayed more than it hid. A swollen, discolored bitemark bloomed upon the royal lip. Hans knew a lover's bite when he saw one. "Tell me you didn't—"

"Didn't what?" Dorilian showed no inclination to waste time on explanations. "It is not what I did that should concern you. It is what *she* did that has led to this! She will have my name within the hour if she has not done so already. I have packed and my horse is ready—I but want the men!"

Hans knew better than to tread upon Dorilian's temper. No good would be done by arguing with him. What had Dorilian done? What had—

"Aubrey?" Hans asked.

Dorilian nodded. He appeared to realize that Hans required at least some explanation, and cursed under his breath. "The lady made known to me that she had information on your ridiculous ritual. I don't know myself what made me do it, she... I agreed to meet her in secret. 'Twas my mistake, for the bitch took the hand I offered and sank her sharp little teeth to the bone, trying to get me to talk. And when I attempted to bring her to you, she knocked me senseless and bound me like some damned beast. Would that I could have made her pay the proper penalty!" Dorilian met the stricken look in Hans's eyes and added, in a voice laced more with frustration than venom, "I should have killed the wench, truly—and would have, but..."

"But what?"

"She's... confounding. Besides which, I *could* not. I am bound by Erydon's Promise. Think about it: I can't attack or kill anyone, not in Amallar. These damn Khelds are far safer from me than I am from them."

So whatever else he had done, Dorilian hadn't killed Aubrey. Hans was glad about that but remained filled with dread. "What did she find out?"

"Nothing yet. But soon. She found my *deiknya*." Dorilian stalked to the hearth to stand in the glow of the firelight, never taking his eyes from the obvious surprise on Hans's face. A twisted smile touched Dorilian's mouth despite the bruise there. "Why does that surprise you? Do you think me not important enough to own one? Or that I would travel with naught but a braggart's tongue to credit my claim? I'm not a stranger to Permephedon. I bear the thing well hidden, but the wench had time enough while I was senseless to find it. And, thanks to you, she knew its secret. I was saved by her ignorance of the design. She nearly ran off with the Rill Stone as well. But I retrieved that too." A shrug. "She did not know the meaning of either but she will pry my name from the pages. She has a book of family crests to consult." Dorilian smiled again, grimly. "Do you think she'll thank me for letting her live?"

"I think she'll hate you even more."

A harsh and indefinable something answered Hans in those storm-colored eyes. It didn't matter that Dorilian had known as much himself: to have someone else say it was to pour vinegar in the wound.

"I suppose you have to go," Hans decided reluctantly. "But what about the Rill? And the alliance? Without you—" He realized what he was saying, what he had not even known he was thinking.

But Dorilian caught the thought, because his expression hardened, his gaze losing patience. "What's this, Handurin?" A stinging edge of reprimand underlaid the words. "Do you feel my talons suddenly gripping the rug of your power, waiting to rip it out from under you? You know that I could. It's what they all expect of me. But how distressing it must be for you to only now remember that."

"The Rill will come. I feel it—I know it. The Rill will be the sign by which all others will know what you intend."

"Good. The lesson sticks. Now we will see if you can continue to believe when all around you doubt and I'm not at hand. Thus, we come to the test: that you have placed your fortunes within the crucible of my word—only tomorrow to find yourself standing alone with nothing but that to hold onto. Which will prove truer, do you think? Your faith? Or my reliability?"

"Both, I should hope."

A bare suggestion of a knock, a whisper of sound, alerted them to the door. Treading quietly across the room, Hans opened the door to admit the Trongorian captain Farrl and poor Robdan, still tousled from the little sleep he'd had but dressed for travel and carrying a hurriedly gathered parcel of his belongings. Thankfully Robdan looked alert enough as his gaze darted from one man to the other.

"What happened?" he asked.

"I'll know by morning." Hans answered curtly. "Are your men ready?" he asked the Trongorian captain.

"They will be, sir, by the time we reach the yard." Farrl stood alert and prepared for action of whatever kind was needed. His long Trongorian sword, its scabbard oiled and polished with use, looked like a tongue of orange flame in the firelight. Upon Farrl's strong Estol face Hans saw the marks of a man ready to do battle.

There was no time for long explanations, nor was one needed, but Hans thought Farrl deserved to know the reason for such sudden departure and haste. Hans indicated Dorilian, who had gathered his gear and was standing ready to go. "It's no longer possible for this man to stay in Amallar. I want you and your men to escort him to safety in Essera."

Robdan's face drained of blood and suddenly looked years older.

Farrl bowed low and when he rose and spoke, it was with solemn gravity. "Such honor is rarely visited upon the likes of myself and my men to be bound to the service of the Highborn Princes." He raised his dark gaze to Dorilian and added, "Far less the ruling Hierarch of Sordan."

Though he paused to study Farrl sharply and with interest, Dorilian made no move to answer. Hans, however, had no shortage of questions. "You knew? All this time, you knew?" Not once had Farrl betrayed even the subtlest sign that he thought Thron Estol other than what he pretended to be.

"Many times I have been to Sordan, Your Royal Highness," Farrl said, "and always I but saw his Thrice Royal Grace from afar, which is why I did not myself detect the likeness until it was made known to me. But when my Lord Elector knew that he must return to Trongor, he told me of Thron's other identity and said that should it become necessary to protect his life, my command should be thus directed." Again, Farrl bowed to Dorilian. "I pray of you, Thrice Royal, be not angry."

Regarding the Trongorian with indecipherable amusement, Dorilian replied. "Angry with whom—you for holding your tongue, or the Elector for not holding his? It is my opinion that the Elector's foresight pardons his lack of discretion. I accept your service and shall reward it handsomely."

Expressing gratitude for the honor, Farrl made his devotion.

Hans turned to Robdan and assisted him with the leather straps and tarnished buckles of his winter riding gear. "I want you to go with them, Uncle." Hans picked up Robdan's gloves and handed them to him.

"No!"

Stung by the interjection, Hans shot a look across the room to where Dorilian stood beside the door. The Hierarch's attitude, his expression, spoke very plainly of the disapproval Hans had stopped him from voicing earlier.

"I am not trundling excess baggage on this trip, Handurin. And certainly not a man who has yet to properly sit a horse! I intend to ride hard and long—those who cannot ride will be left behind! Nor will I nanny a Kheld across Essera."

"And I intend that Robdan ride with you. Do you want to stand here arguing about it? We can drag it out as long as you like."

Dorilian faced Hans for a moment, coldly, weighing the confrontation against its motives, its probable outcomes. He decided that he could not afford the delay of argument. "I am leaving," he announced. As sharply as he had spoken, he turned and left the room. Hans listened to his footsteps retreating down the wooden floor of the upstairs hallway.

"You are going," Hans informed Robdan. He shoved the last of his gold coins into his elder uncle's pocket and pulled him along out the door and down the long, shadowy recess of the hall.

"But he just said—"

"He just gave up the argument. You're going to be my ambassador. Don't look surprised—you're the only man I trust to send on my behalf. Dorilian understands what I'm doing and the need for doing it. He won't give you any problems once he is out of Amallar. Just keep up with him."

Hans and Robdan emerged into a gust of cold and wind. Snow blew against their faces, coating hats and cloaks. Ten riders and two extra horses stamped in the yard. It was in the riders' favor that the compound was on the outskirts of the town—if the men did not ride through the village, it was unlikely that anyone would know of their going. Until morning, that was, and the absence of half of Hans's Trongorian bodyguards would have to be explained.

"Wait, Hans."

Hans turned to face Robdan, who had stopped walking. Robdan rummaged through the pouch of possessions hanging at his belt until he found and pulled forth a large cloak clasp made of iron, which he held out so that it glimmered in his hand.

"Take it," he ordered. "It should be yours. It was never mine, not really, and it shouldn't go north except on the cloak of a leader."

"What is it?" Hans took the clasp into his hand, where it weighed upon his palm like a summons.

"A very great hero crafted this from the spear that killed an Ardaenan king. It has always been worn by the Thegn. My father gave it to me. I never knew why, but it was his deathbed bequest and... I think that he meant that I should pass it into the hands of a Kheld worthier of its history."

"I don't think you could."

"I think I just have."

Robdan climbed onto a horse one of the Trongorians held ready for him. Hans said his goodbyes with more restraint than he felt in his heart, a simple grasping of arms and a few stilted words. Amallar had never used Robdan as well as it should have.

"Godspeed, Uncle." Hans wondered that his words did not betray his emotion. "You are my voice now, the only one he will hear." He was barely aware of the stir behind him as the remaining inhabitants of the main house came out to see what was happening.

Within moments, Arne was standing at his side, wrapped in a blanket and barefooted as he stood ankle-deep in snow. "They're going?"

"Yes."

Arne's gaze shot to Dorilian. "Why's he going before tomorrow? Don't let him—"

"I must. The Khelds will kill him."

"You say that like you aren't one too! What if it's all a lie and he's leaving to let you take the fall?"

"That's a chance I'm willing to take. You should be too, knowing what we stand to gain. His life is the only thing binding the Rill to my word."

Hans walked over to where Dorilian waited, already mounted and looking anxious to leave. None but the Trongorians and Robdan would hear what they said. And Arne, who followed behind him.

"I'll meet you in Essera," Hans promised. "Your army and mine. We'll fight Nammuor together."

Looking down from his tall horse, escorted by soldiers and shrouded by darkness, his Highborn blood once again like a star upon his brow, Dorilian was once more that Hierarch of Sordan whom Hans had left behind so many months ago. Even Dorilian's nod had that crispness, that certainty of movement that then had seemed so much a part of him.

"Yes, I begin to think we will. So let me give you a Promise, and let these men witness it: the day your Khelds march north, not against Sordan but at her side, Essera will be yours, and I will renounce all claim to it, save that of my heirs' right to succeed should you or your mother die without heirs. So long as you do not raise sword against me, nor press claim upon my Hierarchate and its domains, I shall not challenge you, nor your heirs in body, nor their heirs who will follow them. This I promise you, my most solemn vow."

"Shall I promise you the same?"

"When you know what you are promising. We both know that trust is rarer than promises. 'Tis a fair exchange for now." The saddle creaked loudly with cold as Dorilian settled forward. "The Rill is my gift to you," Dorilian said in parting. "Use it well.

Aubrey entered her inn room and closed the door behind her. Removing her cloak, she shook the snowmelt from it and pondered what she'd done.

I allowed Thron to get away.

There was still a chance he had not. Beyond the room's sole window, snow was falling heavily, blown by a stiff wind. *He'd be as much a fool to leave in this weather as I was to let him go. I should find Fran,* Aubrey thought. *He's waiting for my word. Or Nalf, at least, to alert the Witan.* But how could she tell Nalf, or Fran, that a man had made her soft, that she'd let Thron escape rather than let the man the Mother had given her be taken by anyone else?

I know I will meet Thron again. And when I do, I'll call him by the name his mother gave him!

The design revealed by the Staubaun token should provide Aubrey with Thron's family name. It was enough to start with.

Aubrey lit the lamp and pulled two books from under the bed where she had hidden them. She chose the thickest and heaviest book first, cradling it on her lap as she sat on the bed, her back propped against the wall. The book spread over her knees as she pored over page upon heavy page of colored plates. The design she looked for had been so striking that she was certain she would know it if she saw it again. A long time and many hundreds of depictions later, she sighed, rolled her head back against the plank wall and mentally cursed the book as unhelpful.

She had chosen the most complete book to be found on the subject of Staubaun symbols, *Traditional and Modern Staubaun Heraldry: Emblems and Crests in Noble Lines and Houses*, a tome compiled by a fraternity of scholars. Robdan had procured it for a fraction of its cost from a Kheld who had sold off the contents of a Staubaun estate given him by Stefan. The volume was a rare treasure of her uncle's. Robdan would be livid if he knew that Aubrey had packed it in a trunk with her things and carried it all the way across Amallar.

It was complete, all right, Aubrey decided. She had never imagined that there could be so many Estol branches to the Staubaun nobility—even the extinct lines were given space, yet something was not right about the images. The symbols, denoting the families making up Sordan's Staubaun-Estol nobility, were not of the same type as Thron's had been. They were too simple, maybe, or not simple enough. Aubrey sighed and uttered a low groan of dismay, wondering if she had hauled this heavy book all the way from Rhodhur for nothing. Damn the cursed Staubauns for being so complicated and stratified and giving every minor noble and his brother their own crest and listing!

It was then that it struck her: she might have labeled Thron too soon. What if, despite his looks, his *family* was considered Staubaun? Would they count as one of their own a man with foreign blood and eyes? Marc Frederick's line was so regarded. Hans himself carried a similar token, one Aubrey had seen illustrated at the front of this book. She could not rule out the possibility that Thron, for all that he did not look truly Staubaun, might be connected to the aristocracy or lurk on the fringes of the truly powerful. His manner did not lack for refinement.

Aubrey turned back the pages to the front of the Sordan section of the book and ran her fingers across the raised and gilded lettering, feeling the heavy mark of that domain's official seal. The chapter listing alone detailed hundreds of entries. She would be lucky if she knew who Thron was in a month! Absently, not ready to concede defeat but not eager to plunge into yet more fruitless searching, she flipped through the next several pages, finding layers of detailed explanations of the evolution of Sordani heraldry, a nomenclature, and the first of the dynastic colorplates. Aubrey turned from one colorplate to the other, wanting only to get beyond them. They passed beneath her fingers, two thousand years of history in spreads of green and silver, blue and gold. And then....

Her hand froze and the page she had been lifting fluttered down, displaying itself in full spread.

The image fit her memory perfectly, its colors clear and too richly realized, too exactly reproduced, for Aubrey to doubt her own eyes. The design she had seen on Thron's medallion—every detail was there! The golden crown mated to a silver sword, the eagle with its wide-spreading silver wings. The circle of three rings, the second ribboned in green. Even the shell added as if in afterthought. All within the broad green and silver border that had told her it was Sordani and not Esseran. Only now, with the design enlarged severalfold, did Aubrey see that no common nobleman could possibly lay claim to such a crest. A sudden and inexplicable cold poured over her skin.

What if he is one of them, a Staubaun Lord? Master of not just an estate but a title? What then?

Her gaze fled to the printed words below the representation to find out if her nightmare could be true.

Only to discover it could be much worse.

Familial crest of the Highborn Sordaneons with the shell badge of the Royal Ardaenan House of Nemenor. Now the sole emblem of the Sordaneons. The crest designates the male descendants of Labran Sordaneon ê Nemenor, twenty-first Hierarch of Sordan and Sansordan in the line of Derlon, son of Amynas Malyrdys and Leur.

Sordaneon. The godborn *Rill Lords?*

It could not be. *That* was impossible. But the image in Aubrey's mind refused to waver and would not let her think she'd been mistaken. Surely, she had seen.... And then she laughed, relieved.

It's a royal design, the one their rulers use. That's all.

That design must have been emulated by scores of noble houses, maybe hundreds, all of them eager to link themselves with legitimacy and power. It was possible, even, that the Sordaneons gave out such tokens to identify their emissaries.

But if that was so, how was she to know Thron's family or connections? Then Aubrey remembered the ring. The ring! Of course. The ring would tell.

There was a chapter on signets at the back of the book. She had not initially thought to consult it, thinking that the ring was the lesser object. It had not looked like a personal signet and was not as ornate as Staubaun signets she had seen in Neuberland. The eagle talons of the setting and the hint of a silver eagle on the center stone had suggested Sordan, however, and great care had been taken to conceal it. Her fumbling fingers ruffled the valuable pages until she reached the section detailing official and dynastic Staubaun signets and other insignia. Among the first, among the Highborn regalia, Aubrey found what she had hoped she would not. The depiction was perfect, her blindness complete.

...given by Derlon, called Sordaneon, to his son Deben I, naming him Hierarch of Sordan and Lord of all lands south of the Great Telarkans to the Sea of Jubbek am Orm. The Sordaneon Ring is more properly a symbiotic device, called the Rill Stone. The device is always kept on the person of the ruling Hierarch, except in rare circumstances when it may be delivered into the possession of his successor. Because of its prominence and the power it can summon, none but those of Highborn blood are permitted to handle it....

Her mind already screaming, Aubrey flung the book to the bed as if it would burn her hands. *No. No. No.* She picked up the smaller volume she'd set to the side: a simple, straightforward directory of the nobility, written only a few years ago. *Sordaneon.* She didn't even know how many Sordaneons there were. In her mind, only one burned bright, hated above all others. *Sordaneon. Sordaneon.* That name burned its way into Aubrey's eyes even from the page.

Sordaneon ê Nemenor d' Teremareon, Dorilian Derlon Amynas Valyoran. (b. 2/1850/04/17, at Sordan) S1. Deben IV Sordaneon upon Valyane Teremareonea (Sebbord II Teremareon). Hierarch of Sordan and Sansordan, Bas of Sorand'ruil and Harad-Rebir, Lord of Katalderan and Tussah, Prince of Caerdon and of his other realms and territories. After 2/1878 head of the Highborn Council.

There were two other names but Aubrey didn't even read them. By dates alone she knew one was too young and the other too old, dead for years.

The clamor in her mind stopped, replaced by a silence so deep that Aubrey's breathing, quiet though it was, sounded harsh and out of place. Only gradually did her eyes refocus on her surroundings and see her tiny room, the wooden chair, her cloak hanging on a peg on the wall. She could still see Thron, still *feel* him, taking back his ring and calling it a family heirloom.

Heirloom! The Rill Stone ring of the Sordaneons, always in

possession of the ruling Hierarch—wasn't that what the book had said? And those gray eyes were Nemenor eyes, the eyes of the Sordaneons, who had the blood of the Ardaenan kings in their veins.

His wrong coloring and eyes that were not Staubaun had kept them all from the truth.

It's him. It has to be him, who else could it be? And I never guessed. None of us did. How could we? Dorilian Sordaneon was supposed to be anywhere but in Amallar! Is that how he was able to fool us so completely, by using our blindness about him against us? So completely that a daughter of the Khelds gave him a fast tumble in the hay?

Again Aubrey was seized by the incredible feeling of that moment in the forge when she had drawn Thron's mouth to hers. He had not resisted.

Is this what you want? Is it? His body had found hers receptive enough, ready enough. Aubrey could still hear herself saying, *Yes!* Could still feel Thron inside her, smell the warm spice of his skin....

Aubrey sprang to her feet, tears rising behind her eyes, and ran to the hook to grab her cloak. *I let him go, but he won't get far. This is our country still, and our horses know ways his will not. Fran will help me catch him!*

Her footsteps echoed down the darkened hall, down the stairs and out into the yard where the wind billowed drifts of snow from atop rooftops and walls. The cold was deeper, more piercing as the snow moved to the east and Essera's icy breath followed hard upon it, making the inn yard look gray and sullen, lifeless but for her own pounding heart. To the east, though obscured by storm, the sky was not as dark. Dawn was already edging into Neuberland, day already full born upon the eastern steppes of Staubaun legend. *Hurry!* That inner sense told her. *The Highborn are sorcerers. They travel upon the wind itself. He must have left hours ago while you read books, delved into lineages, and fancied yourself clever!*

Aubrey had barely left the inn when an arm wrapped around her from behind and pulled her off-balance into a hard embrace. A hand clapped over her face, smothering her sharp cry.

Surprise helped Hans pull Aubrey around the corner of the Black Goose Inn, into the shadows and up against a wall, where there was just enough light to still give him away. He felt sick having to do this.

Giving vent to her rage, Aubrey twisted free and threw herself at him in full fury. "Dorilian!" she railed, accusing Hans of a complicity of which she was certain. She hurled her fists against his chest. "Dorilian! *Dorilian!* You bastard!"

"Aubrey, stop it!" Hans spoke harshly into her ear, all the while grappling her by the wrists, bodily pinning her, before finally wrestling her into silence. Gods, but she was strong! Even through the heavy clothing he wore, Hans could feel the blows. He no longer felt completely sorry for Aubrey—Dorilian had probably had his hands full.

"He's gone." Hans pressed her to the wall until she broke down in sobs. "He's left Bellan Toregh and nobody is going to be riding after him."

"I hate you," she swore, tears running down red cheeks. "I hate you and I hate your brother! And I hate *him* worst of all! You, because you brought him here and you never told us. And Stefan— he *lied!* Stefan told us Dorilian Sordaneon was horrible and effeminate, a weak-kneed, deformed, perverted lover of men! Stefan said he had fisheyes! He told us he was ugly!"

"Stefan lied about a lot of things." Hans was long past being tired of having to beat back his brother's ghost. "Just look at what was going on, Aubrey. Stefan *hated* Dorilian. And he feared him—Dorilian was everything Stefan could never be. Stefan lied about Dorilian to cover his own inadequacies and, as the years went by, was forced to make his enemy more and more monstrous to justify his own failures. In the end, he convinced himself of all of it. And now his lies are so deeply rooted here in Amallar that Khelds can't see the truth when it's standing in front of them. Look at *you.*" Hans gave Aubrey a gentle shake as she hung her head, refusing to acknowledge any point being made. "You find out his *name*—and you can't even see *him* anymore. The man I know as Dorilian is not even human in your eyes. That's why I can't let you tell anyone about this. Because all they'll want to do is *destroy* him."

Aubrey stared through tears the bitter cold froze on her cheeks.

Hans drew a breath to calm himself. "Now you can either find some way to deal with this and keep quiet about it, or I can find some way to shut you up. You can count yourself damn lucky already that Dorilian didn't kill you after what you did to him. In Sordan, they flay the living skin from those who dare to lay hand upon a High-born Prince. And you smacked him on the head and used ropes on him! What were you trying to do, anyway?"

"I just wanted to find out who he really was," she complained, resignedly. "He wasn't very cooperative, and I had to.... I don't see what you're so wrought up about. He got out of it all right, didn't he?"

Sensing her pain, Hans relaxed his grip. "He didn't hurt you, did he?"

"No." Aubrey turned her face to the icy wall.

"Have you told anyone?"

Defiantly, her gaze met his. "Wouldn't you like to know?"

Hans did want to know. There was a chance Aubrey had told someone. More likely, though, she had not. Knowing that she was staying at the Black Goose Inn, he and Arne had raced here and seen no sign of other visitors. Arne had taken position near the bridge and would warn if anyone approached.

"I don't think you've told anyone—yet. But that's where you were going. Aubrey, please listen." Hans tightened his grip until rewarded by a wince. "You can tell the world what you know or you can tell no one. The choice is yours. But I have a stake in what you do. Every hour since my return to this World, maybe even my return itself—maybe even my life—has been leading to this. The Rill, this hill. I'm not going to stand by while Amallar and Neuberland go off into a Kheldish rage over Dorilian that will throw away our one true chance at putting Amallar on a level with Staubauns. The Rill is on the table, Aubrey, but only if I can match its worth to Dorilian. If I fail, if I cannot find a way to get Amallar to follow me, then Dorilian still has the Rill. He still has Sordan and he still is Highborn. Only *we* will have nothing—not the Rill, not his promise, not even peace. But if I succeed, if *we* do... Amallar will have an uncontested ruler in Essera and peace upon its borders—and the Rill."

Wide-eyed, Aubrey shook her head in disbelief. Almost, she laughed. "Hans! You can't put your life—all our lives—into the hands of the godless man who killed your brother and grandfather!"

With a fierceness he'd not expected to feel, Hans tightened his grip, earning a grimace. "Dorilian Sordaneon did not kill my grandfather! He tried to *save* him. I knew that before I ever went to Sordan. And he didn't kill Stefan either. I *know* this for a fact! If you value my friendship at all, don't say that ever again. If you knew even half of what I know, you wouldn't."

Aubrey ducked her head, probably more confused than chastened. Hans exhaled with resignation. There was so much more he wanted to say but couldn't.

"We can't stand here until daybreak," he warned. "You can make this easy for me, or you can force me to do things I don't want to do. Which will it be?"

"What are my choices?"

"Keep silent, say nothing. Wait with me to see if the Rill comes. Amallar need never know that Dorilian was here, and if they should find out later, it will be after all is done. Or, if you will not be silent willingly, then I will see you locked in a room until this is over. Bound, drugged, gagged—whatever it takes to keep you silent. Arne is right over there, watching my back, and he'll help me. I don't want to do that, Aubrey. I really don't. But there is too much on the line, so please don't make me."

A cold wind tunneled through the narrow walkway between buildings, blowing snow onto their exposed faces. Aubrey stared in mingled fear and hope, caught in the crossfire of past hatreds and uncertain futures, unable to choose clearly between them. In those blue eyes, so desperately searching his, Hans watched anger collapsing into disillusionment.

"Aubrey," Hans pleaded, seeking for one last time to persuade. "You don't hate him. You don't want him killed, murdered by your kinfolk. You don't want his blood—Highborn blood—on your hands. Or theirs. Spilled in Amallar. If you alert the Witan, if you send Fran Gorseddson after him, can you promise it won't be? Or the blood of the ten Trongorian Rangers who, I can promise you, will fight to the death before they allow him to be taken? And what about Robdan?" To the sick dawning in Aubrey's gaze, Hans nodded bleakly. "I sent Robdan with him, as my ambassador. What would the Witan do to him? The punishment for treason is death. Maybe even for me. You can bring us all, and Amallar as well, to ruin."

Wind-whipped strands of dark hair trailed across her face. "I don't want to bring you to ruin. You've done that for yourself. You are young and foolish, and you placed your trust in the wrong man."

"And I cannot prove otherwise, not here. What I am asking of you is to trust *me*."

"I want to," Aubrey whispered. Hans could see how desperately she did want to trust him, to believe that Dorilian, Thron, or whoever he was, had come to Amallar to forge an alliance, to give Hans and the Kheld people the gift of the Rill. Surely the past weeks gave enough reason to believe that Hans was at least partially right— that Dorilian was not in all things or ways the man Amallar thought him to be.

Far away, a dying scream drifted down from the high place atop Bellan Toregh and as suddenly was stopped, leaving only its chilling memory to haunt the predawn silence.

"They make the sacrifice to dedicate the Toregh." Hans saw in Aubrey's lowered gaze that he was right. "You know what they're doing, don't you? The Priest of Lud will sprinkle a little blood around and try to stop the Rill from coming. They know that it's stopped running—it's me they're not sure of." Hans looked to where a cart clattered on the main road not far from this neglected corner of the inn. Dawn would soon bring more people to the streets—and to the Toregh. Might as well let Aubrey in on the rest.

"I know there are warriors standing by in the woods around here. I've heard the talk. I hear more than you think. They don't trust me, Aubrey. They think that I'm in league with Sordan at worst and, at best, that I'm nothing but a king's grandson and brother—good enough to be a figurehead or puppet, but too young or too simple to be making important decisions. They'll follow me only if I go where they tell me to go and they envision themselves in high places. They don't think the Rill will come either. But they're ready with soldiers if it does. They think that if Dorilian sends it at all, he'll send an army with it."

"Can you blame them?"

"No. But I can prove them wrong."

Again, closed eyes and turning away. Did she think the way they did?

Hans released Aubrey's wrists and moved his hands to her shoulders, holding more gently, seeking to convince. "All I ask is for one day. Just one day. Let me borrow it from you. One day of your trust and your silence."

"Trust cannot be lent. It must be given."

"It must be given freely. I cannot force your heart and I don't want to. But can't you find enough trust in me to last until tomorrow? Just enough trust to see if the Rill will come today?"

"It may come and still gain you nothing."

"It may not come, and I lose all. You see, I'm taking chances. But if I'm right, and I think I am, isn't it worthwhile to take that chance? Aubrey, you have no idea—this will change *everything*. And I want to have you there when the Rill comes. I want you to see it."

No longer moved by the intense fire of rage, Aubrey slumped against the cold stones of the wall at her back. The night had to have been rough on her, finding out what she had and being prevented from doing anything about it. Hans could tell that although some part of Aubrey wanted to believe him, to trust that his plan would succeed, she remained unconvinced. The best he could hope to gain was her silence.

"I want to see him again." Stubborn words, stubbornly spoken.

"You will." Without knowing why, Hans was sure of it. Far to the east, despite dark clouds, it was growing light.

"Then you have my sworn word," Aubrey said. "Had I a knife, I would swear the oath upon my hand."

"You have a knife." With one movement he reached inside her cloak, to her belt, and brought forth the slender knife that Aubrey, like all Kheld women who lived on the edge of the wild, wore for protection.

A cool smile answered. "You don't trust me."

"I will, if you use that knife."

Wordlessly, Aubrey took the knife. "I won't cut my palm, if that's what you're asking. Foolish boys make oath-promises that way and half of them end up having only one good hand." She lifted her other hand to grab the neckline of her fine blouse, tugging it down to expose the topmost swell of one breast as she gave Hans a tight smile. "I will give you better. A woman's blood, sacred to the Mother."

The tip of the knife dug into firm breast skin, puncturing it shallowly, parting the soft flesh beneath to release a trickle and then a swell of bright blood. Aubrey pressed both sides of the blade to that blood before showing the anointed knife to Hans and making her vow by pressing the blade to her palm.

"I swear this oath upon my blood, that I will not speak all this day until dawn tomorrow of anything I learned last night. Nor will I reveal to any person that I know the true name of Thron Estol Bevvan, or his origins, or his whereabouts."

Though not an oath that would demand the loss of a hand if she broke it, it was an oath Hans could trust. He knew Aubrey Amundda well enough for that. He also recognized the ritual for being related to the one he had undergone in the Grove.

"You don't know his whereabouts." It was time to walk the empty streets that would take them to the house on the outskirts of the village. Arne emerged from the shadows of the bridge to walk behind them.

A faint, triumphant ghost of a smile returned to Aubrey's pale lips as she pointed to the curving shape that towered over the town. "Not yet. But I will. And I swear to you that his blood will pay for yours if you are wrong."

Hans spent the first fragile hours of morning keeping a close
eye on Aubrey Amundda. Much as he wanted to trust her,
he had only to look upon her tense and angry posture, the
way tears still filled her eyes, to know he had to keep her as close as
his own skin. A vow to give Hans, and Dorilian as well, a chance to
make good on all the promises, to redeem the deception by bringing
forth a miracle, went against Aubrey's grain. She remained
convinced that Dorilian had played Hans for a fool and had already
done what was needed to destroy him.

"You played right into his hands." Contempt crowned each angry
word. "He outwitted you at every turn. You didn't escape—he let
you. And you let him masquerade here, find out our plans, and stall
us from doing anything while he moved an army into Merrydn. He
had you fight his battles in Amallar for him! Nalf was right when he
said that you wouldn't know a bad dog until it bit you in the ass. It
was you, more than anyone, who talked us out of bargaining for an
alliance with the Mormantaloran. That alliance, at least, might have
kept that bastard in his place."

"What place? He was here."

"And you, for what reasons I cannot understand, kept him here! You hid him! Not only that, but you let him get away."

"Actually," Hans pointed out, "that was you. I had time to wave Dorilian goodbye and still catch you at the inn."

Aubrey threw herself down into a chair, still glaring. "I wanted to learn his name. Just not... that one." Her scrutiny sharpened. "You could have had the Rill as ransom and the gods know what else—you know that, right? But what if he's false? You stand a good chance of looking the fool. If that happens, you will lose not only Amallar but any chance of ever standing up to him again!"

"Do you really think he came to Amallar just to set this all up? *My* downfall? He could have done that in Sordan. He came because he needed my help. And I wanted the Rill as the price of that. I tell you the Rill is going to come! The Rill will appear atop that hill tomorrow, and I will make my alliance with Sordan—not Mormantalorus." Turning his back on Aubrey, Hans shrugged into the tunic he would wear that day, a white, long-sleeved garment over which he pulled a close-fitting leather jerkin dyed to a rich shade of blue.

Most Khelds would be wearing what Robdan called 'humble clothes,' deep-hued woolens and leathers trimmed with dark fur, the better to show off the gold and silver symbols of each individual's status and affiliations. Chains of silver spear points were especially appropriate, but sun symbols, golden and framed by rays, were favored, as were crescent moons, plowshares, and keld totems. Circles of Life, wrought by goldsmiths in the shape of interwoven oak leaves, acorns, and branches, or wheat stalks, would fasten the cloaks of Kheld women. Aubrey wore one at her throat in a beautiful, twining swirl of shapes evoking the gifts of the Mother. It was her own, as was the soft velvet gown she wore and the lustrous hooded cloak of blue wool that covered her from head to foot, all fetched for her from her room by a girl Hans had sent to get Aubrey's things. All her things, including those two books.

Hans was glad he had done so. Aubrey was Thegn and high clan. Her apparent support, however coerced for a day, was certain to enhance the Khelds' perception of him as one of their own. That was one reason Hans had chosen to be flamboyant: bright blue to make his eyes look bluer, a white tunic to evoke visions of religious ceremony, and the wide belt of silvered leather that he had brought with him out of Sordan. The crowning touch would be a silver-gray cloak of mountain lynx skins, given him by Herberth before leaving Ogarth. Hans had not worn it before this and liked the look of surprise on Aubrey's face when she saw it.

She rose from her seat and walked across the thick carpets of this wealthy man's house. With wondering fingers, she stroked the supple richness of the gray fur. "You look like a Staubaun prince, wearing this."

"I hope I look like someone who will bring the Rill to Amallar." Hans picked up Robdan's iron clasp from the shelf, only to have Aubrey pluck it from his hand.

"This is the Spear-gift of Treowdan Almarreson." Aubrey's voice held a note of wonder. "I'd heard that Robdan owned it. Aelfric Brodheson gave it to him, though it was Cedrec who became Thegnard. I don't think Robdan ever wore it. But it isn't strange that he should give it to you, a man he believes to be the next leader of Amallar."

"It hasn't sunk in yet, has it, that our uncle is an uncommonly perceptive man?"

"I've thought him merely wishful." With a sigh, determined to assist him, Aubrey worked the clasp into the top of the cloak, taking great care to place it properly so as not to damage the leather, and fastened it expertly into place at the shoulder. "Robdan has passed this brooch, a tradition of his family, one of the most respected among the Thegnkeld, to the son of his brother's son. By doing so he continues the tradition."

"You seem to have a pretty good grasp of it yourself."

"I should. I too can trace my line to Treowdan Almarreson, from whose spear this brooch was cast. I hope you live up to what it represents. I think you could be a good leader for Amallar, maybe a great one. And for Essera as well." Aubrey drew away, her expression reflecting that momentary full faith. Her voice became pensive. "You could get us to follow you so easily, if only you would lead us not to Sordan, but to where we want to go."

Hans shook his head. "If I had a road map to my destiny, I would show you where I am going and why. But I don't. I'm not sure myself where this road is taking me, but I'm the one who must set that path, not let others do it for me."

"But this—"

"I need Sordan. I need them as much as I need Amallar. Those Esseran lords that haven't yet gone over to or been defeated by Nammuor don't believe I'm the answer to any of their prayers. I may

be Marc Frederick's grandson, but Stefan wasn't popular, not among
the noble class—and the fact that I'm his brother, and half Kheld, does
me about as much good there as talking about an alliance with Sordan
does me here. Not all of Essera's powerful lords voted for me to return."

"Then we'll fight them and we'll force them to accept you."

"That'll push them to Nammuor so fast, I'll have to patch up
things with Dorilian anyway just to give *us* a chance against them.
Aubrey," Hans said, trying one more time to explain. "It would be
easy if all I wanted to do was to sit on the throne as Essera's king.
Nammuor would let me do that. All I would have to do is call him
Master, follow his will and not my own. Puppet tyrants suit him just
fine. He lets them get away with their excesses and he gets away
with murder. He killed the Highborn Princes at Permephedon. I
know this, the same way I know about Stefan. Nammuor can't be
trusted. He may not even be human anymore. That thing
Nammuor wears on his head—the crown I keep talking about, that
thing he's becoming—has no concept of morality, no sense of fair
play. Dorilian does. You know that."

"Do I? The man I knew was a lie. He never existed!"

"You posed to him his greatest threat yet—and he let you live."
Hans cut off a tirade he had heard before, several times, during the
early hours of the morning. "By every law that man lives by,
Dorilian should have killed you, if only for his own protection. The
more I think about it, the more surprised I am that he didn't do it,
and I don't mean just because he was honoring Erydon's Promise."
Hans nodded as realization took hold, widening Aubrey's wet-lashed
eyes. "Yes, he mentioned that. That promise *binds* him. But he also
realized his own part in what happened, because he mentioned that
too. The man's got this innate scale in his head; he weighs everyone,
everything, including himself. So I hate to put the spear to your
argument, but Thron Estol Bevvan is probably as close to the real
Dorilian Sordaneon as anyone can hope to get."

After listening to Aubrey all morning and getting Arne's report
on some of the rumors that had reached his ears, Hans was beginning
to wonder if he should be more worried. Did all of Bellan Toregh,
the entire assembly of the Witan, the Priesthood, even the Old
Mothers, wait only upon his failure? Was that why they were
gathering like vultures, hovering about the place where a carcass was
most likely to fall? If he looked out the window, he could see them
converging on the Rill mount, walking on the road to the hilltop

where they would gather beneath arching structures they were convinced would remain empty when the sun reached its zenith. All at once Hans was weary of it, wondering why he tried.

The common folk, at least, believed in him: the woman who had brought them their breakfasts had looked at Hans with shining wonder in her eyes. And following the Witan last night, grown men had wept into his hands. The servant girl this morning, who Hans had sent for Aubrey's belongings, had asked if she could ride the Rill. *They* believed.

Why did so many of their leaders, then, want him to fail?

Because if I'm right, then they're wrong—and they have been wrong their entire lives. He stood to make Kheld leaders look like fools for having preached against Sordan all these years. With one act, Hans could extinguish all that was left of Stefan's power base.

The Rill is my gift to you. Dorilian's words had felt true—so true and real that Hans could almost hold them in his hand. Like some crazy philosopher's stone of Mentan legend, the Rill would turn his lump of lead to malleable gold.

Play it right, Hans, he told himself. *Play it right and they'll see you just like one of the Malyrdeon god-kings who gave them Amallar. Dorilian, even in Sordan, wouldn't have it so good.*

"Hans?"

He barely heard Aubrey speak, so far had he wandered into his own thoughts. When she tentatively touched his arm, he looked into her eyes.

"We'll know soon enough, won't we?"

"Soon enough," Hans agreed.

The door opened. Nalf Rhys and several other men, among them Fran Gorseddson, stood just within the entrance. Arne, past whom they had pushed, elbowed his way around the intruders until he stood at Hans's side. Together they watched the Thegnard rub at the brass studs of his heavy leather gloves. Nalf's ornaments, like those of his companions, flashed prominently against the rich fur of his collar.

"Where are your Trongorians?" Nalf asked, to the point.

Hans sighed. He had known he would have to answer that question. Fran Gorseddson's penetrating look seized Aubrey's cool, unanswering gaze, demanding explanation. Hans answered as directly as he could. "I sent some of them away. I didn't think I would need twenty of them."

"Getting your spy out of Amallar, maybe?" Nalf Rhys guessed. His small eyes skewed to the silent Aubrey.

Though Hans was tempted to dismiss the accusation, to do so would be a mistake. Aubrey had admitted sharing her suspicions with Fran. And the Thegnard was no fool.

Upon receiving no answer, Nalf chuckled. "So, he was one, eh? Well, we'll know soon enough if he did you any good. If he didn't, maybe we can fetch him back for you, get it out of his hide. And I don't see Robdan. Sent him with them, did you?"

"I needed to send a representative."

"Oh, a *representative!* Aren't you getting a bit ahead of your stick! Where are they headed? Sordan, maybe?" Nalf looked to Arne, who clamped his jaw, then back to Hans. "Gignastha? Leseos?"

Hans allowed his gaze to slip momentarily, a slightly tighter breath to expand his chest.

"Leseos. Fran, get some men after them. The snow hid their tracks, but we should pick them up if we ride that way."

Fran nodded, his surly glare hardening on Aubrey as he left. Nalf Rhys pondered Hans with grim new attention, while over his shoulder the remaining Kheld leaders scowled through their beards, their displeasure obvious. "What are you up to, boy?" Nalf growled.

"There aren't that many ways to get the Rill," Hans explained. "I had to do it the best as I could. It's a patchwork job, but I think it will hold together."

"Hans Thegn," one of the Witan elders warned. "You try our patience. We have borne your foolishness and talk, but to bring a spy among us—"

The accusation was not going away. "Was the only way to do it," Hans conceded. "You can at least give me the chance to prove myself. All I ask for is this morning."

Nalf frowned. "Aubrey?"

Aubrey's eyes, bright in her pale face as she looked out from the shadowed folds of her hood, met her uncle's in a clear moment of hesitation. Hans kept his throat clamped hard against the swelling fear that rose from his bowels. Here, in the presence of so many others, Aubrey could speak without fear. He could do nothing to stop her. Her knowledge had become a weapon, to be used against Hans by speaking. And for him by not.

"Let's see if the Rill comes, Uncle," Aubrey said finally. Her cool manner betrayed nothing about having had to think around a secret. "The God Spear will tell us what we need to know."

36

Though it has been many centuries since any can claim to
have heard it speak, the Rill is not a silent Entity. It
expresses being through movement; it commands
economies and silences politics. It demands respect for its
sheer power to move us, whether bodily across the
continent or through the beauty of its passage. It responds
at intervals to human interventions, imparts to human
endeavors its sense of scale and permanence. It speaks the
language of hope.

ZAMENES, *ON THE NATURE OF ENTITIES*

That morning saw heavy banks of clouds pass to the east and
the sun rise above them, dazzling against the too-blue crystal
vault of the sky. The priests were quick to say that the great
god Lud saw fit to bless the proceedings in his honor. A young bull
had been sacrificed at dawn in a secret place, its blood used to mark
the boundaries of the holy ground, its heart burned upon an altar as
an offering, that Lud might strengthen the warriors who gathered in
the forest. Later, the flesh of the bull would be prepared for the
sacred Feast of Warriors to be held that night—after the battle many
expected. For those killed in battle, the bull would be served them
by Lud upon the table of slain enemies.

Bellan Toregh, too, underwent a ritual of dedication. In the light
before dawn, the Faeduadan had sacrificed a young horse and
commanded holy blessings upon the site. Each towering arch and
ring they had marked with blood, sacred runes fraught with great
power and dark magic, called upon for protection against the coming
of the Staubaun-thing. Even the Staubaun gods, they knew, could
be bound by oaths and rituals. The Rill structures, however, caused

all markings upon them to vanish as if they had never been and after three attempts, the priests ceased their efforts.

Throughout the morning, Khelds from far and wide came to witness the calling of power to this place where two great forces dwelt. They came to the High Rock, there to stand in the long shadows of the cold trees, to feel small before the unknown that had forever dwelt there undisturbed, knowing that Stefan's brother, Hans Thegn, had vowed to summon it from its sleep. To all but a handful of them, the Rill was a blur, a breathless whisper of something rumored but never grasped. And to those rare few who had been privileged to see it in motion at Leseos or Dazunor-Rannuli, the Rill was a dream of power that belonged to Staubauns alone. So they came to Bellan Toregh by the thousands, from a countryside throughout which the news had traveled from tongue to tongue, to stand in the snow and bitter cold, not knowing which outcome they awaited.

"Would you look at that!" Arne turned in the saddle to point as Hans and Aubrey reined in alongside. The riders accompanying them, most of the leaders of the gathered cruihcila, crested the ridge behind them and also looked upon the sight. The open, snow-covered hilltop had become a solid fringe of humanity, uplifted arms undulating like stalks bending in the wind as Hans came into view, the day suddenly alive with thousands of voices sounding as one. In Sordan, once before, Hans had seen such a demonstration. He found himself within a repetition of that evening in the Dekkora with the bonfires burning and the masses chanting for the one man in whose lineage they had placed all faith and worship. Dorilian's arrival then had silenced them. But no bonfires burned atop Bellan Toregh. It was cold and daylight, and Dorilian had gone, leaving Hans alone to face the masses. Nor was it the Sordaneon name upon people's lips this time. The name they were chanting was his own.

He glanced at Aubrey and caught her thought.

If you fail them....

A chilling echo of that thought took root. *If he fails me... if he fails me, I fall. But he will fall with me. The longest, hardest fall this World has ever seen—and even I would not dare to rejoice in it. Dorilian and I both stand before some kind of god. Or is it that between us we are making one?*

The official party pushed its way through the crowd. Nalf Rhys loudly wished that Hans had not sent so many of the Trongorians off with the spy. Soon enough, the platform opened before them like a great stage outfitted with fantastic, soaring props, a towering strangeness that dwarfed them all like so many ants upon a broad white plain. Hans reined his horse to a halt as its hoofs sounded upon that smooth paving. He dismounted to face a somber semicircle of the Faeduadan and acolytes, robed in ceremonial splendor to await the man whose prophecy they had come to reveal. Mesmerized by the moment, Hans was barely aware that someone came to take his horse away. The others too had dismounted, their horses led away.

Aubrey's hand and the gentle swipe of her cloak against his gained Hans's attention. "Take care," she whispered. Her lips brushed his cheek in what others would no doubt mistake as a lover's gesture. "The priests can bind you to the decision of the oracle, even to the loss of your hand if you forswear it."

My hand, Hans recalled, the blood upon it dedicated to the god. *Robdan warned me that they had stolen my fate.* He nodded that he understood, then strode across the platform to meet the priests. The surface of Bellan Toregh was hard and snowless. Not even the snow melting from bystanders' boots made puddles. Looking up, he appraised the flawlessly realized, gleaming planes and angles of the sanctuary building. Not so many days ago he had stood here, practically in this very place.

Except that then the mount had lain dormant. No longer.

Hans felt something had changed, a kind of... energy. A pulse. Or was he imagining things?

He wrenched his mind from the Rill for a moment and looked to the red-robed priests. Their faces, their eyes, revealed the true nature of his enemy. Not mercurial Dorilian, now out of reach. Not Nammuor himself, not yet. Not even the Priesthood nor the many adversaries who had plotted or would continue to plot his undoing. They were but agents of that which plagued him. In front of him, staring with the blue eyes of men whose lives he had promised to change, Hans saw the twisted, far-reaching effects of fear. Fear of him, of the unknown, of the forces that moved him. Fear of what awaited. Hans's own fear was nothing compared to the shadow that moved these men to plot his failure.

What have you done? He stared back at them. *Why is the look of blood in your eyes?*

Abruptly, with the same hyperclarity that had sharpened his perceptions all morning, Hans knew what they had predicted: the Rill would not come. Not for him. Their god had told them to come to Bellan Toregh to put Hans to the one test they were sure he would fail.

Lud's Spear.

Hans was to summon the Kheldish god… but the god would not answer. The priests wanted for Hans to stand before this crowd, the hope of thousands pinned to him, so that those thousands would watch him fail. These Faeduadan, their faces wreathed in poorly concealed smiles, sought the downfall of a prince in a battle of deities. Humbled in the sight of all, Hans would be powerless to reverse Lud's judgment. Once that humiliation had occurred, Hans could be chained—forced to submit to the Priesthood and the will of the Witan if he hoped to lead the nation.

It was the sort of plot that Dorilian himself might have devised, given the situation.

Hans got down on one knee before the golden-antlered Head Priest, recognizing him as the red-robed celebrant of the Sacred Grove. Knowing him now, Hans responded with the appropriate formal name and title. "Groddi Wiccena."

"Hans Thegn Erwanson. You remember me."

"How could I forget? I was trusting and you tricked me into a sacred sacrifice. I'm surprised you can call it binding." Enough distance stood between them and the crowd that no bystanders could hear their exchange.

"Not I, but the god led you to your sacrifice. And it *is* binding, or you would not be here." The Groddi Wiccena solemnly noted those who had accompanied Hans. "Some are missing. Is not Robdan Thegn Aelfricson here with you today to witness your glory? And did you not bring with you to Bellan Toregh a company of mounted men to guard you?"

"I need no men, mounted or on foot, to guard me. And I don't think I will lack for witnesses."

From the secret depths of his hood, the Groddi Wiccena studied Hans with barely suppressed displeasure. "Beware. The god frowns upon those who would lead astray the worshippers of Light. Lud would himself tell us that all men exist to serve the Mother."

Hans met the Groddi Wiccena's chiding evenly. There was no way to reconcile the gap in their beliefs. Had Hans wanted to, he could not stop the Rill from coming. Whatever the outcome of this day's events, the Faeduadan would oppose him. "I'm sure you have prepared an oracle to remind me of my duties."

"The god has spoken, Hans Thegn. Prepare for his judgment upon you."

Aware of the gazes of the priests, the assembly of elders, Old Mothers, and the leaders of the kelds, Hans bowed his head before the robed circle. With great dignity, the Groddi Wiccena, High Priest and Summoner of the Faeduadan, turned to face the members of the Witan who stood in places of importance. Behind them spread the many thousands who had come to witness the revelation of the sacrifice.

Lifting high the rod in his hand, the Groddi Wiccena displayed its ornament: the golden sunburst of Lud. "Two wanings past, Hans Thegn Erwanson, brother to Stefan, King to the Khelds and to golden Essera of the Staubaun Lords, did come to the Sacred Grove. There, upon holy ground, he consecrated the Horse. Thus he did dedicate himself to be the flesh of the sacrifice, whose blood above all others it pleased the god to drink and in the sacred dream reveal the fate of his nation! Hear now the oracle of Lud!"

Hans identified the chill that formed in his veins as recognition. A rite of cannibalism through sacred transformation, the horse's blood turned back into his by magic.

The Groddi Wiccena held out his staff. The sun, burning down upon the platform, glinted upon the sunburst of Lud and from there reflected onto the Groddi Wiccena's face, a sudden illumination.

"The man bleeds upon the altar! His spirit is revealed among the stars that attend the burning of his sacrifice. Black are his omens! The Great Bear's paw does strike upon the shield of Alm. A shooting star burns its way across the heavens through the rising smoke of sacrifice. The heart of his horse is divided! Great turbulence seethes among the stars and in his path, war and calamity and blood flowing from the arm of Alm. The Eagle soars above the field, and the heart of Hans Thegn is not whole. The god has shown me Amallar victorious on the field of battle, Hans Thegn burning the northlands upon his shield, gathering them into his cup, sharing with us his birthright and his Kingdom."

A roar rose from the crowd.

"But hold!" The Groddi Wiccena's voice wailed of ill fortune and the crowd's celebration died. Only those baleful words were to be heard. "A shadow falls upon the children of Alm! The Eagle flies before them on the field, but the heart of Alm falters in the breast of Hans Thegn—no longer does it strengthen his arm with courage, give virtue to his victory. The dark half of his heart has worms that twist within! They open him to darkness, weakening his hand. He cannot lift the shield of Alm against the blue towers! They fall and he is lost! And the children of Alm scatter in the wind!"

The Groddi Wiccena dropped his arms, drew the rod before him, the symbol of the sun held so that it covered his face. With the god's visage as his own, he looked down at Hans with stern authority. "Hans Thegn! Hear the judgment of the oracle. Prove yourself worthy if you wish to bear the shield of Alm upon your arm! Lud will decide if in you there is the stuff of Kings. This day the god has decreed that you be stood upon the High Place. Here, if the god sees you as worthy of his aim, you will meet the test of Lud's Spear. Should the god turn away from you and not show you his Spear, the oracle declares that you may be redeemed in the Grove of Fire, there through sacred marriage to make your heart one again with the heart of Amallar."

Hans felt his real heart of flesh sink as though indeed worms gnawed within its bloodless chambers. *So it comes down to that. Amallar's fate depends not on my performance, but on that of the god! If the Rill doesn't come, I stand condemned.*

The oracle thought the Rill wouldn't come to Bellan Toregh. Of course. Why should it? The Rill had not run here since before this World had been spun from the Mind of Leur. Time and time again, Highborn Princes and Staubaun sages had said it never would. Not to Amallar. Not to the land whose people Epoptes would not allow to ride it or even to set foot upon its platforms. It was the nature of gods—even Staubaun gods—to be constant. Running, the Rill was like the sun, indifferent and unchanging in its course through their lives. And if for any reason it were reborn, they knew, it would be no nearer than before.

But it would be deadly to any who stood in its path.

White-faced, Hans rose from his knees and bowed his acceptance of the oracle. Nothing would be gained by speaking, except to further the belief that his heart was not with them. Instead, he turned to Aubrey and Arne—one who supported him because his heart could do nothing else, the other because her promise would not allow her to do otherwise.

"Aubrey, I ask you to stand by me," he said. "And Arne also."

Both walked forward. Aubrey's blue cloak stirred in the icy wind, her hood pushed back and dark waves of hair loose about her shoulders. Proud and with a golden circle of Life ablaze at her throat, Aubrey could have been a Kheld priestess. The clutch of Old

Mothers standing at the edge of the gathering, near but not with the Faeduadan, bowed their heads. Their hands shaped runes of blessing, declaring Aubrey an instrument of the Mother, within the sacred protection of the goddess. If Aubrey looked afraid, it was for Hans, not herself—and because of the Rill. It was Arne whose expression clearly revealed that he envisioned disaster. That in the face of gods, mystery, and fear Arne could still stand by him, Hans counted as the first miracle of the day.

He turned from the Groddi Wiccena to Aubrey. "I know about the test of Lud's Spear, but what are the other things?"

"Trespass not upon the oracle!" the Groddi Wiccena warned.

Aubrey met the priest's angry look with one of her own. "Hans Thegn is still a stranger to many of our ways." She spoke in a raised voice even the clan chiefs could hear. "The laws of our gods are not practiced in ignorance. If Hans is to decide his path, he must know the nature of his choices. Even a prisoner is told these things." She regarded Hans with both concern and reassurance. "The Grove of Fire is an arena of combat. You and an opponent sanctified by the god, often a prisoner who has been promised his freedom, fight to the death inside a circle bounded by man-high rings of tinder soaked in resin, the outer edge of which is set on fire as the combat begins. If you do not kill your man before the innermost ring catches, you would both die of smoke and flames. If you kill your man, you can possibly escape, your heart having overcome its divided nature. If your man kills you—well, it would mean that your heart was not Kheld enough to overcome him. You can be sure your opponent will reflect the oracle's wishes."

Hans heard a few of the gathered priests rumble in protest and knew Aubrey was telling more truth than they wished to be revealed. He needed to know the rest. "And this sacred marriage?"

"Made within the Sacred Grove, upon the altar. The woman would hold clan right. I know little else but that the purpose is to create a child."

Not just *a* child. An heir. The very thing Dorilian had warned Hans of that first day at Rhodhur, these priests through their oracle sought to ensure. *It will come to that*, the Hierarch had said. *It always comes to that.* If these men could not rule through Hans, they would do so through his child. If he let them.

Drawing himself straight, Hans savored for a moment the clean air of winter before he announced in a strong, clear voice that carried to those gathered in witness. "I am prepared to meet the test of Lud. I have said that the Rill will come—and it will!"

"Proudling!" the Groddi Wiccena pronounced. "You put yourself in peril, declaring ahead of yourself the mind of the god!"

"We will see to whom he has spoken."

Looking toward the fringes, he saw Nalf Rhys in the crowd ringing the platform. The Thegnard straightened and thrust out his chest, then shouted. "Damn you, boy. Do it, if you can! I'll not throw a stone to stop you. But if the thing comes with a belly of soldiers, I've ten men standing by with arrows aimed at your gut!'

You're a cagey badger, Nalf Rhys. Hans granted the Thegnard his grudging respect. *And a damn sight more perceptive than your priests.*

With a nod, Hans left the company of his friends and followed the Groddi Wiccena the last few steps separating the platform from the curved depression of the main run. When they reached it, the Groddi Wiccena turned Hans to face the crowd. The hilltop had come alive with human faces, fevered Kheld gazes wanting to see if the Rill would come as promised. If it did, they would know Lud had blessed Hans's hand and laid at his feet the god's own Spear that would lead them to victory.

Or, they would see that the god had found Hans lacking, his heart misled and loyalties divided.

The Groddi Wiccena called for his acolytes, who brought to him a massive staff carved from an ancient branch of oak, inscribed with mystic symbols and bound by rings of gold. An earthenware urn fashioned in the shape of a horse, painted red, was set at the robed man's feet. *Come on, man, stop dawdling*, Hans found himself thinking. *This mystic mumble is taking too much time!*

The Rill was set to come at midday, whenever that was. Khelds, unlike Staubauns, had few measures for small units of time. Hans felt the hour in his bones, however. The shadows along the western bases of the pylons were barely more than stubs.

Noting his impatience, the Groddi Wiccena allowed a tight smile to cross his lips. "You shall not wish it come, when you stand in its path." Grandly lifting high his arms, his red robes flaring impressively in the wind, the Groddi Wiccena addressed the gathered onlookers in a loud, commanding voice. "This is the test of Lud's Spear! Cowardly is the man, and unworthy, who leaps from the path before the Spear burns as brightly as the Sun through the Eye!"

An eerie, moaning chant filled the air, priests and acolytes invoking Lud's dubious blessing upon Hans. Hans stood at the edge where the platform gave way and the slip angled downward. He was aware of priests falling to their knees beside him, arms upraised, chanting, still chanting. Then, without warning, the Groddi Wiccena's hand on Hans's arm twisted cruelly, throwing Hans off-balance and over the edge. He tumbled onto the sloping surface and slid the rest of the way until he'd landed at the bottom.

"Hey!" Arne's voice rang out. Many of the crowd also shouted in protest.

Damn! Hans twisted around and propped himself on his elbows to look up at the Groddi Wiccena, now standing directly above him and confronting Arne's raised fists. To Hans's relief, Aubrey stepped between the two men, one hand on Arne's upper arm. Speaking.

Whatever Aubrey said to Arne, her voice was too low for Hans to overhear. But his gaze met Arne's and pleaded for his friend to back off.

The Groddi Wiccena stood unmoving, watching through the shadow cast by his hood until Arne and Aubrey had rejoined the other onlookers. Once they had, the Groddi Wiccena turned to address Hans. The crowd fell silent again as they strained to hear.

"Be humble before Lud—and your Fate."

With what dignity he still possessed, Hans pushed himself to his feet. Determined to be heard, he raised his voice. "The oracle has decided that I must stand before the god. So it shall be. But I choose where I stand!"

Turning his back on the figure in red, Hans started walking along the length of the slip. Permephedon. Sordan. Had Dorilian known this would happen and prepared him to face it? Or had Dorilian simply followed his own all-consuming paranoia in suspecting the Faeduadan might try to use the Rill as the townsfolk did?

It was a long, long walk, a third of the way to the southern edge and its nested rings, but Hans eventually found what he sought. With every step he had replayed Dorilian's warnings about *charys* movement and ring activation and the best chance to look brave and survive. Though he feared he would miss it somehow, he found it. The slightest change in lucidity, faint but wide. While his heart pounded and his legs threatened to shake, Hans stopped walking at that lucid band and turned to face north. Toward Essera and his fate. Toward Permephedon.

"Here I stand! Beneath the bright sun of Amallar!" Hoping to sound majestic, Hans tried to think of what Dorilian might do, or say, in such a situation. He stood straight and tall for those who could still see him. "Now let the God's Spear come to me!"

The low concave floor of the slip looked polished, glassy, with a sheen like ice. One reason for the term cold trees. That and its thermal properties. But whatever substance formed the wide, shallow trench in which Hans stood, it was durable: three centuries of rough Kheld boots had walked upon it and it remained unscarred, not even scratched.

The wind whipped his hair and Hans tried to put from his mind that the Rill might come at any moment. That he was vulnerable. That he did not know what to do next. "Next" was... something Dorilian knew far better than Hans did.

Satisfied that Hans would stay where he stood, the Groddi Wiccena whirled and swooped upon the horse-shaped urn held by a second acolyte. Taking it up, he unfastened the lid and scattered a trail of charred remains and ashes the length of the platform between Hans and the crowd, a dark trail upon a pure white expanse.

"These are the bones of Hans Thegn's Horse!" The Groddi Wiccena placed the emptied urn back into the acolyte's hands, to be buried as was proper for so sacred a vessel. Taking the rune staff from his acolyte, the Groddi Wiccena stood spread-armed in his flaring robes, the color of blood sacrifice, and addressed the crowd. "Let no man seek to cross to him! No man may place himself between the chosen of the god and the power of the oracle. May Lud strike faint hearts wherever they stand!"

Aubrey turned to Arne and clutched his arm, leaning near to whisper something urgent. Hans watched Arne shake his head, point and spread his hands. Arne looked ready to vomit.

I wasn't supposed to be here, in the run. He's telling her that. Arne knew as well as Aubrey did that if the Rill didn't stop, there wouldn't be anything left of Hans to bury.

Hans looked away, instead faced the Groddi Wiccena across the line drawn with charred bones. The enormity of Hans's gamble had begun to sink in. *Your god should rage at you, Groddi Wiccena. You have placed him in an impossible position.* Even so, a coldness wrapped itself around Hans's spine. The skin of his arms pebbled from the chill. There remained a chance that he was doomed. That Dorilian had erred somehow, that the Rill would not come—or worse, that it would come *wrong*.

All Change resembles Chaos. How not? Chaos is the true
face of Leur—the child of omnificence. All things that are
not permanent, that Change, are gifts of Leur, including
Time, their greatest Creation. Therefore, Chaos is
Creation's forge, both end and beginning. This World was
born of Devastation.

Cibulitus, *Annals of the Return: The Leur-Taryynan*

The Rill mount at Bellan Toregh was already stirring. That
much Dorilian knew.

In the bitter cold pale of dawn, with the now awakening
town a hard half-night's ride behind him, Dorilian reined in his
horse and called his escort to a halt. After moving off the road, they
located a small meadow behind a hillock in which to make camp.
The sun struggled through the trees while the weary party hobbled
their animals and broke out cold provisions for a silent meal, after
which they sought much-needed sleep. Dorilian did not sleep and
instead took watch. He was not yet confident of escape and—more
than that—his mind continuously threaded and tangled memory of
Rill manipulation with conjecture of whether his plan would
succeed, producing an anxiety he could not dismiss. The Rill never
failed. But Dorilian was not the Rill, not a god. He had merely made
a few moments of contact with one.

After placing a bedroll beneath his buttocks and bracing his feet
upon a snowless bit of rock, Dorilian pondered whether he was a
madman or a fool. Reason told him he had been one or the other,
and possibly both, for weeks. And now he was a fugitive, dependent
on strangers. Perhaps in Merath he would regain his proper place
and some semblance of Hierarchal dignity.

Dorilian lightly touched the bitemark on his lip and found it nearly healed. Just as well. If his escort had noticed, they'd said nothing of it. He, however, would remember Aubrey's mark upon his body even after evidence was gone. It had been far too long since he had taken a woman—or been taken by one. Trying to figure which had happened in this instance was too confusing to sort out; he needed more distance, more surety that he could handle the event. And not just the event, the aftermath. *Her.* Aubrey Amundda. A woman for whom Dorilian had accepted lust in place of death, and who now would face just as much danger as that from which he was fleeing. He had done nothing to restrain Aubrey after their heated coupling. Dorilian had left and she had let him leave. For all he knew Aubrey had by now told all Bellan Toregh what she—and he—had done. If so, she might also have told them who he was. Did Khelds have a means of communicating across distances? If so, his escape hung by a thread.

As for Aubrey... she had good reasons, as good as his, to keep any discovery of Dorilian's identity to herself. And she would be better able to lie about it. He still dared to hope she might.

Dor?

Lev. Though the touch came at a bad time, Dorilian wrenched his mind from all other thoughts. There was no way his peril of last night hadn't bled through to the boy in some form. Best now to find out how much. Dorilian pushed aside knowledge that he was too tired for this, that he had exhausted his ambrosia and his rations were too scant to restore him.

I'm here. I'm safe.

Thank Leur! Relief poured through in a wave. *Thank Leur and all gods. I worried all night!*

Levyathan's worry scraped razor-sharp on Dorilian's nerves. He moved to put those fears to rest. *I have fled, with Handurin's help. I and ten men. I am riding to Merath.*

Still in Amallar?

Yes.

You were discovered.

No. Maybe. Whether Aubrey would talk or Handurin circumvent rumor was still uncertain. *If I have not been, we may still salvage this plan.*

The Rill? You don't know yet? Levyathan had calmed, the discourse shifted to assessment of other things.

No. Another hour, two hours. Then we will know. Dorilian thought of something else. *I need coin. Esseran. We travel light and I must buy food for myself and my escort, the horses too. If possible, I would like to pay for an inn.*

Dor—

I cannot replenish without food. Just do as I ask. I must conserve my strength.

A flash of anger. *That horrible woman—*

And there it was, ripe for speculation and misunderstanding. *No. She... it's complicated. One day you will understand.*

She put you in danger! She hurt you.

She let me go. And for that, Dorilian had let Aubrey live. Kept Erydon's Promise. This was way too much for Levyathan to fathom. *Send coin—and await the Rill.*

When the sun neared its zenith, Dorilian roused his escort and ordered them to remount. As their horses stamped in the piercing winter cold and deep snow, Dorilian continued to stand at the edge of the meadow, his gaze raking the trees on the other side.

The road they travelled roughly paralleled the Rill run to the east. The path generated by the Rill could not be seen except where it clipped hilltops or carved through mountains, but even from this distance Dorilian detected the Entity's unmistakable trace. In Sordan, the Rill's vivid presence suffused his life. Here in Amallar it beckoned with a siren's whisper. Just one more time before fleeing this primitive country, he would test the boundaries of his being.

Dorilian focused to the north and west, beyond the meadow and trees. He tugged the glove from his left hand, the one bearing the Rill Stone, and extended it. Cold and wind caressed his naked palm and fingers. Always he touched the Creation. Through the Rill presence that entwined his flesh, he located distant Permephedon's great vastness, something powerful lurking within. Tired though he was, a little more strength was all he needed. He waited—and detected the first flaring of the system.

Yes! Rill power kissed Dorilian's fingertips. Accomplishment flooded his veins as he experienced the sensation of propulsion rings expanding the field, the advance cone thrusting straight at the eye of his connection to the Entity. Upon his hand the Rill Stone flared. Only a breath later, as the Trongorians and Robdan exclaimed their wonder at the sight, a flash born on the horizon burst into passage to the west before it vanished southward toward Bellan Toregh.

Even before that brilliance, Dorilian detected an answering power surge at Trestethion and knew his success. The Rill had performed as he had directed. Lowering his arm, he released the contact and replaced his glove. The Rill Stone hidden once more, he walked back to where his escort waited with the horses.

"You did it!" Robdan declared as Dorilian mounted.

"The Rill has spoken." *I have spoken.* The saddle creaked as Dorilian took up the reins and settled on his roan horse's back.

"And Hans—"

"I do not know. Whatever has happened, or will happen from this day on, we will find out eventually."

Dorilian turned his escorts toward Merath. It was done, this deed Handurin—and Marc Frederick before him—had so wanted to happen. They thought it simple, but Dorilian knew otherwise. He was godborn. Leur's blood. Always he must ask the questions: *What have I destroyed? What have I created?*

Always he must face the answer.

Truth.

Quirin shoved a path through the swarm of robed men that milled between him and Permephedon's somnolent core rings. "Show me the aberration."

Permephedon's Archmage, tense-jawed and wearing an air of impatience Quirin had been tasting for weeks, followed onto the massive, curved walkway. In the vast chamber beyond the walkway, three rings of core arrays hung in shimmering orbit. What resided at the center to hold them in such suspension no person, except possibly Marenthro, knew. The Archmage stopped at a flat console flanked by glowing projections. His index finger hovered above a ripple in the Rillstream's steady signature. "You can see it here, a disruption in the pattern. It resembles the opening signal of an imminence but—" He raised an eyebrow and indicated the remainder of the signature.

Quirin frowned. "No convergence." *Every* Rill imminence was followed by a convergence.

"So—without a convergence, not an imminence. Perhaps another fluctuation?" There had been a fluctuation a few weeks before—a month before—since which the Rill had been silent.

Frustratingly so. For nearly three months, the only Rill activity to appear on Permephedon's screens had been pulses from south of Randpory Crossing. And there had been no access at all to internode communication.

"Did you manage to trace the origin of *this* fluctuation?" Quirin snapped. The earlier event had escaped Epoptean efforts to pinpoint an origin. Or even a simple reason for existing.

The Archmage gestured to the system map with its strand of glowing lines and illuminated circles. "Just as before, that it is occurring in the primary artery."

Between Permephedon and Sordan. Not Hestya—but also not some rogue node outside the current configuration. So... maybe nothing. Merely a bubble or less than that on the surface of a vast sea of Rill data. Had Quirin not seen such before, he would be less fixated—but he had witnessed two unique events. Both times had involved a man he could not dismiss. Dorilian Sordaneon was unaccounted for and capable of far too much disruption for the Order to let down its guard.

The signature on the screen flashed—then erupted with signals. Its slash transected the screen just as the immense rings at the heart of the cavernous chamber awakened and the arcane brackets and spokes around one core array burst into brilliant, contained light. The Rill was back on system. Quirin hurried to the viewing portals on the other side of the chamber wall and watched, heart pounding, triumphant, as the primary run on the platform below released spindles that rapidly rotated and swiveled, threading the translucent shape of a *charys*. Massive. Sublimely tapered. Perfect. The vessel solidified into shimmering wonder, turning opaque before the spindles retracted.

The *charys* completed, power shifted smoothly, then pulsed throughout the run. Quirin did not need projections to know what was happening as the *charys* rose. On the nearly empty platform and all around the operations chamber brothers darted like bees. A light whine, pure as the sound of the Creation being sung into being, filled all ears.

Imminence.

"Has it locked?" Quirin screamed.

"Yes!" one of the brothers tending the projections cried. "But we can't tell—"

"Raise Dazunor-Rannuli!" Quirin commanded the stupefied

brother standing at comms, frozen in place and staring as all of them were doing. The man sat and put on his headpiece.

The *charys* shot through the massive south-facing portal overlooking the city, into the open air, and vanished. Quirin caught a breath.

"What do they say?"

The brother at comms shook his head. "Nothing. Same as before. No response from Dazunor-Rannuli."

Quirin turned to the Archmage, who was staring helplessly at the system screen. "Where did it go?"

"I don't know how... there was no chant... no request," the Archmage stammered. "There." He pointed to a bright two-ringed circle on the map where no circle had been before.

Trestethion.

38

Did I take a risk that day? I trusted in what I knew, or
thought I knew, and that what I wanted to believe was in
fact true. I think the greatest risk any of us take—and we do
it every day—is to put full faith in our own judgment.

Handurin Stauberg-Randolph, letter to Robdan Aelfricson

Men had stood in the run at Bellan Toregh before him, Hans knew. In hope or despair or foolish pride, they had placed themselves upon the anvil of an Entity. They had lived or died according to schedules produced in distant lands where Kheldish deities were unknown, by people who did not even know or care that other gods existed. At first Hans felt only cold, the wind in his hair and on his skin. To every side, the Rill's guardian structures cradled vistas of white and blue within frozen rings and arches. Those unmoving shapes framed him even as they did the azure bright sky above Bellan Toregh, a thing known in passing, his presence noted, analyzed, reduced to what it would take to remove him.

Months ago in Sordan, in an antechamber of the Rill's nerve center and within sight of the Inception, the Psilant who headed the Epoptes had told Hans to leave, that he was not fit to behold the Entity. Now Hans stood atop Bellan Toregh and asked the Rill to behold *him*. Invisible emanations skimmed his mind and teased his skin. Dorilian had warned Hans not to play games or take chances. *Best not to tempt fate. Even when coming to a stop, a* charys *is massive and difficult to outrace.*

Hans could not say how much time passed. Soon after the Groddi Wiccena had ceased his clamor, time had seemed to stand still.

Enraptured by the Entity, Hans surrendered this World for another detected at the fringe of his senses. Myriad fine vibrations tickled tiny nerves under his skin and alerted him to something that pulsed just beyond the reach of human senses. He could not say what it was—the Rill, or something vaster still. Whatever doubts he might have harbored about Bellan Toregh being an active node faded.

Had Dorilian stood even as Hans stood now, in Teremar or Randpory, asking the Rill to see him? *Does he feel the Rill the same way I do? Does everyone?*

And then Hans felt the Rill *move*. All earthly boundaries fell away, all human senses suspended. A vision of a City mightier even than Sordan burst into his mind, towers white and blinding.

Imminence.

Sordan challenged the sky. *Lock.*

Bellan Toregh, tiny and bright. *Go.* Himself, hands open, extended without thinking.

...Convergence...

Hans raised his arms, thrusting his hands into energy so near that he felt his fingers tipped with danger.

The crowd's scream alerted him to the moving structures overarching the hill. He watched as the shapes bracketing him stirred, buckled, and rearranged. Swifter than wind-driven grass and more elegant than dancers, the Rill's rings telescoped, sinuous circles and arches that elongated and flowed.

To the north. Toward....

A pinpoint of light appeared deep in the heart of the corridor of arches. Then it burst upon him. Hans felt a titanic surge as massive energy fields shifted into the deceleration arms.

It's coming too fast!

Helpless in his barbaric finery, Hans stood rooted as the *charys* hurtled toward him in pulses of quicksilver. What had seemed a star in the blink of an eye became a sun, then filled the entire run, as energized brackets cradled the madly expanding proportions. With a barely heard, deep-throated hum, the Rill arches above the mount contracted into elegant new rings.

Stand! As he had so many months before at the Gateway, Hans slammed aside his reflex to flee. Had the *charys* been traveling full speed it would have atomized him in the time that thought had taken. Instead a low-pitched descending whine created by the energy fields shifting between rings split the crowd's screams of warning as the sound of the arriving *charys* belatedly merged with the sight of its silvered shape. The hum died to a series of sonorous drones as the *charys* hit a succession of floating rings, one after the other, that pulled it to a long, still swift but slowing glide high over the Toregh's snow-covered woodlands and meadows. The *charys* sailed above the town and its outlying farms, a breath-stopping, silver shape beyond beauty or myth.

The silent-again rings retreated into their original housings and limbs retracted. The gleaming *charys* entered the run and Hans sensed magnetic fields beneath his feet activate to brake what residual momentum the vessel retained. Overhead, the Rill's vast crown of white arches resumed a status of serene waiting. The *charys's* tapered nose reached Hans just as he put out his hand to touch it. Warm. The temperature of skin. For a moment the vehicle's massive weight pushed against Hans's outstretched hand, and then, as though it obeyed his bidding, it stopped, held fast by the brake within the slip.

"*Mother's Tits!*"

"*Look at that!*"

Cries of jubilation and relief carried to Hans. The platform itself was but silence and gasps. The priests and Old Mothers stood speechless as thousands shouted that Hans Thegn had stood in the path of Lud's Spear—and that he had touched it. Held it in his hand.

Sick and elated, Hans found himself shaking. Had Dorilian erred, even minutely, Hans would have died, unable to escape a vessel that measured its speed in units none could imagine or crushed by its inexorable weight. Instead, he'd not had to move one step. He had passed the test. *The Khelds cannot doubt me now, not now. And it will be damn hard to doubt Dorilian.* Overcome, Hans dropped his head to rest upon the surprising skin of the *charys*. Neither warm nor chill, nor soft nor hard, but something possibly not earthly matter at all. Instead of shattering his fragile human form, it had just elevated him to near godhood.

Father knows how to put on a show. Fahme's words prompted Hans to follow in those footsteps.

With a concerted effort at looking unshaken by his experience, he emulated Dorilian's move from the morning they'd visited the dormant platform, running three steps and swinging himself onto the landing. Ass first, then onto his feet. From there he took a moment to skim his hand along the *charys's* sleek curve. Out of nowhere, a laugh filled his throat and he released it and raised his arms overhead, fists clenched in victory.

The crowd answered with a roar.

The Rill had awakened.

"Hans Thegn!" Nalf Rhys hollered, his voice a bull roar as it emerged from a sea of awed exclamations. Bearlike and imposing, the Thegnard stalked to the fore, ignoring the priests who waved their staffs at him. "Out of the way, faedu!" Nalf growled when the Groddi Wiccena moved to intercede. "You lost your chance at him." Nevertheless, Nalf showed he respected the dangers of flouting holy oracles and took care not to walk upon or otherwise disturb the lay of the cremains the priests had strewn across the platform. "I'm Thegnard here, and I want a look at that damned thing! The holy terror was supposed to come from Sordan, not from the north!"

When Nalf came to stand before Hans, several other Khelds at the front of the crowd looked ready to stampede after the sound of the Thegnard's boots.

"We thought it would be better this way." Even to his own ears, Hans thought his voice sounded drained. The battle rush in his blood was rapidly fading, his senses dulling as his body returned to normal.

"We? Who's we?" Though his gaze devoured the gleaming shape of the *charys*, Nalf stood in too much awe to touch it.

"Dorilian and I. We knew that any *charys* that came from the south would be considered suspect."

"Who says this one isn't?"

"Look inside. It's empty."

Although immense and nearly as long as the landing, the *charys* was wider than it was tall. An apparently seamless ribbon of transparency bisected the car from end to end. Also, three portals on the side facing the station stood open. By simply looking, all could see that what Hans said was true: the *charys* was empty of all but open space and what looked like markings on its interior. The Thegnard grunted, then gave Hans a nod.

"He stopped it, by damn!" Nalf turned to the crowd and raised his staff of office to them. "What do you think of him? Do you believe it? Hans Thegn awakened the goddamned Rill, for love of the Mother! And not a soldier in sight!"

Arne and Aubrey and several others standing on the landing overcame their amazement and rushed toward Hans. As they did so, the Groddi Wiccena planted himself before them, his arms spread in dire warning. "Approach him not! The thing is evil! Lud's Spear cannot be halted in midflight—what Hans Thegn has summoned is a Highborn abomination! He stands yet subject to the voice of the oracle!"

Confronted again by the ambiguous will of obscure gods, the press forward stopped everyone in their tracks. Except for one.

"The oracle didn't stop Nalf Rhys from crossing!" Arne shouted. "And it won't stop me!"

Hans smiled as he watched Arne take a hop across the ashes.

"Thanks." When Arne came to stand before him, Hans embraced him. But Arne wasn't looking at Hans, he was gaping past Hans's shoulder. In Sordan, Arne had never gotten close enough to see a *charys* up close.

"Look at that, will you? He really did it!" Arne burst into a smile that had not quite shed disbelief. "It's real?"

"Real enough to take you back to Sordan in the morning."

Arne retreated three steps, his delight replaced by realization. Before, it had been just a lot of talk. "Oh, no," he protested forthrightly. "I'm not going back there. Not on this thing, I'm not. They didn't want me nowhere near it the first time!"

Smiling broadly, knowing that he would win that argument when he returned to it, Hans turned instead to the priests where they stood as rigid and unmoving as red chess pieces on a stark white board. A nation waited with bated breath upon the fringes of their contest, its fate to be determined by an oracle that had gone beyond its priests' interpretation.

Coming to the line of the ashes of his sacrifice, Hans crossed back over that barrier of remains and shadowy superstition. The charred bones, blackened and brittle, still held a power he was determined to take back and make his own. "I stand upon the word of the oracle!" As he addressed the Faeduadan, Hans made certain all could hear his voice. "I passed the test! Who better to take up the shield of Alm than the man who can hold the god's Spear in his hand!"

The Groddi Wiccena stood as still as stone. "You claim too much. Lud's Spear is not a Rill thing!"

"You're wrong," Hans countered. "You mistake the nature of your oracle. It said that Lud would bestow his Spear upon that man worthy to carry the shield of Alm." He pointed at the *charys*. "That appears to have happened. Because the Rill is very much a weapon— and a shield. The god, perhaps, deserves better prophets."

The Groddi Wiccena's bark was harsh in his throat. "Whose god smiles upon you, Hans Thegn? Not ours. The Rill was stopped and all the prayers of the Staubauns could not move their god to set it free."

Hans grinned, his confidence increasing. "Perhaps their god has left them." Just behind the phalanx of priests, Aubrey pressed her hand to her throat, but whether she was pleading for silence or containing her own secret understanding of his meaning, Hans could not say. The time had not yet come for him to reveal the twisting irony of that truth. The war would begin with such words. "I will not argue oracles with you. It's not my place," Hans told the Groddi Wiccena. "But the Rill has come, as you can see. And if it wasn't Lud who sent it, that doesn't change the fact that it's here. Lud doesn't command the Rill, or you would have had it long ago. His Spear is a weapon men cannot command. I do not command it—but I hold it. For now. The Rill is the weapon I bring to you."

"The abomination comes but at the will of its god."

"Yes, and its god dwells in Sordan. The reason the Rill stands here today is because I demanded a sign of Sordan's goodwill. This *charys* will stay while we talk. All night it will stay. But by midsun tomorrow, we must send our answer to Sordan."

"Answer to what?" Nalf Rhys challenged.

"Whether we're willing to talk alliance."

From the milling confusion of the crowd, Fran Gorseddson came forward, raging as he pointed at the *charys* and an enemy against which his Neuberland army had never claimed a victory. "This thing is a trick! The Sordaneon lies! He casts a dazzling stone in our path and while we fall all over it, gabbling like geese, he moves armies behind our backs!"

"Then throw it in his face!" Hans gave them the option. "Send this *charys* to Sordan, empty as it came, and you'll never see one stop here again! But what if in return for an alliance with Sordan you can have everything your rivals in Dazunor-Rannuli and Leseos have ever had? The tie to the Triempery that made them richer and more powerful than you could even dream of stands here before you! What would it be worth to you, to Amallar and Neuberland, to gain sworn access to the Rill, not just here but in other cities? To have the Rill generate wealth for *our* people? Are you willing to throw that away as well?"

In the silence that answered, the wind swirled in whispers, a dull snapping from the cloaks of thousands. Even the Faeduadan could not challenge the power of the new reality before them. They could not throw it away, because the Rill could not be denied. Bellan Toregh would always be there to remind them of what might have been.

Nalf Rhys scowled and his shrewd eyes passed from Hans to the *charys* gleaming a short distance from where he stood. Just a touch of craft, cautious and yet to be committed, caught hold of his lip and pulled a smile sideways into his silver-streaked beard. When he spoke, it was with a gambler's swagger on his tongue, a long Kheld love of a hard bargain. "No man in his right mind would turn his back on that thing without hearing the matter out," he said, "and you know it, lad. Talk on."

Initially I and most of my advisors regarded the opening of
the Rill into Hestya as a hostile act. In every usual sense, it
was. Certainly, the young Sordaneon prince Dorilian
intended that I and Essera should be alarmed—and
warned. The challenge at such times, however, is to step
back and look at an event with clear eyes: not at the intent,
but at the consequences.

MARC FREDERICK STAUBERG-RANDOLPH, LETTER TO PRINCE REGELON

It took the Witan until nightfall and a little beyond. A generation
of arguments had to be hard fought before they could be won. But
as twilight deepened and the Rill's active glow augmented the
cold white light of the moon, even dissidents fell under the Entity's
unanswerable spell. That, and the growing breadth of the movement
against them. Talk that had shifted between warring views through
most of the afternoon had little by little made possessing the Rill not
merely a possibility but a reality that had fallen within their grasp—
and grasp they did, with a vengeance. Sordan was the enemy, but it
was an enemy with something they wanted, and when Khelds wanted
something, they weren't too proud to go after it. Those who argued
against pursuing a Rill treaty—the Faeduadan, a few old people and
some angry young ones—found themselves hopelessly outnumbered
and shouted into silence. When the Old Mothers weighed in by
declaring that, according to their runes and Wheels, the Rill might
possibly represent the foretold Change, the last nail was hammered.

The Groddi Wiccena, enraged, cast a curse on the abomination
and left before nightfall. But even superstitious Khelds doubted that
the Rill, being a thing beyond their gods, perhaps even of another
world, could be harmed by such maledictions.

"Make up your minds, priests!" Nalf Rhys had been the loudest voice among many. "You can't have it all ways! Either Lud sent this thing, or he couldn't stop it from coming. And it seems to me that if the god sent it, then he means for the Children of Alm to have it. And if the god doesn't want us to have it but he couldn't stop it from coming, then maybe we need a new god! As I see it, either the god gave Hans Thegn his Spear, or Hans Thegn's found himself a god out there who is stronger than Lud!"

In a world where the old gods of men could be threatened by the emergence of younger, stronger deities, such taunts were well aimed. No man wanted to follow a god whose powers were diminished. Reluctantly, the Faeduadan were made to concede that the will of Lud had, in fact, been served, but they held fast that the omens of this day were dark and clouded the future not only of Hans Thegn, but of all Amallar.

Hans was awakened by the sound of knocks at the door, followed by a muffle of voices. Arne led several important Kheld leaders into the room. In the firelight, the metallic fastenings and clasps on jerkins of rubbed leather and velvet overgowns took on a burnished glow, lending these men and women in their cruihcil finery an imposing, rustic authority.

"Thegnard. Noble leaders." Hans hoped he sounded alert. "I'm afraid you've caught me napping."

"No one's caught you napping yet, lad, but you nipped the lot of them by the tail." With a sound between snort and laughter, Nalf Rhys acknowledged an opponent who had beaten him soundly on all scores. "Gods damn you, Hans Thegn Erwanson, but I think we might find there's a king in you yet."

Hans grinned. He had expected Nalf to be a proponent of the Rill, if not the alliance, for the wealth and power to be gained by its acquisition.

"What did you cook up with that Sordaneon bastard, eh?" Nalf's narrowed eyes were more appraising than hostile. "Those god-fiends of the Staubauns don't give away the Rill for love, and they don't give it away for money. They hold it like the Mother's own and they don't let it go! Even when Marc Frederick had their damned Hierarch locked up at Stauberg, they wouldn't yield their precious

Rill! He had to go begging for it. So what are your pockets lined with, Hans Thegn, that the devil himself would give you even one shot at it?"

"I already told you. Dorilian Sordaneon wants to go north into Essera, to defeat his enemy Nammuor the Mormantaloran there. I want Nammuor out every bit as much as he does. But I can't field an army while Amallar's opposition stands in the way. So I told Dorilian to offer something Amallar couldn't turn down."

"That still doesn't say how you got him to do it. Or what we'll have to put up front to get it. He's not giving it away, now, is he? There's some striking to be done, hard bargaining, I'll warrant, ere we come up with something—what he wants, what we want, eh? You wouldn't have a sniff of the flavor of that stew, would you?"

"I might. I did, after all, have a hand at talking him into it. But I can tell you right now that the Rill commands a hefty price."

"He wouldn't be Dorilian Sordaneon if it didn't!" But the curl on Nalf's lips did not deny continued interest. "You've staked yourself on this, boy—you know that, don't you? When you said you would get us the Rill, I said to myself, 'This is it, the brag of them all that will twist Hans Thegn's neck, and all I can say is he built his own gibbet!' But you came up with it, didn't you? We can't refuse at least making a stab at getting the thing. Not when we stand to cram the throats of every bastard Staubaun Lord in Essera and Neuberland that ever looked down their noses our way. The Witan has decided in your favor, Hans Thegn Erwanson. We'll look into this alliance you want. We'll meet with the damned Sordani and see if there is anything to be got by talking with them. But we want to come out of it with that Rill!"

"We will, if I have anything to say about it." Hans felt confident in that boast as well. "Dorilian and I have already reached an understanding of sorts. But his first condition, even before he will agree to talk Rill, is that there be an alliance in place, in writing, fully agreed to and signed. An alliance that will let him go north to fight Nammuor."

"And no discussion before then?"

"No."

"Why?"

"Exactly what you were talking about before. We're talking about a Highborn Prince here," Hans reminded them. "The Sordaneons have held the Rill inviolate for more than a thousand years, long before Alm ever set foot in the World. The Rill is their godhead, a sacred truth. It binds them—to the Hierarchate, to their people, and to Essera. And Dorilian considers it family. He really does. It's his ancestor. Dorilian has said, and I know that he will hold to it, that he will not discuss the Rill with Sordan's sworn enemies."

"He discussed all this with you?"

"I discussed it with him. I practically had to beat him into listening to me. I don't want to have to do that again. I don't think I can."

"This is it?"

"This is it. Make your peace with Sordan, Nalf Rhys, and give Amallar a chance at getting the Rill."

"Amallar to treat with Sordan—and you to lead us?" Fran Gorseddson stood defiantly at the rear of the others. The concealing folds of his hooded cloak hid his expression. "Why?"

"He won't give the Rill to people he can't trust. Why should he trust Nalf Rhys? Or you?"

"Or you?" Fran persisted. "Why the hells does he trust you?"

"Because I've never lied to him." As soon as he said it, Hans realized just how true that statement was—and how profound. He had never placed a falsehood between them. "And he has never lied to me."

"I'll believe that when I see it." But Nalf was clearly weighing those words alongside others in his shrewd but straightforward mind. "Trust that man too far, boy, and he'll take off your head. Them Highborn, they're not human, you know. Not like us. It's witchcraft that they live and breathe, and witchcraft that will get them. We'll take him for his Rill, all right for that, but we won't take him at his word. Be warned, though, we're taking you at yours! If that man turns on us, your back gets it first!"

"You still don't believe in me, do you?"

"Believe in you, what's that? I believe in what happens when all is done. That's what counts. That's what I believe in. If we can come out of this mess with the Rill in our land, then I guess Amallar can make its peace with Sordan."

"The negotiations will be difficult," Hans warned. "Sordan will demand that we make concessions."

"Then we'll demand concessions for us too, damn it," growled Fran.

Although secretly pleased to see the Neuberlander among the

men who had agreed to consider the alliance, Hans knew it was too soon to feel overjoyed. The Witan would appoint any team that negotiated on its behalf. Hans could only function as an intermediary between the hostile nations—a delicate balancing act at best and not one he particularly relished. Just a little of Dorilian's power, enough to say to either side, "This is it, this is what we are going to do," would have been a blessing. He sighed and fingered his Thegn brooch in the firelight, wondering when the type of power it symbolized would come to him. That, too, would emerge from the negotiations. He glanced again at the men facing him, waiting.

"The alliance will be negotiated through the Witan," he concurred. "For now, we must decide who is to go to Sordan in the morning."

No one answered him. Hans looked at the fifteen cruihcil leaders, keld-chieftains and elders, who had elected to come to him with the news of the Witan's decision. Many were old; most had never left Amallar. None of them looked prepared to make that journey or risk their lives on the chance that the Rill still could not be ridden by Khelds. Gazes slid away from his every attempt to meet them, avoiding having to offer their list of excuses. Fran alone met Hans's inquiry, but the Neuberlander was not a suitable candidate: Sordan held warrants for his arrest and execution that were valid enough to be used. And would be, until an agreement could be made granting him and other rebels amnesty.

"We have to send a delegation." Hans tried not to sound short. "I would go myself, but—"

"No," Nalf Rhys stated curtly. "You stay here."

"I had planned to. But if no one else will go, who am I supposed to send? This delegation will represent our agreement to set up talks between our nations. What will Sordan think when I send a couple of villagers and a cow? And I don't want to send Arne alone."

From where he stood beside Hans, Arne spoke out. "And I don't want to go alone, neither."

"I'll go." A firm, female voice drew all eyes across the room. Hans heard the bedchamber hanging fall heavily back into place as Aubrey came to stand before the men. She'd accompanied Hans from the ceremony, mainly because all her possessions were in his custody. Exhausted by a sleepless night and drained by stages of rage and emotion that had torn at her all morning, Aubrey had immediately fallen asleep on Hans's mattress. The sight of her coming from his sleeping chamber, obviously just arisen from bed, still wearing the clothes she had worn at the ceremony that morning, her hair tousled, her mouth faintly defiant, gave rise to a roomful of approving smiles. Only Fran Gorseddson shot her a dark scowl.

"I'll go to Sordan." Aubrey faced Hans as she said it. He alone of all the people in that crowded room understood the reasons why her blue gaze wore that look of passion.

He's not there, Hans wanted to say to her. *You won't find him there.* But surely, Aubrey knew that.

"I don't think—"

"Let her." Nalf's sharp expression revealed that he thought Hans would not send his woman into a trap, if indeed there was one. And if Aubrey did go, Hans would see to it that she, and the others, were held safe, or there would be hell to pay for it later. "She speaks and writes fluent Stauba, and she's sharp. I'll see to it you have six worthy others in the morning, all provisioned and ready to go with her."

It was fair. Knowing what Nalf Rhys was thinking, Hans had no choice but to agree. And who knew but Aubrey Amundda might reconcile Dorilian in her own mind once she had seen Sordan. But somehow, deep within that place in his heart that understood what Aubrey was trying to do, Hans knew that seeing Sordan would only make the man she sought to exorcise less real.

40

The Brotherhood was established by Covenant to
safeguard, facilitate, and administer the Rill's public
aspects: operations; schedules; communications; and the
generation of fees necessary to maintain parts of the system
for which the Order is entrusted. It never fell to the
Sordaneons to provide for or oversee those aspects. The
vital investment of the Sordaneons is generative and
political: communication with the Rill Entity itself, with
the goal of fulfilling the promise of Derlon's original
transformation.

PSILANT AMBIGON DIAMONES,

STUDENT'S INTRODUCTION TO THE ORDER OF EPOPTES

Trestethion.

The mere syllables chewed like worms at the base of
Quirin's brain, coiling within waking nightmares no
differently than Hestya had once done. Following the node's
surprising appearance, he had stared at the system schematic for
hours. So had dozens of Epoptes from each of the Brotherhood's
deeply trained disciplines—from Rill historians to core technicians,
operations savants to philosophers—delving into the whys and the
wherefores and, most importantly, the *how* of Trestethion.

The how was a bit of a mystery—though not to Quirin.

"The node is in Amallar and was never entered," the historians
said. "Even if the node could be awakened, the Sordaneons cannot
go there to perform that action."

One of the philosophers scoffed. "Have you achieved what
generations of scholars cannot and unraveled the full permutations
of Erydon's Promise?"

"The Rill—"

"Is in Amallar, yes," the philosopher agreed. "The Rill is also *Highborn*. And living, even in its current moribund state. So let us hold off on issuing lists of what the Highborn can and cannot do in Amallar."

Now, hours later, Quirin paced the carpet beneath the dome of his waterglobe-lit study. The trappings of his office should have bestowed more of a sense of permanence, of control. Instead he felt the approach of imminent disaster. He knew perfectly well how Trestethion had made an appearance and by meeting's end the gathered Brothers had agreed: Dorilian Sordaneon. Almost as terrifying as the new node was the possibility—perhaps even the certainty—that *Dorilian* had performed the awakening in person. In Amallar. But *why?*

Quirin wanted to know the particulars of *that*.

Hearing a soft cough behind him, Quirin turned his head. The stooped form of Brother Zeddeus stood just inside the room's gilded door panels. Zeddeus bowed and extended a silver tray.

"Eminence. A message has arrived."

On the tray glimmered an envelope of fine vellum ribboned with black and stamped with gold. Grand Mage Phlebbos. A chill of distaste crawled down the back of Quirin's neck but he picked up the message, breaking the seal after Zeddeus had departed. Upon separation, the cracked wax released a faint spark. Quirin's gaze skimmed the black, coded letters and he scowled.

At the Conclave two months earlier, Quirin had removed Phlebbos as Head at Dazunor-Rannuli. His reasons had been twofold: to mitigate Dorilian's obvious retaliation against that mount's perceived offenses, in hope of prompting the Sordaneon to restore Rill service; and to make less obvious the Order's collaboration with the Prince Regent's ally, Mormantalorus. Despite the military and economic advantages provided by that alliance, Mormantalorus was... problematic.

For that reason, so was Phlebbos's request.

Quirin summoned his chamberlain and indicated that he would receive the Grand Mage and his guest in the ceremonial hall attached to the Psilant's residence; the building was private and Quirin ordered there should be no staff in attendance. He would trust to the chamber's *Ir*-warded walls and his personal devices to provide a veneer of safety—times were too dangerous to do otherwise. To enhance his status, he wore his tall cap of jeweled velvet and the richly embroidered cape of his office. Both adornments were heavy; if the meeting went long, he would emerge with a headache.

When the Mormantaloran entered the porphyry-paneled hall, Quirin was seated atop a dais on a high-backed chair bearing the insignia of his office. Carved and gilded images of the Rill and the famed deeds of Psilants past graced the chamber walls. Such a setting would imbue any man with confidence. Even so Phlebbos, after ushering his guest into the room, hung back several steps in an unbecoming way that signaled warning. Quirin tensed.

Arcane power radiated from the visitor. Amber *Ir* gems glinted from lattices clasping the man's exposed temples and forehead and shone murkily from under strands of white hair. Unnaturally dark eyes dominated a face graced with an aquiline nose and arrogant mouth, Staubaun beauty at its purest. A collar of red *Ir* jewels, capable of housing vast energy, hung atop the man's velvet neckline. Rich garments of deep purple leather and silk clothed muscular limbs, a look furthermore capped by a cloak of midnight fur tipped with silver. Each forward step of the visitor's dark boots was accompanied by an aura of malice.

Quirin had met Nammuor Varehos only once, though memorably, at Dorilian Sordaneon's wedding to Nammuor's sister. Even then Nammuor had been renowned for *Ir* magework. People called him Sorcerer, a designation earned many times over. Quirin gestured for Phlebbos to leave and watched with a frown his subordinate's haste to scamper away. The great doors to the chamber closed before Quirin broke the silence.

"Nuarch," he acknowledged. That Quirin spoke first proved little; that he did not bend his neck upon using that lofty title said more. Though Quirin was nominally the host, Nammuor outranked him.

Nammuor brushed aside the disrespect. "Psilant."

"Your visit surprises me. Are you even welcome in this City?"

There was something slightly off about Nammuor's smile. Something sly and knowing. "Permephedon is a neutral City, open to all. A Promise made by the Three."

Nammuor made no acknowledgement of the allegations that might have barred his presence. Perhaps it was true that Nammuor had not been at Permephedon on the day of the Demise. Quirin *had* been here and had not seen him—but he *had* seen Dorilian

Sordaneon. Bloodied. Desperate. Already half-mad. To judge by recent developments, that madness persisted.

Quirin decided to tread carefully.

"I don't know what business you have with the Order that cannot be handled more discreetly by... our usual arrangements. We do not exist to serve governments, even that of Essera's King—or Prince Regent—and we certainly do not serve to advance the interests of a nation that has seceded from this Triempery."

"This Triempery that the Wall and Rill built? This Triempery someone is currently using the Rill to destroy? Yes. Well, I was hoping you would wish to put a stop to that." Nammuor's black gaze weighed Quirin anew. "I do."

"This Order will not—*cannot*—allow ourselves to be drawn into your quarrel with the Sordaneons."

"You still equate them with the Rill?"

"That the Sordaneons are Rillbound is not a matter of what I *or* you equate."

Nammuor's eyes creased with a smile so cold it caused Quirin's skin to pebble. "Not entirely, no. I have had this conversation recently with concerned members of the Seven Houses. Even you surely can agree that Dorilian is not the Rill. Not *yet*. Maybe never. No Sordaneon since Derlon has ever actually achieved integration. Some scholars believe it may be impossible."

Quirin among them. Nammuor surely knew that much if he had studied the matter at all. The letters in which Quirin had published his conclusions had been widely circulated. "And what do you believe?"

"I believe Dorilian knows he cannot do it."

Quirin drew a deep breath. An accurate assessment. For all the Hierarch's bluster, Dorilian fought as fiercely to not engage with his birthright as he did to claim it. That several of Dorilian's talented Sordaneon ancestors had attempted to join bodily with the Rill Entity and *failed* surely factored into his hesitation. No one knew what success would resemble—except obliteration. The question here was not what Dorilian might do, but what Nammuor wanted.

"Nuarch, please. I don't believe you're here to debate Dorilian Sordaneon's divinity."

"No. His instability. His capacity to command the Rill may be limited, but it has become dangerous."

"If you have only now reached *that* conclusion, you are trailing the pack." Dorilian had been dangerous to Nammuor, and the Triempery, for years. This kind of blunt attempt to drive home the point was almost disappointing.

"I but wish to offer my help if you wish to... contain him."

"An offer you made also to the Seven Houses?"

"They declined my assistance."

Quirin would need to learn more about what had been offered—and what the Seven Houses had refused. At the moment, however, he faced Nammuor without access to that information. Quirin steepled his fingers atop his velvet vestments. "We are not interested in assassination."

"Neither am I."

Possibly true. The Sordaneon bloodline was imperiled and even Mormantalorus must see value in preserving the Rill, if only for making Essera or Sordan a useful conquest. Even to that end, however, Mormantalorus held a valuable card: the child Levyathan was Nammuor's nephew. Nammuor already had a strong claim to the bloodline.

"I don't understand what you are proposing."

"Capture. Imprisonment. Neutralizing the threat. It's been done before."

With Labran. Dorilian escaped Stefan's plan. "Do you think we have not pursued such a plan? For ten years we have rendered Dorilian helpless in Sordan." It was important that Nammuor know how well Quirin understood Highborn prisons. In this matter, he knew something Nammuor did not. "Enemies to every side, no path forward, safe in the City of his Entity. You played a part in that, as did the Seven Houses. As did Stefan and the Khelds, until that ended too soon." A look of interest. Nammuor did not know. "Dorilian has broken free. He has fled the safety of his cage."

Nammuor's feral expression hardened. "Do you know where he is?"

It amused Quirin to discover the dregs of the day's revelations could taste sweet. "Not precisely. You are aware, of course, that the Rill was witnessed to have sent a *charys* south from Permephedon, and that it bypassed the Mount at Dazunor-Rannuli?"

"Yes."

"You came to me to find out where it went—and what that might mean to your plans. Don't play me for a fool, Nuarch. I know many things you never will. And I have my fingers on the pulse of a god."

Quirin lifted his left hand which bore the First Ring of Order and displayed that he possessed six fingers, the proof of Aryati blood in his veins.

Nammuor's regard on him turned inward, reflecting. Quirin's barb had landed as intended.

"You call Dorilian dangerous," Quirin continued. "You do not know the half of the peril that misconceived troublemaker threatens to call down upon us. Do you know that the Rill has spawned a new node? A new mount? And that this new mount is in Amallar?"

"Amallar?" Nammuor tilted his head. Doubt, quickly followed by hard-eyed realization.

"There was a dormant node along the primary run. Trestethion. Never opened. A dark blip on the map until it appeared today, bright as a star." Quirin smirked. "The Prince Regent surely noticed the Rill passage. How not? Thousands saw it, saw the *charys* leave and saw it pass them by. All Dazunor-Rannuli must surely be abuzz. Array messages are bouncing throughout Essera, bearing the joyous news that the Rill has resumed running. Naturally, the Prince Regent made certain you heard it from him first. And you are here because only *you* could have traveled to Permephedon so quickly—and expect to be received in person."

Confirmation of that assessment glowered back at Quirin, unamused. "And this *charys* went to that new node? To Amallar?"

"We have every reason to believe so."

"And Dorilian?" Impatience clipped the name to a razor edge. "Is that where *he* is?"

"We do not know. But it stands to reason that Trestethion is where he *was*. Rill nodes do not activate by spontaneous generation." Quirin rose to his feet, adding height to his presentation. Like Nammuor, Quirin too was tall and aware of his advantages. "What is clear is that Dorilian has become a danger to us all. He means to unleash the Khelds upon Essera, upon his enemies and the World. He saw the ruin Stefan caused and he intends to finish the job. He wishes to seize the Rill for his own purposes and his alone."

"I think he has done that already. You will be next, Psilant." Nammuor's sneer revealed perfect teeth. "Dazunor-Rannuli is still silent. Dead to the World. Make no mistake, Dorilian will leverage his Rill to remove you from his path. All of you! What need has he of your Brotherhood now? He may well bear Derlon's gifts in his blood! He will demand a more orderly Brotherhood, or none at all."

Quirin stepped down from the dais onto the mosaic floor and walked to the wall of tall, arched windows that overlooked Permephedon's Rill Mount. A glance over his shoulder at Nammuor standing still in the same place, unwilling to join Quirin in gazing upon the Entity. Beautiful and somber. A coiled shadow. The device Quirin wore behind his ear, concealed by his hat of blue velvet, detected the way Nammuor's malevolence tainted the room.

Does he have it with him? Even the thought chilled Quirin's blood. The Diadem of the Devaryati, fabled and deadly. Nammuor was rumored to have found it. If he bore the device on his person, it made sense that Nammuor would not wish to approach nearer.

The Rill was vivid tonight, aglow for the first time in weeks. An Entity in the full of its power.

"What do you want of the Order?" Quirin asked.

"Of the Order?" Nammuor shook his head. "Nothing. Against the danger Dorilian poses to me and this World, your Order is of little use except as purveyors of mage arts. You make exceptional waterglobes. Your mages are more skilled at large arrays than my crystalliers."

Quirin frowned, then nodded. Permephedon's Sages and Sordan's Rill technicians had studied Aryati installations for generations and possessed great understanding of how to construct stable stationary arrays, though many of those skills had been lost following the Second Ardaenan War and, later, the War of Succession. Now that another war lapped at their heels there was great risk of losing even more of that knowledge. Particularly if Dorilian had his way.

Nor was Dorilian the only misbegotten royal on Essera's crowded game board. Handurin Stauberg-Randolph was emerging as a potentially much bigger problem—hinging on whether the Kheldish prince was still alive, of course. It was entirely possible that Dorilian, while he was in Amallar, might have rid himself of Handurin. Quirin even dared to hope for it.

"Too many pieces are in motion," Quirin decided. "I will do nothing until this situation sorts itself out."

"A pity. I don't plan to wait for that. I have dealt with Trongor in ways you will soon hear about. When news reaches your ears, pay attention." Nammuor's handsome face went flat and cold. "Dorilian has left Sordan. Thank you for telling me."

"He will almost certainly return on that *charys*."

"You are probably right. But he will not stay there. He has

started his war and that means he will be vulnerable— if not immediately then soon." With a flare of his cloak of silver-tipped midnight, Nammuor turned to leave. "Dorilian Sordaneon is about to become your worst nightmare, Psilant—and as much as he wants to be rid of me, he also wants to be rid of *you*. I will see you again when you are ready to be rid of *him*."

END

To be continued in
Book 5 of the Triempery Revelations:

The Walled City

KINDLY TURN THE PAGE FOR
A PREVIEW OF

THE
WALLED
CITY

When night had fallen and the other Khelds had sought their beds, Aubrey remained restless. She roamed the suite provided for her stay until she exhausted its comforts and luxuries. The terrace beckoned, so she sought the coolness and quiet of Rillglow-brightened stone. The Kheld delegation was being housed in the Sordaneons' own wing, and she, being the only woman, had been given an apartment of her own. Even the garden outside her door was isolated and private, meandering between terraces and walks from which the City could be viewed.

Is this where you stood, so many weeks ago, when you contemplated going to Amallar? She could imagine Dorilian here. This magnificence, of all settings, suited his arrogance. *Why did you come to Amallar when you had all this? Is it any wonder that to you we seem so small? Hans is right: we could not have taken this from you. But that man in Essera, the Mormantaloran... can he?*

How powerful, then, Nammuor must be, to pose a threat to this City and the people in it. That had an Entity standing guard. And what of Amallar, which had not Sordan's defenses? How had its leaders allowed themselves to fall into the trap of believing that all Staubaun countries were like Essera, divided and corrupt, without growth and without honor? Was it because they were blind? Or were they merely envious?

"Envy seeks to destroy what might outshine it. Better a world in darkness than one that might seek another star."

Startled, Aubrey spun and pressed her hands against the wall at her back as a shadow emerged from the trees of the garden. She had not seen anyone there nor heard any approach. Her visitor's clothing of muted silver and gray blended with the night. Levyathan studied her as he came into the blended light of the Rill and the moon. Even as it did in Amallar, a full moon rode the skies above Sordan.

"I know you," he told her, "because he did." Something about the young Sordaneon Heir was changed from the boy she had seen earlier. He cocked his head to one side. "He was supposed to come back; he was supposed to be here tonight. Few knew where he had gone, and few knew to expect his return, so no one has questioned.

I have explained it to them and they know better than to dispute what I say. But I knew two nights ago that Dorilian would not be returning, that he had to flee Amallar prematurely. I knew that he had been driven from danger into danger. Do you wonder that I was prepared to hate you?" He sighed and turned, placing his elbows upon the rampart at her side. "I thought you would be awful. But you're not."

Stunned, Aubrey could not help but stare. Two nights ago would be the night she had discovered who Dorilian was. How could that news have reached Sordan so swiftly? Thron—Dorilian—had not had access to the Rill that night, not with the Faeduadan swarming all over the Rill mount, making sacrifices. He would not have taken the chance of getting caught.

"What do you know about that? Did Hans write that in his letter?" It chilled her to think that Hans would have betrayed her.

Levyathan shook his head. "No. Handurin keeps women's secrets as closely as those of men. In time he will become a trove of them. Yours is but one of the first."

"Then how?" she demanded, uncaring entirely that this was a Highborn Prince for all his youth, forgetting that he was a boy. Her tone alone constituted an offense.

Levyathan looked straight at her and spoke in perfect Khelda. "Do you really want to know—lady?"

Mother save me, he even says it with the same tone of voice, the same inflection! Aubrey, though she felt a sudden chill in the cool night air, could not look away from that penetrating gaze. Levyathan was not asking what had happened... because he already knew.

"You don't know what we are," he told her. "You have no idea."

THE WALLED CITY

COMING IN SPRING 2025
from Forest Path Books
https://forestpathbooks.com

Acknowledgements

A great many people go into a story, and most make it out alive. For those who did not, my deepest commiseration. Seeing as she has placed so much of herself in so many characters, this author barely survives most of her stories. So far, the author hasn't killed off any characters partly based on her children or siblings—but that's coming.

In The God Spear, the Triempery Revelations series acquires a new aspect deeply rooted in non-Highborn society. Khelds existed as supporting arcs of the first three books, though some characters and events hinted at their importance. In this book, they emerge as a full society and some Khelds become major players. The Highborn Triempery of old is pronounced dead. Long live whatever happens next.

At this point, the author would like to thank a few of the many people in her non-fictional world who contributed to the creation of this book.

Carol Dascanio, probably the most family-oriented person I know. While writing, whenever I encountered a Kheld mother or grandmother and needed to bring her to life, I would pause to ask: "What would Carol say or do?"

Thanks also to my comrades in bringing this book to publication. Christina Wooden, my first reader, who takes my raw writing without flinching and fearlessly tells me where the commas should go. Her notes and comments are pure gold and elevate the story. And let's not forget Copy Editor Carole, who polishes the edited books and may yet nitpick me into eradicating the other PC - "pronoun confusion." I promise I'm getting better.

Thanks to my publisher Forest Path Books for believing in this series and in me, and in doing such wonderful work in creating quality books for our readers.

I'm also deeply thankful for the artists I have worked with for this book and the series. They have brought so many of my creations to life: my amazing cover artist Larry Rostant, who captures the wonder and beauty of the Second Creation; Margarita Bourkova's magnificent illustrations of the Triempery's magical artifacts; Jamie Noble's vivid portraits of Nalf and a Dog Man yet to appear; Lazare's gorgeous posters of four of the Triempery's fantastical cities; and, of course, Thomas Rey's beautiful map of Amallar which accompanies this book.

My heartfelt appreciation to the readers and reviewers who have given my indie books a chance. João Guimarães, thank you for your support and letting me know you like my work. Joseph Poopinski, for what may be the most fun review of *Sordaneon* to date. Jamedi, of Jamreads Reviews, for contacting me out of the blue and for his continued interest in the series. Rebecca Crunden, for her support of indie writers and books, including mine. Fellow author A.J. Calvin, who, while writing her wonderful series, finds time to also read my series. And readers who might be curious about what I have to say about my books, characters, writing, and life can listen to my podcast interviews with the gang at Prickly Pens.

And of course, I must acknowledge my husband, Steve, for his many contributions to this book. He is my first editor, a taskmaster who excels at calling out omissions or excesses in scenes. Steve keeps characters in their lanes and plots and continuity front and center. As silent partners go, he's the best.

– L. L. Stephens

Triempery Appendix
CHARACTERS

MALYRDEONS—Past

Ergeiron One of The Three, son of Leur and Amynas. After his brother Derlon gave life to the Rill, Ergeiron founded the Wall, sealing dangerous Time Rifts opened during the Gweroyen War, protecting the Malyrdeon stronghold at Stauberg, and serving as a means by which his descendants could discern past and future events.

Cienorr Son of Ergeiron, founder of the Mormantalorus Nuarchate.

Telarion Son of Ergeiron and founder of the Stauberg Principate, first Esseran king and ancestor of current Malyrdeons.

Emrysen Wall Lord and great-grandson of Ergeiron, who bestowed a conditional pardon on the Hen Kyon.

Erremon King of Essera, great grandson of Emrysen. Slain by Ardaenan King Thorondar in the First War with Ardaen

Erydon Great-great grandson of Emrysen, who granted the Khelds the wilderness of Amallar for their homeland.

Endurin Last true Wall Lord and last Malyrdeon King of Essera. Endurin's Heir died unexpectedly, leaving only a natural daughter, who fled to sea and was caught in the Rift. Endurin later brought her son Marc Frederick back to the World.

Ariande Granddaughter of Endurin. Mother of Marc Frederick.

MALYRDEONS—Present (and associated characters)

Apollonia Queen of Essera (family name Halasseon); daughter of Elegiros, Prince of Tahlwent. Wife of Marc Frederick and mother of Jonthan.

Austell Wall Lord, third cousin of Endurin and distaff cousin to Marc Frederick. Brother of Enreddon II. Died in the Demise.

Elegiros Prince of Tahlwent (family name, Halasseon); third cousin to Endurin. Father of Apollonia. Died in the Demise.

Elhanan Son of Rheger Dannutheon; Wall-gifted; one-time tutor of Stefan and Dorilian at Permephedon. Deceased.

Enreddon II Prince of Stauberg; cousin to Endurin and distaff cousin to Marc Frederick. Scholarly, but not Wall-gifted, Enreddon supported Endurin when the aged king named Marc Frederick to be his Heir. Both of Enreddon's wives died in childbirth, failing to produce living sons. Later wed Palaistea. Died in the Demise.

Ionais Princess of Merrydn; daughter of Regelon and betrothed of Jonthan Stauberg-Randolph.

Ostemun Prince of Dannuth (family name, Dannutheon); distant cousin to the Stauberg Malyrdeons. Sired three daughters. Grandfather to Kerr. Died in the Demise.

PALAISTEA Princess of Lacenedon; daughter of Lakron. Married Enreddon II. Mother to Eldon II and Enreddon III, Heirs to Stauberg and Lacenedon. Deceased.

REGELON Prince of Merrydn (family name, Merrydeon); matrilineal cousin to Sebbord Teremareon. Father of Ionais, betrothed of Marc Frederick's son Jonthan. Died in the Demise.

RHEGER Prince of Hespera (family name Dannutheon); brother to Ostemun. Father of Elhanan. Possesses strong spatial ability and is one of few Malyrdeons who can use an enhancer for translocation. Deceased.

MARGARID A princess of Gweroyen who weds Elhanan. Daughter of Kathanos. Sister to Estevan IV Niarchos.

SORDANEONS — Past

DERLON One of The Three; known as the Rill-Giver because he integrated his immortal body and life with Rill's remnants, facilitating its rebirth. Epoptes believe Derlon's integration still directs the Rill's actions, though he has lost the ability to interact with other beings.

DEBEN I/II/III grandson and great-grandsons of Derlon (collectively known as the Three Debens), ushered in a Golden Age of Rill expansion and Triemperal growth that secured the Sordaneon dynasty. Builder/ creators of Leseos, Bynum, Gignastha, and the Vermillion Aqueduct.

PELEOR Son of Derlon; slain by the Aryati, who poisoned his blood and spilled it on the mount at Simelon to be absorbed by the Rill. His blood still stains the platform and Rill structures.

TARLON Hierarch of Sordan during the Second War with Ardaen. The youngest of his three sons wed an Ardaenan princess to secure the truce. Tarlon was the last manifested Rill Lord, able to communicate with and influence the Entity. Opened the Rill node at Randpory Crossing.

SORDANEONS — Present (and associated characters)

DAIMONAERIS Princess of Mormantalorus. Daughter of Camas, the Mormantaloran Nuarch; half-sister of Nammuor. Married Dorilian. Mother of Levyathan II. Deceased.

DEBEN IV Sordan's Heir and regent. Son of the captive Hierarch, Labran, and Ermenthalia, daughter of Mezentius, Prince of Suddekar. Deeply paranoid, Deben had not set foot outside of Sordan's Serat in thirty-five years. Married Valyane, daughter of Sebbord Teremareon. Father of Dorilian and Levyathan I. Died in the Demise.

DELEUS Son of the Heir to Suddekar; great-grandson of Mezentius and grandson of Sebbord. Although a first cousin to Dorilian, Deleus is not Highborn.

DELOS Deben IV's twin brother. Son of Labran. Used the Lacenedon Crown to break the Vermillion Aqueduct and end the siege at Gignastha. Died after that deed from plasm shock.

DORILIAN Son of Deben IV and Valyane. Brother of Levyathan I. At the age of seven, witnessed his mother's murder. His precocious physical and empathic gifts allowed him to save his neonate brother. Determined to right wrongs done to his family.

ERMENTHALIA Daughter of Mezentius and a Mormantaloran princess. Wife of Labran, mother of Deben IV. Bears title of Gracious Hierarchessa. Inclined to favor alliance with Mormantalorus, from which her mother hailed.

LABRAN Grandson of Tarlon; his mother was a princess of Ardaen. He wed Ermenthalia, daughter of Mezentius, Bas of Suddekar, and is father of Deben IV and grandfather of Dorilian. He objected to Endurin Malyrdeon naming Marc Frederick as Heir to Essera and at Marc Frederick's coronation refused to acknowledge him as King. Labran fought his way into the Rill node at Permephedon and was able to command the Rill to stop running, creating wide-spread panic. Taken captive by Marc Frederick and considered too dangerous to release, Labran was imprisoned at Stauberg, far from any active Rill nodes.

LEVYATHAN I Son of Deben IV and Valyane. Grandson to Labran and Sebbord. Brother to Dorilian. When enemies poisoned his mother, Levyathan was born months too soon to survive. Although saved by Dorilian, Levyathan's development was affected, and he suffered neurological deficits. Deceased.

LEVYATHAN II Son of Daimonaeris and Deben, raised by Dorilian as his own son. Heir to Sordan.

MEZENTIUS (family name Suddekeon); Bas of Suddekar. He wed a princess of Mormantalorus. His eldest daughter Ermenthalia wed Labran and gave birth to Deben IV. Died in the Demise.

SEBBORD (family name Teremareon), Prince of Teremar. Possibly Rill-gifted, Sebbord trained as an Epopte and rose to the level of Archmage in service to the Rill. He wed twice and sired three daughters. Grandfather of Dorilian, Levyathan, Deleus and Tiflan.

TIFLAN (family name Morevyen). Bas of Teremar. Grandson of Sebbord but not Highborn. Seven feet tall, he is Dorilian's first cousin and a loyal ally.

VALYANE Princess of Teremar. Sebbord's daughter, wife to Deben IV. Mother of Dorilian and Levyathan I.

LEGON (family name Rebiran) Son of Terveryen, Bas of Anit-Rebir. Youngest of six sons. Sent to Sebbord as a boy to enter Sordaneon service. Dorilian's friend. Commander of the Eagle Guard.

TERVERYEN (family name Rebiran) Bas of Anit-Rebir. Father of Legon and Cressida.

TUTTO (family name Rhunnard) An Estol who served as Sebbord's sword master and now serves Dorilian. Later Bas of Kolgya.

SINON (family name Kouranos) Marc Frederick's administrator in Sordan during that city's occupation; later governor of Neuberland. Stefan's Archhalial Ambassador. Shifted allegiance to become Dorilian's Archhalial Ambassador.

BERSYAS (family name Garheleon) One of Dorilian's generals.

Pandaros (family name Vidyamemnon) One of Dorilian's generals.

Noemi Wet nurse to the infant Levyathan I, later his governess. Mother of Fahme. Deceased.

Raxa Levyathan II wet-nurse, trained by Noemi.

Thuraya (family name Lares) Sage Physician; Dorilian's house physician.

Heran (family name Albos) Mormantaloran agent. Wed Noemi. Father of Fahme.

Fahme Princess of Sordan. Noemi's daughter by Heran. Adopted by Dorilian.

Haeskos (family name Periskleron) Dorilian's Admiral.

Quirin (family name Chrysolemnos) Psilant, or leader, of the Brotherhood of Epoptes.

Pitar (family name Kisthoda) Arch Epopte/Mage; chief at Dazunor-Rannuli.

Tharos (family name Odakkon) Epopte at Sordan.

Pallas (family name Trophoneos) Speaker of the Sordan Halia.

STAUBERG-RANDOLPH (and associated characters)

Marc Frederick King of Essera; great-grandson of Endurin Malyrdeon through his son Estevan II and Brenna Almarresda. Son of Ariande Malyrdeon and William Randolph. Considered a Malyrdeon in recognition of his relation to and support from them, but he is not Highborn. Marc Frederick first married Thora, a Kheld woman. After Thora died of a miscarriage, he wed the Highborn princess Apollonia as a condition to becoming Endurin's Heir. He has two children: Emyli, his daughter by Thora, and Jonthan, his son by Apollonia. Died in the Demise and interred in the Vault of Incorruption.

Emyli Daughter of Marc Frederick and Thora; was betrothed to Deben IV Sordaneon but ran away at age fourteen with charismatic Kheld rebel Erwan Cedrecson. The pair wed and Emyli gave birth to Erwan's son, Stefan. To free Erwan from prison, Emyli helped Kheld rebels gain access to the stronghold of Gignastha, resulting in three Highborn deaths and the bloody siege of that city. She later gave birth to her second son, Handurin.

Jonthan Son of Marc Frederick and Apollonia. Prince of Dazunor. Married Ionais, princess of Merrydn. Their union was childless.

Stefan Son of Emyli and Erwan; grandson of Marc Frederick and adopted by him after Jonthan's death. Succeeds Marc Frederick as King of Essera. Marries Nilla Lowenda. Deceased.

Hans (full name Handurin) Son of Emyli, reputed son of Erwan. Grandson of Marc Frederick. Brother to Stefan.

Gareth (family name Morgen) Marc Frederick's steward, in charge of his household.

Trevor (family name Allen) Captain of King's Guard.

Marenthro Wizard of Permephedon; ageless and possibly immortal. No one knows much about him save that he is apparently benign and possesses both Wall and Rill affinity. Responsible for finding Marc Frederick for Endurin and bringing him back to this World.

MORMANTALORUS (and associated characters)

NAMMUOR (family name Varehos) Ruler of Mormantalorus, half-brother to Daimonaeris. Reputed to have Aryati blood. Has recovered the lost Diadem of the Devaryati. Responsible for the Demise. Is intent on collecting the blood and lifeforces of the remaining Highborn princes.

OARZAS Nammuor's Chief Crystallier.

CORAM (family name Barzanes) Was with Nammuor at the Demise. Nammuor's emissary to Stefan. An adept in mage arts.

BAMATU Archmage at Aral.

SALKREN ZEL Mormantaloran general. With Nammuor at the Demise.

SEVEN HOUSES (and associated characters)

CHYRALANE (family name Rannuleon) Denizen of Phaer, most prominent of the Seven Houses. Daughter of a Highborn prince of Rannul. Opposed to any action that would lessen the cartel's control over the Rill. Very tall.

RHYNOS (family name Tybenos) Denizen of Koillos.

IPHITHUS (family name Kheprion) Nephew and heir to Chyralane.

Geron (family name Thoptis) Denizen of House Thoptis.

PHILEMON LEANDER Wealthy Staubaun merchant, not noble but aspiring to the nobility. His daughter married the Denizen of House Haralambdos.

ESSERAN STAUBAUNS (and associated characters)

ASPHALLADRA (family name Velos) Youngest daughter of the Enlad of Chennor; wed Cullen Brodheson. Sister to Zoranna.

JARON VELOS Enlad of Chennor. Father of Asphalladra and Zoranna. Ambitious nobleman intent on arranging high-ranking mates for his three daughters.

PALIMIA (family name Attora) Daughter of a high-ranking Sordani noble killed to facilitate confiscation of his estates. Later married Eldonus Kastryon. Mistress to Marc Frederick, and later Dorilian. Deceased.

ERENOR THOLEROS Cousin to the Halasseon rulers of Tahlwent; grandson of a natural daughter of Elegiros. Friend of Stefan. Regent to Hans and Prince Regent of Essera.

KONDROS (family name Bragord) Ally of Erenor.

ESTEVAN IV (family name Niarchos) Bas of Gweroyen. Son of Kathanos. Maternal grandson of Estevan III, last Highborn Prince of Gweroyen.

KATHANOS (family name Niarchos) Archon of Peleddor. Father of Estevan. Friend of Emyli. Son of Smaragda.

HEBRON (family name Ursenos). Cousin to Lakron, Prince of Lacenedon, and Palaistea. Bas Regent and later Bas of Lacenedon.

Machon Epirosi Archon of Penrhu. Breeder of blood horses.

Alban Eskeros Gignasthan lord whose lodge Dorilian used during his rebellion.

Phellan Illarion Bas of Serrain, married to Linne, one of Ostemun Dannutheon's daughters. Father of Lucien and Raphelon. Deceased.

Lucien Illarion Heir to Serrain. Supporter of Stefan.

Raphelon Illarion Younger brother to Lucien.

Grenant Aigelleros Minor lord loyal to Ostemun. Wed Raeva, eldest of Ostemun's daughters. Father of Kerr.

Kerr (family name Aigelleros) Son of Grenant and Raeva. Grandson of Ostemun. Nephew of Rheger and cousin of Elhanan and Raphelon.

Burelan (family name Phaeros) Bas of Rannul. Grandson of the last Prince of Rannul. Deceased.

Euella (family name Phaeros) Burelan's sister. Basarchessa of Rannul.

Arton (family name Metagoras) Third son of the Archon of Eddethel (Merrydn). Assistant to Cullen Brodheson. Wed Euella Phaeros Deceased.

Zepheron (family name Elmarachos) Admiral of Essera's Royal Navy.

KHELDS (and associated characters)

Arne Anseldson Friend and companion to Hans; a slave whose freedom Hans purchased in Ben Aranath on his journey to Sordan.

Brec Anseldson Arne's older brother. Nephew of Robdan Aelfricson.

Nalf Rhys Current Thegnard (leader) of the Thegnkeld, the foremost clan of Amallar. Follower of Stefan. Uncle of Aubrey.

Aubrey Amundda Daughter of Amund Rhys and Vallsa Elslethboern. Niece of Nalf Rhys. Cousin of Cullen Brodheson. Friend of Nilla and Lark. Inherited a king's grant in Neuberland.

Lark Rappeleye Friend of Aubrey and Nilla. High clan; Rune Daughter.

The Bog Crone Mythical old woman who lives in the Bogs/Fens. Aubrey, Lark, and Nilla encountered the Bog Crone, who then read their runes upon her Wheel.

Cullen Brodheson Cousin and best friend to Stefan. Keeper of the King's Trade. Enlad (later Archon) of Heddros & Wyre. Wed Asphalladra. Deceased.

Erwan Cedrecson Son of Cedrec Aelfricson; ran off with young Emyli Stauberg-Randolph. She later bore his sons, Stefan and Hans. Died at Gignastha.

Tobold Forbasson Thegnard (leader) of the Thegnkeld, the foremost clan of Amallar. Died at the Demise.

Lowen Toboldson Son of Tobold and father of Nilla.

Cedrec Aelfricson Late Kheld representative to the Triemperal Archhalia. Father to Erwan. Grandfather to Stefan and Hans. Died at the Demise.

Nilla Lowenda Daughter of Lowen Toboldson and niece of Goff Horvadson. Marries Stefan. Murdered by Erenor.

ROBDAN AELFRICSON Cedrec's youngest brother; a scribe. Uncle to Stefan and Hans.

RESSANY ROBDANSDA Robdan's oldest daughter; widow of Bren Forbasson, a Kheld noble executed for Stefan's murder. Holder of good land. Mother of seven.

TRELLA ROBDANSDA Robdan's middle daughter, mother of Remi

WYTHA ROBDANSDa Robdan's youngest daughter.

GERD RALFSON Innkeeper at Rhodhur Hall. Formerly cooked for Cullen Brodheson.

WODD Chief of Aubrey Amundda's holdermen; his wife Hild serves as steward of Aubrey's holding in Neuberland.

FRANWELF GORSEDDSON Foremost general of Neuberland's Kheld forces. Friend and former lover of Aubrey Amundda.

MOTHER EWLYS One of the Old Mothers of Rhodhur's Barrowwood.

MOTHER AEGDNIS Chief of Rhodhur's Old Mothers.

OTHER CHARACTERS

THAA non-human. Rift Guardian; the Dark Watcher. Aligned with Marenthro.

ENDELARIN (family name Nemenor) King of Ardaen, brother to the throne queen. Romantic and rumored to have one hundred wives. Cousin to the Sordaneons and fond of reminding them of it.

HERBERTH (family name Tammet) Elector of Trongor.

FARRL (family name Hennek) Captain of Trongor.

MELENTHAS (family name Helaosun) Princess of Merced, daughter of King Galanthius. Prospective bride for Dorilian Sordaneon.

GALANTHIAS (family name Helaosun) King of Merced, father of Melenthas. The island nation of Merced, while economically allied with Sordan, embraces ties with Nammuor.

JOOAR ZETHARNNA A prince of Lahgael, not in the line of succession. Governor of Ben Aranath.

BARAN REDHARG Hen Kyon leader, Lord of Gloanneach. Looks human.

ENTITY-BOUND DEVICES

THE LEUR'S RING Fashioned from the body of The Leur as last living act. Rejects non-Leur flesh and can only be worn by the Highborn. Used at coronations to identify the true king of Essera (Heir of Ergeiron). Manipulates real world/Leur's Creation. Removes barriers. Opens doors. Reveals truth and restores Leur's reality.

THE RILL STONE Device created by Derlon, who encapsulated his immortal blood in Rill matrix. The Rill Stone will identify a Sordaneon who wears it by glowing green. The Rill recognizes Sordaneon wearers and will not arm itself or lock locations against them. Can be used to burn a permanent Eagle mark onto any other substance, including human skin.

THE **WALL STONE** Shard of the Wall containing Ergeiron's immortal essence. It connects directly to the Wall, regardless of proximity, and must be used carefully by individuals open to its gifts. Allows wielder to peer into discreet temporal flows. The Wall Stone unlocks the Aidion and provides access to the Archive, which it assists in revealing.

OTHER ENTITIES

THE **DIADEM** The Undying Crown; the Diadem of the Devaryati. Pre-Devastation device created in secret by the Aryati from the immortal core that remained of Vllyr after that god was destroyed by Amynas and the Leur. Generates and commands arcane forces. Vastly powerful when fully tapped into an immortal being. Retains vestige of Vllyr's godhood. Malevolently self-aware and fixated on destroying that which destroyed Vllyr. Succeeded in corrupting the Aryati, destroying Mulsor and the First Creation.

GREATER ENHANCERS

SORDAN CORONAL Also called Derlon's Crown. Most powerful of the Greater Diadems. Now in possession of the Sordaneons.

STAUBERG CORONAL Also called the Star Crown; Ergeiron's Crown. Now in possession of the Malyrdeons.

MORMANTALORUS CORONAL Also called the Crown of Fire; Ciennor's Crown. Now in possession of Mormantalorus and its ruler.

LACENEDON CROWN Also called Ulnossi's Bane. Used by Delos Sordaneon to break the Vermillion Aqueduct.

OTHER DEVICES

DERLON'S ARMOR The fabled Eagle Breastplate, helm, gauntlets & greaves. When activated sheaths the wearer's torso and limbs. Kinetic negation. Any blow to the armor is absorbed. Invincible to nearly all weapons.

SWORD OF AMYNAS Also known as Derlon's Sword or the Gweroyen Sword. Greatest of the tullun blades made from Vllyr's skeleton. Most effective when paired with more powerful enhancers.

RINGS OF ORDER Three rings created by Derlon Sordaneon before the Inception. Used in accessing Rill stations and communicating with the Overlay. The Head Epopte (Psilant) keeps one of the rings.

BACKGROUND — Highborn Origins

ARYATI Human strain engineered to replicate the powers and immortality of Leur. Creators of greater and lesser devices that generate quasi-magical powers. The Aryati rose to extraordinary heights through genetic manipulation and technology but were arrogant and acquisitive; they ultimately destroyed their world. A remnant of the Aryati survived into the new Creation but most were slain following their defeat by the Highborn during the Gweroyen Wars. The survivors scattered. No pureblood Aryati survive but the strain persists in noble Staubaun lineages.

LEUR Immortal beings that created the World. Elusive, mostly hidden from humans until technological advances revealed them. Leur magic built the Five Cities, each in a day, and, combined with Aryati technology, engineered the living matrix of the Rill. During the Devastation brought by the Aryati, the Leur sacrificed itself to create the temporal disjunction that preserved the Creation. The lone Leur survivor mated their immortal bloodline with that of the Aryati clone-prince Amynas, conceiving three immortal sons known as The Three.

MALYRDEON Descendants of Ergeiron, one of the three sons of the gods Amynas and Leur; Ergeiron settled in what is now Stauberg, where he created the Wall as a barricade against the Rift. The Wall exists throughout all Time. Some descendants of Ergeiron are able to "walk the Wall" and by that means divine future events or reveal the truth or import of past events.

SORDANEON Descendants of Derlon, second of the three sons of the gods Amynas and Leur. Derlon settled Sordan, home to one of the surviving Five Cities of Leur, from which he gave life to the Rill by melding his immortal body with that of the vast machine. The descendants of Derlon carry the potential to connect with and communicate with the Rill, which would allow them to alter the god-machine's operation and physical structure.

HUMAN RACES

HIGHBORN Males descended from the immortal sons of Leur and the human Amynas. Leur traits pass only to male offspring, who must mate with human females to reproduce. For this reason, the adage is that the Highborn take the race of their mothers. Almost exclusively, the Highborn have chosen to reproduce using Staubaun lineages.

STAUBAUN A people originally created by (and related to) the Aryati and still manifesting some traits of the parent race. Some can wield lesser devices. Tall, fair-skinned, brown or gold-eyed blondes, beardless (with little body hair), Staubauns are intelligent and long-lived. They also, after generations of success and prosperity, tend to be rich and privileged.

ESTOL An amalgamation of races, the general population. Disdained as mongrels by Staubauns, Estols nonetheless rise to positions of influence and become minor nobility. Most are servants, laborers, soldiers and craftsmen. Because they are of mixed blood, Estols can have any human color of eyes, hair, or skin.

KHELD A barbaric people that entered Essera through the Rift during a period of instability following the First War with Ardaen. Khelds generally have blue or green eyes. They also have dark hair, sturdy builds and are shorter. Adult males are usually bearded. Their language is completely separate, as are their ways of life. Kheld naming differs from the Staubaun, as does their system of inheritance.

NEMENOR A seafaring people that forms the ruling families of Ardaen, Callorn, Lahgael, and the Isles of Maskos. Traditional enemies of the Triempery in the past, a marriage by treaty to a younger son of the Hierarch of Sordan instilled Ardaenan Nemenor blood into the lineage of the Highborn Sordaneons.

NONHUMAN RACES

LEUR A magical race, as explained above, creators of the original World and the tripartite Creation they fashioned to salvage it from destruction. Originally the Leur people inhabited the area now known as the Bogs, a marshy delta where the Dazun River flows into the sea. The last Leur was slain by the Devaryati and the race is now only legend.

HEN KYON The Dog Men, created by the Aryati as hunters and servants, specifically to track down and kill the magic-gifted offspring of Amynas and Leur. Intelligent and reclusive, the Hen Kyon are bipedal, often with fur covering parts or all of their bodies. The most true-to-breed have long, wolfish faces with well-developed olfactory organs. They have incredible stamina and strength. They can interbreed with humans, from which race they were originally fashioned. The Hen Kyon nearly eradicated the young Highborn race. Though they later repented their deeds, the Dog Men were abhorred and hunted nearly into extinction until the Malyrdeon King Emrysen cloaked them in obscurity and gave them the haunted wilds of the Kragh in which to live unmolested. They have since become feared and avoided.

PLACES (background)

(MENA)TROHIANA The Second Creation. The present World that moves forward in Time.

(MENA)TANTAUREUS Archived world/Past world, living remnant of the First Creation. Birthplace of Marc Frederick.

GSCH The World of Fire. The moment of Devastation, forever happening, never completed. A single moment in Time that has both already occurred and will never occur.

FIVE CITIES Eternal cities built in the First Creation by Leur and continuing in the Second Creation. Îs (vanished), Permephedon, Sordan, Mormantalorus, and Mulsor (destroyed).

MULSOR Destroyed in the Devastation. As a Leur creation part of it remains eternal. A ghost city whose appearance portends doom.

DALN BARRIER Created by Leur to separate the World in Time. Past World/Gsch/Current World.

THE RIFT Transient instabilities in the Daln Barrier that permit passage between the Past World and the Current World. The appearance of Mulsor is one such occurrence.

TRIEMPERY A confederation comprised of three aligned Highborn empires: Essera, Sordan, and Mormantalorus.

ESSERA

STAUBERG Capital city of Essera. Home of the Malyrdeons. Major seaport. Location of the Wall. Site of a dormant Rill mount.

ASAE ERANOS The Malyrdeon Serat or Malyrdeon Tower. Royal palace in Stauberg.

AIDION Heart of the Wall. Located under the shrine at the Gate of Transformation. Where gifted Malyrdeons walk the Wall.

GATE OF TRANSFORMATION Original city gate of Stauberg. Transformed by Ergeiron and now site of a shrine.

ELEUTHERON Domain also ruled by the Prince of Stauberg. Rich and deep in history.

BYNUM Foremost city of the Eleutheron.

DANAE PALACE Princess Palaistea's seat. Near Bynum.

GWEROYEN Domain in Essera, north of Stauberg. Former stronghold of the Aryati.

ENNSA Capital city of Gweroyen.

IDDOLEA Destroyed city in Gweroyen. Former capital of the Aryati.

PERMEPHEDON City-State presided over by Marenthro. One of the three remaining Five Cities. Neutral seat of the Triempery and home of the Triemperal Archhalia. Northernmost Rill city and a major Rill hub.

HIGH CITADEL Central redoubt of Permephedon's city core. Also called Marenthro's Tower. The Leur Arcana and Harmonic Hall are here, as are the Archhalia Chambers.

JEWEL TOWER Malyrdeon tower. Floats above the Mirror in Permephedon's city core.

SORDANEON TOWER Sordaneon hold in Permephedon's city core. Congruent with the Rill, which it is near.

LACENEDON Domain in Essera, north and east of Permephedon.

KENELM Capital city of Lacenedon. Site of a dormant Rill mount.

SERRAIN Domain in Essera, just west of Permephedon

SIMELON Capital city of Serrain. Site of a dormant Rill mount.

RANNUL Domain in Essera.

TERNA Capital city of Rannul.

DAZUNOR Principality in Essera, holding of Essera's Heir.

DAZUNOR-RANNULI Pre-eminent city in Essera due to its position on the Dazun River and presence of a major Rill node. Home of the Seven Houses.

DAZUN RIVER Largest river north of the Telarkan Mountains. Major economic resource and highway. Has no navigable egress to the sea.

THE FAN Egress of Dazun; fens, marshes and channels that go nowhere. Also called the Bogs. No one knows how or where the Dazun empties into the sea (or even if it does).

RILLHOME Sordaneon palace in Dazunor-Rannuli

CUSTOMHOUSE Seven Houses seat in Dazunor-Rannuli.

ILLYSTRI PALACE Malyrdeon palace in Dazunor-Rannuli, located on island in the Lago.

LAGO Lake in heart of Dazunor-Rannuli near the Rill mount.

EMRYSEN PALACE Esseran monarch's residence in Dazunor-Rannuli, on the Upper Canal

UPPER CANAL Large canal north of the Rill mount and Lago, where the wealthy live.

LOWER CANAL Main canal of Dazunor-Rannuli. Largely commercial properties along it.

BEARD FEN Kheld neighborhood in Dazunor-Rannuli

MERRYDN Principality in eastern Essera. On the Dazun River. Home to the Merrydeon Princes. Site of a dormant Rill mount.

MERATH Capital city of Merrydn. Famous for its palace and walls of blue stone.

DANNUTH Principality in Essera, holding of the Dannutheon Princes.

KYRBASILLON Capital city of Dannuth. Famous for its beauty and public places. Four gateways of Virtue: Arch of Mercy, Arch of Truth, Arch of Courage, Arch of Justice.

TAHLWENT Principality in Essera. South of Stauberg and on the sea. Home to the Halasseon Princes.

ARAL Capital of Tahlwent. Major sea port.

HALASSEON SERAT Palace of the Halasseon Princes.

GUSTAN Town on the Dazun River near the Fan.

GUSTAN MANOR Marc Frederick's personal residence, which he designed and built using materials from his home world.

TRULO Major city on Dazun River. Seat of the Princes of Dazunor.

GOLDEN PALACE Highborn palace in Trulo.

KRAGH Badlands of high hills and dangerous gorges. Home of the Hen Kyon. Near Trulo. Site of the destroyed Aryati city of Gyges.

THE MAW Huge hill in the Kragh

AMALLAR Semi-autonomous domain of the Khelds. Considered part of Essera.

THE BOGS Kheld term for The Fan; endless marshes of terminal Dazun River.

RHODHUR Capital of Amallar. Site of Rhodhur Hall.

EASTMEARY BRENNA City in Amallar.

AURDOLLEN Sanctuary near Rhodhur and site of a school for girls.

THE HILL Temple complex at Aurdollen devoted to the Mother. Children conceived under the Hill, through anonymous couplings sanctified by the Mother's Priestesses, are considered destined for fortunate lives.

The Sacred Grove Oak grove and temple complex near Aurdollen devoted to the god Lud. Home of the Faeduadan Priesthood.

BELLAN TOREGH Town on eastern edge of Amallar. Site of a dormant Rill mount.

FLOH River that flows through Bellan Toregh. Tributary of Dazun River.

ORQHO Mines in southern Amallar near Leseos.

NEUBERLAND Esseran domain/protectorate. Kheld and Staubaun populations often in dispute over land.

SAEMOREGH Kheld town in Neuberland.

AMUNDHAL Kings grant holding of Aubrey Amundda. Near Saemoregh.

GOBBA Frontier holding east of Neuberland, loosely affiliated with Essera.

ANNECH Frontier holding allied with Gobba, increasingly at odds with Essera.

LESEOS City-State. Former Principality of Essera, now a semi-autonomous Basarchate. Rill city. Located south of Amallar and west of Gignastha.

GIGNASTHA Former Principality in Essera. Made a Crown Protectorate after its Highborn Princes were murdered by Kheld rebels.

SAR'PRYANNIS Poisoned lake in Gignastha. Gignastha is built on cliffs overlooking this lake.

VERMILLION AQUEDUCT Raised by Deben II Sordaneon to provide water to Gignastha and also power the locks securing the impregnable gate of the Watergilt Palace. Broken by Delos Sordaneon during the Gignastha War.

LOWER NEUBERLAND Part of the Principality of Gignastha, south of Gignastha and bordering Randpory, the northernmost territory of Sordan.

HORCROD Fortress in Lower Neuberland.

SORDAN

SORDAN One of the three remaining Five Cities. Called the City of Light, City of Amynas. Site of the Inception, originating point of the Rill, and a major Rill node. Island city surrounded by a large and very deep lake.

SORDANEON SERAT Palace of the Sordaneon Hierarchs, in Sordan, and congruous with the Rill. Portions of the palace are part of the immortal Citadel forming the core of the city.

VIRIDIAN RIVER Man-made river contained within the Serat. Site of numerous features, including a waterfall over the Serat walls.

WELL OF BIRDS Located in a courtyard of the Sordaneon Serat.

THE PRISM Rainbow-laced waterfall and gorge on grounds of the Serat.

VA HAIRA First Creation underground passage connecting the Rill, Citadel, Serat and other pre-Return structures in Sordan's city core.

THE INCEPTION Sordan's Rill mount. Largest Rill complex, where Derlon's presence has fully completed its transformation. Multiple levels, platforms, and crown of portals.

KING'S HOUSE Palace near the Serat, connected to the Va Haira. Former residence of the Malyrdeons.

SARKUAN Lake surrounding Sordan.

SORAND'RUIL River that flows from Sarkuan to the sea.

SANSORDAN Domain attached to Hierarchate. Largely desert/wasteland. Western coast poisoned by destruction of Mulsor.

IRIDONOS Fabled treasure city of the Aryati, rumored to lie in poisoned Sansordan.

ILMAR Domain of Sordan. Located at mouth of Sorand'ruil.

IVERNESSE Capital city of Ilmar.

NEREID PALACE Sordaneon palace in Ivernesse.

KOLPOS Gulf between Sansordan and Ardaen. Also known as the Gulf of Mulsor.

LAHGAEL Kingdom of the Lahgai, a Nemenor-Estol people allied with Sordan.

BEN ARANATH River port of Lahgael on the Sorandruil.

SUDDEKAR Principality located on the southern shore of Sarkuan. Borders Mormantaloran domain of Othgol. Home of the Suddekeon Princes.

BATRAZ Capital city of Suddekar; location of the Palace of Dawn.

ILDURRIA Domain located on northern shore of Sarkuan.

TOLLECH Principality located north of Ildurria.

RANDPORY CROSSING City-State. By agreement a free trade city because of its Rill mount.

RANDPORY RIVER Navigable river that forms the border between the Sordan Hierarchate and Trongor.

ANIT-REBIR Domain located north of Teremar. Mountainous.

TEREMAR Principality located on eastern shore of Sarkuan. Rich and powerful, home of the Teremareon Princes.

ASKORRAS Capital of Teremar.

TULAMANTA Palace at Askorras.

HESTYA River port in Teremar. Site of an active Rill mount.

TIRIS Estate on Sordan island given by Dorilian to Daimonaeris.

RHONDDA Sordaneon estate on Sordan island. Personal estate of Dorilian.

TRONGOR Independent nation of sea folk located on Kolpos north of Sansordan, west of Randpory, and south of Amallar. Separated from latter by the Telarkan Mountains.

OGARTH Capital city of Trongor. Site of a dormant Rill mount.

ARDAEN Monarchy located on large peninsula west of Trongor. Seafarers known as the Sea Kings.

SKALMRIMVOR (see Caerdon)

AMROSET Capital city of Ardaen.

CALLORN Region of Ardaen.

CAERDON Principality. Former region of Ardaen, ceded to the Sordaneon Hierarchate as part of a treaty and now included among the Hierarch's title domains.

MERCED An independent island kingdom near Ardaen, loosely allied with Ardaen.

MORMANTALORUS

MORMANTALORUS One of the three remaining Five Cities. Sits on an active volcano and is livable only because the City itself creates an environment conducive to human habitation. The environment immediately outside the city's bubble is toxic.

DZALARAD The volcano.

ILGAON Main tower of the Citadel of Mormantalorus, where Nammuor creates his arcane crystals and devices using the energy of the volcano.

NUARCH'S TOWER Residential tower of the Citadel of Mormantalorus.

MAGISTRY Part of Ilgaon tower where mage work is done.

ORM Domain. Borders Suddekar.

OTHGOL Domain. Borders Teremar.

TELEG Southernmost domain of Mormantalorus.

NALAPAR Eastern domain of Mormantalous.

XEBBETH Large island domain west of Mormantalorus.

ULAN-JANA Mountainous domain south of Teremar and northeast of Mormantalorus. Gifted by Nammuor to Dorilian and Daimonaeris on their wedding.

WORDS and TERMS found in the Books

CHARYS Rill conveyance. Created by the Rill at need and uncreated when no longer needed.

CRUIHCIL Kheld unit of government; leaders in a community charged to speak for that community as a whole or at a Witan.

DEIKNYA An oval medallion created by Marenthro that displays the royal or noble house to which that person is bound. Given exclusively to Highborn, royal, or high nobility.

FAETHA Kheld word meaning 'learned' (female); used for women who have mastered one of the Faces of the Mother: Knowing; Healing; or Life.

FAEDU Kheld word meaning 'learned' (male); used for men who have devoted themselves to the god Lud and are sanctified to perform his rituals.

FRA'DON Means 'royal brother.' Used by the Highborn for another of their kindred.

GYNEKOS used for a Highborn lineage that has reverted to purely human. This happens when a Highborn sires daughters instead of sons.

ORBUS/ORBI Balls of light Highborn princes generate in their hands. A minor power.

THRICE ROYAL Proper form of address for a Highborn prince regardless of age or rank. Highborn are considered royal three times over: Father. Mother. Entity. Generally, a Highborn prince is born to a royal father and mother, though the latter is not always the case... but it usually is.

TULLUN Material created from the god Vllyr's skeleton. Can be sharpened to an edge that can cut anything but itself. Shaped by the Aryati into blades from daggers to swords. The Sword of Amynas is a tullun blade mated with device matrices.

L. L. Stephens

has been writing science fiction and fantasy full-time for several years. Published works include a debut science fiction novel in the deep dark past and a medical journal, as well as lots of short stories, and local brochures, newsletters, and pamphlets for everything from local politicians to an international airport.

The Triempery series, which begins with *Sordaneon*, is a six-part series and life's work. For excerpts from existing or upcoming books, lore, maps, and other related content, visit the L.L. Stephens website at:

https://triempery.com

Twitter: @triempery
Facebook: L.L. Stephens Author

Independent Publishers Rock!

We appreciate your purchase of a Forest Path Book. We do our best to cultivate distinctive and compelling stories for our readers.
If you enjoy our authors' efforts, kindly consider that a reader review at your favorite online outlet can help spread the word. To keep track of our latest releases, sales, & happenings, please join

INTO THE FOREST
https://forestpathbooks.com/into-the-forest/
(The Forest Path Books reading group and newsletter)

When you sign up for the newsletter, as our 'thank you!' you'll receive a code via email for 25% off your first purchase at our store!

https://forestpathbooks.com